The clone turned and lunged at him again, sword drawn, grinning like a dog, and as the Icefalcon stabbed him through the chest he realized that the man was possessed of a demon.

The demon came out of the man's mouth like a glowing mist that thrashed and clawed at the Icefalcon's eyes and face for a moment and then was gone. The body of the dead clone lay in the snow at his feet.

Shouting on the other side of the snow ridge. The Icefalcon, Cold Death, and Loses His Way fled. Later, after the sergeant had looked at the dead man, cursed about barbarians, stripped off the dead man's clothing and weapons and gone away again, they returned to look at the body.

"He makes his warriors out of air." Cold Death knelt to touch the hairless face. "Or wood and dirt and dead flesh, as the case may be. But he can't make a man's soul. It was only a matter of time before the demons found a way into the living flesh . . ."

# ICEFALCON'S QUEST

## Barbara Hambly

A Del Rey® Book
THE BALLANTINE PUBLISHING GROUP • NEW YORK

A Del Rey® Book
Published by The Ballantine Publishing Group
Copyright © 1998 by Barbara Hambly

All rights reserved under International and Pan-American Copyright Conventions. Published in the United States by The Ballantine Publishing Group, a division of Random House, Inc., New York, and simultaneously in Canada by Random House of Canada Limited, Toronto.

www.randomhouse.com/delrey/

Library of Congress Catalog Card Number: 98-93461

ISBN 0-345-38824-0

Map by Christine Levis

Manufactured in the United States of America

First Hardcover Edition: February 1998
First Mass Market Edition: January 1999

10  9  8  7  6  5  4  3  2  1

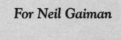

*For Neil Gaiman*

THE NORTHERN ICE

Tiyomis          Shilgae

The Night River

The
Cursed Lands                              FELWOODS

                        Gae

P L A I N S
        Sarda
        Pass
                        GREAT
Dare's Keep                              Prandhays
in Renweth                               Keep
Vale

Black Rock Keep

                              Penambra
GETTLESAND

                    THE ROUND SEA

THE
ALKETCH
LANDS

Khirsrit

                              Christine Levis

# CHAPTER ONE

Had the Icefalcon still been living among the Talking Stars People, the penalty for not recognizing the old man he encountered in the clearing by the four elm trees would have been the removal of his eyes, tongue, liver, heart, and brain, in that order. His head would have been cut off, and, the Talking Stars People being a thrifty folk, his hair taken for bowstrings, his skin for ritual leather, and his bones for tools and arrowheads. If it was a bad winter, they would have eaten his flesh, too, so it was just as well that his misdeed occurred in the middle of spring.

The Icefalcon considered all this logical and justified: the laws of his ancestors were not the reason that he no longer lived among the Talking Stars People.

All the horror that followed could have been avoided had he minded his own business, as was his wont. Sometimes he felt that he had spent entirely too much time living among civilized people.

It had been a bad year for bandits. The summer following the Summerless Year had seen more than the usual bloody strife in the rotting kingdoms that once made up the empire of the Alketch in the South, and bands of paid-off warriors, both black and white, drifted north to prey on the small communities along the Great Brown River. It was said they had penetrated far to the east, into the Felwoods, though few came so far north as the Vale of Renweth. Now it was spring again. When a woman's screams and a man's thin cries for help sliced the cold, sharp air of

1

the Vale, the Icefalcon guessed immediately what was going on.

In the round clearing in the woods about three miles up-slope from the Keep, he found pretty much what he expected to find. The scene was common in the river valleys these days: an old man lying with a great bleeding wound in his head by the remains of a small campfire, a donkey squealing and pulling its tether, and a burly, coal-black warrior of the Alketch in the process of dragging a buxom red-haired woman into the trees. In the filmy eggshell brightness of the spring afternoon the old man's blood glared crimson, the warrior's yellow coat in brilliant contrast to the emerald of the grass, the beryl of the close-crowding trees. The knife in the woman's hand blinked like a mirror.

Seeing no point in making a target of himself by crossing the meadow openly, the Icefalcon ducked immediately back into the belt of hazel and chokecherry that ringed the clearing and kept to cover as he worked his way around. The woman was putting up a good fight. She was as tall as her attacker and of sturdy build, dressed as a man for travel in trousers and a padded wool jacket. Still, the man got the knife away from her, twisted her arm behind her, and seized her thick braids. The woman cried out in pain—she had not ceased to shriek throughout the encounter—and the Icefalcon simply stepped from behind an elm tree next to the struggling pair, flipped one of his several poignards into his hand, and slit the warrior's throat.

The woman saw him a split second before he grabbed the man around the jaw to pull his head back for the kill. She screamed in what the Icefalcon considered unreasonable horror—what did she think he was going to do?—as the man's blood soused over her breast and belly in a raw-smelling drench, and jumped away as her attacker collapsed between them. The Icefalcon had already turned, sword in hand, to scan the woods behind.

"Shut up," he instructed. "I can't hear anything." A single bandit was even rarer than a single cockroach.

But there was no second attack. No sound in the woods, at least as far as he could tell over the woman's hooting gasps.

He glanced back at her after the first quick check and pointed out, "Your companion is hurt."

"Oh!" she cried. "Oh, Linok!" and rushed across the clearing to where the old man lay.

After looting the fallen body of weapons, the Icefalcon followed more slowly, listening, watching all around him, tallying sounds and half-guessed movements in the shadows of the trees. She'd made noise enough to have brought the armies clear from the Alketch, let alone from higher up the Vale.

He came up on her as she was dabbing clean the old man's scalp. The cut looked ugly, blood smeared all over the round, brown, wrinkled face and matted dark in the salt-and-pepper hair. "Hethya?" moaned the old man, groping for her arm with a shaky hand.

"I'm here, Uncle. I'm all right." Her jacket had been pulled nearly off her shoulders in the struggle, her tunic torn to the waist. She made nothing of her half-bared breasts, round and upstanding and white as suet puddings under the terra-cotta spill of her hair. The Icefalcon put her age at perhaps thirty, a few years older than himself. She had a red full mouth and the porcelain-fair skin of the Felwoods and an easterner's way with vowels as well.

"We're all right for now," corrected the Icefalcon, still listening to the too silent woods. "Your visitor's companions will be along at any time. How is it with you, old man? Can you back the donkey?"

"I—I believe so." Old Linok had the well-bred speech of the capital at Gae, before the Dark Ones destroyed it along with most of the rest of the works of humankind. He sat up, clinging to his niece's fleshy shoulder for support. "What happened? I don't . . ."

"Your niece will explain on the way to the Keep."

Impossible that the bandit's companions weren't only minutes away—the Talking Stars People would have already left the old man behind. The Icefalcon had with some difficulty been taught to follow the dictates of civilized people about those too infirm to look out for themselves, but he still didn't understand them. "Get him on the beast and don't be a fool, woman," he added, when she turned to gather up bedrolls and packs. "The bandits will have those one way or the other."

"But we carried those clear from . . ."

"No, no, Hethya, the boy is right." Linok struggled with maddening slowness to get himself upright. "There will be others. Of course there will be others."

The Icefalcon already had the donkey over to them. He reminded himself that among civilized people it was not done to grab old men by the backs of their clothing and heave them onto pack-beasts like killed meat, no matter how much more efficient such a procedure might be for a speedy getaway. His sword was in his right hand, his attention returning again and again to the place in the trees where the birds were silent—somewhere between the big elm with the lightning scar and the three smaller elms close together.

"You're from the fortress, aren't you, young man?"

"Be silent, both of you." He was too preoccupied with trying to track potential attackers by sound to inquire where else they thought he might have emerged from, if not the monstrous black block of the Keep, whose obsidian-smooth walls were visible from nearly any point in the lower part of the Vale.

They were there. He felt their presence as one sometimes felt the spirits of holy places, felt their eyes on the little party with all the training of his upbringing in the Real World, the empty lands beyond the mountains. He'd killed their companion and was in charge of two and perhaps three sets of weapons and a donkey, far rarer than gold in this devastated world. He and his companions were outnumbered . . .

So why didn't they attack?

And why didn't these two idiots he'd rescued shut up?

But they didn't. And the bandits kept to the trees, invisible and unheard. As far as the Icefalcon could tell, they didn't even follow them as they moved from clearing to clearing down the ice-fed stream, until they came to the open land that surrounded the Keep of Dare, the last refuge of humankind between the Great Brown River and the glacier-rimmed horns of the Snowy Mountains, somber towers blotting the western sky.

"You were fools not to come to the Keep when first you entered the valley." The Icefalcon glanced at them, man and woman, for the first time taking his eyes from the surrounding woods. "Where were you bound? You must have seen it."

"Now listen here, boy-o," began the woman Hethya, apparently indignant at being called a fool, though the Icefalcon would have been hard put to devise another term that covered the situation.

"No, niece, he's right," Linok sighed. "He's right." He straightened his bowed back—he was a little, round-faced, stooped man, with blunt-fingered hands clinging to the ass' short-cropped mane—and looked back at the Icefalcon walking behind them, long, curved killing-sword still in hand.

"A White Raider, aren't you, my boy? And clothed as one of the King's Guard of Gae."

Civilized people, the Icefalcon had discovered, loved to state the obvious. In the improbable event that a man of the Realm of Darwath—and they were a dark-haired people on the whole—had been flax-blond *and* grew his hair long enough to braid, it was still unlikely in the extreme that he'd have had dried hand bones plaited into the ends of it.

The bones were those of a man who had poisoned the Icefalcon, stolen his horse and the amulet that guarded him from the Dark Ones, and left him to die. The Icefalcon saw no reason for civilized people to be shocked about this, but mostly they were.

"Had you journeyed as far as we have, young man," Linok went on, shaking a finger at him, "in such lands as the Felwoods have become in the seven years since the coming of the Dark, you'd beware of anyone and anything you don't know, too. Cities that once were bywords of law and hospitality are nests now of ghouls and thieves . . ."

His gestures widened to dramatic sweeps, like an actor declaiming. The Icefalcon wondered if Linok sincerely believed that the Icefalcon had somehow missed these events or if he simply liked to hear himself talk, a failing common among civilized people who didn't have to deal with the possibility of death by starvation or violence as the result of ill-timed sound.

"The very Keeps themselves are no longer safe. Prandhays Keep, once the stronghold of the landchief Degedna Marina, was breached and overtaken by outlaws who nearly killed us when we came there seeking shelter. There is no trust to be found anywhere in this sorry and desolated world."

"Still," said Hethya softly, "it is not so bad as it was." Her voice altered, the broad dialect of the Felwoods lands transmuting into something else, her carriage changing, as if she grew taller where she walked at the donkey's head. "*Nathión Aysas intios tá,* they used to say: The Darkness covered the very eyes of God."

The Icefalcon tilted his head at the unfamiliar words, of no language that he knew or had ever heard. There was the echo of dark horror in the woman's eyes, and her whole face, in its frame of cinnamon curls, grew subtly different.

"You mean in the days when the Dark Ones rose," he said.

Her laugh was soft, bitter, and strange, out of place in the lush-featured face. "Yes," she said. "I mean when the Dark Ones rose."

Around them in the open meadow a half hundred or so sheep fled bleating, and the dozen cows raised their heads to regard them with the mild stupid curiosity of bovine kind: all the livestock left to a community of some five thousand souls. The pasturage had been shifted again, as the rubbery, alien growth called slunch spread into what had been the Keep's cornfields, and only a few of the fields themselves remained. The ice storm that struck in the Summerless Year had accounted not only for most of the stock, but for all but a few of the fruit trees as well, freezing them to their hearts. Even the spells of the Keep's mages had been unable to revive more than a handful. Raised by magic three and a half millennia ago, the black walls of the Keep itself stood isolated in the desolation.

Still, they stood, impervious to horror, night, and Fimbul winter in a world of glacier-crowned rock, and Hethya looked on them across the meadow with sadness and knowledge in her eyes.

"Not the rising of the Dark Ones that you remember, barbarian child," she added softly. "Not their brief, final rising, when they wiped out the last of humankind before themselves passing on into another dimension of the cosmos." Her hand shifted on the donkey's bridle, and she seemed oblivious now to the dead bandit's blood crusted on her clothing.

"I remember the days when the Dark Ones rose like a black miasma and did not depart. Not in a season, not in a year, not in a generation. I remember the days when humankind shrank to handfuls, not daring to leave the black walls of its Keeps for years at a time, fearing the night, fearing the day almost as much. When the world we knew was rent asunder and all the things that we cherished were swept away so that not even the words for them remained.

"I remember," she said. "It was three and a half thousand years ago, but I remember what it was like, at the original rising of the Dark. I was there."

"I don't know how young I was," said Hethya, sipping the tisane of hot barley that Gil-Shalos of the Guards brought her, "when she first started speaking to me in me mind."

She drew up her legs under the borrowed skirts of homespun wool—worn and mended like everything in the Keep these days—and looked around her at the notables of the Keep assembled in the smallest of the royal council chambers.

"Six or seven, I think. I know I startled Mother—and horrified me aunties—by some of what I'd come out with, things no young girl ought to think or know."

Her wry grin summoned back for a moment that red-haired child, with her pointed chin and wide-set cheekbones and innocent hazel eyes, in a house whose diamond-paned window casements would have been left open after dark to catch the evening breeze. In her smile the Icefalcon, seated with Gil-Shalos and a couple of other warriors near the door, could glimpse the reflection of parents and siblings who had mostly died uncomprehending, terrified, one night when the thin acid winds blew cold from the shadows and the shadows themselves flowed out to drown the light.

Minalde asked, "Does she have a name?" She leaned forward, dark braid swaying over the faded red wool of her state gown, twined with the pearls of the ancient Royal House.

Hethya's tawny brows tugged together. "Oale Niu," she said at length. "Though I don't know whether this is her name or her title. She calls herself other things sometimes."

The Icefalcon saw the glance that passed around the room, the murmur of wonderment and question like wind rustling the aspens by the orchards. Even the Keep Lords, the few members of the ancient Gae nobility who'd managed to make it to the Keep with food stores and servants and miniature armies of retainers and guards, were impressed, and they tended not to be moved by anything that didn't directly impinge on their real or imagined privileges. Lord Ankres muttered something to Lord Sketh, who nodded, blue eyes bulging. Three of the Keep's four mages—Rudy, Wend, and Ilae—leaned forward on their bench of smooth-whittled pine poles, draped in mammoth and bison-hides. Wise Ones, the Icefalcon's people would have called them, they had summoned spots of glowing witchlight to augment the flickering amber of the small, round hearth, but the blue-white light burned low, giving the big double cell the intimacy of a private chamber.

"Oale Niu," Minalde repeated softly, tasting the shape of that name with a kind of wonder. The Lady of the Keep and widow of Eldor, the last High King of the Realm of Darwath, had changed a great deal from the shy seventeen-year-old the Icefalcon had rescued from the Dark Ones seven years ago. Thin-boned and delicately beautiful, with lupine-blue eyes that had seen too much: a pawn who had worked her heartbreaking way across the chessboard to become not a queen, but a king.

"And you remember to her?" asked Altir Endorion, Lord of the Keep of Dare.

He had his mother Minalde's eyes, large and blue as the hearts of the deepest-hued morning glories, and her coal-black hair. Of his father, he had the memories of the House of Dare, memories of the line that stretched unbroken back to the original Time of the Dark; memories uncertain, patchy, in no particular order, memories of other people's mothers, other people's griefs. Some members of his house had been spared these memories, the Icefalcon had been told. Others had had them only in flashes, or sometimes in the form of hurtful, restless dreams. Minalde had them, too, inherited from the House of Bes, a collateral of Dare's line. Sometimes Tir's eyes were three thousand years old and more.

He'd be eight in high summer and looked it now, small face filled with wonder as he gazed up at this newcomer from another world.

Hethya smiled looking down at him, and her expression softened. "I don't remember *to* her, me little lord," she said. "I—I *am* her, in a way of speaking. Sometimes. She's like in a room in me head"—she tapped her temple—"and sometimes she only sits in that room talking to me, and sometimes she comes out, and . . . and then *I* have to sit in that room, and listen to the things she says, and watch the things she does with me hands, and me feet, and me body."

Her brow creased again, and some remembered pain hardened a corner of her mouth. She looked aside from Tir's too innocent eyes.

After a moment she went on, "Sometimes she'll tell me things, or show me things, things about the Times Before. It's hard to explain the way of it, between her and me."

"Rudy?" Minalde looked across to the young mage who was her lover, seated at a discreet distance with his two colleagues in wizardry out of respect for the sensibilities—religious or political—of the Keep Lords and the Bishop Maia. "Have you ever heard of such a thing?"

Rudy Solis shook his head. He, too, had changed, the Icefalcon thought, over the past seven years. Like Gil-Shalos he was an outlander, son of an alien world. When they had arrived in the train of Ingold the Wizard on the morning following the final destruction of Gae, the Icefalcon had guessed immediately that Gil-Shalos, who now sat beside him in the loose black clothing of the Guards, would survive. He had seen the warrior in her eyes.

Rudy he had not been so sure of. Even after the young man had found in himself the powers of the Wise Ones— powers that evidently did not exist or were not accessible to humans in his own world—the Icefalcon would not have bet the runt of a pot dog's litter on Rudy's survival. He might do so today, he thought, but not much more. For all that Rudy had been through, under Ingold's tutelage and on his own, like many civilized people he lacked the cutting blade of hardness in his soul.

"I've never heard of anything of the kind," he said. "Neither has Ingold, as far as I know. At least he's never mentioned it to me." He shook his long dark hair from his eyes, an unprepossessing figure in his laborer's clothes and his vest of brightly painted bison-hide. "When we're done here, I'll contact him and ask."

"It is a most inopportune moment," put in the elderly Lord Ankres dryly, "for Lord Ingold to have absented himself from the Keep."

Gil-Shalos stiffened at this slight to the mage who was her lover, her life, and the father of her young son, but as a member of the Guards it was not her place to speak out of turn to one of the Keep Lords. Rudy answered, however.

"When you come to think of it, my Lord, there never *is* an opportune moment for Ingold to go scavenging. I mean, hell, nothing ever happens in the winter because the bandits and the White Raiders are as locked down by the weather as we are, but then *Ingold* can't get out, either. The only times he *can* get to the ruins of the cities is in summer. Are you saying you'd rather he didn't find stuff like sulfur and vitriol to kill the slunch in the fields? Or books?"

"He could leave the books for another time," responded the stout Lord Sketh. "There are things we need more."

"Like a new brain for you, meathead?" muttered Gil under her breath.

"Be that as it may," Minalde intervened, with her usual artlessly exact timing, "the fact is that Lord Ingold *is* at Gae just now and can be contacted easily by any of the mages here. Wend? Ilae? Have either of you heard tell of such a thing, that one of the wizards of the Times Before should possess the mind and soul of someone in our times?"

Both the dark-eyed little ex-priest and the slim young woman shook their heads. Their ignorance was scarcely a surprise, as neither had received formal training in wizardry. The Dark Ones had been hideously efficient in wiping out the schools in the City of Wizards and everyone else with obvious ability in the art.

"Well, I've never heard of such, either," said Hethya. "And believe me, your Ladyship, I've *looked*."

"It is a rare—a very rare—phenomenon." Uncle Linok spoke for the first time, from the corner by the hearth. He adjusted the shawls and blankets wrapped about him, wool and fur and the combed and spun underwool of the mammoth, yak, rhinoceros, and uintatheria that the Keep's hunters trapped and speared in the winter when the great lumbering animals migrated from the North.

"But it is by no means unheard of. As a collector and collator of old manuscripts myself, I've found mention of it only once, in the Yellow Book of Harilómne."

"Harilómne?" Brother Wend straightened up, dark eyes growing wide. "Harilómne the Heretic? He was a mage of great power, who sought out and studied all records of the arts of the Times Before, in the days of Otoras Blackcheeks, my Lady," he explained, turning to Minalde. "It was said he knew more about those lost arts than any man living, though no one knows how he found it out. No one has ever found his library . . ."

"And just as well," said the Bishop Maia. "Just because a thing was wrought by the mages of those times does not mean that it was wholesome, or worthy of being found. The Times Before were years of great evil as well as great knowledge. Some of the knowledge Harilómne uncovered was used to great ill, as anyone will tell you, my Lady."

"But three of his books were supposed to be at Gae," put in Rudy. "That's what that merchant guy last month told Ingold. That he'd seen them in the cellar of a wrecked villa there. That's why Ingold took off the way he did."

"And well he should," said Linok. "All knowledge, all magic, is precious in these times." He made a gesture then, of stroking his ragged beard, and something in his movement—the way his hand came up, wrist leading like an actor's—snagged at the Icefalcon's mind. An impression, gone immediately, that he knew this man. Had seen him somewhere before.

But the round face, the wide-set eyes, and the snub nose were not familiar.

Someone who looked like him? A kinsman?

But he knew as soon as he phrased the question that it wasn't that.

Linok went on, "The single reference in the Yellow Book

speaks of a girl in the reign of Amir the Lesser who was 'possessed of a spirit of her ancestors,' who apparently spoke languages unknown to any in the world. She could identify and explain an 'apparatus' that was 'said to have stood in the vaults beneath the Cathedral of Prandhays since the founding of the city.' What this apparatus was the book did not say, and the apparatus itself is now long gone, but it was said that the thing produced a great light, and while the light shone none could enter or leave the Cathedral, nor certain areas of its grounds."

"A force field?" Rudy looked across at Gil—the word he used was unfamiliar, in the tongue of their own world that neither spoke much anymore. "I'll be buggered. You ever hear Ingold mention that?"

She shook her head.

"And was it an apparatus," asked Minalde, folding small slim hands in her embroidered lap, "that you came to the Vale of Renweth to seek, Hethya?"

The woman hesitated for a long time, her eyes seeking Linok's. The old man nodded.

"I think we can trust these good people, my child."

One could have heard a snowflake fall in that lamp-lit golden room.

"She—Oale Niu—says there were caves or something in the cliffs on the western side of the valley." Hethya brought the words out hesitantly, as if dredging them from deep within her mind. "She says she and some other people, wizards I think, hid up there from the Dark Ones. They walled up things, weapons and . . . and other things I'm not understanding, to hide them there from enemies, after they got the Keep built."

The whole room was an indrawn breath. Hope, wanting, flashed between Rudy's eyes and Minalde's, palpable as the leap of summer lightning from cloud to cloud.

Lord Ankres said, "But we have all been to those caves, my Lady Queen." He leaned forward, narrow hands resting on his knees. "Lord Ingold himself has gone carefully over them and found nothing but marks and scratches on the floor."

Hethya looked puzzled, biting her lip.

Rudy asked her, "Whereabouts are these caves? Down near the old road?"

She shook her head immediately. "No, those were the ones the people stayed in, where there was the water. These were up higher, and farther on, I think. I'd know the place if I was to see it again."

Rudy looked down at Tir, sitting rapt at Minalde's feet. "Any of this sound familiar to you, Ace?"

The boy shook his head, eyes shining. "What kind of things?" he wanted to know. "Machines?" For the past two winters he had been enthralled by the mazes of levers and pulleys, belts and steam turbines, that Ingold was constructing in his laboratories in the heart of the Keep crypts next to the hydroponics gardens that fed the population. The few fragments of ancient machines that had been found provided only tantalizing scraps of information, hints and clues and the tiniest seeds of speculation, which, the Icefalcon knew, drove Ingold and Gil insane.

The Icefalcon himself had little opinion of machines. They could not be made to work and took up a deal of space, and, upon two or three occasions, trials of their virtues had resulted in nearly killing everyone in the room. Gil and Rudy had both attempted to explain to him why it was necessary that such machines as Gil saw in the record crystals from the Times Before should be made to work again, but the Icefalcon still distrusted them.

It was said among his people that it took a brave man to befriend a Wise Man, and after eleven years' friendship with Ingold Inglorion, greatest of the wizards of the West, the Icefalcon had concluded that one had to be slightly mad as well.

Hethya was still speaking, telling Tir and Rudy and the Lady Alde about machines that would draw water from deep in the earth or generate heat and operate the pumps that circulated air and water through the unseen black ducts and pipes of the Keep. Though Maia was shaking his head in disapproval, she spoke of apparatus that would melt snow and cause plants to fruit and put forth crops twice and sometimes thrice in a year—the sort of things the more foolish of the people of the Real World west of the mountains attributed to their Ancestors, as if anyone's Ancestors would be interested in such matters. The Talking Stars People had more sense.

"I know not whether these things will remain," Hethya said, the Felwoods brogue dissolving again, the antique inflection returning as the pitch of the voice itself deepened and slowed. "We hid them deep, for the world in those days was full of foolish men and the acts of a few evil wizards had brought down the persecution of the Church on them all. A world of time has passed over them, and time contains many things. We thought, me Uncle Linok and meself . . ." She was all Felwoods again. "We thought to lay hold of some of these things, to buy ourselves at least a place to dwell, now the eastern lands are all warfare and bandits and death."

Her nostrils flared a little, and the hazel eyes darkened again, and her fingers clenched the faded gilding of her chair arm.

"You need not trouble yourselves about the purchase of refuge." Alde rose from her own chair and held out her hand, her full garnet oversleeve falling straight. Against Hethya's height and strength she had a fragile look, like the chair she had sat in, the delicate workmanship of a world fast slipping away. "Whatever you seek, be sure that you will have our help. Whatever you find, be sure that it will not be taken from you so long as your use of it be honest. That I pledge you."

Hethya curtsied deep with her borrowed skirts and kissed the Lady's outstretched hand. Linok carefully unwrapped himself from his many shawls and made his bow, an elaborate Court obeisance that once again tripped something in the Icefalcon's mind.

But then, it was the sort of silliness that civilized people did, and he had lived among them for four years before the coming of the Dark Ones. There were many in the Keep— not just the Keep Lords, either—who scrupulously maintained the old forms, and it was not unreasonable to suppose that such a one might have a niece with a roving eye and a Felwoods turn to her tongue.

It was the mark of civilized people to make such allowances and not live with one's hand forever on one's sword-belt. Commander Janus of the Guards, and the Lady Minalde, and others over the years, had told the Icefalcon repeatedly that every snapped twig did not necessarily presage the swift onset of bloody disaster.

But the reflection that he was right, and they wrong, was of little consolation to the Icefalcon in the face of what was to come.

# CHAPTER TWO

"If you mean, do I think she was faking," said Gil-Shalos half an hour later, walking along the broad Royal Way at the Icefalcon's side with her gloved hands stuck in her sword-sash, "the answer is yes."

At midday the mazes of the Keep were sparsely populated, especially in spring. The rasp of files and saws, characteristic noises that rose and faded with the turnings of the fortress' tangled hallways, were stilled as the men and women who labored all winter in their dim-lit cells joined hunting parties or optimistically cultivated what arable land there was—anything to add to the Keep's slim stores of food and, especially, clothing. With the destruction of the entire sheep herd in the Summerless Year, the Icefalcon had immediately reverted to the wearing of leather and furs, dyed black as the clothing of the Guards of Gae was always black; others were following suit.

Uneasy torchlight flung shadows over the black stone walls but couldn't pierce the gloom collected under the high ceiling vaults. Here and there vermillion slits of poor-quality-oil light marked the rough louvers or curtains that closed off doors of the dwelling cells. Raised largely in the open, the Icefalcon had had a difficult time getting used to living under a roof in his years at Gae. The Keep was like dwelling forever in a cave.

A very safe cave, of course. But a cave, nonetheless.

But he had played in caves as a child, up in the Night River Country. He had memorized their most intricate twists and turnings, their tiniest holes and pass-throughs,

in order to ambush his playmates, even as the children
here learned to run the mazes without lights in the course
of their games. He still practiced several times a week,
finding his way about the back reaches of the Keep blind-
folded. Following his example, as in many other things,
Gil did this as well.

"It is not exactly what I mean," the Icefalcon said, as
they turned left and descended the Royal Stair. Many
people had trouble keeping abreast of the Icefalcon's
long-legged stride, but Gil was fast. "But tell me why you
think this woman lies about the Ancestor who dwells
within her head."

"There's too much of a difference between her uncle's
class and hers."

"I thought of that. It is not inconceivable, o my sister,
that the man's sister could have married beneath him."

"Maybe." She didn't sound happy about it. She understood watchfulness as few civilized people did, the awareness of patterns and when a single trace or scat or spoor
looked not as it should. "But anybody can make up gib-
berish and say it's an unknown language. Religious fakers
in my world have been using that one for centuries. And
logic would tell anybody that people had to live *somewhere* while the Keeps were being built. If you think about
it, it would have to be in caves."

The Icefalcon nodded. It was, he reflected, part of a
storyteller's art, and he'd frequently teased Gil about the
fascination all civilized people had for stories that sounded
true but weren't.

They passed under clotheslines draped with garments
hung between the Royal Stair's spacious arches to take advantage of the updraft of warm air and on into the Aisle.
Hundreds of yards long and over a hundred wide, its
ceiling vanished high in darkness above them. The obsidian walls, like those of the densely twisted corridors,
glittered dimly with squares of scattered lamplight; doors,
and windows. Multifingered streams trickled dark and
clear as winter midnight under railless stone bridges that

cut the black expanses of floor. At the Aisle's far end, pale
daylight leaked through the Doors, the single entrance to
the whole of the Keep's great inner dark: two pairs of massive metal portals separated by the twenty-or thirty-foot
thickness of the outer wall itself.

Dare's Keep. The final stronghold. Unbreachable by the
Dark that had shattered the world.

"Both she and that uncle of hers have been eating pretty
good," said Gil, and twisted a tendril of her dark hair
around one of the sharpened sticks that held it out of the
way. "And there's a limit to what you can pack on a
donkey. But mostly what tips me off is that she thinks—or
she says this Oale Niu bird says—that the Keep is powered by machinery. She thinks that the heart of the Keep is
a machine. And that would be true for Keeps like Prandhays and the Black Rock Keep in Gettlesand. Keeps
where a wizard, a mage, didn't sacrifice himself or herself
to enter into the heart of the Keep as a source of magic to
keep it going. If Oale Niu really were a mage from the
Times Before, she'd know about that. She'd know about
Brycothis."

She spoke softly the name of the wizard who had sacrificed herself: Ancestor in a way, the Icefalcon thought, of
all those who lived here. When first he had been told the
secret of the Keep, known only to a handful, he wondered
why he had not guessed it already.

There was life here in the lamp-sprinkled midnight
among the catwalks overhead, life in the flow of the
moonless water along the streams of the floor, life in the
breathing of the air. The life of the Keep, like the spirits
that dwelled in rocks and trees, in the ocean and in each of
the thousand thousand stars. It was the only time he had
heard of a human being transforming herself into a spirit,
the *ki* of a place, but it did not surprise him.

The spirit was the mage Brycothis, who had abandoned
her body and been absorbed into the magic walls to draw
power from the earth and channel it to the uses of her
people within those walls forever.

Sometimes he wondered that everyone in the Keep did not guess.

At other times, after he had been dealing with these civilized people for a while—mud-diggers, the Talking Stars People called them, these people who had lived so long so fat and easily, with their wheat fields and their furniture and their clothing that tied up one's sword-hand—it did not surprise him at all. Civilized people would have trouble guessing what was amiss should a uintatherium take up residence in their parlors.

"But why here?" he asked. "Why make up such a tale?"

"Because we've got food here." Gil shrugged. "And we've got the only setup that guarantees production of food. Since those bandits took over Prandhays Keep last summer, we're just about the last stronghold for the length of the Great Brown River, from Penambra to the Ice in the North, and the most productive. You know how many bandits these days are from the Alketch, soldiers displaced by fighting there since the old Emperor's daughter gathered troops and threw out the general who thought marrying her against her will would be a good way to become Emperor himself, the more fool he."

"They are fools," said the Icefalcon dismissively, "the Alketch." The original owner of the finger bones he wore in his braids had been a prince of the Alketch.

A door in the Aisle's south wall, and a dark vestibule, led them into the watchroom of the Guards. The triple-sized cell was bright with glowstones—ancient crystal polyhedrons that shed a kind of stored magelight—and redolent of the warm reek of potatoes, venison stew, and sweaty wool. Sergeant Seya was playing pitnak with one of the rookies—Gil glanced at the sergeant's tiles and shook her head.

"If our girl Hethya was passing herself off as some kind of ancient wizard to gain status wherever she lived," she continued, turning back to the Icefalcon, "Alketch bandits' religious scruples might not have stretched to keeping her around, especially once they found out she couldn't come across with anything useful. You know what the Church in the South does to wizards. My bet is she and Uncle Linok had to get out of there fast."

"So they stole a donkey," said the Icefalcon, "and came here . . . For what purpose? To hoax us?"

"At a guess. To buy status. Maybe they thought we wouldn't let them in. Everyone loves a good story."

"Civilized people do," retorted the Icefalcon, who wasn't about to admit to a weakness of that kind. "They could make a good living," he added thoughtfully, "just selling the donkey." Knowing some of the speculators who operated in the Keep, Linok had probably already been offered the little animal's weight in gold, which was cheap these days, since it would neither hold an edge nor stand up to the heat of a cook fire. It was just possible that someone would make an attempt to steal the creature, though with so few animals in the Keep such a theft would be difficult to hide.

It occurred to him that he could have killed both the old man and the woman and sold the donkey himself to the highest bidder, always supposing anyone in the Keep possessed anything he wanted that badly.

None of the Talking Stars People were particularly interested in things they couldn't carry two hundred miles on foot. The habits of the Icefalcon's upbringing died hard.

Gnift the Swordmaster came in, calling together his afternoon practice, and now that her son Mithrys was able to walk—and learning to talk, may their Ancestors help them all—Gil had returned to training regularly with the Guards and taking her turn on the watches. While she and the others were stripping to their undertunics and wrapping their hands and wrists, the Icefalcon again put on the soft jerkin of black-dyed wolf-hide he wore on patrol, marked with the white quatrefoil emblem of the Guards of Gae, and pulled on over it a heavier vest, and his gloves. Though it was April, in these high valleys the wind blew cold, colder now every year. There was still chance of snow.

Janus, the stocky, red-haired Commander, called out, "You're not on now, you know," and the Icefalcon shrugged.

"I'm just going up the Vale to see about those bandits."

"There can't be a lot of them." He straightened up from lacing his boots. "The watchers at the Tall Gates never saw them. Neither have any of the patrols."

"Even so." He gathered up his bow, a blanket, a quiver of arrows, and then, because he had been raised among the Talking Stars People, added to the sword and water bottle at his belt a leather wallet of dried meat and flatbread, enough for a hard day's walking, and some dried fruit. Like most of the Guards he carried a firepouch at his belt, the whole cured hide of a woodchuck lined with horn and clay, in which was packed a smolder of rotted yellow birch that would burn for a day.

There were few enough guards, and Renweth Vale stretched eighteen miles from the sapphire wall of the St. Prathhes' Glacier down to the spruce forest at its lower end. A fairly large force might hide in the pinewoods or the rock caves above, and it was not impossible they could have come in over the ice-crowned spine of the peaks, rather than the eastward pass.

It would be as well to know where they were and what they were up to. The regular patrol had departed only an hour before—the Icefalcon briefly considered rounding up a band to go with him, then dismissed the thought. On simple reconnaissance, he would do better alone. Besides, he thought—the reasoning of a White Raider, Ingold would tell him, but he *was* a White Raider, and the reasoning was logical—bandits might have weapons and horses that could be appropriated.

Instinct made him seek the trees as quickly as he could. From the stones called the Four Ladies at the glacier's foot one could see all the clear land of the Vale. He worked his way carefully under cover of the woods up to the round meadow where Linok and Hethya had camped. He did not seriously think that anyone was watching from the Four

Ladies, but there was no point in giving anyone a hint of his movements or intentions.

He had not seen tracks of bandits yesterday, he thought, nor the day before. The watchers on the Tall Gates that guarded the lower pass to the east had not sighted them, either.

Odd.

From the edge of the trees he scanned the pale sky northward, orienting himself. His upbringing in the Real World had taught him to learn every facet of his surroundings, tree by tree, gully by gully, mudflat, spring, and stone. He knew Renweth Vale as well as he knew the ranges of his childhood, the Haunted Mountains and the Night River Country. Had the sky-shadowing devil-birds of legend carried him off and set him down anywhere in the range of the Talking Stars People, he would have been able to determine where he was, where the nearest cover lay, where to find water and in what direction to walk to come to the steadings and horse herds of his people were it winter, or their summer hunting camps wherever they might be, depending on the rains and the grass.

Therefore he knew exactly where the lightning-scarred elm tree and its three sisters lay.

And above them, there were no carrion birds.

Scrupulous bandits? In his experience bandits didn't even bury their camp garbage, let alone their dead.

When he wanted to, the Icefalcon could travel very swiftly, but the terrain here was rough, cut with streams and dotted with pale boulders among the trunks of pine and fir. It took him over an hour to reach the place, and when he did the sun was barely a hand span above the marble-white knife of the Great Snowy Mountains in the West.

The bandit still lay at the meadow's edge, arms flung wide, head twisted over to the side. Both face and head had been shaved a little less than a week before, and though the man's face was young, the beard and hair stubble were white, a common color among the Black Alketch. No bird had torn his eyes or his belly, no fox chewed the soft parts

of his face. Nothing, as far as the Icefalcon could see, had
invaded the gaping flesh of the severed throat or begun to
eat at the corpse.

It had simply rotted where it lay.

*In four hours?*

He knelt beside it, pulled off his glove to touch the
cheek. Liquefying flesh had already begun to drip away,
showing the pale jawbone and teeth.

*Plague?*

Not a pleasant thought. Particularly not with Ingold a
week's journey off in Gae seeking Harilómne the Heretic's
books. This man had seemed healthy enough to try to rape
Hethya, if that had indeed been his intent.

He pulled off the man's glove, and most of the hand's
flesh came with it. The odor alone told him that all was not
as it should be. The wars with the other peoples of the
northern plains, the torture sacrifices by which his people
periodically communicated with the Ancestors, the hunts
of mammoth and dire wolf and yak, would have been
enough to teach him the stench of the dead, without the
Time of the Dark when corpses lay like windfall plums in
the streets.

This stink was only vaguely similar, not like human
flesh at all.

He sat back on his heels. Birds were beginning to cry
their territories before settling in for the night. A squirrel
ran up a tree.

The bandits had gone.

The sun slipped behind the white horns of the glaciers
that shawled Anthir, northernmost of the three peaks that
guarded Sarda Pass. Blue shadow poured east to drown
the Vale, though light still filled the sky. The Icefalcon
rose and traced the bandit's prints back into the trees.
Here, where the yellow pine-straw covered the ground,
there was no good surface for tracks, a situation not helped
by the fact that the bandit had not worn boots. Like the
poorest beggars in Gae before the Dark Ones came, he had
wrapped his feet in strips of hide. Still, where the man's

marks crossed one of the dozen meltwater streams, the Icefalcon found in the mud of the water's verge the tracks of three others.

All four had stood there together, not long before the one bandit had gone to meet Hethya, Linok, and his destiny in the clearing. The other men had gone southwest.

The Icefalcon frowned. The light was sufficiently dim that he had to crouch for a closer look.

There was no mistaking it. All four men were the same height, judging by the length of their strides, and all four exactly the same weight.

The Icefalcon had grown up able to differentiate between the tracks of his grandfather's white mare Blossom Horse and those of his cousin's mare Flirt and those of any other horse owned by anyone in the family. He had been able to recognize the prints of individual dogs, of anyone in the family or in the larger People, and of many of the members of the wild herds of reindeer, yak, bison, and mammoth as well. Tracks, and scat, and individual habits of beasts were the topic of most conversations around the longhouse fires in winter and under the summer stars while hunting in the Cursed Lands or the Night River Country. They were the heart and business of the Real World, told over the way civilized people told over Gil's useless tales of enchantment and romance. The Icefalcon could no more have been mistaken than he could have thought that a prairie chicken's feather belonged to a red-tailed hawk.

Three of the four bandits had wrapped their feet in the same way, and the hide wrappings were thin enough to show him that they all walked in the same fashion as well. Not just that they all toed in slightly, but that they all put their weight on their heels in the same way. Had all worn boots, the pattern of wear on the soles would have been identical.

*Brothers?*

No brothers he had ever encountered had been *that* similar.

Save for those of the bandit he had killed, all turned upstream. There was a path along the gorged mountain flank
that would take them to Sarda Pass and the little-used way
that led down into the plains and badlands of the West.

*Why that way?* He couldn't be sure, for the light was
more and more uncertain, but he thought the hide wrappings were new. The dead man's were, without ragged
edges or the blurring of long wear.

Disquieted, the Icefalcon got to his feet and drew the
bandit's dagger from his belt. Alketch work, beautifully
tooled and quite old. He called to mind the bandit's
clothing, yellow coat and crimson breeches, slightly too
big, looted from an earlier wearer. Boots were expensive
and required more work to accommodate to another size.

Then he realized what it was that had tugged at his mind
about Linok, what it was about him that he had recognized, or thought he recognized.

It was too dark to see tracks in the meadow now, and in
any case there might be very little time. Turning, he made
his way toward the Keep at a run.

The Icefalcon was one of the tallest men in the Keep,
long-boned and rangy, and he ran fast. He was still a mile
from its walls when he saw blue witchlight dance in the
meadow by the stream, and voices carried to him, too far
to make out words, but recognizable in their timbre and
pitch. He turned aside, his heart cold in him with dread.

There was only one reason people would be outside the
Keep after nightfall.

Though the Dark Ones had been gone for seven years,
the trauma of their coming ran deep. Almost no one who
had passed through that horror would willingly remain
outside of shelter once twilight gathered. Moreover, with
the Sunless Year had come changes in the world. Huge
patches of slunch emitted a sicklied radiance all along the
valley's floor, and the mutant creatures that grew from it
were not all harmless. Even without such beings, there
were always the perils of the mountains themselves: dire

wolves, saber-teeth, the bears that were coming out of hibernation, now thin and hungry and angry.

Fog lay in the low ground of the meadows, dense and white. The moon would not rise for some hours. The voices came clearer, and the magefire showed him the faces of the man and woman scanning the damp earth for tracks.

"Sometimes he goes exploring where the old road used to run along the west foothills," said the voice he recognized as Rudy Solis'.

*They're talking about Tir.*

"He says sometimes he remembers things there."

Gil-Shalos. In seven years they had almost completely dropped the tongue of their own world, even when speaking to one another, save for words that had no translation in the Wathe, like *tee-vee* and *car* and *Academy Awards.*

"You think he might have gone out with Hethya? I saw her talking to him."

"He might have, if she described something he thought he recognized."

"Yeah, but why wouldn't I have . . ."

Even as Rudy was speaking the words, the Icefalcon was thinking, *Why would Rudy need to search? He's a Wise One. He has his scrying stone. He should be able to call Tir's image . . .*

*Unless Tir is with another Wise One.*

He'd guessed before, but the confirmation was like taking an arrow in the chest.

"It's Bektis." He stepped out of the trees.

Gil-Shalos was already turning. No fool, she.

"Bektis?" She looked nonplussed as she spoke the name of the Court Mage who had years ago sold his services to the power-mad Archbishop Govannin, had followed her to the Alketch and, so rumor said, had assisted her when she carved an unshakable sphere of influence in those war-torn lands. "What does Bektis have to do with Tir being gone?"

The Icefalcon hadn't even broken stride, forcing Rudy

and Gil to fall into step with him as he led the way fast
through the knee-deep ground fog and on toward rising
ground, the shouldering bones of the hills that guarded
Sarda Pass and the road down into the West.

"We have been had for dupes." The Icefalcon's voice
was bitter, anger at himself tempered by fear. "Made fools
of by a shaman's illusion. The old man Linok was Bektis
the Sorcerer. I thought I recognized his voice and the way
he stroked his beard. Were we to waste time going back
across the meadows we would find his tracks—long and
thin, not the tracks of the little short-legged man we saw.
The whole thing was a fakement, a lure, a tale, so that he
could get into the Keep."

Gil swore. Rudy, who was a little slower on the uptake,
said, "Well, I'll be buggered. But he isn't in the Keep. He
and that broad Hethya disappeared about two hours
ago . . ."

Gil concluded for him, guessing, but at the same time
sure. "And they took Tir with them."

# CHAPTER THREE

"I was a fool," said the Icefalcon.

It didn't take them long to cut Bektis' tracks. Snow still lay thin where the shadows of the Hammerking mountain fell on the trail, and the prints of the old man's boots were there, long and narrow, with the heel and nail-work characteristic of Alketch bootmaking. Prints that had to be Hethya's mingled with the wizard's, along with the marks of a second donkey, and the three identical bandits with hide wrapped around their feet.

"Where's Tir?" Rudy held his staff close to the sparkling ground. The magelight playing around the pronged metal crescent at its tip glittered on the crisp edges of the new prints.

"On a donkey." Gil forestalled the Icefalcon's reply. Night wind coming down cold off the glacier tore long wisps of her smoke-black hair where it escaped from the leather cap she wore. "We're lucky the herdkids were just bringing in the horses from pasture when Bektis was getting ready to get out of there, or we'd have lost a couple for sure." She bore a lantern and a firepouch like the Icefalcon's, though the lantern was dark; like the Icefalcon, Gil believed in never making assumptions about who she'd be walking with or what she might need.

Some way farther, they saw Tir's tracks where he'd gotten off the donkey to relieve himself behind a boulder.

"Are they keeping a guard on him?" The Icefalcon scanned the ground by the witchlight's glow, seeking other tracks near the small boot prints, the little puddle of frozen urine.

"My guess is Bektis has an illusion on him." In the bluish witchlight Gil's thin face, scarred across cheek and jaw, was impassive, her gray eyes steely-cold. "He probably thinks Rudy's with him and that everything's okay."

Rudy cursed. He'd been silent most of the way up the glacis, but the Icefalcon knew that the Prince was like a son to the young wizard and that Alde would be frantic with anxiety for her child.

Winds blew down the peaks, pregnant with the scent of coming snow. Not unusual for this time of year, reflected the Icefalcon bitterly, but too useful to a Wise One fleeing over the pass to be accidental.

"I should have known him," he said grimly, "long before they reached the Keep."

Gil regarded him in surprise. "How could you?" she asked. "Wend and Ilae—even Rudy—didn't see through the illusion. I didn't, and I saw him just two years ago in Khirsrit."

"Neither Wend nor Ilae ever saw him before the Wizards Corps was organized for the war against the Dark." He moved off again, leaning a little against the iron hammer of the wind, a bleached, silent-moving animal in the wild dark. "Nor did you, or Rudy, know him much longer. Not to know his voice, or his manner of movement. Not to recognize the way in which he speaks. As court mage to Lady Alde's brother he was about the palace from the time of my coming there. I knew him well. And in any case," he added dryly, realizing too late yet another truth, "why would they have camped for the night within five miles of the Keep they claimed to be seeking? I should have recognized a fakement when I saw one."

"Bektis is a wizard," retorted Gil. "It's his job to deceive. Don't be so hard on yourself." She tucked her hands under her armpits, cold despite the gloves she wore. She was a thin woman, all bone and leather; cold until you saw her smile. Many of the Guards had affairs with the women of the Keep, the weavers and brewers and leather workers and those who tended the hydroponics gardens. The Icefalcon's affairs, when he had them, tended to be with women in the Guards or in the military companies of the other Keep Lords. At one time he had considered Gil, though it had been obvious to him from the first that her heart was given elsewhere. His only serious love, many years ago, had been so also, and this time he had not deceived himself.

Now he returned her gaze with some surprise. "I speak only truth," he said. "Had I gone about my business and left these people to their own devices, the Keep would not now be in danger of losing its link with the memories of its Ancestors."

The pass had grown steeper, Gil and Rudy falling behind the Icefalcon's swifter strides, though Rudy was tough, as most wizards were, and Gil a proven warrior. From the top of the boulder-strewn slope the pass ascended, a narrowing corridor of gray-black cliff and blacker trees, losing itself in night. Wind bellowed in the pines and all the world smelled of snow, hard spinning granules of it flying through the white circle of the staff's light. The *ki* of Sarda Pass were said to be capricious, malignant, and stern, hating equally mud-diggers and the People of the Real World.

Rudy propped his staff against a juniper in a boulder's shelter and fumbled through the slits in his overmantle to get to the pockets of his vest. Carefully—his hands awkward because of his gloves—he drew out the slip of amethyst that served him for a scrying stone and tilted it back and forth a little until the light of his staff caught in its central facet.

"Wend?" he said. "Wend, can you hear me?"

Watching shamans and Wise Ones communicate always reminded the Icefalcon vaguely of the games children played. Evidently the priest-wizard replied, speaking in Rudy's mind, for after a time Rudy said, "Look, we've found Tir's tracks. Linok and Hethya took him. Linok put a spell of some kind on him to get him to go with them. The Icefalcon says Linok is actually Bektis, and, you know, looking back I think he's right."

There was a pause, occupied, the Icefalcon presumed, by Brother Wend's exclamations of astonishment—useless in the circumstances. Spits of snow stung his cheek.

"Tell Minalde what's going on." Rudy scrubbed a nervous hand over his face. His profile, a little craggy with the bump of an old break in his nose, cut blue-black against the witchlight, flat white triangles of which reflected in his eyes.

"Tell her he seems to be okay. Whatever they want him for, it isn't to kill him, or they'd have done it already. They're taking him over Sarda Pass and calling down a storm to close the pass behind them."

The Icefalcon could well imagine Minalde's reaction to that information. She loved both her children with a passionate ferocity: he clearly recalled, during the last desperate stand against the Dark Ones in the palace at Gae, her holding Ingold against a wall, the tip of some dead man's sword pressed against the wizard's breast, crying that she'd kill him if he did not save her child's life.

Bektis did well, he thought, to summon the anger of the snows. It was certain that nothing less would stop her.

"Gil and the Icefalcon are with me," Rudy went on. "We're going to try to overtake them and hold them if we can. Tell her to get Janus and a party of Guards out after us ASAP."

He used a colloquial shortening of the phrase *as soon as possible* transliterated from their outland tongue—the outland trick of using the initial letters of each word in a phrase to represent the phrase itself was one that was creeping steadily into the Wathe as well.

"Tell her not to worry." Another foolishness, in the Icefalcon's opinion. "We'll bring him back."

Given that Rudy was a seven-year apprentice in arts that Bektis had studied through his lifetime, the statement was wildly optimistic to say the least, but the Icefalcon did not remark on it. Rudy started to put the crystal away, then changed his mind and gazed into it again, bending his head and hunching his shoulders to shield his eyes from the wind.

"Ingold?" he said softly. "You there, man?"

The merchant who had brought Ingold word of the library cache at Gae had said that it was in a villa on the town's far side, an area largely under water now. The Icefalcon had accompanied the wizard on last summer's quest—when Gil's baby Mithyas had been only a few months old—and had familiarized himself with the city in its new state: sodden, ruined, head-high with cattail and sedges and creeping with ghouls. The old man would have to watch his back.

Ingold was evidently there.

"Look, you got to get back here. A wizard showed up at the Keep—Bektis, the Icefalcon thinks, and I agree with him. He's snatched Tir."

At least Ingold seemed to have no extraneous comment to make.

"He's taking him over Sarda Pass. Me and Gil and the Icefalcon are on their trail, and we're going to try to hold them until the Guards come up, but it's gonna be rough. I don't know what's going on, but I got to get going now. I'll be in touch, okay?"

"How did he look?" Gil asked when they were climbing again. Rudy dimmed the glow of his staff to a marshlight flicker, barely enough to permit his non-mageborn companions to see. There was no sense in advertising their location, but no sense in getting lost either, and the night was without light. Flakes of snow filled the air, blurring the donkey and boot tracks.

*Women,* thought the Icefalcon. *They had to ask.* Gil-Shalos was a fine warrior and had a logical mind, but she was a woman to her bones when it came to matters concerning the man she loved.

"I would assume," he said, bending to examine what

might have been marks of someone leaving the party—
they showed only the later investigation of that medium-
sized black bear that laired on the other side of the
Squaretop Rocks—"that he looks like a man of seventy
who has been sleeping on the ground for three weeks
without trimming his beard." Gil slapped his arm with the
backs of her gloved fingers and turned back to Rudy.

"Not bad. Couple of scrapes and cuts, and his left hand
was bandaged, but it looked like he could use it okay.
What the hell is Bektis doing here anyway, Spook? I
thought you said he was working as Bishop Govannin's
gofer down in Alketch."

"He was. God knows what influence she had over him,
but she ordered him around like a servant. Yori-Ezrikos—
the Emperor's daughter—used his power, too; used her
friendship with Govannin. But he hated Govannin. I could
see it in his eyes."

"He hated everyone," remarked the Icefalcon. Blown
snow was swiftly obscuring the trail, but there was nowhere to go in the pass but ahead if they wanted to get
through before the storm closed it. He wondered how long
the Court Mage would keep up the illusion that Rudy was
with the little party—if that was in fact the glamour he had
cast over Tir's mind—and that all things were as they
should be. Or had Tir realized already that the man he
thought was his stepfather and mentor was in fact only a
ghost wrought by a mage's cleverness?

Tir had never seen Bektis—or at least he had been only
an infant when the Court Mage had departed in disgrace
from the Keep—though he had heard his name. He would
understand soon enough that something was wrong, when
the man he had seen first short and pug-nosed gradually
melted into another form, tall and thin with long white
hair, an aristocratic, aquiline nose, and haughty dark eyes.

Why take him over the pass?

"Why take him over the pass?" That was Rudy.

Gil's reply came raggedly, her words fighting the storm
winds. "They have to want him for what he remembers

from his ancestors. If it was just to cripple the Keep, they'd have killed him before they reached the pass and split up to get out of the Vale undetected."

"But he doesn't remember everything!" protested Rudy. "And we don't know what he *does* remember! Bektis should know that."

The Icefalcon led them into the lee of a small cliff under the Hammerking's flank, where the wind was less and the snow thinner underfoot, allowing them better speed. Unseen above them the glaciers that armored the Hammerking's shoulders sent down their slow, glass river of cold.

"More important," said Gil, "*Govannin* should know that. Unless she figures to have Bektis put a spell of *gnodyrr* on Tir, to dig into what he doesn't remember consciously. That's the worst kind of black magic, and God knows what it'd do to a kid that young, but that's never stopped her before."

Rudy cursed, viciously and with every step as they scrambled up the protected trail.

By the ground's shape underfoot and the way the wind roared and shifted, the Icefalcon recognized where they were and steered the others hard to the right. To the left streams had cut gorges in the floor of the narrow, U-shaped canyon. The forty or fifty feet that separated this gash from the mountain's hip were safe enough to navigate in fine weather but perilous when visibility was poor.

This far from the Vale wolves lived, too, and saber-teeth. The Icefalcon listened for their voices above the sea-howl of the trees.

"There they are," said Gil.

Light flickered and whipped against the rocks ahead and made buzzing diamonds of the snow. As the Icefalcon had suspected, the donkey had slowed them, as had the presence of the Alketch warriors, unhandy in cold weather. Of a certainty none of them knew the pass.

"How many are there?" asked Gil.

"Warriors? Three." The Icefalcon glanced around him,

calling to memory what the terrain ahead would be like. The deepening gorge, the cliff, the stream; the waterfall that would probably be frozen still and the shouldering outcrop of rocks beyond it, narrowing the pass to a gate thirty feet wide. Remembering the wisdom of Gil's alien upbringing, he added, "They were alike, in stride and weight, even to the way they walked. More alike than any brothers I have ever encountered."

"Clones?" Gil spoke an outlander word and looked to Rudy for confirmation. His eyes were half shut, as the eyes of Wise Ones were who concentrated on the casting of a spell.

"Come on." He seemed to wake from reverie and pressed on again, striding ahead of the Icefalcon now, pushing against the pounding winds. "I put a Word on the donkeys, but I'm not sure how long it'll last. Bektis can use a counterspell . . ."

"*If* Bektis figures out why the donkeys stopped." She was running beside him, a lean dark gazelle leaping up the sheltered goat trail. "He'd have trouble figuring out a Chinese finger puzzle," a judgment that meant nothing to the Icefalcon but that made Rudy laugh.

"Are we anywhere near that big spur?" he asked in the next breath. The light from his staff dimmed to nothing, but sparks of blue lightning crept along the ground at their feet, barely illuminating the way. "If I can get a rockslide going ahead of them, we can hold them . . ."

Thunder cracked as blinding light split the darkness. The Icefalcon grabbed Gil by one arm and Rudy by the back of his bearskin mantle, thrust them forward as the snow-roar in the swirling obscurity above told him that Rudy wasn't the only one who knew how to start avalanches. Rudy yelled "Damn it!" and cried out other words, magical words, answered from far off above the storm.

"Rudy!" It was a child's voice, piercing and terrified.

The winds checked, failed. Rudy made a pass with his hands, and cold blue light showed the crowding enscarpments of the Mammoth and the Hammerking bizarre in the harsh shadows, the glistening headwalls of the glaciers above. Dune and drift snow clogged the way, and against the thrashing trees, the scoured shelter of the rock-spur and frozen falls, their quarry could be seen.

The donkey was rearing and fighting in terror, the second animal dragging at its rein. Tir was fighting, too, on foot in the clutch of a black-faced Alketch warrior whose grip held him almost up off the ground. Two other warriors, who even at this distance could be seen to be of the same height and build, stood with drawn swords, blinking in the magic refulgence, waiting.

"Bektis!" yelled Gil. "Where's . . . ?"

A crash of rock splintering. White lightning cleaved the already fading brilliance of the air, and the Icefalcon shoved Rudy in one direction and Gil in the other, springing clear himself as a levin-bolt skewered the ground where Rudy had stood and steam exploded from the snow in a hissing cloud. The renewed glare showed up Bektis, tall now and thin in Linok's rough furs and quilted trousers, arms uplifted on the rock pinnacle beyond the ice-locked falls. The bandaged head wound—an illusion from the first—was gone. Now his head was flung back, his long white hair and patriarchal beard transformed to flags by the battering wind, and lightning laced his fingers in blue-glowing flame that hurt the eyes.

Rudy shouted a word of stillness, swept away and drowned. The storm winds took the fire he threw and hurled it in all directions, and boulders rained down out of the sudden fall of renewed night, crashing against the walls of the gorge. The Icefalcon, very sensibly, flattened into the overhang of the eastern cliff and stayed there. Levin-fire ripsawed the blackness, granting brief visions of Rudy and Bektis, and it seemed to the Icefalcon that Bektis wore a device of some kind on his right hand, a thing of crystal and gold that caught and focused the searing light. When Rudy threw answering fire, the jewels seemed to engulf the old man in a protective coruscation of rainbows. The

Icefalcon did not watch the battle. Rather, with every explosion of brightness he worked his way a little distance farther toward the donkeys, the warriors, and Tir. They'd all be watching Bektis, too.

It might give him a chance.

The Icefalcon was not a believer in luck. No one was who had been raised in the Real World. He knew Rudy's chances of defeating the more experienced wizard were negligible, and it was doubtful that he could even hold him in combat long enough for the Icefalcon to get in bowshot of Tir's captors. Thus he was neither disappointed nor angry when a final incandescence smote the night behind him, a riven cry and the sound of falling rock. He thought he heard Tir scream, *"Rudy!"* Then the wind's force smashed the pass with redoubled fury, burying all in night.

The Icefalcon wedged himself into a crevice and waited, conjuring in his mind the slow progress of Bektis down the ice-slick boulders on the other side of the rock-spur, across the winter-locked stream. The temperature, falling all this while, plunged still further. He unslung his blanket from his back to wrap around him like a cloak, his gloved fingers aching and clumsy. There were broken brush and branches within the crevice, sheltered from the storm and still fairly dry, enough to form a crude torch, though it took him a long while to break kindling into suitably tiny fragments and he had to wait to open the firepouch until the winds eased somewhat for fear of killing the flame within. When he got a torch kindled at last—the Icefalcon was a patient men—he raised it high.

Gil's voice called out, "Here!"

By the sound she was at the edge of the drop-off into the gorge.

Black lines of charring scored the rocks and earth, as if the ground had been beaten with red-hot rods. Despite the snow already filling the scars, the air stank of burning and coals winked in the ruins of blasted firs all around. The pattern showed clearly how Bektis had driven Rudy leftward to the cliff's edge, until he could retreat no more.

Gil had kindled her lantern, and its feeble glow revealed a great final scorch on the rocks above the gorge, the boulders themselves split with the heat. Snow hissed and melted as it touched them. The wind's main force was easing, but the snow came down harder now. The pass would be choked long before day.

It took Gil and the Icefalcon nearly two hours to work their way down into the defile. Rudy lay on ice-sheeted rock beside the still obsidian ribbon of the stream. He had dragged himself to the shelter of a toothed overhang, where spruces clustering on the rock above further broke the wind and snow. Remnants of a heat spell lingered in the place, melting the snow where it skirled around his body.

"You still with us, punk?" Gil pulled off her gloves to touch the long-jawed face with its bent nose, brushed back the blood-matted hair. Her face was expressionless as bone, but she had gentled, the Icefalcon thought, since the Summerless Year. "Don't check out on me now."

They had been friends for seven years, coming together from that other world where Ingold had found them, unthinkably different from both the Real World and the world of the civilized mud-diggers in their cities and their palaces. Both had told him of their former home many times, but still he could not picture it, other than thinking it uncomfortable, crowded, noisy, and utterly lacking in sense. Gil-Shalos was a woman whose heart was a sealed fortress, able to survive any loss, but this man was as much family as any she had in this world.

Under her hand, his fingers moved.

The week preceding had been fine and dry. The snowstorm, magically summoned, had not lasted long enough to soak the fallen branches in the crevices and rock chimneys along the walls of the gorge. The Icefalcon made a dozen trips, digging under deadfalls and dragging tinder to the shelter of the overhang, where he piled branches to catch the snow and so form a protective wall, as his people did in wintertime. While he did this Gil probed and manipulated the broken bones and smashed ribs, ascertaining damage and making sure Rudy could breathe easily. The Icefalcon was personally a little surprised that the young wizard had survived the fall at all. By the light of Gil's fire he could see the side of Rudy's face was scorched, as it had been in last autumn's explosion in Ingold's laboratory. His gloves were burned away completely, and his clothes blackened and torn.

"I doubt the Guards will be here until day." The Icefalcon sat back and pulled on his gloves again. "The wind's fallen, but it's snowing more heavily now. In a few hours the pass will be utterly blocked."

Gil said nothing for a time, but her eyes seemed very blue in the firelight. Stars of snow spangled her ragged black hair around her face. She and the Icefalcon regarded one another, each knowing the other's thought and what had to be done.

"Will you be well here until dawn comes, o my sister?"

She nodded.

"It stinks," she said, and her breath blew out in a jeweled sigh. "I'm sorry, Ice."

"I shall do what I can to leave a trail in case some do make it through. And I shall at least be on hand to help should the boy attempt to flee."

"That's good to know." She was already sorting out possessions: the lantern, most of Rudy's arrows, and his bearskin overmantle as well, for the niche was warm now from the fire and there was wood to last well into the next day. She offered him part of her own rations, which at his advice she had started carrying whenever she left the Keep, but he shook his head:

"We cannot know what will befall, o my sister. Your own life may depend on it."

"Myself, I think Tir has too much sense to run for it once they get to the other side of the pass," she said, adding a fish hook and a couple of her own hideout knives to the Icefalcon's already formidable collection. "He's only seven and a half. There anybody I should pray to?"

"To your Straight God of civilized people." The Icefalcon adjusted the last of his accoutrements, his mind already on the ice-rimed rocks beyond the waterfall, the
angle of wind in the pass. "He is the guardian of Tir's Ancestors, and of those who shelter in the Keep. The knowledge Tir carries may very well be the saving of them,
should some peril arise in the future."

"And what about your Ancestors, Ice?"

He'd spoken of them to her, Black Hummingbird and
Holds Lightning, and all those silent others whose blood
stained the carved pillars of the crumbling Ancestor
House at the foot of the Haunted Mountain. Had spoken
of those *ki* that could be felt there in the close silences, or
heard when the wind stirred the hanging fragments of
bone and hair and wood. Noon, the warchief who had
raised him, and the shaman Watches Water had spoken
of their deeds around the fires of the winter steadings,
with the eyes of the dogs glowing like lamps, for they listened, too.

He was fond of Gil but was not sure she would understand how it was with Ancestors.

"My Ancestors would think it only right that I pay for
my stupidity with my life," he said in time.

And Rudy's. And Tir's. And the lives of everyone in the
Keep. That was the way Ancestors were—or the Icefalcon's Ancestors, anyway.

"But I have not prayed to my Ancestors in eleven
years," he went on slowly. "Nor would they listen now to
supplication on my behalf. I sinned against them and
against my people. And so I departed from the lands where
I was born. I will be returning to those lands now, but it
will be my death should I encounter my own people
again."

He embraced her briefly and then began his slow ascent
of the icebound rocks, long pale braids snaking in the
wind, to regain the way that would lead down Sarda Pass
to the world he had forsaken forever.

# CHAPTER FOUR

Eleven years previously, the Icefalcon had departed from the Talking Stars People, under circumstances which, if they did not absolutely preclude his return, guaranteed a comprehensively unpleasant welcome home. Because it was unreasonable to suppose that any of those who dwelt in the Real World—the Twisted Hills People, or the Earth-snake People, or those other peoples whom the mud-diggers referred to collectively as the White Raiders—would trust one whose Ancestors had been enemies of their Ancestors, there had really been no place for him to go but across the mountain wall in the east.

As a child he had heard tales of the people of the straight roads, the mud-diggers, the dwellers in the river valleys, though the ranges of the Talking Stars People lay far north of the ragged line of mud-digger mines and settlements that stretched from Black Rock among the Bones of God to Dele on the Western Ocean. Noon and Watches Water had told him the mud-diggers were crazy—which he had found later to be by and large true—and also lazy and stupid about important things, and almost unbelievably unobservant about the world around them.

In the warm lands where water was easy to come by and plants were coaxed in abundance from the earth, there were kings and walls and warriors to protect those who didn't bother to learn to protect themselves. People could afford to be lazy and to make an art of telling fanciful stories about things that had never actually happened, at least for as long as the kings were alive and the walls were standing.

After the coming of the Dark Ones things changed, of course.

But in the high summer of his seventeenth year, when the Icefalcon made his way east over the pass that now he traveled west, the Dark Ones had been only one tale among many to the mud-diggers and in places not even that.

In that summer the cover had been better, pale aspens bright among the firs, with brakes of hazel, dogwood, and laurel to conceal him and his horse. He'd moved mostly by twilight since the people of the straight roads kept guards in the pass at that time, fearing quite rightly the depredations of bandit troops from the West. In those days the Raiders had very little use for the mud-diggers' cattle. There had been gazelle and bison, red deer and wild sheep then in the northern plains.

The Keep of Dare was the first structure the Icefalcon beheld on the sunrise side of the mountain wall. It had surprised him, he recalled, and smiled a little at the recollection. The houses of the mud-diggers that he had seen before had all been wood structures of two or at most three floors, or in the South low buildings of adobe roofed with pine poles or tiles. He had not expected the Keep. It was some time before he learned that civilized people on this side of the mountains did not all dwell in great dark solitary fortresses, untouchable by enemies.

Sunrise found him in the thin stands of birch and aspen at the western foot of Sarda Pass. Reaching the place nearly an hour short of first light, he found a spot where chokecherry grew thick around the white boulders that marked the ascending road from the West and, crawling in, rolled himself up in Rudy's mantle and his own blanket to sleep. The snow lay behind him. Clouds piled the gray-and-white western cliffs of Anthir, and bitter wind nipped

at him like a Wise One's leftover curse. He hoped Gil
would be well.

Squirrel chitter woke him. He had a sling tied around
the bottom of his quiver, and it took him nearly two hours
to kill four squirrels: spring wary, and spring thin as well,
no more than a few mouthfuls each. Still he roasted them
and ate everything that wouldn't keep: guts, hearts, brains.
He'd need the meat later. Some of the innards he used
as fish bait in the pools of one of the many springs that
came down from Anthir's climbing maze of hogbacks and
scarps, and the fish he caught he cooked also. Time-
consuming, but he knew himself incapable of rescuing Tir
alone if there were a Wise One in the enemy party, and the
tracks of Bektis and Hethya weren't going to fly away. He
shaved—his beard had not begun when he'd first crossed
the mountains and he'd never liked going furry—and tried
to bring down one of the raccoons that came to thieve his
fish but failed in the endeavor. The sun was high before he
filled his water bottle and Rudy's from the spring and set
out on what he already knew would be a long pursuit.

He'd taken three horses when he left the Talking Stars
People—Little Dancer, whom he had owned for years,
Sand Cat, and Dung For Brains. Sand Cat had been shot
under him in a brush with Gettlesand bandits, and Dung
For Brains he had killed himself when the animal went
lame. His dog, Bright Feet, had also been killed by the
bandits in Gettlesand: the spirit-bag he still wore under
his clothing, next to his skin, contained some of Bright
Feet's hair.

He found horses corraled near the shining jet walls
of the Keep, his first day in Renweth Vale. Stealing two
was no difficult matter. These he'd named Brown Girl
and Wind.

Then, knowing he was going to live east of the wall for
some time, he set himself to observe the mud-diggers who
lived in the Vale. It became obvious to him at once that
these were a war party of some sort, though he could not

determine who their enemy was and where they lay. They
had neither flocks nor herds (except for their horses), nor
did they plant fields of the corn, cotton, and beans that
grew in the mud-diggers' settlements in the South. They
had a few dooic as slaves—the slumped, hairy semi-
humans that the Talking Stars People would have killed
out of hand—but he did not see children among them, or
old people, though that could have been accounted for by
famine or plague.

The men and women of the Keep, back in that far
summer, wore either black clothing marked with a small
white four-petaled flower or red with one or three black
stars. There was a tall man who wore red much of the time
and sported a chain of blue gems around his neck and a
long black cloak that spread about him like wings when he
walked, and he seemed to be in command of the men and
women in red. It was a day or so before the Icefalcon realized that another man—equally tall but thin, clothed no
differently from all the other wearers of black, save that
the emblem on his breast was an eagle worked in gold—
was commander over them all.

This man was the one they called Eldor, or Lord Eldor,
and this was the man who, the Icefalcon realized on his
second day in the Vale, was stalking him.

"It only needed that!" stormed Blue Jewels on that
second day, when the two horses were reported missing.
He made a great expansive angry gesture that would have
startled game and drawn enemies for miles around, and
Eldor folded his long arms and regarded him in self-
contained quiet, his head a little on one side.

"Bandits in the Vale! I told you how it would be did you
reopen Dare's Keep, Lord Eldor. It dominates all the valley
for miles. Instead of expending effort and supplies to
make it fit for a larger garrison—which I understand, with
the depredations of the bandits growing in the West—you
would do better to leave it locked and expand the fortifica-
tions at the western foot of the pass."

His deep, melodious voice carried easily to where the

Icefalcon lay along the limb of the great pine tree that still grew between the Keep and the stream. It was the custom of the Talking Stars People periodically to send warriors south to kidnap men from the settlements, whom they kept as prisoners for a winter to teach the children the tongue of the Wathe. These men they usually initiated into one or another of the families so that when the time of the spring sacrifices came nobody who had actually been born into the families had to be tortured to death, though the hair of such men usually wasn't long enough to make good bowstrings.

"As sure as the Ice in the North," Blue Jewels went on, "if you leave the Keep open, either bandits will take it as a hold or some troublemaker landchief will."

"If it was bandits." The tall Lord Eldor followed the offending sentry back to the horse lines, speaking to Blue Jewels as they walked. "Tomec Tirkenson tells me bandits as a rule are too greedy for their own good. They'll lift the whole herd, not two out of the middle where they wouldn't be noticed until the count."

After a little more bluster, Blue Jewels—whom the Icefalcon later knew as Alwir of the House of Bes, one of the wealthiest and most powerful lords of the Realm— ordered out a party of his red-clothed warriors to search the Vale, and the Icefalcon made his leisurely way back to his camp near the standing-stones, to move it before they got there.

He later came to know both Eldor and Alwir well, but it sometimes seemed to him that all the years of acquaintance only deepened, rather than altered, his initial impression of them: Alwir declaiming and jumping to an incorrect conclusion, Eldor standing a little distance from him, withholding judgment, an expression of observation and a detached amusement in his steel-colored eyes.

Winter still held the land below the pass. The Real World that stretched between the Snowy Mountains and the Seaward was an unforgiving land, a land of little water in most places and few trees, a land of hard, steady winds punctuated by summer tornadoes and, so he had heard, of winter ice storms these past ten years that tore man and beast to shreds and froze them where they fell.

Herds of bison and antelope wandered the open miles of grassland, and as the winters lengthened and deepened, mammoth, yak, reindeer, and rhinoceri joined them, followed by the great killers: dire wolves, saberteeth, horrible-birds. Since the Summerless Year slunch had spread, the wrinkled, rubbery, faintly glowing sheets of it swallowing the ground for miles, sucking the life from any plant it engulfed. The slunch in its turn put forth a kind of life, strange creatures that wandered abroad but did not appear to either eat, or seed, or excrete. These things died and rotted with a strange, mild, sweetish stench and left patches of slunch where they lay.

The Icefalcon's hackles raised like a dog's to see how the slunch and the cold had altered the land. Many of the groves that dotted the western foothills were now dead, buried under the whitish masses. As he followed the westward road that first day, the stuff stretched on both sides, in patches or in sheets miles broad, and neither rabbits, nor lemmings, nor antelope moved over the dying grass that lay between.

By the debris left where Bektis and his party stopped to rest, the Icefalcon learned that in addition to what Bektis and Hethya had carried on their two donkeys they'd helped themselves to the Keep's stores of dried meat, cheese, and potatoes. With his sling he killed two kites that came down after the cheese rinds and potato parings and added their meat to his satchel, and the rinds and parings as well. With slunch growing abroad in the lands food would be even more difficult to find, and he knew he could waste none. Only in the camps did he see Tir's tracks and guessed by the marks in the thin dust that they were keeping the boy's hands tied.

In a way it was just as well, he thought. Whatever Gil might say, the boy might have tried to escape while the mountains still loomed in the east, and his chances of survival would be nil in these desolate lands.

After black-cloaked Alwir with his blue jewels had declared him to be a bandit, hunting parties went out to search the Vale of Renweth for the Icefalcon for three days running. The Icefalcon had been more amused than anything else, patiently moving his camp every few hours— the invisible camp of the peoples of the North, which left no sign on the land—and watching them. He watched, too, the trains of mules that came up the gorge of the Arrow River through the smaller range of peaks west of the Vale, food and seed and saplings; watched the training of the black-clothed Guards under the tutelage of a little baldheaded man with a hoarse voice; watched Alwir and Eldor walk around the walls of the Keep and the edges of the woods that surrounded its knoll, talking and making notes on tablets wrought of wood and wax.

Alwir continued to complain of the size of the Keep and its uselessness as a garrison against the Gettlesand bandits. "In times of siege it's a jail!" he declared, striding up and down the shallow steps that led to its single pair of dark metal Doors. "To be sure, no one can get in, but the defenders are trapped! Unless there's a secret way out? A tunnel for sorties, perhaps, or a hidden door?"

His blue eyes glinted eagerly. He was a man who loved secrets, thought the Icefalcon, lying in the long grass beside the stream. Himself, he would never have entrusted any secret to this Alwir, who seemed to consider himself above the laws of common men by virtue of his descent from the lordly House of Bes.

"None that I know of," replied Eldor calmly and went on with his surveying, knee-deep in the long meadow grass.

This Eldor was a man of thirty-five, as tall as Alwir and just slightly taller than the Icefalcon himself, who at seventeen was an inch or so short of his final growth. Eldor wore his brown hair cut off about his shoulders, as was the fashion of civilized people, and had an air of lean strength. Sometimes he would fight practice bouts with his warriors, either the black-clothed or the red.

Observing them in the light of the fires and torches—which illuminated the whole western face of the Keep and would have made them an easy target for the arrows of any foe on earth—or in the twilight before full dark, the Icefalcon saw with approval the hard stringency of the teaching. The lithe bald man in charge corrected and explained and shouted criticism as if the combatants were stupid children barely able to bat one another with clubs, or put them through endless drills with weighted weapons that the Icefalcon quickly saw were designed to most quickly and efficiently increase their strength and speed. It was a method of teaching he had never encountered among his own people, and it fascinated him. He would go down to the camp by the black walls every evening, after the work of planting and clearing had been done and after the stupid patrols had been called in, and he would watch them for hours. In his own camp he whittled a sword of the length they were using, with a two-handed hilt, balanced differently from the short stabbing-swords used on the plain and made for a different sort of warfare. He practiced everything he had seen the previous night, timing himself against the calls of the night-birds or striking against a tree trunk.

Then he would go back and listen, and heard for the first time the music these people made, with harps and pipes, different from the simple reed flutes of his people, intricate and beautiful if completely useless.

They would also tell tales, of valor and violence and love, and it was some time before he realized that these were made up and had never really happened to anyone. It was an art with them, he learned later—and also among Gil's people, evidently—to make such fictions sound as if they were true. The tales of civilized people were beautiful and fascinated the Icefalcon in spite of himself, but he told himself they were useless.

Then one night the Icefalcon had returned to his camp
to find Wind and Little Dancer gone.

That Eldor hadn't taken all three animals, as one would
do to an enemy, outraged him. *I think you'll need a horse,*
it implied. That he had left Brown Girl, the worst of the
three, was a slap, given teasingly, as a man might slap a
boy in jest. And he knew it was Eldor who had taken them.
While he was watching the sparring in the evening, he
thought, annoyed, as he searched the place the next morning for tracks.

He found them, but it was difficult. The man had covered his traces well. Eldor had distracted him with the
large search parties while making solitary reconnaissance
of his own.

The Icefalcon guessed they were expecting him to try to
steal back Little Dancer, at least, from the cavvy. They always tethered her and Wind in the middle. He noticed the
Guards were now more numerous. So he waited and
watched, until one evening Eldor rode forth from the Keep
alone on Wind, a tall black stallion that the Icefalcon had
seen was a favorite of his. He followed him up the meadows to the rising ground above the Keep and shot him in
the back with an arrow.

The Icefalcon smiled again, thinking about it now as he
made a cold camp in the ditch beside the west-leading road.

Of course Eldor had been wearing armor, steel plate
sandwiching a core of cane and overlaid with spells of
durability and deflection. If it hadn't been twilight, blue
shade filling the long trough of Renweth Vale like a lake of
clear dark water, he'd have seen the awkward fit of the
man's surcoat or wondered why in summer he'd worn a
cloak. Eldor had carried a pig's bladder of blood, too, and
smashed it as he fell from Wind's back, so the Icefalcon
smelled blood from where he hid in the trees. He'd
thought it sheer bad luck that his victim had fallen on the
reins, holding the horse near. The "corpse" had hooked his

feet out from under him and put a knife to his throat. The Icefalcon never believed in bad luck again.

"Alwir thinks you're a scout from a bandit gang," Eldor said, without relaxing his grip. "But you're alone, aren't you?"

The Icefalcon said nothing. He supposed if he had to die at least this was better than the fate he left among the Talking Stars People, but his own stupidity filled him with anger.

"I've heard you people don't ride with bandits."

Still nothing. It was true that none of the people of the Real World had much use for bandits, not wanting the possessions that lawless folk so stupidly craved, but it was not the way of his people to speak with enemies.

"I don't want to kill you," said Eldor, though he didn't relax his grip or move the knife. "It would be a waste of a good warrior, and I need good warriors. I saw the practice posts you've made at your camps, to go over for yourself what Gnift has been teaching the Guards lately. Would you like to learn?"

The Icefalcon considered the matter and pointed out, "I am your enemy."

Eldor released him then and got up very quickly, stepping clear even as the Icefalcon rolled to his feet. "Why?" he asked.

The Icefalcon thought about the reasons that he had left the Talking Stars People and about where he might go, and what he might do, now that it was impossible for him to go back. He found that he did not have any reply to Eldor's question.

Eldor Endorion.

The Icefalcon drank a little water and settled himself in the bayberry that grew in the ditch. The silence of the prairie drifted over him. He listened, identifying the crying of the coyotes and the greater voices of wolves farther off, the susurration of the ceaseless wind and the smell of dust and growing needlegrass.

The world of his childhood reassembling itself, scent by scent and sound by sound in the darkness.

He was home.

Eldor Endorion.

He hadn't been at all surprised to learn that the man who had overpowered him, the man who had put himself in danger in order to trap a possible spy, was in fact the High King of the Wathe. Even when he learned the size of the Realm, and the rich complexity of the world Eldor ruled, he had felt no surprise at the acts.

They were typical of the man.

Eldor remained an extra week in Renweth Vale with the men and women he had sent to regarrison and reprovision the Keep, in order to train with the Icefalcon, to get to know him, to test him as leaders test warriors whom they seek to win to their sides. The Icefalcon had trained hawks. He knew what Eldor was doing.

He never felt toward the King the reverence that the other Guards did or stood in awe of that darkly blazing personality. But he knew the man was trustworthy and respectworthy to the core of his being. He was content to attach himself to the Guards.

He spent four years in the city of Gae, training with the Guards. He exchanged his wolf-hide and mammoth-wool clothing for the fine dense sheep-wool uniforms, black with their white quatrefoil flowers; wore the hard-soled boots of civilized men (though they were less comfortable than moccasins and left more visible tracks). When his beard came in the following year, he shaved, as civilized men did, though he never cut his hair. He learned to use a long killing-sword and to fight in groups rather than alone.

In Gae he met Ingold, Eldor's old tutor, unobtrusively mad and—he quickly learned—probably the finest swordsman in the west of the world. He saw him first sparring on Gnift's training floor and took him for some shabby old swordmaster down on his luck, which was what he invariably looked like. Later, after he trounced the Icefalcon roundly, they'd have long discussions about animal

tracks, the habits of bees, and where grass grew. Just to
watch the High King spar with the Wise One was an edu-
cation. Now and then he would see Alwir's sister about the
palace compound, a pretty, quiet schoolgirl who read ro-
mances and never left her governess' side and had not a
word to say for herself. Three years after his arrival in Gae
she was married to Eldor, for the benefit of both their
houses. Their child was Tir.

Though no one knew it, time was running out for civilized folk, like water from a cracked jar.

It was during this time, too, that he became acquainted
with Bektis, who was much more a fixture at court than Ingold. Ingold was in and out of the city, but Bektis had
a suite of chambers in Alwir's palace in the district of
the city called the Water Park—less crowded and smelly
than the rest of Gae, which had taken the Icefalcon years
to get used to. Bektis scried the future and the past (he
said) and learned through magic of things far away, and
he also worked the weather for court fetes and advised
Alwir about shipping ventures, something that made the
Wise Ones mistrusted by merchants and farmers throughout the civilized realms. Shamans among the Icefalcon's
people also worked the weather, insofar as they would
avert the worst of the storms from the winter settlements
and the horse herds, but such workings were known to be
dangerous. Besides, working the weather might let enemies guess where you camped.

Alwir and Bektis referred to the Icefalcon as "Lord
Eldor's Tame Barbarian" and made little jests about the
things that were, to him, simply logical, like always having weapons and a day's supply of food on his person,
keeping to corners and never being where he could not immediately get out of a room. Their jokes did not offend
him. Merely they informed him that they were fools, as
most of the people of the straight roads were either mad or
fools.

And most of them died with the coming of the Dark
Ones.

                        *    *    *

Wind moved over the land, bitterly cold. Above the overcast that veiled the sky most nights now, the waning moon was a ravel of luminous wool. It had taken the Icefalcon most of a year to separate the reflexive terror about being outdoors after nightfall, developed by those who had passed through the Time of the Dark, from the reasonable wariness he had possessed before. Now he listened, identifying sounds and smells, gauging the scent of greenery and water somewhere beyond the slunch to the northwest that meant he might hunt tomorrow, measuring it against the certainty that there would be predators there as well. A small glowing thing like a detached head on two legs ran by along the top of the ditch—most slunch-born things glowed a little. A night-bird skimmed past, hunting moths.

Tir was out there in the dark, in the camp with Bektis and Hethya and those three identical black warriors.

Eldor's son.

Eldor was not the kin of the Icefalcon's ancestors. By the standards of the Talking Stars People, he would be considered an enemy. But he had not been. And he was the only person in Gae—the only person in all that new life the Icefalcon had lived among civilized people for four years—to whom he had spoken about why he had left the Talking Stars People and why he could not go back.

Speaking to him had made him less of an enemy. But what he would be called, the Icefalcon did not know.

The Dark Ones ringed this place.

Tir forced his eyes open, forced himself to look out past the campfire that seemed to him so pitifully inadequate; forced himself to look out into the darkness.

*They aren't really there.*

He had never actually seen the Dark Ones. Not that he remembered by himself—his mother had told him they'd all gone away when he was a little baby. Sometimes in nightmares he'd be aware of them, amorphous waiting stirrings in the shadows and a smell that scared him when he smelled things like it sometimes, some of the things the women of the Keep used to clean clothing with.

He saw them now. The memory was overwhelming, like a recollection of something that had happened to him only yesterday: clouds of darkness that blotted the moon, winds that came up suddenly, seeming to blow from every direction at once, carrying on them the wet unnatural cold, the blood and ammonia stink. On this very stream bank— only the gully wasn't this deep then, and the stream's waters had lain closer to the surface, gurgling and glittering in the light of torches, a ring of torches—he had watched them pour across the flat prairie grass like floodwaters spreading and had felt his heart freeze with sickened horror and the knowledge that there was no escape.

*They aren't really there.*

He faced out into the darkness, and the darkness was still.

The memory retreated a little. He felt weak with shock and relief.

"For the love o' God, Bektis," said Hethya, "let the poor tyke eat."

She stood in the firelight, hair dark except where the reflected glare made brassy splinters in it, red mouth turned down with irritation. Bektis said, "I'm not going to risk the child running away." He was rubbing and polishing the device that he wore over his right hand with a chamois; the great jointed encrustation of crystals and gold locked around his wrist, gemmed the back of his hand and his arm, and the knuckles of two of his fingers, with slabs and nodules of coruscant light. Polishing meticulously, obsessively, now with the leather and now with one of the several stiff brushes he took from his satchel, as if he feared that a single fleck of grease from dinner— which Hethya had cooked—would lessen its lethal power.

He had killed Rudy with it.

Tir shut his eyes.

He had killed Rudy.

When he shut his eyes he could still see his friend, his mother's friend, the man who was the only father he'd known.

Hand lifted, the pronged crescent of the staff he bore flashing light, levin-fire showing up the crooked-nosed face, the wide dark eyes. Working magic, fighting Bektis' spells so that he could rescue him, Tir, get him away from those people who'd somehow made him think that Rudy was with them all the way up the pass, that Rudy was there telling him it was okay to go with them.

He could still see the fake Rudy melting and changing into a black-skinned bald man, a man he'd never seen before, like those two other identical black warriors who'd come out of the woods to follow them toward the pass. Could still feel their hands on him, grabbing him when he tried to jump down from the donkey and run.

Then Rudy had been there, with Gil and the Icefalcon, witchlight showing them up among the rocks and snow and inky shadows of the pass. Rudy running, zigzagging away from the lightning bolts Bektis threw at him, straightening up to hurl fire from the head of his staff, crying out words of power.

The lightning bolt had hit him. And he'd fallen.

Tir clamped his teeth hard to keep from crying.

"Here you go, sweeting." He heard the rustle of Hethya's clothes—she'd changed back into trousers and a man's tunic and coat—and smelled the scent of her, thicker and sweeter than a man's. He smelled, too, the roasted meat and the potatoes she carried in a gourd bowl and opened his eyes.

"Please untie me," he whispered. He wriggled his wrists a little in the rawhide bonds, trying to ease the pain. The coarse leather had blistered his skin during the day and the slightest pressure was a needle of fire.

"I'm sorry, me darling." She picked a fragment of meat from the dish; she'd already cut it up for him. "His High-And-Mightiness seems to think you'll run off, and then where would we all be?" She blew on the meat to cool it. Steam curled from it, white in the firelight.

"Please." He tried not to sound scared, but panic scratched behind the shut doors in his mind. The Dark Ones coming. The wizards in the camp setting out flares, setting out what looked like stones, gray lumps woven around with tangled tentacles of iron and light. Fire columning up from them, the wizards' faces illuminated, tattooed patterns lacing their shaved skulls and grim fear in their eyes. His father's warriors bracing themselves with their flamethrowers and swords, and the one wizard who'd been engulfed by those rubbery tentacles, falling away from their grip only a heap of red-stained, melted, smoking bones.

It was only a memory. It had happened thousands of years ago. The Dark Ones weren't coming back.

Hethya made a growl in her throat, glanced back at Bektis, and pushing Tir around by his shoulders, yanked the knots free of the bindings. The rawhide jerking away brought tears to his eyes, and the cold in the open cuts was excruciating.

She turned him around back. "Just till you finish eating, mind," she said.

Tir whispered, "Thank you."

"Not so fast, child."

Bektis rose from his place by the fire, crossed to where Hethya sat tailor-fashion in front of Tir, Tir kneeling with the food bowl between his knees. Tir got to his feet; Hethya too. Tir tried hard to keep his voice steady. "I won't run away. I just . . ." He couldn't finish. Couldn't tell this tall bearded man how badly it terrified him, not to have the use of his hands, not to be *able* to run in this place where the Dark had descended on them, this place at the far end of that blind corridor of memories.

Bektis said softly, "See that you don't."

The flourish of his arm, wrist, and elbow leading—like Gingume at the Keep who'd been an actor in Penambra

before the Dark came— seemed to reach out, to gather in
the formless prairie night.

Gold eyes flashed there. Ground mist and shadow coalesced. Something moved.

Tir's heart stood still.

"You know what I am, don't you, child?" murmured
Bektis. "You know what I can do. I know the names of the
wolfen-kind; I can summon the smilodonts from their lairs
and the horrible-birds from where they nest in the rocks.
At my bidding they will come."

The camp was surrounded with them. Huge, half-unseen
shaggy shapes, snuffing just out of the circle of the firelight. Elsewhere the glint of foot-long fangs. A snarl like
ripping canvas. Tir glanced back again, despairingly, at the
pitiful handful of flames, the three black warriors crouched
beside it, staring around them into the dark with worried
silver-gray eyes.

Hethya put her arms over his shoulders, pulled him to
her tight. "Quit terrifyin' the boy, you soulless hellkite."
She ruffled Tir's hair comfortingly. "Don't you worry,
sweeting." Bektis glared at her for silence—after hesitation she said, "Just you stay inside the camp and you'll be
well."

Stomach churning with fright, Tir looked from her face
to Bektis' cold dark eyes, then to the lightless infinity beyond the fire's reach. Movement still padded and sniffed
in the long grass. Waiting for him. He didn't want to—
she'd kidnapped him, dragged him away here, lied to him,
she was part of Bektis' evil troupe—but he found himself
clinging desperately to this woman's arm.

She added, a little more loudly, "He's such a great
wizard, he can keep all those nasties at bay, sweeting.
They won't be coming near to the camp, just you see. Now
come." She drew him toward the fire, opposite where
Bektis had resumed his seat. "Have yourself a bite to
eat, and roll up and sleep. It's been a rough day on you, so
it has."

She meant to be kind, so Tir didn't say anything and

tried to eat a little of the meat and potatoes she offered him. But his stomach hurt so much with fear he could barely choke down a mouthful, and he shook his head at the rest. When he lay down in her blankets next to her, with the swarthy guards keeping watch, he could still hear the *hrush* of huge bodies slipping through the grass, the thick heavy pant of breath. Could smell, mingled with the earth smell and rain smell and new spring grasses, the rank carnivore stink. All these interlaced with the clucking of the stream in the gully and lent a horror to dreams in which Rudy's death—over and over, struck by lightning, endlessly falling from the jutting rocks into blackness—alternated with the slow flood of still darker blackness spreading to cover the wizards' flares, to cover them all.

Then he'd wake, panting with terror, to hear only far-off thunder and the endless hissing of the prairie winds.

# CHAPTER FIVE

On the third day out from Sarda Pass, Bektis and his party were attacked by a scouting band from the Empty Lakes People.

This didn't surprise the Icefalcon. He had never rated the intelligence of the Empty Lakes People much higher than that of the average prairie dog.

He had overtaken Bektis around noon of the second day, though the wizard was not aware of the fact. Sometimes the Icefalcon trailed them north of the road, sometimes south, taking advantage of the gullies that scored this land and the low clumps of rabbitbrush and juniper that lifted above the waving green lake of grass.

The three black warriors, he saw, carried heavy packs—blankets and provisions for many days—bad news given his own need to hunt as he went. When they halted for nooning, he briefly considered helping himself to their stores but gave up the idea at once. Like most of the warriors of the Real World, he carried talismans to give him at least some protection against the illusions—and the scrying abilities—of Wise Ones, but such amulets were only as good as the shaman who wrought them, and he suspected Bektis would be able to see through such wards without much trouble if he had any suspicion that there was a reason to look. Even could he slip past whatever guardian-wards Bektis might put around the camp, the mere fact of the thefts would alert them that they were being watched, and with a Wise One in the party this was far too dangerous to permit. He was eking out his small supplies of meat and fish with the roots of last autumn's water plantains and cattails, but even they took time to gather and prepare, and he could feel hunger gaining on him.

Toward sunset of the second day they left the road and turned north to Bison Hill, a mound in the midst of the prairie covered with elder and cottonwood and used by travelers as a campsite—and by bandits as a handy place to find travelers—since time immemorial. Deer grazed in the woods, as did the small swift antelope of the plains.

He worked his way up to the knoll through stream cuts and bison wallows and under cover of the long prairie grass, making a mental note to speak to Janus about changing the clothing of the Guards from their traditional black to the colors of the earth. From a thicket of wild grapes some distance back he watched Hethya and one of the three black warriors—*clones*, Gil had called them, meaning identical people who were presumably common to her world—unload the donkeys while Bektis built a fire at the edge of the shelter of the trees.

Only an idiot or a Wise One would build a fire in such a place, where anyone could take advantage of the cover to come up on them, even as the Icefalcon was doing. But he supposed that with the advantage of wizardry it was possible to remain comfortably out of the wind and not worry about who or what might be deeper in the woods. Any of the Talking Stars People would have camped some distance from the knoll, where they could see in all directions, even had they had a Wise One in their company.

There was never a guarantee that some other war band wouldn't include a shaman more Wise than one's own.

"I can help you," said Tir, as Hethya lifted him down from the donkey. "I promise I won't run away." He spoke matter-of-factly, but with a friendliness in his voice that told the Icefalcon that this woman must have used him kindly over the past day and a half. Indeed, the woman's face was not cruel, and by the way she patted Tir on the shoulder, and the closeness between them as they stood, it was clear that she was used to children and liked them.

She glanced now over at Bektis, who was ordering the warriors about placing the blankets. It was the closest the Icefalcon had been to them—less than a hundred feet—and he studied the weapon of crystal and gold on the sorcerer's hand with wary interest. A device of similar workmanship around Bektis' neck, a high collar fitted up close under the ears, was visible only briefly when the wizard pushed down the furred hood of his coat and tried to untangle his beard.

"I think best not, sweeting," Hethya said in a voice so low the Icefalcon had to guess at some of the words. "But thank you; 'tis kind of you thinking of it." She ruffled his hair again. "Sit you down there under the tree a bit. We'll be having supper soon, and I'll untie you to eat. Are you tired?"

Tir shook his head, though he looked beaten with weariness. He followed her, his hands still bound behind his back—the Icefalcon could see where his wrists were bandaged under the thongs—while she unshipped a little nest of cook pots. "Does Oale Niu just tell you things?" he asked her as she worked. "Or do you see things, or smell them sometimes, and . . . and remember? Or think you remember but you don't know what it is?"

"Like what, honey? Here, you, Akula," she called out, and all three of the guards turned their heads. "One of you go fetch me water from the spring, would you?"

The men stared at her, scorn in their faces, for in the Alketch men do not take orders from women. Bektis snapped, "Do as she says," and all started off in search of the boiled-leather pail that had hung, filled neatly with potatoes, on the second donkey's pack saddle. Watching their aimless movements, it occurred to the Icefalcon that none of them were very bright.

"Like this." Tir nodded toward the rolling wonderment of green beyond the scrim of birches. They had left the great slunch beds behind them, and for the most part the land was as it had been since the world's dawn: long grass bright with spring, widely dispersed clumps of rabbitbrush, the dark lines of treetops marking stream cuts sometimes sixty feet below the level of the surrounding plain. "It smells like something . . . One of those other people was here once." "Those other people" was how the boy thought about his ancestors, those memories of ancient days.

"Only it was in the winter, I think," went on Tir softly. "Everything was brown. Did Oale Niu come here?"

"She did that." Hethya settled back on her hunkers, and her voice changed again, slowed and deepened, as she said, "I was here. Twelve of us rode down from the flanks of Anthir mountain. The mages ringed our camp with a circle of flames to keep the Dark Ones at bay."

Tir frowned. Even from this distance, the Icefalcon saw in the set of his shoulders, the stance of his compact body, the memory of distant things. "He was here with his daddy," he said, so softly the Icefalcon almost could not make out the words. "His daddy knew the way. The road was that way, north toward the mountains, by those little hills."

Two of the warriors came back with water; Bektis gave them very exact instructions about mounting guard on the camp, things that to the Icefalcon seemed obvious. The Icefalcon slipped back among the trees, carefully picking hard and sheltered ground, and crawled snakewise on his belly through the grass to the bison wallow that he knew from other days lay just south of the road. Bandits—or more likely the Empty Lakes People, whose spirit wands he had seen twice in these lands—would be along in the morning.

And they were.

The Empty Lakes People didn't attack until nearly noon, but the Icefalcon was aware of them when they came up the coulee to the northwest as a redstart and a raven flew out of the trees. They waited there for a time, for the party in the grove to pack up and move on.

When Bektis and his group didn't pack up, but rather collected more firewood and water, like people who planned to remain where they were for the day, the Empty Lakes

People—being the Empty Lakes People—decided that the
thing to do was attack rather than make a closer observation
of the grove, in which case they'd have seen that there was a
Wise One in the party and thought again about the idea.

Or maybe not. These were the Empty Lakes People,
after all.

In any case they attacked, with predictable results. The
Icefalcon heard a cry from the wooded hill, and Hethya's
scream. The woman always seemed to be screaming. A
man broke cover on the eastern side of the hill and ran
across the road with his deer-hide jacket in flames. He fell
in the long grass. Another warrior rode full-tilt out of the
grove on a dun-colored mare that reared in sudden terror at
something it saw but the Icefalcon didn't.

*Illusion.* There were amulets against such spookery on
the mare's bridle but clearly Bektis' powers were greater
than the amulets' maker—and since the Dark Ones' sys-
tematic destruction of mages, many of the talismans had
outlived their effectiveness years ago. One of the black
warriors pelted from the trees and grappled briefly with
the warrior, dragging her down from her horse. She cried
out in terror and pain, and struck at something—again
illusory—in which moment the black man plunged his
sword into the woman's chest. She fell, coughing blood. A
war-dog, probably hers, raced from the trees, coat blazing,
crying and yipping in pain.

In the grove other shapes were running around or struggling in the trampled underbrush of wild grape and snake-
weed. More barking, war-dogs terrified and confused by
enchantment. Fire flashed, or perhaps only the illusion of fire.

Tir, very sensibly, climbed a tree. The Icefalcon saw
the boy's bright blue jacket sleeves among the limbs of
the cottonwood under which Bektis had built last night's
fire. He was glad that someone—probably the woman
Hethya—had untied Tir's hands and hoped none of the
Empty Lakes People remained in the coulee, which was
just within bowshot of the hill. The boy probably knew
that running away from Bektis would be a waste of time.

*Bide your time, son of Eldor. Watch for your chance.*

*The coyote who waits can eat the flesh of the saber-tooth who plunges ahead into a fight.*

The attack was over before the shadows had shortened the last inch or so to noon.

Leaning up on his elbows, the Icefalcon watched the three black warriors load the bodies of the slain onto the horses that remained in the grove and carry them out to the coulee to dump them. Then they returned to Bektis' camp, tethered the captured horses, and set about gathering water and making lunch.

*Thank you,* thought the Icefalcon. *Now stay put so I can eat, too.*

He crawled through the grass—noting automatically that rains had been scanty here and so the herds would not be plentiful later in the year—to the edge of the coulee, which at that point was some twenty feet deep. Even a few years before, the stream at the bottom had been wider and stronger than it was now. Barely a trickle flowed over gray and white rocks, and the sedge and cattail along its verge were thin and weak, though on the whole the bottomland that lay for thirty or forty feet on either side of the water was lusher than the prairie above. Cottonwood and lodgepole pine made light cover from bank to waterside; lungwort, fleabane, and marigolds gemmed the grass.

The half-dozen bodies lay jumbled below in a clump of chokecherry. Their dogs had been thrown down with them, the heavy-headed, heavy-shouldered fighting brutes of the Empty Lakes People. The Icefalcon took a very cautious look around, then slithered down the bank some hundred feet from the place, which he circled twice before coming close. Carrion birds were already gathered. He wondered if Bektis would notice when they flew upward.

They settled again on the limbs of the cottonwood just above the bodies, below the line of the prairie's edge.

There had been six in the scouting party. Five lay here, fair-skinned like all the peoples of the Real World, bronzed from the sun, their hair—flaxen or primrose or the gay hue of marigolds—braided and dabbled with darkening blood. Four had perished of stab wounds, and one bore the same lightning burns that had marked Rudy's face. The sixth would be the man who ran out of the grove with his shirt burning, to fall in the long grass.

The Icefalcon waited, listening, for some little time more, then moved in and made from them a selection of trousers, tunic, jacket, gloves, and cap wrought of wolf or deer hide, whose colors blended with the hues of the prairie. He changed clothes quickly and buried his black garments in a muskrat hole in the bank, piling brush to conceal where he'd driven the earth in. His weapons and harness he kept; his boots as well, for none of them had feet of his size, and boots would outlast moccasins on a long hunt.

He collected also all the food they carried, scout rations of pemmican, jerked venison and duck flesh, pine nuts, and bison and raccoon fat sweetened with maple sugar. He hung the buckskin pouches and tubes from his belt and shoulders, working fast, with one eye on the birds overhead.

When they flew up, he retreated, picking again the stoniest line of departure, which would show no mark of his boots.

Rather to his surprise he knew the man who slipped down the bank from above and stole up on the bodies, taking far fewer precautions about it than the Icefalcon considered necessary, but what could one expect from the Empty Lakes People?

It was Loses His Way.

Loses His Way was a warchief and one of the most renowned warriors of the Empty Lakes People. He had given the Icefalcon the scar that decorated the hollow of his left flank in a horse raid during the Summer of the Two White Mammoths. He'd been a minor chief then, and the Icefalcon had encountered him twice more, once in a battle over summer hunting and once at a Moot. If the Icefalcon hadn't left the Talking Stars People, they'd probably have fought again at another Moot. He was a big man, some ten years older than the Icefalcon, with massive shoulders and tawny mustaches braided down past his chin; the finger bones of a dozen foes were plaited into his hair.

He moved painfully now, and the Icefalcon saw the red blister of burned flesh through the black hole that had been the back of his tunic.

When he saw the bodies had been disturbed, he looked around quickly, short-sword coming to his hand.

Conscious of the possibility of sound carrying, the Icefalcon whistled twice in the voice of the tanager, a bird native to the oakwoods along the Ten Muddy Rivers, where the Empty Lakes People had originally dwelled, though it was never seen in the high plains. Loses His Way turned his head and the Icefalcon stepped from cover, crossed swiftly to the pile of bodies at the foot of the cottonwood tree. "I am an enemy to the people who did this," he said, as soon as he was close enough that their voices would not be heard. "I am alone."

Loses His Way raised his head, grief and shock darkening gentian-blue eyes. "Icefalcon." He spoke the name as it was spoken among the Empty Lakes People, *K'shnia*. He was like a man stunned by a blow, barely taking in the presence of one who was his enemy and the enemy of his people.

"The air was full of creatures that tore at us," he said, and turned back to the dead. "When we rode away, the horses threw us and ran back. Our dogs attacked us and savaged one another." He touched the torn-out throat of a big gray dog, as if stroking the hair of a beloved child. "There was a Wise One, a shaman, among them."

"The shaman is called Bektis," said the Icefalcon, framing the words carefully, haltingly, in the tongue of the Empty Lakes People, which he had not had call to speak for years. "An evil man, who has carried away the son of one who was good to me."

Loses His Way seemed scarcely to hear. His thick scarred stubby fingers passed across noses, lips, brows. "Tethtagyn," he said, framing the name in the tongue of the Empty Lakes People; *Wolfbone* it meant. "Shilhren . . .

Giarathis . . ." Under long, curling red brows his eyes filled with grief.

"Twin Daughter," he whispered, and touched the face of a warrior whose hair was as red-gold as his. "Twin Daughter."

Gently lifting the thick ropes of her hair—three braids, as was the fashion of his people—Loses His Way took from around the young woman's neck a square spirit-pouch, decorated with porcupine quills and patterns in ocher and black. Worn under the clothing and out of sight, spirit-pouches were almost the only article decorated by any of the peoples of the Real World. With his knife he cut off some of Twin Daughter's hair and put it into the pouch. Then he sliced the palm of her left hand, and with his thumb daubed the congealing blood in the open center of the pouch's worked design.

This he did for all the others in turn, saying their names as he did so: Wolfbone, Blue Jay, Shouts In Anger, Raspberry Thicket Girl. The Empty Lakes People, the Icefalcon remembered, did not revere their Ancestors, but rather the *ki* of various rocks and trees in the country of the Ten Muddy Rivers. It was to them that these spirit-pouches must be dedicated and returned.

The Icefalcon privately regarded such customs as unnecessary and a little dangerous. Dead was dead, and any member of the Talking Stars People would have been able to find his or her way home without the assistance of a spirit-pouch. But he saw, in the big warrior's face, the need to do these things for his own peace of mind.

One of the things that the Stars had told the Ancestors of his people was that every people had their custom, and though all other people were wrong, it was not polite and frequently not safe to say so. At least Loses His Way didn't feel it necessary to take fingers the way the Twisted Hills People did.

"You took all the food?" he asked then, and the Icefalcon nodded. "Then let's go away. I thought you departed from the Real World for good," he added, as he and the Icefalcon followed the cliff wall northwest, seeking an inconspicuous place to regain the prairie above.

"I departed," said the Icefalcon. "Though I fail to see how my comings and goings are the affair of the Empty Lakes People."

"Blue Child is now the warchief of the Talking Stars People," said Loses His Way. "Even before the coming of the Eaters in the Night this was reason enough for concern among those of us who hunt the same mammoth and pasture our horses in the same ravines. Now that the mammoth move south, and white filth grows in the ravines of the homelands—now that the Ice in the North rolls south to cover valleys that once belonged to the Empty Lakes People—it is a matter for concern that she rules your people instead of you."

The cliff was lower toward the northwest, and the Icefalcon recalled how squirreltail grass grew thicker in that direction, amid stands of juniper brush that masked the cliff's rim from the direction of Bison Hill. Under cover of these junipers the two men scrambled up and glided through the thickets to higher ground.

At the cliff's top a dark shaggy shape rustled up to them out of the grass, a yellow-eyed war-dog, burned like Loses His Way over his shoulders and back, like Loses His Way mourning his losses and his pain in silence.

He licked the warchief's hand and wriggled with grateful joy to have his ears rubbed—sniffed the Icefalcon suspiciously but followed in silence. The Icefalcon raised up on his knees to put his head above the clusters of leaves but saw no sign of travelers as far as he could look west along the road.

They were evidently staying put for the day.

"For one thing, the Empty Lakes People never owned a thumb-breadth of the land in the North," he pointed out. "The starlight wrote our names on forest and stone from the Haunted Mountain across to the Night River Country, and ours it remains, Ice or no Ice, forever. Will these take you and your brother here back to your people?" He

nodded to the dog and held out to Loses His Way two
tubes of pemmican and one of the several sacks of pine
nuts. "I hunt this Wise One and his warriors, and in the
North I am told the white filth grows thick. There is no
hunting in it. I need all I can carry."

The brilliant eyes narrowed. "You hunt this Wise One? I
thought you had returned to find Gsi Kethko."

"Gsi Kethko?" The name had two meanings. In the
tongue of the Salt People it signified the hallucinogenic
pods of the wild morning glory, but in the more melodic
(and altogether more perfect) language of the Talking
Stars People it meant the Antlered Spider, one of the fifteen Dream Things that sometimes carried messages from
the Watchers Behind the Stars.

"The Wise One," Loses His Way amplified.

"He was a member of Plum's family," remembered the
Icefalcon, not sure why the warchief thought he should be
interested. "A little man so high who dressed his hair with
elm twigs. He stayed with us when we camped on the
Night River just before the Summer Moot, the year that I
departed. I don't think he was a very good Wise One. We
nearly starved to death waiting for him to charm antelope,
and his information about the salt grass along the Cruel
River left a great deal to be desired. Why would I seek out
the Antlered Spider?"

"I thought he might have spoken to someone else concerning the spells he laid on the dreamvine that your old chief
Noon took, at the Summer Moot in the Year of the White
Foxes, the year that you left." Loses His Way turned the end
of one of his mustache braids around his finger, but his eyes
did not leave the Icefalcon's face in the piebald shadows of
the thicket. The Icefalcon felt a coldness inside him, as if he
already knew what else his enemy was going to say.

"The draft is prepared on the night the chief takes it,"
the Icefalcon said, his soft, husky voice suddenly flat. "He
himself gathers the dreamvine before he goes up to the
mountain. There can be no spells laid on it since no one
else touches the pods."

"According to Antlered Spider, Noon always gathered the pods in the same place," the warchief replied. "Along Pretty Water Creek, between the white rock shaped like a tortoise and the three straight cottonwoods."

The place flashed at once to the Icefalcon's mind, and he realized that what Loses His Way said was true. Noon had taken him there a hundred times in his childhood and told him of the properties of the low-growing, innocuous-looking vine: how it was prepared by the warchief on the mountain and what it did.

"The Antlered Spider said that Blue Child took powdered elf-root and had him lay words on it, so that when the powder was mixed with water and painted on the pods of the vine, the face that Noon would see in his vision at the Summer Moot would be yours. And it was your face that Noon saw, wasn't it?"

"How do you know this?" The cold in him deepened, a dream remembered and repressed—the old man's face impassive, eyes dead, empty with grief. The Icefalcon, and his cousin Red Fox, and their friends Stays Up All Night and Fifty Lovers, sitting by the Moot Fire, the talk soft and nervous as it always was at such times. Then Noon walked out of the night into the red world of the firelight, the white shell held out stiffly in his hand and death in his eyes.

Always just stepping into the firelight. Always just holding out his hand.

"My son . . ."

*My son.*

But he had known almost before Noon spoke what he was going to say. They had all looked at him, his kindred. Looked at him, and moved away.

The cold crystallized within him to a core of ice, as the cold had then.

"Why did he tell you this?" It astonished him how normal his voice sounded. But he was the Icefalcon, and it behooved him not to show his feelings, particularly not to one of the Empty Lakes People.

"He was dying," said Loses His Way. "Fever Lady had

kissed him at the winter horse camp. The snow was deep outside, and I could not leave."

"What was he doing in your horse camp?" The Ice-falcon drew a deep breath. Far off over the badlands, thunder rolled, soft with distance. The scent of the storm came rushing at them on the blue-black cloak of the wind.

"He wasn't really one of Plum's family." Loses His Way shrugged. "He was the son of my maternal aunt's husband's stepbrother. The Empty Lakes People drove him out in the Year of the Crows for putting a barren spell on his sister because she had more horses than he did. No one liked him. Blue Child took him in."

"Blue Child took in a Wise One of *your* people?" The Ice-falcon was shocked to the marrow of his bones. "Took him in and had him put a spell on the *chief of her own people*?"

Loses His Way nodded. The Icefalcon was silent. Winter-night silence. Death silence. The silence in the eyes of an old man who has just been told by his Ancestors that the boy he has raised from childhood, the young man he looked upon as his successor, is the one They want, the one They have chosen to bring a message to them written in the crimson extremities of pain.

The torture sacrifice, the Long Sacrifice of summer, that the people may live through the winter to come.

Lightning flared, purple-white against the nigrous mountains of cloud. Gray rain stood in slanted columns over distant hills. The wind veered: Bektis, at a guess, witching the weather to turn the storm away. Shamans of the Talking Stars People generally didn't care if they got wet.

The Icefalcon observed it all, staring into distance, feeling nothing.

"I don't know whether Gsi Kethko told anyone else of this," said Loses His Way, after a time, stroking his long mustache. "But for two years now I have been watching for you, waiting to see if you will return to your people and claim your due."

*    *    *

"Are you all right, honey?"

Tir sat back on his heels, trembling, small hands propped on his thighs. Hethya ran a competent palm over his clammy forehead, then helped him to his feet and led him away from the little puddle of vomit among the ferns at the base of the big cottonwood tree. Some distance off she knelt down again and took the boy in her arms.

She was a big woman, like the farmwives and blacksmiths in the Keep. Her arms were strong around him and the quilting of her coat smooth and cold under his face, and her thick braids, tickling his chin, smelled good. Tir rested his head against her shoulder and tried not to feel ashamed of himself for getting sick.

It was weak, like the little kids. He was seven and a half. With the deaths of Geppy and Thya and Brit and all the other older children in the Summerless Year, he had stepped into a position of semicommand in the games of the younger.

Tears stung his eyes, remembering his friends. Remembering Rudy.

"There's no shame in it, being afraid." Hethya's big fingers toyed gently with his hair, separating it into locks on his forehead, as his mother sometimes still did. "Even great kings and heroes get afraid. And sometimes that happens, after you've been real afraid."

Tir was silent, trying to sort out what he had felt clinging to the limb of the tree. He was still sweating, though under his furry jacket he felt icy cold, and his stillness alternated with waves of shivering that he could not control.

"You did well," she said.

In fact, when Bektis had spun around and cried out "Raiders!" and the three Akulae whipped their curved southern swords from their sheaths, from those dark hollows in his mind Tir heard someone else's voice, one of those other people, say as if thinking it to himself, *Get out of everybody's way.*

Lying on the branch of the tree, he had felt curiously little fear. Too many memories of killing men himself—of those other boys killing men—lay too near the surface. Memories of terror in battle, memories of grief and remorse, memories of the grim rush of heat that drove in the knife, the spear, the sword. Watching Hethya, watching the Akulae, cutting and hacking at the men and women who ran stumbling from Bektis' unseen illusions filled him with emotion that he could not name, closer to sadness and horror than fear. But strong. Horrifyingly strong.

The emotion, whatever it was, left him wrung out, shaken, sickened, so that as soon as the fighting was over he slid down the cottonwood's trunk and vomited, not even knowing what it was that he felt. He could see the faces of the dying men still. Their faces, and the faces of all those others who had died in ages past by the hands of those whose memories he touched.

One day he might have to kill somebody himself.

His face still buried in Hethya's shoulder, he heard Bektis' sonorous voice repeating summoning-spells, then the soft scrunch of hooves on leaves and the whuffle of horses' breath. Looking up, he saw Akula leading two beautiful bay stallions by the bridles, so beautiful they took his breath away. The Keep boasted few horses. Four more stood, eyes rolling, among the trees. Another Akula was tethering them.

This Akula had a bleeding wound on one arm. Hethya made a little exclamation under her breath and, with a final quick hug, released Tir and stood. "Here," she said, going to the man. "Let me get that covered."

"My dear young lady." Bektis strolled over to her through the trees, stroking his long white beard and considering the six horses with a self-satisfied smirk. The jeweled device still covered his right hand. He was seldom without it, even if he had no magic to work, and he seemed to enjoy just looking at it, turning it reverently to catch the sunlight, like a vain adolescent admiring a mirror.

During the fight Tir had seen how lightning and fire had flowed out of it, how strange smokes and rainbow lights seemed to leap from it around the heads of the White

Raiders, making them cry out and slash at things only they could see, making their dogs attack one another or bite the legs of the Raiders' horses. Tir had been badly scared by the Raiders' dogs.

"It's scarcely worth your time. The man will be dead before the wound heals."

Hethya opened her mouth to retort, then glanced down at Tir and shut it again. The Akula looked from Bektis' face to Hethya's without much comprehension, a thick-muscled man with grim pale eyes. Tir wondered if Akula—any of them—knew enough regular speech to understand what had just been said.

He'd just begun to learn the ha'al language of the Empire of Alketch and could say *Please* and *Thank you* and a number of prayers, though since God presumably spoke all languages he couldn't imagine why he had to learn, with great difficulty, what God could just as easily understand in the Wathe. But his mother, and Rudy, and Lord Ankres said that the language was a useful thing for a King to know.

"And now that we have horses in the camp," said Bektis, drawing close around his face the fur collar of his quilted brown coat and tucking his beard behind a number of scarves, "I think it best we keep the boy tied up until his Lordship arrives. See to it."

"Please, Lord Bektis." Tir stepped forward, his heart pounding. "Please don't tie me up. If something else happens, if the Raiders come again, I don't want to be tied up."

"So you can run away in the confusion?" Bektis had already started to turn away. There was contempt in his voice, and Tir felt his face flush.

"I know I wouldn't get far," he said with dignity. "Even if I stole a horse, you could just make it turn around and come back to you, couldn't you? Or scare it, like you scared those people with stuff that wasn't real, so they couldn't protect themselves."

The wizard's dark eyes flashed with anger at this implication of cowardice and cheat. "And a fine predicament you'd be in if I hadn't, boy. We're not playing children's

games. Do you think the White Raiders would spare a
child of your years? I've seen children younger than you
with their guts staked over five yards of ground. Tie him
up," he added to Hethya. "And give him a lick or two, to
mend his manners."

He walked away to the edge of the grove, where he
settled himself under a tree. Tir saw him take something
from a velvet purse under his coat, polish it on his chamois
cloth, and set it on a little collapsible silver tripod where
the dim sunlight lanced through the thin leaves. Scrying,
as old Ingold scried for things in his fragment of yellow
crystal. As he'd seen Rudy scry, hundreds of times.

At the thought of Rudy his throat closed and his eyes
grew hot, seeing him fall again through the whirl of snow
and darkness. *Don't make him be dead,* he prayed. *Please
don't make him be dead.*

Hethya's hand dropped gently onto his shoulder. "Come
on, honey," she said. "We'd better do as he says. I'll make
it as easy on you as I can, and if we're attacked again I'll
see to it you can get to safety."

Tir nodded. He wondered sometimes, lying beside her
in the warmth of her blankets, feeling safe while Bektis'
wolves and saber-teeth snuffled around the verges of the
camp, if she had a little boy of her own.

"Who's his Lordship who's coming?" he asked softly,
as she led him toward a thin sycamore tree where there
was shade and grass. "And what's he going to do? Why
does he want me?"

"Never you mind that, honey," said Hethya. "I'll make
sure you're all right."

But her eyes avoided his as she said it. She wasn't lying,
he realized. She just knew that she had no power to do
that, if Bektis—and his Lordship, whoever he was, and
whyever he wanted him—decided to kill him.

# CHAPTER SIX

Shadow passed over the grass.

The Icefalcon turned, scalp prickling, then scanned the sky. There was no sign of a bird.

The chill wind of morning rippled miles of grass and brought the smoke of the camp on Bison Hill. They were waiting for someone, the Icefalcon thought. Or for some event, as Wise Ones waited for conjunctions of stars and planets that would increase and focus their power. Above the coulee, black birds now gathered in clouds, but none circled anywhere near the hill.

A smoke-colored flicker in the corner of his eye, and this time he was sure of it. Ears tilted inquiringly, Yellow-Eyed Dog raised his nose from his paws and sniffed the air. The sky was empty overhead.

"What is it?" whispered Loses His Way.

The Icefalcon drew breath and relaxed a little, as much as he ever relaxed or could relax.

"Cold Death," he said.

It was after noon, the day following Tir's abduction from the Keep, that a mixed company of Guards and other Keep soldiery under command of Janus of Weg finally reached the gorge where Rudy lay. Once it grew light enough to see, Gil climbed the rocks two or three times, snow still falling heavily, to lay out branches and rocks and to carve laborious notches with her footprints in the snow, showing where they were. She had just returned from gathering more wood when she heard voices on the rocks above. "Gaw, what a mess," said the familiar back-country drawl of the Commander—and a heavenly choir of angels playing the back half of "Layla" on electrified harps couldn't have been sweeter to her ears—"I thought you said you could chase the snow-clouds out onto the plain, me dumpling."

"They should have gone." Brother Wend's soft voice was puzzled. "It's unheard of for weather to cling this long after the Summoner has departed. I think . . . I'm not sure, but I think there are spells of danger up ahead as well, avalanche and anger among the beasts of the mountains."

Janus cursed. "Bektis was never that strong," he said. There was a scuffle, and a couple of little snow-slips tumbled down the rock face. Then Gil saw the black shapes of the Guards, and a couple of the white-clothed warriors of Lord Ankres' company, scrambling down the way she had marked.

Wend knelt beside Rudy and exclaimed in shock, pulling off his heavy gloves at once to weave spells of healing and stasis over the great burns and cuts on Rudy's face and chest. Meanwhile, Janus and the others spread out along the frozen stream to cut saplings for a litter. The Icefalcon's makeshift wall had served to keep the niche under the overhang warm through the night and into morning, but Rudy's face wore the look of death. "Don't die on me, man," Gil whispered, in her disused English, as she watched the priest-wizard's fingers trace again and again the lines of healing and strength over the still, hawk-nosed face.

She'd have to face Alde, too.

The Lady of the Keep awaited them on the shallow steps of the black fortress, wrapped thick in the faded rainbow of her coat of quilted silk scraps. Like a crooked scarecrow, the Bishop Maia of Renweth stood beside her, and on her other side her friend and maidservant Linnet unobtrusively held her hand. There were other people as well—the Keep Lords, and Ilae, and the entrepreneurs who functioned more or less as neighborhood bosses—

but as she walked beside Rudy's litter with the scrag-end of the storm winds lashing at her face, Alde was all Gil saw.

The younger woman's jaw set, body stiffening, drawing in on itself for protection, when it was clear to her that Tir wasn't among the returning Guards.

"Rudy's alive," Gil called, as they came near enough for her voice to be heard without shouting. "The Icefalcon's gone after Bektis and Tir. Tir seems to be all right."

"Thank you." Gil could only guess at Alde's reply by the movement of her lips. Wind lifted the Lady's hair, a shroud of night, as she descended the steps to grasp and kiss Rudy's nerveless hand.

Undemonstrative herself, Gil did the only thing she could think of to do to help her friend through the hours of the evening and the night. She stayed beside her in the cell to which they brought Rudy, a chamber in the Royal Sector whose round tiled heating stove and larger bed made it more comfortable than the young mage's narrow quarters off the wizards' workroom on first level south. Neither Ilae nor Wend had had early training in their craft, both having denied or neglected their talents in the days before the coming of the Dark Ones. But Wend had, through the years of his priesthood, practiced sur-reptitiously the healing magic on those members of the small western community who had been in his care, and both he and the red-haired girl had seven years of formal teaching. Together they worked spells of strength and sta-bility on Rudy's heart and nervous system, and of healing on his flesh, drew runes and circles of power around the herbs they prepared to combat infection.

Through the night Minalde stayed quietly in a corner of the room, fetching water or lint, feeding the fire or holding the knots on bandages when such things were called for. Linnet disappeared to look after Gisa, the daughter Alde had borne Rudy in the Summerless Year, who at eighteen months was old enough to know something was desperately wrong, and to care for Gil's son Mithrys; Gil remained at Alde's side. She didn't say much—she had never known what to say to someone in grief or pain—but once Alde reached out and took her hand and squeezed it hard enough to hurt.

Later she asked, "Did you see Tir?" and Gil shook her head.

"I heard him call out Rudy's name," she said. In the soft double glow of lampflame and witchlight, Alde's face seemed thin and old, an echo of the old woman she would one day be. A woman who had lost the husband she adored and feared and had seen the brother she had worshipped turn tyrant and monster, who had survived the crumbling of her world and found in its wreck a love like the rising of the stars.

"We saw his tracks a couple of times, when they let him off the donkey. I think that Hethya woman must have gotten him out of the Keep to look at the caves along the north side of the Vale, and Bektis put a glamour on one of those warriors he had with him to make Tir think it was Rudy."

Alde only nodded, her face an ivory death mask.

"I never thought Bektis would possess the power to hold storms so long after he had gone." Brother Wend turned on his three-legged stool, drying his hands on a coarse hempcloth towel, a dark-haired little man whose priestly tonsure had grown in when he left the Church, only to be replaced by his hairline's early retreat. "Of course, he will always be a greater wizard than I, but . . ." He shook his head.

"He had a . . . a device of some kind," said Gil. "This kind of crystal *thing* strapped on his hand. It may just have been reflection, but it looked like it lit up when Bektis threw lightning or defended himself against Rudy's spells. He's a stronger wizard than Rudy is anyway, but if it was a magnifier or amplifier of some kind . . ."

Ilae looked up from grinding dried purple-bead roots in the mortar. "Does such a thing exist?"

"Who knows?" Gil replied. "We don't know what's

been stashed away all these years, left over from the Times Before. Ingold is always finding references to stuff the Church confiscated and hid and never talked about."

"And with good reason, if legend is anything to go by." Maia stood in the doorway, his long face lined with concern. "How is he?"

"About the same." Gil shrugged, hiding fear and anxiety, as the Icefalcon did. "Maybe other people hid stuff, too, out of fear of the Church or of their neighbors. Now those places have been broken open, and nobody's keeping an eye on them anymore." She glanced sidelong at Maia. "Why do you think Ingold's been in such a panic to find books and implements and whatever other apparatus he can?"

"There were certainly records in my episcopal palace of things I did not understand, hidden in places lost to anyone's memory," the tall Bishop agreed. "We do not even know what may still be hidden in this Keep, untouched since the Dark's first rising."

"And it's a good guess Govannin had a couple of secrets on hand. For all she carried on about mages being soulless tools of Evil, she was quick enough to use black magic in anything *she* considered a good cause. If Bektis ever did manage to break her hold on him, you can bet your best fur booties he'd help himself to whatever he could stick in his pockets."

"How soon will the storm clear?" Alde, who had sat all this while with bowed head in silence, now looked up at Wend. "How soon can a party go over the pass in pursuit?"

"I'll go out there in the morning," the physician promised. "Even the strongest spells disperse, if their maker is not there renewing them. I'm not the weather-witch Bektis is, but I should be able to hasten their breaking."

"How soon?" Her eyes were like the heart of the night, her voice porcelain, cold and friable, as if it would shatter at a touch.

"Tomorrow afternoon?"

She whispered again, "Thank you." Her small hands closed around Rudy's brown, cold fingers, seeking reassurance, perhaps hoping to hold his spirit to his flesh. She hadn't touched the tisane Linnet had brought, or the supper, either. Gil knew better than to think that she would unless forced.

*I'd better get some sleep,* thought Gil. *And pack.* She remembered the three identical warriors. Were others waiting to join Bektis once he got over the pass? A dozen or a hundred, cookie-cuttered out of some unguessable spell? Ingold had never mentioned such a thing to her, nor Bektis' jeweled weapon, either.

How could she, and the Guards, and a novice like Wend cope with those and whatever else the sorcerer had up his fur-lined sleeves?

But the concern turned out to be moot. An hour or so later Ilae put down her herbs and sat up straight, her hand going to her temple, her eyes suddenly flaring wide. *"Damn,"* she said.

Alde, her hand still locked around Rudy's where she sat on the floor, a pillow at her back, looked up sharply at the note in the girl's voice. "What is it?"

"I . . ." Ilae hesitated, frowning, listening hard to sounds only she could hear. Then the witchlight brightened behind her head as she dug in the purse at her belt for a scrying stone, a ruby Ingold had found in the ruins of Penambra, which she turned and maneuvered in the sharp glint of the light. "Damn," she said again, more forcefully, and pushed her rusty hair out of her eyes. "There're men coming up the road from the river valley, my Lady. Lots of men—horses—spears glittering in the moonlight . . ."

*"What?"* Alde surged lithely to her feet, crossed the room in a flurry of petticoats, and looked over Ilae's shoulder as if she too could see in the jewel. "Where?"

"They've just passed the wards we set up in the Arrow Gorge. Hundreds, it looks like. Carts and tents." She looked up into the Lady's face with baffled eyes. "It's hard to see in darkness, but I think they're black-faced, black-skinned, the men of the Alketch, and the brown men of the Delta Islands with gold beads in their hair. They're coming fast."

Alde cursed, something she seldom did. "Send for Janus," she said. "We need to meet them at the Tall Gates and hold them there, if we can. Thank you, Ilae . . ."

Gil was already out of the room, striding down the Royal Way toward the Aisle and the lamplit watchroom of the Guards.


The Icefalcon and Loses His Way watched Bektis' camp through the night, turn and turn about with hunting small game in the coulee. They worked mostly in businesslike silence, though Loses His Way asked about the conditions of grass on the eastern side of the mountains, and the movements of mammoth and bison herds, always a fruitful topic among the peoples of the Real World. He asked, too, about the pedigrees of the horses at the Keep and shook his head sorrowfully when the Icefalcon informed him that the Keep horse herd had been acquired at random from the South and that even before the destruction of the original herd, the ancestry of horses was not a concern of most mud-diggers.

"It is very foolish not to know whether your horses are the sons and daughters of brave beasts or cowards," he said gravely, stripping the skin from a woodchuck he had shot while Yellow-Eyed Dog slaveringly feigned disinterest. They sheltered in another bison wallow, not the one southeast of the hill but an older one to the southwest, full of curly buffalo grass and pennyroyal, with a good view over the broken lands to the south. "How can you know what they will do if you don't know about their ancestors before them? These mud-diggers of yours want all the wrong things and don't know what is important."

"They are not *my* mud-diggers," pointed out the Icefalcon. "And I have told them this many times."

"Then why do you follow this shaman? This child is not your kin. He may even be your enemy." He used the word *dingyeh*, "not-kin," *oktep* in the tongue of the Talking Stars, and set the strips of woodchuck flesh over the hot coals of last night's fire to roast.

"The child is . . ." The Icefalcon was silent a moment, trying to phrase his relationship to Eldor—and to the people in the Keep—in terms that could be understood in the Real World. There was much about his new life that he could not explain in terms of the old.

At length he said, "The child's father helped me and gave me shelter when I departed from my own people."

"Did you need shelter?" asked Loses His Way.

"No. But for his sake I would not like to see the boy come to harm. What troubles me now is that Bektis must be watching his back trail . . ."

And then they were no longer two, but three. The Icefalcon couldn't even tell how long she'd been there.

She was a diminutive woman, with the black hair that sometimes marked Wise Ones in the Real World. From babyhood her parents had shaved it off, so she had never learned to regard it. It was hacked off short now, straight as water and heavy as the hand of fate. When the Icefalcon had seen her last, it had not yet been touched by gray. Her eyes were black, too.

"Little brother," she said.

"Elder sister." He inclined his head. "You know Loses His Way, our enemy from the Empty Lakes People."

She nodded. Everyone in the Real World knew everyone else, pretty much, or at least knew of them.

"It pleases me to see that you were not devoured by the Eaters in the Night, o my sister. I had heard that they singled out the Wise."

She smiled, small but very bright, like a star. "Then I suppose I am not all that Wise." She picked a pink-edged flower of bindweed and turned it in her fingers, smiling at the silkiness of the petals under her touch. "Do they still haunt the lands east of the wall of snows, little brother?"

He shook his head. "At the end of that first winter a Wise One there sent them away to the other side of Night, where no people live and it is night forever. They have not returned again."

"Good," said Cold Death briskly and worked the flower into the end of the Icefalcon's braid among the bones. "I thought it must have been something of the kind. Now who is this Bektis, and why does it concern you that he watches his back trail?" She sat down cross-legged between them and picked the woodchuck's heart out of the coals, devouring it with an expression of ecstasy. "Was it he who slew five of the Empty Lakes People and put their bodies in the coulee, or was that you, little brother?"

"It was Bektis," the Icefalcon said a little grumpily because he loved woodchuck hearts with a great, strong love. "And those with him." He gave her a quick summary of the events of the past four days, finishing with "He is a fool, but not so much a fool that he would not watch his back trail, knowing that he was observed in carrying the boy away. He knows that the warriors of the Keep will bear stronger amulets against his spells of battle illusion and battle panic than the warriors of the Empty Lakes People, whose shaman Walking Eyes was killed by the Eaters seven years ago, yet he displays no concern over the matter. He waits here for something."

Cold Death tousled the dog's ruff. "For the rest of the black warriors," she said. The dog sniffed at her and licked her hand.

"T'cha!" scolded Loses His Way amiably. "You kiss your people's enemies, o my brother?"

"He tastes her that he may devour her later," explained the Icefalcon, and the warchief nodded.

"Very well, then."

"Ninety-eight of them are a day south of here," Cold Death went on. "Tonight you'll be able to see their fires. As for why he shows no concern about pursuit . . ."

She frowned. She had sharp little flecks of brow, pulling together over a short snub nose.

"There is power in that band," she said. "They have twelve wagons covered in blue canvas, and surrounding them . . . not darkness, but a movement that bends the shape of the air." She shook her head and tried to shape some kind of meaning with her square brown short-fingered hand. "There is evil in them, such as I have never before seen. Demons follow them, and the elementals of water and air and earth. Blue Child follows these warriors and their wagons at a distance."

"And does the Blue Child," asked the Icefalcon softly, "ride these lands?"

"These lands are ours," said Cold Death. "Unto the Night River Country and down to the Bones of God."

Loses His Way hackled like a wolf at the suggestion that the larger portion of the Real World did not in fact belong to the Empty Lakes People, but Cold Death continued unconcernedly, picking another flower. "It was Blue Child who sent me scouting, to see who or what awaited this dark captain, with the hook for his hand, at Bison Hill."

Bison Hill was the only place the mud-diggers used for meetings, the only landmark large enough to catch their blunted attention. The Icefalcon only asked, "A hook?"

*Vair na-Chandros,* he thought. *It had to be.*

"A big man with hair that curls like that of a bison's hump, gray with age, not white in youth as many of the black warriors. His eyes are yellow and his voice like dirt in a tin pot. He has a silver hook in place of his right hand, and his men call him Lord. You know this man?"

"I know him." The Icefalcon's face was impassive as he turned the woodchuck meat on the flat rocks among the coals. "In the days of the Dark Ones, this hook-handed one commanded the forces of the Alketch that came to help humankind against the Dark. He abandoned them in the burning Nests that he might preserve his own followers when he went to war in the Alketch. After that I am told he tried to make himself Emperor of the South by wedding the old Emperor's daughter against her will. Now he rides north, does he, with less than six score men, and wagons filled with uncanny things?"

He sat up a little and gazed south across the broken

lands, green miles of chilly springtime where a red-tailed hawk circled lazily and a couple of uintatheria, ungainly moving mountains with their tusked and plated heads swinging back and forth, ambled from one gully to another in their eternal quest for fresh leaves.

But what he saw was the rainbow figure descending the steps of the Keep in the mists and the hatred in those fox-gold eyes when they looked on Ingold Inglorion. He saw too the upraised hooks, scarlet with firelight, summoning back his troops out of the darkness of the burning Nests. Saw Ingold—and hundreds of others—engulfed and borne away by the Dark.

It came back to him also what Gil-Shalos had told him about the Emperor's daughter of the South.

"I like this not, o my sister," he said at last. "This Vair is an evil man, and now you tell me he rides with an evil magic in his train. Whether this be a mage or a talisman or an object of power, I would feel better if I knew something more of his intent, before he takes the boy into his grasp. Will you remain here, my enemy, and look out for the boy? If they await Vair's coming, having brought Tir this distance, he should be safe enough."

"I will abide," said the warchief. "He owes me somewhat, this Wise One."

"Good." The Icefalcon rose. "Then let us ride, o my sister," he said.

Bright against the green-black trees, a red scarf flashed, slashing to and fro.

"They're in sight," said Melantrys of the Guards.

As when wind passes over a standing grove, with a single movement the men and women on the north watchtower bent their bows, hooked the strings into place. Another movement—another wind gust—the soft deadly clattering of arrow shafts. The same wind moved Gil, automatic now but still rich with heightened sensation in her mind and heart: the spiny rough feathers, the waxy smoothness of horsehair and yew. From the watchtower's foot the narrow road led down to the Arrow River Gorge, champagne-pale between clustering walls of mingled green: fir, hawthorn, hazel, fern.

Rustling muttered above the breeze shift of the trees. Sharp as the red arbutus in the ditches came the whinny of horses.

"The fat bleedin' shame of it," sighed Caldern, a north-country man so big he looked like a thunderstorm in his black Guards tunic and coat. "Whatever you do, lassie, don't kill the horses. We can aye use 'em."

Rishyu Hetakebnion, Lord Ankres' youngest son, whispered to Gil, "Do you think we'll turn them back?" He'd spent hours dressing and braiding his hair for this occasion. He hadn't liked being put in the north tower company as a common archer, but his father had insisted upon it: *If you're going to give commands one day you must first learn how to obey them.*

Gil shook her head. "Not a hope."

The leading ranks of the Alketch army came into view.

It is no easy matter to count troops and estimate matériel through a hunk of ensorcelled ruby an inch and three-quarters long: scrying can tell a wizard where and if, but seldom how many. By the time Melantrys and Lank Yar, the Keep's chief hunter, returned from reconnaissance with the news that the Alketch troops numbered nearly eleven hundred strong, the enemy was only hours from the Tall Gates. They were armed for siege, too, Melantrys said. Mules and oxen hauled two "turtles," constructions of log and leather designed to protect soldiers while they undermined towers and walls.

With a full muster of the Keep's available warriors and all able-bodied adults to back them up, Janus estimated they could hold the Tall Gates for a time, but against trained men the cost would probably be terrible. "With all due respect to Mistress Hornbeam and Master Barrelstave," he'd whispered to Minalde at the tense convocation that had followed Melantrys' return, "one seasoned warrior properly armed can account for half a dozen volunteers. Leavin' aside that we can't afford to lose a soul here, their line'll cave. And for what?"

The commander of the Alketch troops was a stocky golden-skinned Delta Islander in an inlaid helmet bristling with spikes. He drew rein just where the road curved on its final approach to the Gates, and Gil could see the choke of men behind him, armored in bronze and steel and black-lacquered cane in the milky light of the overcast morning.

Looking at the Tall Gates.

"That's it," murmured Janus, a few feet along the make-shift wood rampart from where Gil stood. He wore full battle gear, something fewer than half the Guards possessed: black enameled breastplate and helm, rerebraces and pauldrons and gloves, unornamented save for the gold eagles of the House of Dare. "Think about it real good before you come on, me jolly boy. Surely there's another party you can go to instead?"

But Gil knew there wasn't. With the slow-growing cold of the Summerless Year, even the settlements along the river valley had waned, dying out or succumbing to bandit troops. She had heard that the situation in the Felwoods was worse. The Keep of Dare in its high cold vale was the last organized center of civilization for many, many leagues, the last large, stable source of food production. Elsewhere was only banditry, White Raiders, and spreading chaos.

There was no other party to go to.

For the past seven years, the people of the Keep had been working on the watchtowers of the Tall Gates. They'd repaired the old stonework as well as they could without proper quarrying tools and raised palisades of sharpened tree trunks around the platforms on top. Bandit troops had burned the towers twice, but even before the disaster of the Summerless Year it had been hard to get draft animals to haul stone up from the river valley.

Gil would have bet a dozen shirt-laces they would be in flames again within an hour, had she been able to find a taker.

Between the towers another palisade stretched, a rough

chevaux-de-friese of outward-pointing stakes, hastily cut
and sharpened, fired hard, braced in the earth, and inter-
woven with all the brush that could be gathered to make
the hedge thicker yet.

Eleven hundred troops, thought Gil, her gloved fingers
icy on the arrow-nock. They weren't going to turn back.

Battle drums echoed in the high rocks of the pass, omi-
nous, palpable in the marrow of the bones. The golden
commander edged his golden horse aside. The ranks
parted—ebony soldiers from the Black Coast, ivory from
the White, and the red-brown D'haalac borderlanders.
Variegated banners lifted and curled in the morning wind.

For some reason Gil remembered old Dr. Bannister of
the UCLA history department, dry and fragile as a cast
cicada skin, standing at the lecture-hall podium saying,
"Henry II marched his armies against Philip Augustus . . ."

Just that. *Marched his armies.* No wet boots and feet
that ached with cold. No rush of adrenaline or hammering
heart at the thought *What if I die . . . ?*

*Marched his armies.*

The turtles lumbered eyelessly to the walls.

They were sturdily built, Gil had to give them that. She
couldn't imagine how they'd gotten them across the Arrow
River. She saw the overlapping hides black with water—
they must weigh tons—and heard the squeak of the over-
burdened wheels. Arrows rained down from both gate
towers, answered from slits in the walls and roofs. Gil
wasn't fooled. The men inside only waited for the real attack, the attempt by soldiers on foot to take the turtles.

"Come on, Ilae," whispered Melantrys, drawing,
nocking, firing like a machine behind her tangle of beams
and brush, "do your stuff."

The nearer turtle lurched and rocked a little, then came
on. Gil guessed that Ilae's spells of damage—broken
axles, jammed wheels—wouldn't have much effect. If
Bektis could lay a weather-spell on the pass that would
hold a storm there for almost forty-eight hours—and by
the clouds still roiling over the Hammerking it was even

yet going strong—his counterspells of ward on the turtles
would be more than sufficient to thwart a novice like Ilae.

Certainly when the men poured forth from them and
began hacking and rending at the chevaux-de-frise between the towers, they showed no immediate signs of
being affected by whatever panic and terror-spells the girl
could muster. Rudy could probably have summoned
better ones, but again, if Bektis had had sufficient time
to manufacture wards and amulets against such spells,
probably even Ingold couldn't have done much.

On the other hand, Ilae's fire-spell transforming the entire barricade into a wall of flame worked just fine.

Men scattered back, dropping their shields and falling
under the steady downpour of arrows. Gil's forearm stung
where the bowstring smote the leather guard. Her fingers
smarted, and smoke teared her eyes and made it hard
to aim. More warriors pressed forward from the throat of
the pass, armored and bearing big man-covering shields.
Camp slaves, unarmored and dragging brush, came up
behind them, piling the tinder around the walls of the
watchtowers: "Right," said Janus softly. "Time to be off,
children. I guess they really, *really* want in."

There was no surprise in his voice, nor did Gil feel any.
No commander would muster a force that large, or con-
struct siege equipment, on a chance raid.

A second volley of arrows burst from the trees on both
sides of the pass as Lank Yar and his hunters responded to
Janus' signal to cover. Slaves fell, dying, innocent of the
war that spilled their blood. Smoke rolled up the inside of
the tower like a chimney as the archers streamed down the
winding stair inside, Gil coughing, heat beating on her skin.
This in some ways was the worst, and the only time when
she felt in genuine danger. She slung her bow onto her back
and joined the files of Guards—and of Ankres' mixed troop
of his own men, Lord Sketh's, and the Church warriors who
made up the archers on the south tower—in the fast march-
run across the open Vale, to the Doors of the Keep.

*Dr. Bannister should see me now.*

If the turtles got through the burning barricade too fast
and made a path for the horses, there was a chance that
Janus' retreating force could be ridden down and killed.

But they weren't. Gil didn't dare look back, with men
and women running on both sides of her, two and a half
miles up the rising ground from the Tall Gates to the Keep
on its knoll. On reaching the steps she turned, panting,
troopers streaming past her and through the Doors, and
saw the small Alketch cavalry galloping in futile pursuit.
In the aspen groves that surrounded the towers Lank Yar's
hunters were still showering the attackers with missiles,
bales of which had been hidden in the caves northwest of
the Keep and in a hundred other caches, where the little
corps of volunteers would be able to get to them in the
sniping guerrilla campaign to come.

Once the Doors were closed and the Alketch troops took
the Vale, Lank Yar and his hunters would be on their own.
They'd do a certain amount of damage, thought Gil, as the
Guards and the white-clothed warriors of House Ankres
filed past her, but they certainly wouldn't drive the invaders away.

The fires around the towers were losing their first force.
Smoke poured white into the sapphire sky, pierced now
and again by flame, like many-colored silk thrashing in
high wind. A few trees caught, as they generally did.

"Are you having second thoughts?"

Minalde stood at her side, white-faced and drawn. She
held her daughter Gisa firmly by the hand, the dark-haired
child looking about her with wonderment in her dark-
blue eyes.

Gil drew in her breath, and let it out. "No," she said. "If
it's a choice between in or out . . ." She hooked her hands
through her sword-sash. "You're losing Wendie's help inside as it is. If something goes wrong, I think I'll be more
use inside. I don't think I'd make that much difference
when the guys go over the pass to find Tir."

Alde looked away and nodded. Gil could feel her tension at the boy's name.

"Hey," said Gil softly. "The Icefalcon will find him. He'll bring him back." *Charles Lindbergh probably said the same thing to his wife.* Of course, Charles Lindbergh didn't have the Icefalcon looking for his vanished child, either. "How's Rudy?"

"Alive." The gesture of Alde's fingers tried to brush the topic aside, unbearable to the touch. There was silence before she could go on. "The same, Wend says. I . . . I suppose all we can do now is sit tight, as you say."

The last stragglers passed them, panting and joking among themselves, still high with the rush of escape. A hundred yards off the cavalry wheeled, helmet spikes flashing in the sun.

Pale spring sun, thought Gil, bright on the thick new grass of the Vale. The translucent glister of glaciers, opal walls along the black cliffs, miles high; grizzled pines and quicksilver streams; the mirror flash of bogs and glabrous acres of slunch. A hawk turning, infinitely tiny against the sky. Morning light.

She drained it deep, like her high school friend Sherry Reinhold going on one last binge before the diet that always started tomorrow . . .

In or out. One choice, for who knew how long and under what circumstances?

"Time to get inside, me Lady." Janus pulled off his helmet, graying rufous hair hanging in sweaty strings in his eyes. Calculation in that pug face, and worry; the smell of his sweat and the armor's leather straps. Once the Doors were shut—once the Alketch army was free to surround the black walls of the Keep—everyone's options would be limited.

From the twin columns of smoke under the eastern mountain wall dark worms of men crept out. Weapons caught soft flashes of sun, banners a faded echo of the wildflower carpet they trampled. Scrying down the road Ilae had seen their supply lines—Prandhays Keep was far enough away, God knew, but not nearly so far as the South.

The great Doors shut behind them, and Janus and

Caldern turned the locking-rings. Hidden bolts and bars echoed, less a sound than a deep vibration in the glowstone shadows of the gate passage: Gil put her arm around Alde's shoulders. The two women were the last to enter the Keep.

The second set of Doors, thick metal wrought in ancient years, clanged, and all was sealed.

"All over now; nothing more to see . . ." The Guards sounded petty against the hugeness of the Aisle, the loom of speculation and fear.

Someone saw Minalde and set up a cheer that clattered among the high catwalks of the upper levels, the cavernous sable walls. *After you've fought a battle in the morning,* thought Gil, *it's difficult to just get out the laundry or do your gardening in the afternoon.*

*("Everyone in the village would come into the castle during the siege," said Dr. Bannister, nervously chewing on the fat end of his tie.)*

The whole Aisle smelled of hay and the musty heaps of the tiny fodder-potatoes that for thousands of years had been this world's only acquaintance with the spud family, until Rudy's rediscovery of genuine potatoes—food-staple potatoes—two years ago. With that discovery the Keep had become completely self-sufficient. People still tilled corn and wheat outside, but that was for surplus and variety—lagniappe. With the cattle and sheep inside, they could hold out indefinitely. A couple of women were arguing about whose turn it was to shovel sheep dung. A man who hadn't been in the battle was explaining to Lord Ankres how the attack could easily have been turned. Rishyu Hetakebnion, hair a shambles of sweat and smoke, was quietly throwing up in a corner.

Minalde glanced back over her shoulder, at Melantrys and Janus setting the locking-rings of the inner set of Doors. "And now we wait," she murmured. She rubbed her hand over her forehead—Gisa pulled on her other hand, wanting as usual to dart away into the doorways that led to the compounds where cattle and sheep were housed. "As soon as the storms clear, Yar will send men to help the Icefalcon . . ."

"If he needs it." Gil grinned, and Minalde was surprised into a wan answering smile. "It can't possibly be more than a day or two, till they can start. Meanwhile Yar and his boys can give the guys outside a hard time. We'll be okay."

"We'll be okay." She repeated the words as if forcing herself to believe and drew a long, shaky breath. "And in time, these people . . . What can they do? They can't get in. They'll strip the Vale of game, very soon I should think, and what then? Wait until winter? Until they get tired? Until Ingold arrives?"

Gil folded her arms, looking around her at the heaps of fodder and provisions, twice head high and still dwarfed by the Aisle's vastness. (*"Provisions would be brought in from the surrounding countryside . . ."*) Men and women were settling down around the little piles of glowstones, with bales and bundles of sticks and feathers and flint, to listen to storytellers while they made arrows, a wintertime occupation when there was no game or when a storm kept them in. At the Doors Ilae stood in a halo of witchlight, checking communication through her ruby with Brother Wend, outside with Lank Yar's guerrillas. Janus and Lord Ankres went to her, asking—asking about the black river of men, of soldiers and slaves, of siege engines and provision wagons pooling before the Doors.

The only way in or out.

Impervious from the founding of the Keep.

Gil wondered if she should keep silent. But she knew she had to say what she thought. It might just be true.

"The problem is, Alde," said Gil, "the warriors of the Alketch have to know that all they *can* do is sit outside till winter comes and they get buried in snow. They have to know that we have wizards here and would be able to see them coming, and get ourselves stocked up and locked down. So my questions is: *Why doesn't this bother them?*"

Alde sighed, her shoulders slumping a little, and her face was again the face of a young girl. "I wish you hadn't asked that," she said.

# CHAPTER SEVEN

"I expected to be killed, you see, o my sister," said the Icefalcon, his voice no louder than the stirring of wind in the grass that curtained the rims of the maze of coulees through which they rode. "At the Moot, after Noon had gone up to the Haunted Mountain, I overheard Blue Child tell one of her friends, 'I will see that you get Little Dancer and Sand Cat.' I forget what favor he promised her in return. But I knew that she meant to kill me. Thus when Noon came down from the mountain and kissed me with the kiss of death, I was . . . suspicious. It fell, you understand, rather too pat."

It was good to ride again. Cold Death had three horses with her, of the short-coupled gray line of Evening Star Horse, bred by Frogs Singing and his family in the Pretty Water Country; they traveled sure-footedly and in silence through the red clay hills, the grasses of the bottomlands shoulder-high and prodigal with wildflowers. Loses His Way, though in the Icefalcon's opinion not notably quick on the uptake, would at least be a more than competent guard for Tir.

The Icefalcon's mind turned uneasily from what he knew of Vair na-Chandros and the potential evils of Southron magic to what else might be waiting for him—for them all—here in the Real World.

Cold Death listened without comment to the Icefalcon's account of his life east of the mountains both before and after the coming of the Dark: of his meeting with Eldor, of Ingold, of the Guards, and the Keep, and Tir. She listened, too, without comment as he revealed what Loses His Way had told him concerning the Wise One, Antlered Spider.

"Noon raised me as much as you did, when Cattail and the Yellow Butterfly were killed." He named their parents, as was the way among the Talking Stars People. "As much for what Blue Child did to me on that day, I owe her for what she did to him. His death was in his face when he came to me in the firelight." He hesitated a moment. "When did he die?"

"The following summer," she said. "At the Place Where the Rocks Look Like Grapes. He grew too ill to keep up with the hunt and drank black hellebore, after giving his amulets and his horses to Blue Child."

The Icefalcon was silent, seeing again the old man as he stepped out of the night, hand outstretched, fingers shaking around the white shell, sorrow beyond sorrow in his sky-blue eyes.

"The Stars told our Ancestors," went on Cold Death quietly, "to send messengers to them at certain times. The bravest and the strongest, strong enough to pass through the Long Sacrifice without flinching or fleeing. They called you a coward."

"Blue Child did, I expect." His voice turned hard.

"They all did."

The Icefalcon said nothing, staring straight ahead past his horse's ears to a rumpled wall of cottonwood, noting automatically the shape of limbs, the thickness or paucity of leaves.

"How could Noon abide when the one he raised as his son refused to undertake the journey to the other world for his people's sake?" She spoke reasonably, though he knew Cold Death had for all the years of adulthood absented herself from the Summer Moots, when the Long Sacrifice was made. "Without the messenger, our people would be at risk all the winter."

"Did disaster befall?"

"O my brother," she sighed, "there are always disasters. No, the people passed safely through the winter, save for the old men and the children, who died as old men and children always die. But with each death, Noon grieved. He was a man staked between two fires, my brother, glad that you lived and yet ashamed of that joy."

"I was not chosen," the Icefalcon said stubbornly.

"He thought you were." She watched all around her as she spoke, aware of every circling hawk, every basking lizard, every bobbing blade of grass. The three horses moved within the aura of her spells and so were able to travel swiftly without much fear of being seen, but neither Cold Death nor the Icefalcon neglected the common cautions of travel in the Real World: covering their tracks, holding to the cliff walls, speaking in the soft-murmuring hunting voices in which all the children of the peoples of the north were raised. As the Icefalcon had seen in Sarda Pass, no matter how powerful a shaman one kept company with, there was always a stronger waiting somewhere.

Her black eyes slid sidelong to him, and he could see reasons within reasons there, for asking what she asked.

At length he said, "I could prove nothing. I didn't know how it had been done. But Blue Child knew. And Blue Child was always my enemy, even before the death of Dove in the Sun at the Place of the Three Brown Dogs. The Dove perished through her own weakness, and no deed of mine could have saved her, but Blue Child blamed me for her death. And before that time, Blue Child always considered herself Noon's successor. It was in her eyes, o my sister. You were gone at the time of the Summer Moot, or I would have sought you out. Indeed, I thought of doing so, only after the Summer Moot, Noon and Watches Water and all of the others pursued me, and I had to flee."

Still Cold Death said nothing, her small brown hands resting easy on her muscled thighs, speaking to her horse with her mind as Wise Ones did. Winds slewed and cried among the crossing watercourses, and the high hills cut off visibility, making the Icefalcon prickle with nervousness, as he did wherever he did not have a clear view of his surroundings.

"I expected to be challenged at the Summer Moot," he said. "I was a match for Blue Child's strength even in those days, though she is nearly ten years older than I. Had she attacked me from ambush, or put poison in my food, or come on me when I slept, it would have been better than what she did. Not only did she cast me out of the people, o my sister, and not only did she rob me of the right to lead them, which Noon would have passed on to me. She made Noon the weapon of her will, an old man in the last summer of his strength. And he went to his death thinking me a coward and all his training of me gone to nothing. For that I will not forgive her."

Slunch grew thick on the hills to their right, the rubbery blanket of it slopping down into a small stream. From this a shambling band of bloated things toddled on swarms of wriggling legs. The Icefalcon's horse—Scorpion Eater he was called—flung up its head and snorted, but Ashes, the mare Cold Death had ridden these many years, only snuffled disapprovingly. Like one of the Talking Stars People, she refused to be impressed by anything.

Or perhaps, thought the Icefalcon, in these days such sights were common enough in the Real World.

Rain swept over the country, a spring cloudburst common to those lands, though the Icefalcon had noted already that they were fewer than they had been twelve years ago. Resting under a hazel brake at the foot of a hill, the Icefalcon asked Cold Death to scry along his back trail, to Sarda Pass and the Keep, though he was almost certain no one had followed him over the pass. Clouds still sat on the mountain, livid below and blinding-white above, longer than the Icefalcon had ever known a Wise One to tie weather-spells in place. Cold Death broke off a blade of needlegrass and brushed it across the silver pool left in the old bison wallow and sat for a time with her brown legs drawn up, gazing into the sandy shallow.

"The pass is thick with snow, o my brother." She glanced at him under long straight eyelashes, like a thoughtful fox pup. "There are tracks of deer and rabbit in it, but the tracks of men always end in avalanche spills—one, two, three of them. Nor does anyone come on the road from the place west."

"I thought Bektis seemed calm about it," remarked the Icefalcon. "There is a shaman in the Keep, an outlander named Rudy Solis, the son of alien stars. Can you reach him? Speak to him?"

She repeated the name once or twice to herself as was the way of shamans, then brushed the water again with the grass: the Wise Ones of the Real World did not use crystals as civilized mages did, but rather things that came and went, like water and fire. Only among the Salt People did the shamans make elaborate mirrors of blood and obsidian glass.

Water roared fresh in the stream they'd left, and wind still smelling of storm stirred the miscut crests and locks of her inky hair. Her face was like a child's intent on a game. In time she shook her head. "He doesn't reply."

"There is a woman named Ilae, then," the Icefalcon said. "She has red hair and plays a deer-bone flute; she was born in Gettlesand in the Spring of Many Lemmings."

Cold Death went a third time to her gazing. The Icefalcon saw that she still bit her nails. His earliest recollections were of her, a tiny plump girl whom no one ever saw during the time of the summer hunts, such were the spells that she put on herself after their parents died. Black-haired children were frequently shunned in the Real World, and sometimes abandoned to die because they showed up against the dry prairie grass. Though Cold Death had cared for him diligently, still Noon and his wife had taken him into their household under the impression that Cold Death had disappeared, so unnoticeable had his older sister become.

"Are you Ilae?" said Cold Death suddenly, speaking to the pool. "Wonderful! I am Cold Death, sister to the Icefalcon. Yes, he is here. He asks after the outlander Wise One Rudy Solis. She says he lives." The last remark was addressed to the Icefalcon. "I love your hair—you really ought to braid it with blue penstemon, in a crown on top," she added to Ilae in the pool. "It would look gorgeous. She says he is unconscious still." She turned back to her brother.

"He has been so ever since the Guards carried him in. It is all she can do, she says, to hold him in life until their eldest Wise One comes. He is on his way, she says, from the City of Walls."

"And does she have an explanation," asked the Icefalcon sarcastically, "for the fact that no one has followed me over the pass to assist my rescue of Prince Tir? Should I perhaps give over the hunt and return to the Keep again, if the matter is of so little concern?"

Cold Death conferred with her pool again. Ashes and the horse Scorpion Eater cropped the grasses around the thicket, while the third mount, Afraid of Flowers, who had followed at Cold Death's bidding, grazed peacefully a little distance off, soft ears turning with the turning of the wind.

"The Wise One Ilae says that no one followed after you because no one could, o my brother." Cold Death raised her head to look at him, and she looked amused. "Every time parties seek to enter the pass there are avalanches, not just those few whose marks I saw. Moreover, the Keep is now surrounded by a lot of men in armor who came up from the valley below, black men and brown and golden. They sit in front of the gates of the Keep with all their weapons pointed at them, ready to slay the first person who opens those gates, and everyone within eats potatoes and complains about the smell of the sheep and shouts at one another over what ought to be done."

The Icefalcon stared at her as if she'd slapped him, and she grinned back like the demons that occasionally one saw in the coulees, the little ones that seemed mostly harmless. "Indeed I see them now, o my brother," she said. "The smoke of their campfires hangs blue in the air and the glitter of their spears like stars in the turning light.

Warriors of the Alketch lands, I think, like your Vair who rides north."

Her grin broadened, and she clicked her tongue softly, at which faint sound Scorpion Eater and Ashes trotted over to where she and the Icefalcon sat. "I do love coincidence, don't you?"

"Show me one," said the Icefalcon dryly, "and I'll let you know."

The sun westered, stretching out their shadows on the grass. Bison raised their heads as they passed, curly-wooled black humps higher than a mounted man's head, but clearly saw only other bison. In more than one place the Icefalcon saw signs of beasts not common to these lands twelve years before, rhinoceros and mammoth and the broad-horned elk of the Night River Country; the winds blew chill on his back.

"The North has driven us out, o my brother." Cold Death bent forward with the rhythm of her mare's stride as they climbed from the coulee to the plain above. "Blue Child led us south from the winter steadings when the bison and the mammoth ceased to forage. There was an ice storm the winter after you left that killed all of Plum's band, and another in the spring. Now the Ice in the North covers all the Night River Country down as far as the Ugly Hills. Everything is changed there."

The Icefalcon had heard this from Loses His Way—and a great deal about the grazing conditions around the Sea of Grass as well—but it still touched him with a finger of sorrow. Gil-Shalos sometimes talked about why this would be, a curious tale of the stars, and the sun's heat failing, like other tales she told around the watchroom hearth fire, fascinating in spite of its illogic. Everyone in the Real World had known for generations that the Ice in the North moved, though seldom so quickly.

The Stars had told his Ancestors, years beyond years ago, *Change is all that there is. Do not hold anything, for everything will go away in time.* But he hadn't thought of this in terms of the Night River Country. It was an uncomfortable reminder how far he had fallen short of the wisdom of his Ancestors—of the perfection for which he had always striven—to realize that despite all his upbringing he hadn't *quite* thought of it in terms of Noon's death.

In a coulee still muddy from the rain they found the prints of horses, a war band a hundred and thirty-five strong, moving south ahead of them. "The Empty Lakes People," said the Icefalcon, slipping from Scorpion Eater's back to study the marks of the moccasin stitching and to note that Barking Dog, a minor warchief of that people, was still riding that long-tailed dun that overreached its own stride on the left side. Loses His Way had detailed to him a good deal about the pedigrees of that animal—whose name was Saber-tooth Horse—and most of the rest of the bloodlines of the herds of the Empty Lakes People, beasts inferior to the herds of the Talking Stars People, but some of the information was useful.

He swung back up onto his mount, followed Cold Death down the wash. "Loses His Way and his party must have been scouting from the main hunt."

"More grief to them, then," said Cold Death. "Here." She nodded toward the ridge of hills before them, identical to all other ridges in these lands, a civilized person would have said. "From here we let the horses free and walk."

She slid from Ashes' back and gave her round flank a smack. The mare—and the Icefalcon's stallion—trotted off to join Afraid of Flowers. They wouldn't go far.

From the top of the rise they could see Vair na-Chandros and his party.

It was a considerable train, especially in these times. Each of the twelve wagons was pulled by a team of mules. *No wonder the Talking Stars People are interested,* thought the Icefalcon. Remounts, relief teams, and a small herd of sheep followed, under a heavy walking guard; the sun glinted off their bowtips and spears. Vair na-Chandros

himself rode up and down the length of the line on a black
horse—the Icefalcon remembered that the man always
chose blacks. He was helmed and armored as for war, a
scarf of scarlet and blue wrapped over the spiked helm,
and the silver hooks that had long ago replaced his severed
right hand were concealed by the billowing cloak of white
wool. He was much as the Icefalcon recalled him, elegant
and dangerous to the soles of his gold-stamped boots, and
the deep, hoarse bark of his voice brought back the cold
wind under the Keep walls as the remnant of the armies of
the Wathe trained with their flamethrowers for the assault
on the Nest: the smell of the fog that last morning, assem-
bling to march to the flooded ruin of Gae to meet the Dark.

The shrieking of men in darkness as they were devoured.

"Ninety-eight men," remarked the Icefalcon, resting his
chin on his hands and peering thoughtfully through the
long stems of the needlegrass on the ridge. (The Talking
Stars People did not deal in estimated numbers.) "And
more than a thousand sent to besiege the Keep that they
cannot hope to take. What is he hunting here?"

Cold Death shook her head. Wind shimmered silver and
dark in her wolf-hide tunic. "All I know is that I've tried to
scry into that tall wagon there, the one with the guards
walking on both sides, and cannot."

"Another Wise One?" The Icefalcon knew that the Wise
could not scry one another. He didn't like the idea of
trying to get Tir away from two.

"It could be. If so, it is a power I have never seen. Even
in daylight I see around it a sicklied glow, like marshfire
but dimmer." She worked herself back down the slope
until they could follow the ridgeline without being seen.
They walked along the slope of the hill like the shadows of
birds, paralleling the train. "You say that this Keep, this
fortress, cannot be taken?"

"It was built long ago by the Ancestors of the mud-
diggers," said the Icefalcon. "The Ancestors of the Wise
Ones had devices of magic, as if Wise Ones themselves

were made of crystal or gold, indestructible and able to be used like tools by other Wise Ones. Vair na-Chandros visited the Keep seven summers ago and knows there is no way for human armies to break its walls. Yet you tell me he has sent the greater part of his force east to do that very thing, and he is not a stupid man."

"He is if he thought a girl he wedded against her will would forget the experience when she came to womanhood."

There were times when Cold Death reminded him of Gil-Shalos. "He appears," said the Icefalcon dryly, "to have been educated in that respect."

A few hours' further travel brought them to rolling upland prairie, where the wagons formed a circle into which the cavvy was driven. The Icefalcon observed the guarded wagon carefully, but saw no sign of any Wise One riding within. The sheep were pastured nearby under heavy guard. Three riders went out with arrows and spears, circling upwind of a small cluster of bison grazing at the foot of one of the hills, riding like fools in a group. The Icefalcon, lying wolflike in the grass, shook his head and said, "Two arrows says they stampede them."

"I may be your sister, but I'm not a fool," grinned Cold Death. "You keep your arrows, and I'll keep mine. They've been trying to kill bison since they crossed Summer Water Creek. They'll get deer, though, in the coulee, if the Empty Lakes People don't ambush them there."

The coulee that wound away to the east, dotted thick with aspen and cottonwood, was the logical place for the Empty Lakes People to be camped. The Icefalcon said, "They won't ambush the scouts. If it's Barking Dog's hunt, they'll attack the camp at midnight."

"Only fools would try to attack them here," protested Cold Death. Through the screening grasses Vair could be seen talking with one of his scouts, a thin young man with white hair done up in elaborate crests and braids, like an egret in mating time; the young man pointed back toward the hills. "Even without wizardries, the camp is on high ground with no cover around it."

"We're talking about the Empty Lakes People. Two arrows."

"You're prejudiced," sniffed Cold Death. "On the other hand, it *is* the Empty Lakes People. I say dawn."

Despite the camp's favorable position Vair na-Chandros seemed to share the Icefalcon's apprehensions. The tracks of a hundred and thirty-five mounted warriors probably would have that effect, even if one didn't know of Barking Dog's proclivity for midnight raids. The men slung chains between the wagons and drove the sheep into the enclosure. From the eaves of every wagon roof, and on poles set around the perimeter of the camp, the expedition's bald-shaved priest hung demon-scares of glass and beads, such as the Icefalcon had seen on the waists and necks and house eaves of nearly everyone in the southern lands. Most of these amulets were of only limited efficacy—southerners being overly concerned with demons, which could, at most, frighten you in a dark place—but the Icefalcon had been aware all day of a faint nervous edginess, an awareness of being watched.

From the slight rise where he and Cold Death lay, he observed the men as they erected a large square tent against the side of the biggest blue-roofed wagon. Still he saw nothing of any mage, or anything to tell him of Vair's intent. "Do they seek to blot out light from within?" he breathed as they draped the tent inside and out with layer after layer of black cloth. "Will they drape their fires, too, that they be not seen?"

The matter was overseen by a stocky white man, bald-shaved as Bektis' clones and the priest were, but with a small trim fair mustache. He had the animal stride of one trained to fighting, and the Icefalcon recognized, when he took off his heavy leather jacket, the triple scarlet belt around his waist and chest that in the southern lands marked a professional Truth-Finder. He passed into the tent, and came out, and went in again. When he emerged a second time Vair crossed to him and spoke to him for some time, then gave instruction of some kind to a thin tall elderly man with long white mustaches, who seemed by the ribbons on his clothing and the gilded spikes of his helm to be his second in command.

White Mustaches shook his head and shook his head again.

Whatever it was that Vair willed him to do, after speaking to the Truth-Finder, at last he assented. As the men were building their cook fires and unrolling blankets the Icefalcon saw him going about the camp, pausing now by one warrior, now by another, speaking to them with his arm around their shoulders, nodding, his face grave. This Vair did, too.

The bison at the foot of the hills duly stampeded into the distance. The hunters came back to camp with three deer. The sky turned a thousand livid shades of gold and salmon, mad ensanguined glories that had begun in the Year of Two Earthquakes, the year before the Summerless Year.

Gil had explained to the Icefalcon that the colors of the sky had to do with the world growing colder and the movement of the Ice in the North, and why there had been no summer the year before last, but her explanation had left the Icefalcon with little more than a conviction that the Ancestors in charge of the sky had inexplicably become fond of reds and golds. As for the Ice in the North, it had always moved a few feet, sometimes many yards, a year. What was the point of telling over the memories of one's Ancestors, if not to know things like that?

Darkness came. The men in the camp were experienced in warfare and stayed away from the fires themselves, even with the winds that quested the prairie like hungry ghosts. The Icefalcon saw them glance, every now and then, at the square black tent against the side of the tall wagon, from which no light issued. Sometimes after so doing a soldier would make a sign of blessing in the air.

In the coulee the brush flickered in little stirrings against the flow of the wind. Something like smoke curled close to the earth among the cottonwoods, and above the glitter of the water there, but when one looked at it straight there was nothing.

A crack of saffron showed where the tent flap and inner curtains were raised. The reflections sparked a hundred answering notes of light from the demon-scares on poles and wagon eaves and from the eyes of the men on guard.

White Mustaches stepped forth. He stretched out his hand to one of the men to whom he had spoken at the setting of the camp, sitting by the fire among his friends, and somehow the Icefalcon was reminded of Noon, coming out of the dark with the white shell in his hand.

"They don't like it," whispered Cold Death. "Watch them."

Mageborn, she could see better in the dark than he, but creeping to a higher vantage point in the windy desolation the Icefalcon saw indeed how the warriors within the wagon circle fidgeted and looked about them and muttered to one another. Not one slept. Those not on guard sat up in their blankets, or kept two and three together as close to the fires as they dared. Though they played at sticks—a game even more simple-minded than the dicing that went on incessantly in the Guards' watchroom—it was clear none of them gave much attention to the proceedings. The Icefalcon experienced a momentary regret that he could not slip into the camp and set up a high-stakes game.

The moon rose late, meager as a sickly infant like to die; the muzzy stars watched through slitted yellow eyes. Between the second and the third hours of the night came the screaming.

The Icefalcon had seldom heard worse, even during the Long Sacrifice.

"Skinning?" he whispered to Cold Death.

"Sounds like it."

Pressed to the earth among the grass roots, he and Cold Death bellied as close to the camp as they dared. Something moved behind them in the darkness, a wisp of brightness glimpsed from the corner of his eye. When he turned it was gone—or had never been—but a few moments later the grass bowed in the starlight where no wind touched.

*Demons.*

The scream changed. The Truth-Finder must have tightened the screw on the gag.

"Is that how they sacrifice among the mud-diggers?" Cold Death wanted to know.

The Icefalcon shook his head. Out of academic curiosity he listened more closely, trying to sift sound from sound in the shuffle of hushed camp noise, but could hear nothing now from the black tent. "The Truth-Finders work for men, not in the service of the Ancestors," he said. "The mud-diggers call their Ancestors 'saints,' and in the South they sacrifice to them by dedicating gladiators to their names, making them kill one another and letting these 'saints' of theirs choose whom they will take and whom they will spare. In the North, in the Keep of Dare, they only promise the 'saints' things, like money or certain acts."

"But why would their Ancestors want things?" asked Cold Death. "They're dead. And why would they care what their children do?"

The Icefalcon shrugged. "Their priests explained this to me, but it made no sense. There are those who will kill a goat, or a pair of pigeons, to these saints, but this they do secretly, and in the North not at all anymore, pigeons being hard to come by now. When I was in the South, I heard of those who killed human beings to appease demons or to bribe them for favors."

"You can't get favors from demons." Cold Death glanced over her shoulder, to where something riffled suddenly at the water down in the coulee, as if a thousand fish had all snapped at once. "They're bodiless, and you'd have to be a complete fool to trust them."

"People in the South are fools." The Icefalcon shrugged

again. "Most people are, if they think they'll get their own wills."

The bright line slit the night again, a red malignant grin. Vair na-Chandros emerged, leading by the arm a man who walked uncertainly, like one whose legs trembled, but the Icefalcon was almost certain, as they passed the fire, that it was the first warrior who had gone into the tent. Almost certain because the man was bald now and without the mustaches that he had worn. Vair's arm was around the man's shoulders, and though no words could be distinguished the tone of his harsh voice was soothing and kind. As far as the Icefalcon could tell the man made no reply.

Together they came toward the guard who stood just outside the ring of the wagons, within a dozen yards of the Icefalcon and his sister. "Drann," said Vair, greeting the man on guard; he went on in the ha'al tongue of the South, which the Icefalcon knew slightly, patting the man he led on the shoulder as he transferred the guard post from one to the other, then taking Drann by the arm. Drann looked back at the new guard and seemed to hesitate as Vair led him back across the camp to the black tent.

A finger of outstreaming light, and the silhouetted shape of the Truth-Finder inside. Then darkness.

There was no further outcry, but when the wind shifted the Icefalcon smelled blood.

The Empty Lakes People attacked at dawn. Halfway between midnight and morning the Icefalcon resigned himself to the fact that Cold Death was going to win two arrows from him. But then, he had never been able to win a bet with his sister.

The first he heard was an outcry among the mules, and the hard steely *whap* of the southern recurve bows, then shouting. He and Cold Death had moved two or three times during the night and were stationed now in a thicket of rabbitbrush between the camp and the first of the rolling hills. They saw men running and struggling amid a tangle of mules, horses, and sheep within the circle of the wagons.

Animals leaped over and crashed into the chain barricades, driven by howling war-dogs. Then the bulk of Barking Dog's riders swept up out of the coulee, striking like a spearhead at the wagons.

Arrows poured from behind the wagons. Riders plunged out, mounted and ready, dozens of them, old White Mustaches leading with curved sword upraised. When the warriors of the Empty Lakes came near to the wagons, men rushed from the cover of the heavy wooden wagon-boxes, swords flashing, Vair at their head, urging them on. Twenty, thirty, forty men . . .

"Where were they hiding all night?" demanded the Icefalcon, startled. There were close to a hundred and fifty of the Alketch warriors, outnumbering their attackers where they had been outnumbered when the sun went down.

Equally nonplussed, Cold Death shook her head.

They were there, however, and when swords began to cleave and men to struggle hand to hand, it was clear they were no Wise One's illusion. After pushing back the initial charge they held their position between the wagons, refusing to be drawn out, striking only when the Empty Lakes People rode close enough to be hit. The Alketch riders wheeled their horses, driving the attackers toward the spears. The Empty Lakes People promptly scattered in all directions for the hills. One nearly rode over the two watchers in their rabbitbrush blind.

"Can he make men from air?" the Icefalcon whispered. He saw enemies he knew—Gray Mammoth, Herd of Wild Pigs, Long-Flying Bird, and others—fall bleeding in the long grass. Saw, too, the sudden thrashing of the grass near the dying and the spots of trailed gore all around the bodies that spoke of demons.

"It seems he can," said Cold Death, bemused.

Not something that boded particularly well, thought the Icefalcon, for those under siege in the Keep of Dare.

# CHAPTER EIGHT

"She says she has never heard of such a thing in her life."

The Icefalcon sniffed. It was true that Ilae's life had not so far been very long, but it was true also that Thoth Serpent-mage had taught her for five years in the half-ruined Black Rock Keep in Gettlesand, where most of the world's few remaining wizards now dwelled. It was also true that she was Ingold Inglorion's student now.

"Ask her how it fares with the siege."

Over the wide plains the sun stood a few fingers above the mountains. Wood smoke gritted on the air, and the smell of corn porridge. The elementals of earth and water that oozed forth at the stench of blood and pain had sunk away into their native stone and streams, and the demons faded into the bright air. The Icefalcon guessed they had not gone far. Could Cold Death see them, he wondered, as the great shamans could?

"It fares well, she says." A little frown puckered between Cold Death's sparse brows. "She says the southern warriors have not even essayed to break the Doors."

"Have they not?" The Icefalcon settled his back to one of the rocks among which they crouched, down in the coulee where the night lingered blue, and folded his long arms about his drawn-up knees.

He felt no surprise.

The merchant came to mind, the brown-faced southerner who had claimed to be from Penambra, the man who had told Ingold about the cache of books in the villa in

Gae. He had spoken the name of Harilómne the Heretic. And Ingold had gone.

It didn't take a Wise One or a scrying glass to deduce that the man had been dispatched by Vair.

Overhead, vultures made a slow silent pinwheel above the bodies of the slain.

The Icefalcon plucked a little dried venison from his bag and chewed it thoughtfully. "How fares Rudy Solis?"

Cold Death relayed the query to Ilae. The Icefalcon imagined Ilae herself, sitting in all probability in the long double cell the wizards used as a workroom, with its battered table of waxed oak and its great cupboards filled with scrolls, tablets, books salvaged from every library and villa they could get to, from the western ocean to the Felwoods. Rank after polyhedronal rank of record crystals glittered frostily on shelves, the images of the Times Before for all those who could read them. He wondered if Gil would be there, too, studying the crystals by means of the black stone scrying table in the corner, seeing in it the faces of the mages who by their spells and arcane machinery had raised the Keeps against the first incursion of the Dark.

Single-minded and essentially lazy—for it was reasonable to rest and conserve energy when not either in an emergency or preparing for one—the Icefalcon regarded Gil's obsessive studies with some bemusement. She had for years now been piecing together histories, both of the three and a half millennia that had transpired between the first arising of the Dark and the second, and of the Times Before, trying to learn what she could of the world the Dark had long ago destroyed. This she did, she told him, as he would have sought knowledge of a trail long cold, by scratches on rocks or seeds in crumbling dung. That she would or could do so while maintaining the brutal training required of the Guards and caring for a son now able to toddle purposefully in the direction of anything that could conceivably be complicated was, to the Icefalcon, merely an example of the alienness of her nature.

"She says he still lies unconscious." Cold Death's sweet murmur brought him from his thoughts. She held out her hand and he passed her the leathern tube—Cold Death was much enamored of venison sweetened with maple sugar. "The Lady Alde tends him, she says, and has not slept. She is much distressed."

"The child Tir is her son."

A shift in the voices of the men, the doleful complaint of mules, snagged his attention, and he swung up the stones of the low cliff until he could just put his head over the grass on the rim. But it was only breakfast ready, not breaking camp just yet. They were lazy as bears in summer, these southerners. Some of the men gathered around the cook fires, holding out wooden plates and bowls made of gourds. Their heads were bald as new-birthed babies, their feet not clad in boots but, like the feet of Bektis' three clone warriors, wrapped in rawhide.

It was too far to distinguish clearly, but he thought they were all of the same height, the same build.

In the morning stillness the walls of the black tent hung straight, seeming to absorb the light of the pallid sun. The demon-scares flashed on their poles like the corpses of crystal insects, sinister and bright.

He slipped down the rocks to Cold Death once again. "Can you speak with the Wise One Ingold Inglorion?" he asked. "He was once called Olthas Inhathos, the Desert Walker, among the White Lakes People."

"Ah," said Cold Death softly, and smiled. She licked the venison grease from her fingers and plucked another grass blade, which she passed over the tiny pool in the rocks, no more than a cupped handful and frozen with last night's cold, and considered it with bright-black prairie-dog eyes.

"Olthas Inhathos," she said. "Desert Walker. You do not remember me, but . . ."

And she smiled at whatever it was that the Desert Walker replied.

"Even so," she said. "I am in the badlands a day's ride south of Bison Hill with my brother Nyagchilios, the Pilgrim of the Skies, the Icefalcon of the Talking Stars People. The hook-handed bad man Vair na-Chandros is here . . . No, not with me but camped close by, and it appears that he can make warriors out of air. It is he who sent the army against the Keep in Renweth Vale, we think. He also—so my brother says—sent out the peddler whose story took you to Gae, that Bektis could enter the Keep undetected to steal the child Tir."

Her smile widened with delight, and to the Icefalcon she said, "The Desert Walker learned to curse from the Gettlesand cowboys, I think. My little brother is confused," she went on, turning back to the puddle of ice, "and does not know what to do."

"I never said so," the Icefalcon said frostily. *Sisters.* "Tell him of the black tent and the things that passed in the night."

While she did so he climbed the rocks again to watch the movements of the camp.

Under ordinary circumstances the Icefalcon would have felt no hesitation about his ability to creep into the camp itself, even by daylight. But the magic that hung so patently about the walls of that square black tent kept him at a distance. Among his people there was a story about a coyote who went hunting with a saber-tooth and feasted in the end not only on the eggs of the horrible-bird while it was busy killing the saber-tooth—who after the fashion of such creatures didn't wait to see if there was unseen danger nearby before closing in—but on the entrails of the larger and more hasty beast itself.

"He is troubled, your Desert Walker," Cold Death said when the Icefalcon eased himself down into the crevice again. "He says he will make for the Keep with all speed. In the meantime he begs you, guard the boy Tir."

"And what of the black tent?"

"He says there is a tale about an old woman who wrought warriors out of bread dough and brought them to life with the blood from her left little finger, but he does not think this is the case. He says the Guild of Bakers would never stand for such a thing. He says he will meditate." She handed him back the bag.

"Thank him for me," retorted the Icefalcon, exasperated, and slung the bag over his shoulder again.

"Our enemy Loses His Way abides still by Bison Hill." Cold Death stood and tossed her grass blade aside. "He seems at peace, so I can assume that you were right, that the shaman Bektis awaits the coming of this Vair and will do naught to the boy in the meantime. Will you return thence now, little brother?"

"No." The Icefalcon looked around him, gauging the defensibility of the coulee. A water cut led from the main stream to their left, and having hunted here once in the past he knew there was a sort of cave under its bank a mile and a half upstream, hidden by chokecherry brambles.

"I have watched and seen no sign of another shaman," he said quietly. "Yet Vair himself is not mageborn, and there is power of some kind there. Ingold and Minalde need to know of it before Vair achieves his meeting with Bektis. Things may change after that, for better or for worse." He unfolded his lean height—Cold Death didn't even top his shoulder—and sniffed wind and weather, listening to the voices of the camp and the sounds made by the vultures and the kites.

"If there is some magic there that demands sacrifices of pain, I think I had best know this, too, before they take possession of the child Tir."

Cold Death's face sobered, and she nodded.

"Can you work on me a spell of shadow-walking?"

Her mouth was still, but her dark eyes flickered to the brightening sky.

"I know. I have heard the Wise Ones of the Keep, Ilae and Ingold and Rudy, speak of such spells. They are more difficult to perform by daylight, but daylight would render me less easy to detect, as it does demons. I can sleep in the cave there, if you will weave the spells around me and stand guard above my body."

Still she was silent. He saw the concern for him in her eyes.

"I need to know," he said, speaking to her now not as his sister but as a shaman. "We all need to know. And *I* could not protect *you* while you slept."

"Even so," she said, and sighed, knowing he spoke truth. "But if it is a demon in the camp that they have summoned . . ."

"Whatever is there, it is no demon." He gestured to the amulets, like unholy fruit glittering in the new light. "And if there are ward-spells in the camp, or some other form of spirit power that will tell them of my presence, the best time for me to enter is while they are breaking camp."

She spread her hands palm out in surrender. "So be it, then," she said. "Come."

"You go quick, now." Hethya unknotted the rope that pinched agonizingly around Tir's wrists. "He's looking into that crystal of his, so he'll be busy awhile. Don't go far."

"I won't." Tir was sufficiently grateful that this woman let him go into the woods alone to relieve himself, instead of taking him on a rope as Bektis did, that he wouldn't have gotten her into trouble by running away. Besides, he knew perfectly well there was nowhere to go. He might only be seven years old, but he knew he could not survive alone in the badlands. Whatever was happening, he was safer with Bektis—which, as Rudy would say, was a pretty scary mess to be in.

He could not rid his mind of the image of Rudy being struck by Bektis' lightning, buckling slowly forward over the cliff, falling into whirling darkness. Beside Hethya's soft-breathing warmth at night he saw it over and over again, as if it were caught like the images in Gil's record crystals, repeating itself exactly the way it had happened for all eternity. He wanted Rudy and he wanted his mother and he wanted his friends and his home, and he knew that he might never, ever see any of them again.

He knew not to go far into the woods. Hethya was watching him—turning around he could see her broad face, her rough rusty curls and the topaz-and-snuff patterns of her quilted jacket—but he knew, too, that if any trouble arose, like the White Raiders who'd attacked them the day before yesterday, that she was too far off to help. From Tir's earliest memories there had been bandits, dire wolves, saber-teeth, and sometimes even White Raiders in the Vale of Renweth, in spite of all the patrols by Janus and the Guards. He had a healthy respect for the green-on-green isolation among the cottonwoods, boulders, and fern.

He was coming back toward camp when he found one of the Akulae dead.

The man lay on his side at the bottom of a little slope, in a nest of fern and wild grape. Tir could see no blood. It wasn't the man who'd been wounded in the fight, but Tir didn't know which of the other two it was. His white-stubbled face, half turned up toward the dapple shade of elms and cottonwoods, was calm, stoic, and a little stupid, as it had been in life.

Tir looked around quickly. There was no danger in sight. ("It isn't the saber-tooth you see that kills you," the Icefalcon would have pointed out.) Taking a deep breath, the boy scrambled down the clayey slope. Closer to, the body smelled of death, but not of blood. It smelled of something else, too, an ugly decay Tir couldn't recognize or define.

What if the Akula had died of the plague? Gil and Rudy and Ingold all said plague got spread by bugs too tiny to see. What if they were all over this body just waiting to jump off like fleas and onto him?

But at the same time he thought this, he was looking around, pulling a handful of big leaves off the wild-grape vine—from underneath where it wouldn't show—to shield his hands. He unbuckled the dead man's belt and pulled his dagger free, sheath and all. The leaves were awkward, and he threw them away—if he dropped dead of the plague, he thought, it couldn't be any worse than what might happen to him if he didn't have a weapon in an emergency.

He buckled the belt on the dead man again, and with some difficulty worked the dagger down into his own boot, on the inside of his leg, and pulled his trouser over to cover the hilt. There wasn't time for more. Hethya would be watching for him the moment his head disappeared from the bushes. He scrambled fast up the bank again, calling out, "Hethya! Hethya!"

He remembered to sound scared, so they wouldn't think he'd gone down to the body.

She appeared at the top of the bank and held out her hand for him, big and strong and warm. He pointed down the bank. It wasn't hard to fake fear; he was trembling all over and could hardly breathe, but he managed to say, "He's dead!"

Then Hethya did a strange thing.

She clicked her tongue—"Tsk!"—and shook her head a little and took his hand. "Let's get back to camp, sweetheart."

And that was all.


The Icefalcon crouched near the cave's entrance under the chokecherry bushes—it was too low to stand straight— while his sister marked out the four corners of the narrow place with guardian wards, then knelt to burn a pinch of the powder of dried olive leaves on which certain marks had been made to cleanse the air. Ideally, when a scout undertook to shadow-walk—as scouts did occasionally in war, when the other family or band had a particularly powerful Wise One in their midst—he or she would lie on earth and under open sky, where neither the demons of the air nor the elementals that imbued the ground could dominate. Given Cold Death's strength as a shaman the Icefalcon did not doubt that he would be safe from elementals. Still, the damp place, closed in, green-dim, smelling of earth and foxes, made him uneasy.

The Icefalcon had never shadow-walked. It was not

considered safe for boys to make the venture before they reached full manhood, and he had left the Talking Stars People in his seventeenth year. He had seen it done only twice before in his life, when the Talking Stars People had been at war with Black Pig's family of the Salt People.

On the first occasion, the shadow scout had returned safely, with information about the layout of Black Pig's summer hold in the Cruel River Country that could not be ascertained by ordinary observation.

The second time, six or seven years later during another war, the scout's friends—it was the same man who had gone before, who had experience—and Cold Death had waited by the body through three nights and two days, Cold Death weaving such spells as would draw back the scout's spirit to the empty and silent flesh. After that the tribe had had to move on for fear of being raided by Black Pig. The next time the Talking Stars People had camped in that place Cold Death and the Icefalcon—who was sixteen then—and three or four of the scout's friends returned to the place where the body had lain and seen a few of the man's bones. What became of his spirit they never knew.

Thus it was with a certain degree of trepidation that the Icefalcon lay himself down between the four cold balls of spirit-fire that Cold Death summoned from the air and watched her drawing out Circles around him. There was a Circle of Protection, to keep at bay the elementals and the demons that would have taken over his still-living body once his spirit was no longer in residence. "You have to watch out for them while you're walking," Cold Death said, once she had completed the marks and stood wiping ocher and blood from her fingertips. "They'll try to distract you, to get you lost once you're out there. They feed on fear and pain."

There was a Circle of Ancestors. "Do our Ancestors actually guard us when they are summoned to a Circle?" He was drowsy now with the growing effect of the spell and with the warmth of the heat-spells she'd called to keep his body from dying in its sleep. He and Cold Death had watched by turns through the previous night, and neither had slept after midnight.

"I've never seen them." She leaned over him to paint the first lines of the Circle of Power across his face, his hands, his breast under the wolf-hide tunic, in a paste of mud and powdered wildcat blood. She wove his name into them, and the image of the pilgrim-bird that dwells in the high cliffs near the glaciers, overlaid with sigils of protection. These signs were repeated, over and over, in the lines that spiraled out from him to form the anchoring power-curves of the Circle, running up the wall and, it seemed to him in his half-dreaming state, away into the earth around him, like shining roots.

The sharp air from the cave's low opening filled the tiny space with fog, through which the wan blue spirit-fires glowed like tiny suns on a day drowned in mist. Sleepiness closed over his mind.

"You'll want to stop and look at everything." Her fingertip was cold over his hands. "Don't. You're vulnerable to everything—demons, elementals, rain, wind. The sight of the sun itself. If you get lost, you'll never find your way back. Look for the ground first. Don't forget to watch your back trail."

*Back trail,* he thought dreamily. Like tracking in strange country. He tried to remember what that long-ago scout had told him.

"No one is ever really prepared for what it's like." She stuck blades of grass and twigs of the elder tree—whose ancestor was one of the Fifteen Dream Things—into the crossings of the lines. "Not the first time, not the tenth time, not the twentieth. You will be terrified. You have to remember what your flesh was like, every moment, and there will be many things to make you forget. You cannot become unconscious, and you cannot sleep. Do you understand?"

He murmured, "I understand."

"Take three deep breaths, then," she said, sounding very

far away. "And on the third your spirit will go out of your body. Remember that I'm here waiting."

One.

Two.

He was alone, hanging in the brilliant air. Sunlight pierced him like lances, needles of pain. He was colder than he could ever remember being, empty, and terrified.

He couldn't breathe. *(Of course, you fool, you have no lungs.)* But having no lungs did not mean that he did not feel as if he were trapped underwater in that final second before the lungs give out and inhale death. Only that second went on and on.

It was like being naked in bitter winter.

It was like the first moment after one has been thrust from the only home one has ever known, the curses of those inside ended only by the silence of the closing door.

It was like falling, only he did not seem to be getting any closer to the ground.

*Look for the ground first.* But the first thing he saw was the sun. It stood just above the eastern horizon still, but filled the dry air with powdered gold. He found he could look at it without injury to his eyes *(You have no eyes),* and the novelty of that sensation kept him looking, drinking in its light, shaken to his heart by the dense glory of its fire.

He watched it rise. Grandly, slowly, calmly . . .

No wonder they didn't let young adolescents do this.

He was the Icefalcon, he thought. He was the Icefalcon. He had to rescue Tir.

He had to meet Blue Child in battle, when all was done.

He had to return to his people.

*Look for the ground.*

He looked down and was swept by wonder and delight. The world was a jewel of topaz, sepia, and a thousand breath-fine gradations of burning green. Threadlike silver lace marked the bottom of the little water cut, the greater water into which it flowed a jumble of diamond-sewn brown silk down the coulee's heart. Every leaf and twig of the chokecherry bush over the cave-mouth blazed clear and individual, as if incised, and the tiniest, most fragile wisps of the mists from the heat-spell were each an infinite enchantment to be studied, reveled in, adored. The grass-lands were a wonderment beyond wonderment, shape and texture and scent that made him want to rub his face against them as against velvet, the bison shaggy houses with frost in their curly fur. Far off, minute and perfect, lay the exquisite ring of a prairie-dog town.

The twelve blue wagon-tops made a circle in the emerald grass, the horses, streaming out from the opening, a school of brown and black and golden fish. Foreshort-ened warriors in bronze or sable leather milled about the pale daytime cook fire.

The black tent was a square of horror against the wagon's square of midnight blue.

*Ah.*

Then like silver fire a demon struck him, an eel blazing out of invisibility to rip his flesh from his bones. The Ice-falcon cried out, thorned ropes of pain tearing through his heart.

A human's bones protected a spirit. Flesh and muscle were armor, and he had none now. The demon pierced him as the sunlight had done, the pain coring him, dizzy, smothering . . .

*They feed on fear and pain.*

He could feel them eat. Smoky shapes, toothed fantastic horrors encircling him, he was falling, plunging, dying . . .

*What happens when I hit the ground? I have no bones.*

Cold-headed reasonableness came back. *I have no flesh. The pain is an illusion.*

It was a lifelike one.

*Damn the lot of you. Starve and die.* It was hard to say it, but he was—he reminded himself—the Icefalcon, who would have been warchief of his people, and he made himself say it, and believe.

He was still falling, but now he stopped himself from doing so, as he sometimes could in dreams, and walked down the air as down a flight of steps. A demon bit his foot, the pain exactly as if he'd trodden a dagger-blade, but his mind remained locked on the shape of his body and bones, waiting for him in the cave.

*Starve and die,* he told them again.

They spit at him and swirled away. He knew they'd be back.

The smell of grass and sod met him as he reached the ground, a great intoxicating earthy rush. He saw the ants creeping between the grass blades, sunlight on pebbles like reflective glass. He could distinguish the separate perfumes of needlegrass, squirreltail grass, buffalo grass, the scents of each flower one from another—even the differing odors of clay and mold and rock. A madness of beauty as intense as the terror of the pain before.

A man came up out of a bison wallow (*flesh, clothes, sweat, leather*), carrying the dead body of one of the Empty Lakes People over his back, and walked ahead of the Icefalcon toward the camp. The Icefalcon followed him, feeling naked, as if every man among those wagons could see him clearly.

As they approached the circle of wagons the Icefalcon understood why Cold Death had kept her distance from the place and had told Blue Child to do the same. Even as the demon had been visible to him, certain things looked different now, and he was almost certain that it was not a mage that had kept Cold Death from seeing into the camp. Some of the demon-scares—not all—blazed with ugly radiance, the air between them latticed with spells of pain. Past them he beheld the black tent and the wagon against which it stood, lambent with an unhealthy glow, a living rot that pulsed like a heart. Cold Death had told him that her spells would guard him against the demon-scares, but the fear of them still grew as he walked up to their line: he would be trapped, shredded, lose himself . . .

But if he was the Icefalcon, he could and would endure.

Another man walked past him. A golden-skinned Delta Islander, carrying over his shoulder the body of Long-Flying Bird. Not permitting himself to think, the Icefalcon followed him into the camp, pain dicing him, disorienting, breathless . . .

But he was through.

The camp stank of magic. The very air there was dark, and moved.

All about him warriors saddled, harnessed, rolled blankets, unfastened the chains from the wagon-beds. Boxed up gourd bowls and trudged up from the coulee with barrels black-wet and slopping over with flashing frigid springwater. Checked their gear and got it and themselves into marching order.

It was hard not to lose himself in the clamor and noise, hard to remember why he was here and what he needed next to do.

White Mustaches was explaining something patiently to a pale-skinned warrior from the White Coasts: how to harness the mules. The Icefalcon caught words he knew: ". . . same . . . both sides . . ." He was demonstrating the strap lengths. "Balance." The pale warrior only stared, puzzled, from him to the half-harnessed mule and passed a hand over his slick pate. White Mustaches demonstrated again: "balance."

What warrior, after traveling nearly eight hundred miles from the Alketch, would still not know how to harness mules?

Another man came up carrying bowls—the same man. Not just a pale man of the White Coasts, but identical in face, in body, in the way he walked. A black sergeant in red-laced boots had to tell him where to stow his burden. The Icefalcon looked around. There could not be so many pairs of twins in a single company of warriors. Not just twins: sets of three and four, as alike as millet seeds.

*Clones,* Gil had said.

The Icefalcon looked again. Never more than four to a set, and only one of any set wore boots. The other three had rawhide rags wrapped around their feet, as had the clone warriors he'd followed from the mountains.

The rawhide strips were all new.

The men with full heads of hair, and boots, tried not to look at those without them. Sometimes they'd mutter but most often only turned aside.

Vair na-Chandros passed him, close enough to touch, the reek of blood and attar of roses mingling in his clothes. He was making for the black tent, the Truth-Finder walking quietly at his side. The Icefalcon would sooner have picked up a live coal, but he followed them as they lifted the black curtains and passed within.

Masses of lamps hung from the roof, like hornet's nests in a building deserted for three generations, but fewer than half still burned. Most of the candles ranged on planks along the walls, or, standing clumped on iron holders, were guttered to yellow phantasms of twisted wax, and the smell of spent oil, smoke, and tallow mingled with the stench of rotted blood. You could have cut the block of air contained within the tent with a wire, like cheese.

As the Icefalcon had already guessed, the blue cloth of the wagon-cover had been tied back so that the wagon itself made a raised annex onto the square chamber of the tent. There were demon-scares everywhere, depending from every lamp-cluster and pole-end. Being in the tent was like being devoured by ants. A couple of the clone warriors were taking down lampstands and packing up candles. They'd be breaking the tent soon.

The tent contained what was almost certainly apparatus that dated from the Times Before.

*Gil will be pleased,* thought the Icefalcon.

It resembled in workmanship the little that the Icefalcon had seen at the Keep, the pieces from which Rudy had constructed flamethrowers to fight the Dark Ones, and some of what had turned out to be lamps in the crypts where the hydroponics tanks were.

A deep vat, or sarcophagus, occupied most of the wagon-bed. Wooden stairs went up to it, the straw on them, and on the floor of the tent itself, so soaked in blood that it squished under the feet of the men. The vat's curved sides were wrought of what looked like the same black stone as the outer walls of the Keep, but within—the Ice-falcon climbed cautiously to the wagon-bed to see—it was lined with silvery glass, and like fragments of twig and leaf caught in ice, there seemed to be transparent crystals, shards of iron, and tiny spheres of amber and obsidian embedded in the darkly shimmering inner layer.

A canopy of three linked half arches surmounted it, intertwined metal and glass—two men were taking them down now. They wore boots and moved with more intelligence and purpose than did the clones, and packed the apparatus carefully into great wooden crates, stuffing in wadding of dry grass, wool, crumpled parchments, and rags of linen and rawhide. At their apex the arches had been joined by a many-sided obsidian polyhedron and linked down their sides with dangling nets of what appeared to be meshed gold wire, worn thin and tattered, and woven with more spheres of glass and amber. Two more polyhedrons, glass or crystal, tentacled in gold tubes and set on wooden plinths—the plinths were raw-new—stood at the opposite end of the tub. One of the booted warriors boxed them up as the Icefalcon watched.

To the Icefalcon's spirit sight, the whole of the apparatus shimmered with magic, and he understood why Cold Death spoke of it with uneasiness and fear.

There were petcocks and drains on the vat, and the straw underneath them, sodden and stinking, was being cleared away. Sockets, too, made dark little mouths in the corners of the vat to accommodate what looked like poles with ingeniously geared crank-wheels, but these had already been dismantled. *Where had they gotten all of this?* the Icefalcon wondered. And how had it survived the centuries—decades of centuries, Gil said—since the Times Before?

Hidden away, as Gil and Maia had said?

It looked built to last, like all the possessions of the mud-diggers, who could not abide the thought of anything they owned passing into dust.

In the lower part of the tent, on the straw and rough

carpets of the floor, the Truth-Finder was packing up a little box. Coming near, the Icefalcon saw that it contained needles made of crystal, dozens of them, each with a bead on its head: amber, iron, crystal, black stone.

White Mustaches, whom Vair greeted as Nargois, came into the tent and asked a question in which the Icefalcon recognized the words for *corpses*—only Vair used the word *carcasses*, the bodies of animals—and *barbarians*. Nargois assented, and Vair seemed pleased.

Nargois asked something about the Keep of Dare, and Vair shrugged as he replied. Though he knew of it—how not?—the siege was clearly not a matter that deeply concerned him.

*Eleven hundred men? Why not?*

Blood-stench, magic, cold, and pain twisting at his mind, the Icefalcon left the tent. He saw no reason why he could not go directly through the walls, and he was right: the scrape and itch of every layer of the cheap black cloth and canvas, darkness, then the bright dry sunlight of the plains morning. He investigated the other wagons as the men loaded them. Most contained food; one held weapons. Two were packed with clothing, heavy furs and densely quilted jackets in addition to the loose, bright-hued hand-me-down trousers and tunics worn by most of the men.

In another wagon he found crates of the type he had seen in the tent: heavy wood, draped with demon-scares, and dimly glowing with the sickish pale light that played around the apparatus in the tent. Some other apparatus, clearly. *May their Ancestors protect the folk of the Keep if it prove as evil.*

But, of course, he thought, the Ancestors of the Keep folk could not protect them. The protection lay only in Tir's memories—and it was the Icefalcon's failure that had separated Tir from them.

Outside, men were taking down the demon-scares from their poles, the last thing done before moving on. One or

two pocketed them if they thought they were unobserved.
It was an easy matter for the Icefalcon to leave the camp.

So Vair had machinery from the Times Before.

And a woman who claimed to be possessed of a spirit
from those times, though Gil, who was wise in many matters, considered her a fraud.

From a rise in the windswept lands, the Icefalcon
watched the caravan draw away. The snapping of whips,
harness leather creaking, and the ceaseless bleat of sheep
pierced him, musical as the light and the smells and the
terror of the demons who now, he saw, materialized from
the air and drifted after the wagons like thinly glowing
sharks. The cold had grown on him, crippling and ex-
hausting, drawing him toward the unfulfilled promise of
the sun's ascending disk.

Slowly he let himself drift upward, until he hung like
his namesake hawk far above the smooth curves of the
land. His sight could follow the trace of the trail, a grass-
filled groove paler than the surrounding hills, all the way
to the dark tuft of Bison Hill in the distance. In the other
direction that pale groove drove south, arrow-straight, the
scuffed smudges like footprints marking Vair's previous
camps. Every draw and wash and coulee formed serpentine patterns of red and sepia, silver agonizingly bright
through the dust-green cottonwood and sedge. He could
see the rabbits in the brush, the fishlike glowing sinuosity
of water elementals in the stream. He was aware of the
Empty Lakes People, riding in all directions still, scattered
and broken after their defeat and going back to their
hunting trails, telling themselves they were fools who followed fools when mammoth and uintatheria roved the
draws.

And below him, on the flank of one rolling hill, he saw a
single rider, sitting a single gray horse.

She watched the wagons also, no expression on her fire-
scarred face. A big woman, rawboned and heavy-muscled,
shoulders as wide as a man's under a tunic of wolfskin, a

shirt of mammoth wool she'd woven herself on a walking-loom, for who can trust another's luck and goodwill in something that will abide against one's skin? Somehow he could recognize her, as even from this height he could count the black spots on prairie hens. A harsh face, with mocking pale eyes, framed in hair that was white where the fire scars ran up under it. She sat at ease, her hands resting on her thighs, and when next the Icefalcon looked she was gone.

Blue Child.

Lover of Dove in the Sun, who had died on a hunting raid under his command.

Usurper of his birthright, who had branded him a coward and pulled darkness over the last year of old Noon's life.

Engineer of a hoax upon their mutual Ancestors that could have cost all the people dearly through the winter.

And warchief of the Talking Stars People.

*Some day,* thought the Icefalcon, *and I think the day will be soon, there will be a reckoning between us.*

The sun called to him, climbing in its splendor at noon. But the air seethed with demons, smoky forms invisible in the dazzle, and he would be a fool, he thought, to challenge them. So he sought the earth again, and the warm cave under the cut bank, where Cold Death sat beside his body, murmuring spells to keep demons and death at bay.

# CHAPTER NINE

"Any change?"

Minalde shook her head. "I tell myself it's better that way," she whispered, though Gil suspected, looking down at the still bronze face of the man on the bed, that Rudy was beyond being waked. A single pine knot burning in an iron holder smeared gritty yellow light on the younger woman's features. With no guarantee how long the siege would last, use of torches and pine knots was kept to a minimum.

There was no need for more light in this room anyway. Ilae came in several times a day to check on her patient and renew the spells of healing, the spells of warmth that kept him from sinking into cold and death, but as a mage she could see in the dark. When Alde sat here, as she came in many times a day to do, she needed no more light than the single lamp could provide.

Even by its forgiving radiance she looked horrible, wasted and white and beaten. Gil knew she kept up a good face where others could see her. In the Keep they called her brave. Here she wept.

Rudy had been Gil's friend for seven years, since their first unfortunate meeting in the California hills. He was the final link that held her to the world they both had abandoned, the world neither ever quite forgot. She had shed tears in this room herself.

"Look, I hate to bug you about this," she said, "but Lord Sketh will die of grief if he doesn't see you. I can tell him to get lost if you want."

Minalde shook her head and squeezed out the rag that

lay soaking in a bowl of scented vinegar water to wipe down her face. "I'll have to eventually," she said. "My old nurse always told me, *'There's no sense putting off.'* " She got up. When she was working—meeting with the Keep Lords, hearing the endless squabbles and quibbles that the Keep dwellers brought to her for justice, conferring with the hunters and the wardens of the hydroponics gardens about the division of food and labor—she dressed in one of several formal gowns, cut and styled after the fashion they had learned in the days of the Realm's strength to associate with dignity and authority. She was so dressed now: train, flowing sleeves, lavish embroidered trapunto- and jewel-work patterns, though few people in the Keep knew that she took delight in making the gowns herself. The green wool looked muddy by the smoky light, the red velvet of the pillows behind her like old blood.

"We might as well get it over with." Alde readjusted the elaborate braids of her coiffure, pinned over them the veil that had been part of her trousseau, pale-green silk that fell past her hips. "I know what Lady Sketh wants."

Generally when Lord Sketh asked for an audience it was Lady Sketh's idea.

"We haven't even asked their intention," declared the tall, pear-shaped man, folding his hands before the worked silver buckle of his belt. "We've made ourselves prisoners here, living like jailbirds, for nearly a week now, when the matter may be one that can be adjusted by compromise."

"Two siege engines," Minalde pointed out in her low sweet voice, "and eleven hundred men marching fully armed up the pass does not bear the appearance of compromise to me." In the cool white splendor of the glow-stones that hung from wire baskets in her small conference room, she looked worse, thin and stretched, dark smudges under her eyes. "Had they wished to parley at any time in the past week, a man could have come to the steps of the Keep and knocked on the doors. Ilae?"

She turned to the wizard in the low chair to her left. Ilae looked older, and more queenly, with her red hair braided

up into a crown on her head. Maia, erstwhile Bishop of
Penambra and now head of the Church in the Keep, sat
at Alde's right, the position of honor. Minalde had embroidered his formal tabard, too, as a gift on his forty-
second birthday last year. The carved black chair in which
Tir usually sat during his mother's audiences had been
taken away.

"In my scrying crystal I see them, my Lady," said the
girl, and touched the ruby tucked in the palm of her left
hand. "Men with drawn swords stand guard on either side
of the Keep doors. Master Wend tells me there've been
fights, too, 'twixt their men and Yar's archers, and
yestere'en they tried to ambush those as had tried again to
get through the pass."

"Well, naturally there's been fighting," said Enas Barrelstave, who had accompanied Lord Sketh to his audience.
Barrelstave was one of the wealthiest commoners in the
Keep, and something of a demagogue as well. "We meet
them with a rain of arrows; our hunters are shooting at
whoever gets too far from the main camp. We assumed
from the beginning that their intentions were ill." He
glanced accusingly at Janus, on one side of the door that
led to Alde's private chambers. Gil guarded the other, their
black surcoats a silent reminder of the Guards' support.
"Of course they're expecting more trouble."

"The least you can do, my Lady," said Sketh, "is arrange
a parley."

"No."

"May I remind your Ladyship," said Barrelstave, "with
all due respect, that perhaps his young Lordship might
have a different opinion were he here to disagree?"

*Cheap shot,* thought Gil, angry at the not too tactful reminder that Minalde, as regent for Tir, was now nothing
more than the widow of the last King, seven years dead.
Without Tir, her official position was considerably weakened. *I'll remember that later, pal.*

Alde's jaw tightened for a moment, then she said in a
pleasant, conversational tone, "Very well. Would you,

Lord Sketh, or you, Master Barrelstave, like to be the one
who goes outside?"

The two men looked at each other, having quite clearly
envisioned someone of lesser status in the role of messenger. Still, Gil had to give them credit: faced with *Put up
or shut up,* both volunteered, and Lord Sketh, who knew
some of the ha'al tongue, was given the job.

Janus picked Melantrys as Doorkeeper for the opera-
tion. She could catch flies in her hands and had been shot
at enough by bandits that whizzing arrows wouldn't
bother her. Gil, Minalde, and Ilae stood just inside the
inner set of Keep Doors, backed up by a sizable contingent
of Guards, swords drawn and ready. Ilae wrought two
small fire-spells, placing them just between the armed
warriors standing at the outer Doors—not easy to do,
working at a distance with a scrying stone. The Alketch
guards clearly knew there were mages in the Keep because they ran at the first flicker of flame between them.
Ilae, tongue between her teeth with concentration, put a
second burst of sparks a little lower down the steps to get
them to keep their distance, but whoever was in charge of
the Alketch troops had evidently thought of that one because the whole area around the Keep—and every foot of
ground in the camp, set far enough from the walls to make
spell-casting difficult for amateurs, said Ilae—had been
swept and plucked of last year's dead leaves and weeds
like a king's garden on his daughter's wedding day.

On the heels of the second flame-burst Lord Sketh
stepped forth, raised high the white flag of truce, and cried
out in the ha'al tongue, "Parley! We beg a parley!" while
at the same moment Janus slammed shut the inner Doors
and twisted the locking-ring.

Gil was watching Ilae's eyes. She saw them flare wide
and heard the gasp of her breath and knew Lord Sketh had
been fired on or otherwise attacked in the doorway. Minalde, watching, too, said in her very clear sweet voice, "I
told that imbecile."

"He's safe in," said Ilae a moment later. "Melantrys got the Doors shut."

Janus and Caldern worked the locking-rings and opened the inner Doors. Sketh and Melantrys emerged from the glowstone-lit passageway between the outer Doors and the inner, Sketh blanched and trembling with shock, Melantrys pulling a crimson-feathered arrow out of the extravagant hide flap of her boot-top. Their feet crunched on the dry hay and tinder with which the gate-passage was heaped. Gil guessed his Lordship's pallor was due in part to fear that Ilae would get his signals wrong and prematurely ignite this last-ditch incendiary defense.

"Satisfied?" demanded Janus, who hadn't forgotten Barrelstave's imputation of warmongering.

Minalde hurried forward and took Lord Sketh's hands. "Thank you, my Lord," she said, lifting her voice just a trifle so all around the gate could hear. "That took courage, braving the enemy. So now we know."

"They never even listened," whispered Lord Sketh. He looked about to be sick. Lady Sketh hurried up, a stout blond woman almost as tall as her husband, the decoration and jewelry on her clothing making Alde look like a poor relation. "Never so much as paused. The moment I stepped forth, they started shooting, ran up the steps, swords drawn, with no intent to parley."

"Now we know," repeated Minalde, patting his hand like a sister.

Janus muttered sotto voce to Gil, "Like we didn't know before. They pounding at the Doors now, Ilae, me love?"

The mage shook her head, still standing under the nearest glowstone basket, scrying stone cupped in her palm. "They didn't even come up to them. The minute they closed, they stopped."

Janus whistled through his front teeth, eyebrows raised. "So what then?" he asked. "They know there's but the one entrance. What're they waiting for? Someone inside to betray us?" He looked around, his reddish-brown eyes questing the faces of the Guards, of Lord Sketh, of Enas Barrelstave, who stood nearby looking equal parts shaken and indignant, and Lady Sketh who, in the process of enfolding her husband in several acres of fur-lined sleeves, was careful to include Minalde in the embrace as well.

Gil was silent, a thought coming to her, but she said nothing until she and Minalde were walking back to the Royal Sector through the vast near darkness of the livestock-scented Aisle. As they crossed the last of the railless stone bridges, turned their steps toward the laundry-hung arch of the Royal Stair, Gil said softly, "Alde, we're always hearing how the Doors are the only way into the Keep—how the Keep was built that way to be the perfect defense against the Dark Ones. Do we *know* those are the only doors?"

"Yes," said Minalde, startled. She stopped at the foot of the Royal Stair, plum-dark eyes wide, pinpricks of reflection swimming in them from the votive lamps of St. Prool's statue in a niche. "I mean, Eldor said . . . All the records of the Keep say that it was built that way to keep the Dark Ones from entering . . ."

"I know," said Gil. "But *we don't have records from the building of the Keep*. Only traditions, and hearsay, and tales." She folded her arms and glanced back toward the Doors, where the Guards still crowded around Ilae. Men and women kept coming up to them, weavers and tubmakers and gardeners, asking questions and divesting themselves of their opinions with much arm waving and jostling. "Are we *sure* there's no other way in? Because those people outside the gate sure act like they think there is."


"It's nothing to worry about." Bektis carefully replaced his scrying ball in its bags of silk, fur, and velvet, folded up the silver tripod, and stroked his milk-white beard. "Lord Vair was delayed by a White Raider attack on his camp, that's all. They're on the road again and should be with us by sunset."

Hethya started to look around her, but the wizard said casually, "Oh, I'm sure the other two have succumbed as well." Tir looked around, too, and indeed neither of the other Akulae were in sight. But his movement caught Bektis' attention: "And what is that child doing with his hands free?"

"I took him into the woods to pee," said Hethya, eyes flashing with annoyance. "I was never more than a foot and a half from him." Under Bektis' cold glare she led Tir back to the sycamore tree where he had been tied, put his hands behind his back and bound them carefully tight, then ran through them the rawhide rope whose other end was knotted to the trunk. "Stuck-up old blowhard. Are you all right, sweeting?"

"I'm fine," said Tir, sitting down tailor-fashion and trying not to look conscious of the dagger in his boot. "Are the other Akulae dead?"

"Looks like." Seeing the fear in his eyes, she stroked his hair and added, "It's nothing for you to worry over, honey. Nobody killed them. And they weren't . . ." She hesitated, searching, Tir thought, for an explanation that wouldn't explain too much.

"They weren't really people," she said at last. "They—the things they are—don't live very long, and they didn't hurt or anything when they died."

"What are they?" Tir didn't know if this information would make him feel better or worse. When Toughie, matriarch of the Guards' cats, died, his mother had comforted him by telling him that cats didn't live as long as people, which to Tir's mind was awful. The thought that there were things that looked like people but weren't people scared him, too.

He saw her eyes shift again and knew this was a secret she couldn't tell him. "Don't worry yourself with it, sweeting." She walked back to Bektis, scooping up a big handful of her curls and twisting them out of her way on top of her head with one of the jeweled bronze hairpins she carried in the pockets of her coat. She kept her voice down talking to the wizard, but by her gestures she was angry—angry and scared. She was a person who talked with her hands, and the wave of her arm at the pale-trunked cottonwoods on two sides of them, the slash of her hand across her throat, told Tir as if he'd been at her elbow what she was talking about.

White Raiders had come at them once. Bektis shook his head and made his little pooh-pooh flick with his fingers, as if brushing gnats aside, and touched the crystal device that hung by golden mesh straps at his belt. But Tir had heard enough stories from Ingold, from Rudy, from Janus and the Icefalcon, to know that the White Raiders were still watching Bison Hill. Their dead were rotting in the coulee away from the camp—birds hung over the place— but they wouldn't simply say, "Those people are too strong for us, let's leave them alone."

White Raiders never left anyone alone.

But it wasn't the White Raiders who rode out of the southern badlands with the sinking away of day.

Bektis was impatient by then, pacing around and snapping at Hethya; it was Hethya who did all the camp work. She fetched water and made food at noon, though Tir, still tethered under his tree, noticed that she didn't go far into the trees. She brought up the horses, too, and Bektis laid spells around them: Tir thought Ingold's method of keeping horses from running away or being stolen was more efficient, but didn't say so. He noticed Bektis slipped the bright-flashing handgear of crystals on to execute the guarding-spell, and to make the fire, too, and wondered a little about it because Rudy had told him that those kinds of spells didn't take much magic.

When the light turned red-gold and the shadows grew long, Bektis walked to where the slope sank away toward the grassy prairie, the gems still on his hand, and shaded his eyes to gaze to the south.

"Ah," he said, pleased. "At last."

*I have to be brave,* Tir told himself, watching the line of riders, the swaying dark tops of tall wagons, the double file of men with weapons glittering in the harsh dry fading light. *I have to be brave.*

It was an army, bigger than the biggest band of outlaws Tir had ever seen. They were all men—unlike the Guards and the bandit troops Tir had heard about—and they were mostly black-skinned, some with white hair, some with black, some bald as eggs as the Akulae had been. Tir remembered Rudy's description of the black-skinned prince who had offered to marry his mother, back when the lands of the Alketch still had an emperor.

Remembered, too, the name of the Alketch general with a silver hook where his right hand should have been. He had betrayed the armies of daylight when they went against the Dark Ones in their Nests, pulled his men out of the fighting so that he could have his own army strong, left the men of the Keep to be killed. There were a lot of orphans in the Keep whose fathers and mothers had died there in the holocaust of fire and shadow.

The man in the long white cloak who dismounted his horse and walked up the hill to meet Bektis had such a hook, though that was not the most fearful thing about him. He had yellow eyes that did not care whether you lived or died.

"My Lord Vair." Bektis' voice had a caressing note, as if Vair were the most important person in the entire world, and he made the formal salaam that mostly only the Keep Lords made.

"You have the boy?" A voice like rocks rubbing over each other.

*(I have to be brave.)*

"We have him safe and sound, illustrious Lord. I behold within my scrying crystal that your forces surround the Keep of Dare."

This was a shock to Tir, another cold drench of panic.

"It is well done."

Lord Vair gestured impatiently. "Were you followed?"

"Only as far as the crest of the pass, my Lord. The

wizard Ingold not being at the Keep, they sent another of
the Keep mages after me. I slew him with the lightning
of my hands and buried the pass under a blizzard of
snow." The final sunlight leaped and sparkled from his
flourishing hand.

"Daily since then have I scried the pass. The spells I laid
on it still hold strong."

"And Ingold?" His words came out like slaps in the
face. His speech, though recognizably the words of the
Wathe, had a different intonation, the sounds bent and
changed and the accents differently placed.

"He is in Gae still."

Tir's heart sank, but he bit back tears. Those cold wolf
eyes cut over toward him, measuring him as they mea-
sured all things and, as they found all things, finding him
wanting.

"Demon-fornicating son of Evil. And the wench?"

"I am here, Vair na-Chandros of the Southern Realms."
Hethya stepped forward, drawing herself tall. "*Aniòs ith-
bach amrâmmas a teyélsan*, 'The ignorant speak easily of
that which they do not understand.' " The sonorous words
flowed from her tongue like the magic speech of wizards,
and her face seemed to grow longer and thinner, a different set to the mouth than Hethya's broad grin, the hazel
eyes unsparkling, cold as a priestess'. "The girl Hethya,
Uranwë's Daughter, is here with me also, but *I* am here, I,
Oale Niu; here in this place where I stood three thousand
years ago, and I will not be slighted."

The men who had come up behind Lord Vair murmured
among themselves, and one or two bowed their heads.
After a moment Lord Vair inclined his, just slightly, as
well. "I meant no disrespect, Lady," he said. "And indeed
I apologize for the clumsiness of my tongue. The apparatus you instructed us in worked well, as you see."

He signed toward the men gathered around the wagons
at the foot of the slope. It was a little difficult for Tir at first
because all were strangers to him, bald and without facial
hair of any kind, and he was not used to the sight of so

many black faces, but he realized that many of them had
the same features, like the Akulae.

A word came to his mind unbidden, from the dark
hollow of memory: *tethyn*. They were called *tethyn*. And
there was something awful about them—or about it—
something that made him feel sick inside, something he
didn't want to know.

"I trust that the other apparatus will function as well."

"How many things function as once they did, with the
passage of years?" She looked him coldly up and down
and spoke in the voice of Oale Niu, strange coming from
Hethya's lush mouth. "Not men, certainly, nor the bodies
of men. But the machines we built in the ancient days are
wrought of power and adamant," she went on, as if she did
not see Lord Vair's face cloud with anger. "They will do as
they were made to do, my Lord. Be sure of it."

On these words she turned her back on him and strode
serenely off into the woods, swallowed up by the shadows
of the trees, leaving Tir alone.

Vair flicked his left hand—Tir noticed already that he
kept his hooks low at his side or hidden within his sleeve
or the folds of his white woolen cloak. "Set the camp. Nargois, Bektis . . ." The sorcerer stepped closer, as did another man, tall like Lord Vair, extravagantly mustachioed
and cloaked like him in white, his clothing adorned with
ribbons and jewels of rank. "Let's see the brat."

Tir wanted to shrink back and conceal himself behind
the tree but knew it wouldn't do any good. Besides, it
wasn't brave. When Vair, Nargois, and Bektis were halfway across the clearing to him he was swept by a wave of
dread that this awful lord would know all about Akula's
knife hidden in his boot. He looked away, trying to
breathe, and the next moment Lord Vair's iron fingers in
their white leather glove had his chin in a grip like a machine, forcing his head up.

For a moment Tir looked into those honey eyes and saw
in them worse things than he'd ever known in his life.

Then, very deliberately, Vair released his chin and

struck him across the face, hard enough to knock him down. Tir fell, crying out with shock and pain, and the silver hooks flickered out of their concealment, catching Tir's sleeve and ripping the flesh of his shoulder underneath as they pulled him to his feet again.

Vair slapped him twice more, Tir sobbing but too terrified to cry. The hooks pulled him to his feet again and then jerked free of his sleeve, Vair's left hand grabbing his collar while the hooks on their ivory stump whipped around and slashed across his face, opening the flesh from temple to cheekbone in a single vicious swipe. Tir screamed in pain, and Vair shook him, his head jerking back and forth, his breath strangled in the twist of his collar and his neck half broken by the man's strength. Then Vair caught the hooks in his face again, less than a finger-breadth from the corner of his eye.

"Listen to me, little boy," said that cold grating voice, and Tir, weeping in terror and feeling as if he were going to faint or wet himself, stared up into those vulpine eyes. "Do you know how easy it would be for me to pull half the flesh off your face? So that it flaps back and forth like a pancake?" He shook him, only a gentle wobble this time, but horrible as a blow. "Or to dig out one of your eyes? You'll only need one for the job you're going to do for me. Nod your head."

Blank with fear, Tir nodded, and felt the metal pull in his flesh.

With a movement of his wrist Vair freed the hooks and shoved Tir facedown on the grass. With his hands still tied behind him, he couldn't break his fall. His face felt as if it had puffed up to the size of his head, the air like cold metal against the pouring heat of his blood. He lay crying, not daring to look up or move or breathe. Something shoved at his chin, hard.

Above him the cold voice said, "Now kiss my boot, and tell me that you love me."

Tir had to wriggle forward on his shoulders, sobbing so hard he could barely speak. "I love you," he made himself say and kissed the leather. It was cold and smooth and smelled of wax and old blood.

Vair kicked him. "Say it so I can hear you."

"I love you." He had to do it right. He had to do it right or this man would kill him.

"Again. Bektis and Nargois want to hear, too."

"I love you!" screamed Tir, and bunched himself together, knees to his tucked-down chin, sobbing.

Vair kicked him again and walked away; Tir could hear the scrunch of his boots on the trampled grass. "Fix that cut," he heard him say. "Then see me in the wagon."

Bektis came over, pushed him upright against the sycamore trunk, and very quickly smeared salve on Tir's face, as if the injury were somehow Tir's fault. He pushed the edges of the two lines of cut flesh together and wrapped a bandage around Tir's head, but he worked very fast: "Stop crying," he ordered, "lest my Lord return and make you cry in good earnest."

He hastened away to the wagon. Later, when he thought about it, Tir realized Bektis must be almost as afraid of Lord Vair as he was. Now he only put the uninjured side of his face against the tree trunk and cried.

Boots crunched the grass again and Tir whirled in nauseated terror. It was Hethya, dropping to her knees beside him and gathering him in her arms. There was another man behind her, one of the black warriors, a young man as big as a tree.

"He all right, Lady?" He held out a gourd of water.

"I think so. Thank you, laddy-buck." She took the water, held Tir close against her. He buried his head against her breasts, wanting to hide himself in her body, wanting to be a baby again and be taken care of, wanting to be dead. He heard the water from the gourd drip on the grass and wondered if they'd beat him if he didn't drink it or say thank you.

"I got these." The young man's voice had the same inflection as Akula's, awkward over the tongue of the Wathe. "Dates, understand? Dates?"

He felt Hethya move, reaching, and heard the warm smile in her voice. "Thank you."

"My own father, he beat me. Bad. But not like that." There was a clumsy pause, and Tir felt the man's rough fingers touch him very gently on the hair. Then the grass crunched again as the young soldier walked away.

Tir curled himself into a ball, trying to make himself as small and impervious as an apple seed, and cried until he fell asleep.

# CHAPTER TEN

They harnessed the wagons with the first of morning light and traveled north.

The Icefalcon, who had seen the furs and quilting, the snowshoes and ice axes packed among the stores, was not surprised. "They journey to where the land is cold, o my enemy," he said, from the bison wallow south of the road where he and Cold Death had joined Loses His Way shortly before sunset. "With your permission, when they have passed from sight we will visit your kin again in the coulee and see what other clothing they can lend."

But as the wagons drew close to the coulee Lord Vair raised his arm and called a halt, and the Icefalcon saw men descend into the bottomlands and presently return dragging and carrying the swollen, crow-gouged bodies of the slain.

"What hunting is this?" rumbled Loses His Way, and Yellow-Eyed Dog, lying beside him with his nose between his paws, pricked his ears at the anger in the man's voice.

"Cold hunting for us." Icefalcon propped his chin on his crossed wrists. He had shaved that morning, but after six nights sleeping on the ground he could have done with a long soak in the baths on first level south, or a session in one of the sweathouses at the winter steadings of his people. "I for one am not eager to try to slip into their camp, within my body or out of it, to borrow furs."

The chieftain shook his head. "No need. When we prepared to attack we left our blankets and heavy clothing and our spare food in a fox burrow in the bank, a mile up the gulch," he said. "They will be there still. But this . . . Can they not let even the dead sleep in peace?"

"The dead are not disturbed when the kites strip their bones," remarked Cold Death, and tweaked the fur between Yellow-Eyed Dog's paw-pads just to see him turn his head and look at her patiently. "Your family sleeps still."

"Pah!"

"They took the bodies of the slain yestermorning as well," the Icefalcon said thoughtfully. "They're in that wagon there, the last in line . . . Look." Bektis, resplendent now in a coat of quilted velvet with an immense collar of ermine and gloves of white kid on his hands, stepped down from the wagon he rode in and came around to the last wagon in the line, which even in the spring chill could be smelled from the bison wallow.

"Does he make magic with the bones of the dead?"

"Puts a spell on them to arrest rot, more like."

"He should put one on his own heart, then." The warchief's tawny brows pulled down till the weather-reddened face seemed little more than the arched crag of a nose projecting from a great fiery tangle of braided gold and a glint of angry blue. "And on the heart of that black saber-tooth that would hurt a little child."

Bektis lifted his gloved hands, making graceful passes over the wagonload of carrion, long white hair streaming in the freshening wind. *It would be a mass of snarls by nightfall,* thought the Icefalcon—braiding was the only way to deal with the plains wind. Then the sorcerer climbed back aboard his own wagon, wrapped himself carefully in blankets, and pulled up his hood. Nargois of the long white mustaches wheeled his horse and raised his hand; there was a great cracking of whips along the line, and the caravan moved off.

Since there was no possible way they could lose the train in the empty universe of prairies, the Icefalcon, Loses His Way, and Cold Death, after retrieving the coats and blankets, the pemmican and short, heavy war axes from the fox burrow and loading them onto their horses, investigated the camp as well.

"These clones, as you call them, fell and died yesterday," said Loses His Way, poking in the midden of scraps and ashes. "They slumped down where they stood, like men taken suddenly by sickness. But neither the woman nor the Wise One made a move to cleanse themselves, nor to shift their camp. I smelled no smokes of healing."

"And they carried the bodies away with them." The Icefalcon studied the ground where one of the clones had lain, close by the trampled ground and dung of the horse lines. The yellow leaf-mast was stained with the liquid of unnatural decay, and the marks of heavy boots and men's feet in rawhide strips showed where the corpses had been lifted and carried to the wagon in the night. "The apparatus Vair carries with him makes warriors, not out of air, I think, but out of the flesh of the dead."

"It is an evil hunt." Loses His Way stroked the end of his enormous mustache. "And now you tell me that my people have scattered to the far corners of the wind, not knowing what is being done with their flesh and their bones." He touched the place on his breast where, under his deer-hide shirt, lay the flat embroidered spirit-pouches of Blue Jay, Wolfbone, Twin Daughter, Shouts In Anger, and Raspberry Thicket Girl. "It is one matter, o my enemy," he said, looking down at Cold Death, who barely came up to his breastbone, "to feed the vultures with your flesh. The vultures are our sisters, too, and so all things return to the home of our Ancestors. But this shamanry, this evil . . ." He shook his head.

"This I will not forgive."

Cold Death called the names of the horses into the wind, and the horses came, trotting up from the long grass of the coulee, snuffling and ears pricked. Ashes, Scorpion Eater, and Afraid of Flowers had been joined by two others, southern horses who had escaped during the raid, and they, too, were laden with blankets, furs, and supplies.

So they mounted and rode north, into the rocks and gorges and lava beds called the Cursed Lands. The caravan moved, and the Icefalcon followed, and the stink of the corpses could be smelled in its wake until Bektis repeated his spells while wearing the crystal hand. The moon waxed to full and began to wane again, and somewhere behind them, the Icefalcon was aware, drifted the Talking Stars People, like vultures riding the thermals and waiting for a sick animal to fall.

No road existed in the Cursed Lands, yet the wagons made their way north and slightly west unerringly, without halts and queries and casting about. The Icefalcon remembered the pale trace in the gamma grass, invisible from the ground but straight as a bowstring. At night, or with the first dove-colored light, the frost a silver dust in the grass, the Icefalcon would see Vair na-Chandros and the woman Hethya come out from among the wagons with Tir between them, Tir thinner and more haggard by the day. The Icefalcon never came close enough to hear—with Bektis in the train he did not dare—but it seemed to him that it was Tir who pointed to the gaps in the hills and gave directions by the dim-shining stars.

The land grew harsher. Gullies and washes creased the bare clay hills, steeper than before, dividing the scattered prairies where slunch glowed filthily in the dark. Twice the Icefalcon shadow-walked, investigating the edges of the camp and seeking a way to extricate Tir from Vair's grip. But Tir was kept bound much of the time, and there were many guards, facing all ways, inward and out. Cold Death was as fearsome a warrior as she was a shaman— something no one ever thought, to look at her—but with Bektis' crystal hand, even her aid might not suffice to get the boy away safely. Vair would kill Tir rather than permit his escape. And, for all her frivolousness, the Icefalcon was fond of his sister and would not like to see the lightning of that cursed crystal hand skewer her as it had skewered Rudy. There would and could be only a single attempt, and it had better succeed.

Whatever it was that Vair wanted, it lay in the North.

His mind returned to the trace he had seen from the air. The work of the Times Before, built in the ancient days beyond the memories of the People of the Real World. He asked Cold Death about it, but Cold Death, who knew the properties of every herb and root in the great grasslands of the Real World, and the names of the *ki* of each tree and stream, could only say, "I have never heard of such a thing, o my brother."

And Loses His Way, who could (and nightly did) detail the family histories of every horse belonging to his own people and any number of other clans and tribes from whom the Empty Lakes People raided horses—who could recognize the prints and scat of king mammoths and individual musk oxen and reindeer in half a dozen herds and tell stories about them—only shook his head and said, "That's foolish. Nothing lies in the North but the Ice. Why would anyone build a road thence?"

"That's what I'm trying to figure out," the Icefalcon snapped, exasperated, though he knew he would have received a similar reply from Noon or any of his friends in his family—Red Fox or Stays Up All Night or Fifty Lovers. And though Loses His Way could, like any of the people in the Real World, speak of the habits of animals long dead, or the small details of war parties and hunts for generations back, or recount from memory weather conditions mentioned to him in passing forty leagues to the south, he had very little interest in the slunch-born things that roved the hills abandoned by gazelles and rhinoceri, the lumpy misshapen beings that Gil said were broken echoes of life as it had been years uncounted in the past.

*Why?* the Icefalcon wondered. Lost dreams, Gil called them, woven in the slunch and repeated without meaning— but whose dreams? And what had the world been like that had spawned them?

He had been affected, he thought, a little embarrassed, more than he knew, by the habits of civilized folk and did not like to speak of this to his sister or to Loses His Way.

And indeed, it was not the way of the Talking Stars People to show interest in such matters, which had no bearing on life as it was lived in the Real World.

Still, the road was there. And as the cold grew more piercing, and the great sheets of slunch that even the wind could not rustle lay more and more frequent and their voiceless denizens took the place of the creatures that had once grazed these dying prairies, the Icefalcon welcomed the far-off plaints of the Alketch sheep and the squeak of wagon axles, the only living sounds to break the stillness of these lands.

It was high spring, and they rode through a world filled with light. But the temperature fell, and the thunderstorms that at one time had crashed and raged daily over these lands were mute and absent as the vanished birds. There was only the wind itself, bearing the smell of stone and sleet.

By day they followed, and by night they worked by the tiny light of hidden fires, cutting hickory saplings where they found them for snowshoes and sled runners and slicing up coats of bison or musk ox or sheep to sew with sinew the pieces into double-layer garments, fur inside and out.

Twice the train halted for a day, by streams full enough that Vair, and Nargois, and Hethya, and some of the others could heat water and bathe in a tent set up for the purpose, and the priest held rites in praise of the Straight God.

Then one day in the distance the Icefalcon saw a glittering rind of blue-white, flashing in the heatless ghost of the sun.

It was too soon, he thought, far too soon. They should only be drawing near to the aspen groves, the woods of birch and maple, the streams and meadows that lay to the south of the Night River Country, his people's summer range and the home of his heart.

Loses His Way had told him this; Cold Death, too. But he understood that his heart had not believed. The land of his childhood's joy, the place that would have been the

center of his defenses as warchief of his people, was lost
to him, buried under the rolling weight of time and snow
and fate.

He could not deny to himself that he looked upon the
Ice in the North.

"I was ill on that journey." Hethya gazed somberly into
the leaden morning distance, with what Tir had come to
recognize as Oale Niu's eyes. "The Dark Ones came, surrounding our encampment. We, the mages, fought them,
ringing the camp with walls of fire and lightning. Their
power was terrible." She turned her face a little aside and
passed her hand across her brow, as if to erase the mark of
pain that appeared there. "We survived, but some of us lay
like the dead for many days afterward, unable to move or
speak."

She looked across at Tir, changeable eyes inscrutable,
her mouth half hidden behind the heavy quilting of her
collar. "Do you not remember this, Lord Altir?"

Tir shivered, though he was bundled thick in a coat of
furs, a princely garment wrought in the fashion of the
South. Vair had given it to him, for the cold was deepening
daily, and though it was May there was frost every night.
Even through the layer of brocade, and the soft padding of
lynx-hide that protected his narrow shoulders, the pressure of Lord Vair's hooks reached his flesh. It wasn't as
bad as the tall man's pale eyes, which he felt pierce the
back of his head.

"I don't . . ." he began, and then saw something else in
her gaze.

Not Oale Niu's eyes. Hethya's, peeking from behind
them as behind a mask. Scared.

He swallowed, nodded. "I don't . . . I don't remember
their names." It was the first time he had lied about his
memories. He looked away quickly, gazing at the plain before them. Sheets of water covered the rock and stunted
grasses, milky with pulverized stone and floating with

cakes and chunks of pale-blue ice, dyed straw and primrose and the fragile pink of sand lilies with the coming
day. Blots of slunch festered on such dry land as there was,
further blurring and confusing the landscape, but some
things had not changed.

*Put everything else out of your mind,* Rudy had told him
once. *Don't worry about what you think we need around
here, Ace, or what Gil's trying to find out about those guys.
Just tell me what you really see, whether it makes sense
or not.*

It was hard to put Lord Vair out of his mind.

"The road ran that way." He pointed toward the broken
wall of black talus and scree, four days' journey across the
drowned plain. Through every fang and promontory of the
broken dark hills ice glimmered, an unearthly, unholy
aqua in the nacreous dawn. "It went around the right side
of that hill. The Big Guardian, they called it. There was a
valley going back."

"If I may point out," said Bektis, stroking his beard,
"the logical course for a road to follow would be to the left
of that promontory, not the right. The watercourse begins
there, as you see, my Lord. The way will be easier for the
wagons as well."

"Which is it, boy?" Vair's voice was a razor, opening
the side of Tir's face again in his imagination, peeling
away the half-healed flesh to expose bone and brain and
the trembling pulp of self. "Left or right?"

Tir closed his eyes. His throat, his chest, his stomach
all clenched on themselves with terror of another beating,
another session with the hooks. Since his earliest awareness Rudy had taught him to trust his memories, to call
them forth gently and easily, letting come what would:
*If you don't see anything, just say, "Hey, man, I don't
remember."*

Tir didn't like to think about what would happen if he
said to Vair na-Chandros, *"Hey, man, I don't remember."*

But lying about what he saw was something else.

The hooks pricked through the heavy brocade, the pro-

tecting furs. "Left or right?" Tir felt panic flood him and
tears fill his eyes.

"Grant the child a moment to consider," cut in Oale
Niu's dry, matriarchal voice. The glimpse of Hethya he
had seen was completely gone. "How correctly could you
have answered your schoolmasters, my Lord, with a knife
against your face?"

"It was right." Tir's voice peeped like a mouse from his
constricted throat. "I remember us leaned over walking
like this . . ." He balanced his weight sideways, seeing in
his mind the train of mules and horses, the square black
shape of his father's shoulders—that other boy's father,
with the long tail of gray hair hanging down his back—
higher on the slope than the thin small bald-headed man
who rode beside him.

The way their heads bowed against the rain. The way
the bald-headed man gestured while he talked. He was
there. He'd been there, the Big Guardian looming crookedly
against harsh gray sky.

They had gone around the Big Guardian—differently
shaped now, shorter and wider at the base, but still recognizable after three thousand years—to the right, although
from where they stood he could see no sign of road in the
broken, rock-covered slope.

Because she had helped him he added, "The men had
trouble because they were carrying—carrying a . . . a lady
mage in a litter." He half closed his eyes again, extrapo-
lating how it would have been, and said, "The men on this
side"—he gestured with his left hand—"were higher than
on that." He waved his right and then was still, trembling
with terror, praying Vair wouldn't hurt him anyway.

"You are not," said Vair softly, "trying to lose us in the
wilderness, are you, child?" The metal of the hooks,
freezing cold in the bitter air, brushed the side of his
cheek. "Or making a game of us? Because I tell you, it will
go worse for you if you are."

Tir's trembling increased. Tears began to trickle from
his eyes and snot from his nose, and he found it impossible

to speak, fearing the results of whatever he might say. This happened to him often these days, and he was always overwhelmed with shame when it did, but he couldn't help himself. He shook his head.

"Tell me yes or no, child," pressed that inexorable voice.

It took everything he had. "No, my Lord."

Lord Vair's silences were terrible, for they were unreadable, containing cloaked violence and rage without reason. The men went in fear of him, too, fear almost as great as their love for him. But this time he said, "Then we will pass to the right," in a perfectly normal voice. "Is the way safe, Bektis?"

"I believe it to be, yes, my illustrious Lord." The Court Mage made another of his formal salaams. After the second or third time he'd tried to ensorcel the carrion wagons, he'd taken to wearing the crystal device all the time on his right hand—with no glove under it, as if he could not stand to lose contact between the jewels and his flesh. He was always cradling it and stroking it with his left, continuously but unconsciously, the way he caressed his beard. "In all my scrying in these lands I have not seen sign of the White Raiders, after those first attacks."

"That doesn't mean they aren't there." The words came out of Tir almost involuntarily, and he wanted the next second to stop up his own mouth and never speak again.

The hooks twisted in his collar. "*Are* you mocking at us, child? Or making a game of your elders?"

"No, my Lord." His throat closed, bringing his voice down to a whisper again. "Really no." *Please don't hurt me,* he thought, but he'd already learned that pleading only made everything worse. Sometimes. Not always. "Just that the Icefalcon told me that a lot of the White Raiders carry amulets, or have their Wise Men and shamans ride with their scouting parties, so the shamans of their enemies can't see them."

"I believe," said Bektis, with stiff sarcasm, "that my

skills are *somewhat* more advanced than those of barbarian bone-scryers."

"Even Ingold can't see Raiders coming up on the Vale half the time," said Tir. "Really."

The Icefalcon himself never spoke of it, but the other children of the Keep—mostly the herdkids who had been his friends before they had all perished in the ice storm of the Summerless Year—whispered stories about what the Raiders did to captives. Though he would have loved to see Lord Vair come to grief, he knew they'd kill Hethya, too. All the men in Lord Vair's train, many of whom he was coming to know, like Ugal, who'd brought him the dates, were blameless as well and didn't deserve slaughter. Being here wasn't their fault.

"Bektis?"

"I think the child is merely being difficult," the wizard stated coldly. He pulled his coat collar more closely around his face; the end of his nose was red with chill. "Yet it could not hurt to keep more men on patrol."

Vair na-Chandros pulled his hooks free of Tir's collar and turned back to the camp, followed by the wizard, the child, and Hethya. Hethya still bore herself with the haughty mein of Oale Niu, but she put her arms around Tir's shoulders as he walked; Tir was already crying, involuntarily, from reaction to fear. He hated himself for it and tried not to do it where the men could see. He was Eldor Andarion's son and didn't want them to think him a sissy. Since Lord Vair had told him, many days ago now, that Bektis had seen in his scrying ball that his mother and Rudy were dead, and his sister Gisa with them, it seemed to him that he couldn't stop crying.

The Keep was under siege, they said, and would be broken open soon, and everyone killed. He had nowhere to go, and no one to turn to now. The only people he knew in all the world were Bektis, and Hethya, and Lord Vair.

They entered the Night River Country, and the clones began to die. Nearly three weeks had passed since the attack by the Empty Lakes People. The Icefalcon wondered whether clones only lived for a few weeks or whether they were more than humanly susceptible to the cold. Ahead of them, the ice stood behind the badlands hills in a luminous wall.

The copses and meadows along the Night River had been the easternmost of the summer grazing lands of the bison and wild sheep herds of the Talking Stars People, the place of summer memories of rich pasture and short light-filled nights. It had been the place, too, of raids by other people attempting to poach on the herds that were the birthright of the Talking Stars People or to steal horses whose pedigrees equaled the bloodlines of great chiefs. Loses His Way pointed out the place where he nearly speared the Icefalcon during the Summer of the Two White Mammoths, and the Icefalcon said haughtily, "You missed me by ten inches, and your spear was too dull to have pierced my tunic," at which they both laughed. The lands were barren now and sheeted with meltwater from the glaciers, where it wasn't blotched with slunch. There was no hunting. All three were living on pemmican and dried lemming, and even Yellow-Eyed Dog looked thin.

A few days previously the Icefalcon had cut the tracks of the Talking Stars People, and though they'd covered their traces well he still recognized the hoofprints of Blue Child's horse Merrykiller in their midst. Logically, if they were trailing the caravan, they'd move up Dwarf Willow Creek, or what was left of it. Scrying and scouting the lands around them, Cold Death claimed she also had seen a band of the Earthsnake People, two hundred and two strong, led by their chieftain Pink Flowering Vine. The Icefalcon wondered whether they were aware of the presence of Blue Child and her warriors, or she of theirs.

In the nights the phosphor sheen of the slunch reflected in the thin meltwater lakes, and across those glowing sheets, by the light of cloud-dimmed summer stars, the Icefalcon half saw, half guessed the beating of demon wings. Few demons dwelt in the Vale, and those that did seldom impinged on human affairs, but since his experiences of shadow-walking he felt a greater awareness of their presence and a greater uneasiness of them. They piped and hooned and whistled on the water and called out in the semblance of those the Icefalcon had known here or echoed the voices of those who had once ridden through these lands.

Sitting on guard in the heavy jacket of mammoth wool that had been woven by a woman of the Empty Lakes People, he thought he heard Noon's voice: *I thought to make you truly my son.* Or was it, *You have betrayed us all, my son?* Another time he thought he heard Blue Child's cold slow tones, whispering the promise to give someone his horses and, later, the free joyous laugh of Dove in the Sun.

Beside him, Cold Death said softly, "Is it true that you left Dove in the Sun to die?"

He looked around quickly. His sister was one of the few he could not hear come up on him. She sat down at his side, tiny in her great coat of musk ox–hide, with her black eyes peeking out from beneath her skraggy black hair.

"She could not have lived, injured as she was," he explained patiently, as he had explained before, twelve years ago and many times since. The brilliance of the moonlight was such that he was able to knot thongs on a pair of snowshoes, a task he could have accomplished by touch in the dark; these he now set aside.

"White Bear of the Salt People speared her through, and she and her horse fell together off the high rocks in the Place of the Brown Dogs. I saw them lying on the highest of the three ledges there. The others in the band were pinned down by arrow fire, farther along the canyon. By the time I reached her she would have been dead. She was too young to have come on the raid. She had not the strength to keep up, nor to save herself when she was in trouble."

"Yet you allowed her to come."

The Icefalcon shrugged. "She thought herself ready."

Cold Death considered him with those bright prairie-dog eyes. "Did you love her?"

The Icefalcon looked away.

"Or did you allow her to come with your raiding party

only because you knew Blue Child did not permit her to ride with hers? Because you wanted—out of love for her and a desire to show up Blue Child—to give her what Blue Child would not?"

The Icefalcon was silent. The doors of his heart shut, like the adamantine doors of the Keep, locked with hidden mechanisms of steel and guarded with the ghostly runes of ancient spells. Endlessly distant, some slunch-born nameless thing floated over the sterile landscape that spawned it and there was a bodiless crying of demon voices on the air. For a time it seemed to him that he could see the diminutive Dove standing with her arms upraised in the dawn of the Summer Singing, blood running from the ritual cuts in her palms and sides, her hair the color of the new-lifted light and her clear voice carrying to the heavens.

He picked up his snowshoe again. "There was a time when I loved her. She had the heart of a young hawk, wanting to be a warrior, wanting to prove herself, to find her own name. She thought Blue Child was keeping her back on purpose, even while she loved her."

He knotted the leather and pulled it tight, fingers gauging the tension and the shape of the bowed wood. His fingers were blistered with cold already; he tucked his hand in his armpit. "I told her that this was not so. By then I knew that they were for one another, heart and soul, and I had given over that love."

"Did you think her ready to take on a warrior of the Salt People?"

The Icefalcon shook his head. "I made an error." He went back to lacing the leather and the wood, not meeting his sister's eyes. "I have regretted it since. But Dove in the Sun made her own choice to ride with us. Blue Child knew this."

Beside him, Cold Death sighed. The glacier wind that whisked her breath like a white banner from her mouth bore on it the stench of the carrion in the wagons of Vair na-Chandros, the stink of the few sheep remaining, the smell of mules, and the waste of men who are eating badly of dried meat and slops.

"Blue Child knew this and hated me." The Icefalcon glanced back toward the shallow depression in the ground where Loses His Way slept, sharing his huddle of earth-colored robes with Yellow-Eyed Dog, invisible in the darkness. "What Blue Child did was worse than murder. The day will come when I will have a reckoning with the chieftain of the Talking Stars People."

Cold Death left him and went to sleep on the other side of Yellow-Eyed Dog. The Icefalcon blew on his frozen fingers and continued to work, finding comfort in the undemanding task and listening all the while to the night.

At the end of that summer, when the Talking Stars People were once more in the ranges they'd disputed with the Salt People, he had returned to the Place of the Brown Dogs, though this was not the custom of his people, and had borne down the bones of Dove in the Sun, with some trouble, for they had been much scattered by coyote. He buried them farther back in the canyon, at the place where wild roses first appeared in spring. The Dove had loved wild roses, risking the bees that swarmed over the shallow streams to lie on the rocks and smell the blossoms.

The place, the Icefalcon realized, was not many miles north of where he now sat.

Around the fire pits of their hunting camps and the long-house hearths of winter, the Icefalcon's kindred had all his life told stories: about the habits of bison and the fat-rumped black sheep and the big antelope of the North, about tracking hares and how musk oxen breed, about weather conditions at different times of the year in Dwarf Willow Creek or in the Sea of Grass, about the Ancestors. Useful matters having nothing to do with old kings or wild roses.

The Stars had spoken to the Ancestors, giving them spells and cantrips to keep their souls from being drunk away by the Watchers Behind the Stars and their eyes from being deceived by the illusions of the Dream Things.

But above the glowing ice, the milky sheets of water that lay at the feet of those black barren hills, the Stars kept their counsel.

# CHAPTER ELEVEN

Vair na-Chandros and his men made camp beneath the diamond wall of the end of the world, the Ice in the North. From the sheltering curve of the shoulder of rock that had once been known as Daylily Hill, the Icefalcon watched them take down the wagon-boxes from their wheels and cut trunks of birch and elder to make sled runners.

"Are all of them mad?" Loses His Way propped his shoulder against a deadfall spruce. "They cannot hope to get those wagons up the wall of the ice."

"It is an elaborate madness," murmured the Icefalcon, folding his arms. The wind that streamed cold and steady from the ice stirred his long braids—he had left off shaving, finally, a few days ago, to let his beard protect his face. "And Vair na-Chandros would seem to have convinced a goodly number to join him in his fantasy."

Though Daylily Hill lay a fair distance from the camp, it was still possible to see what the tiny figures did: chopping trees, slaughtering the remains of the sheep herd, making additional sledges on which wood for fires was being lashed. One man was occupied in taking something from one of the wagon-boxes. "Boots for the mules," said the Icefalcon.

The Chieftain of the Empty Lakes People stared at him as if he'd said they would provide the mules with pink satin ball gowns. "They give their animals boots and let these wretched clones of theirs wrap their feet in hide like slaves?"

"To keep them from skidding on ice," said the Icefalcon. "It is a thing the mud-diggers do in the wintertime, when they wish to take a heavy load from one place to another."

"Why don't they take their heavy loads in the autumn before the fall of the snow?"

"Because they are fools," said the Icefalcon. "They are mud-diggers." But they had carved the bones of the hills to build their road and laid the foundations of bridges that still lay in the riverbeds as fords, even though that road led to the emptiness of the North. They had built the Keeps, proof against all the evil magic of the Dark.

"They are asking for trouble," he added after a time. "Even a child knows you draw and dress an animal if you plan to eat it."

"Perhaps they're in a hurry. They may have seen the horses of the Earthsnake People."

Someone in the Earthsnake People had a spell that kept the horse herd close by their hidden camp, away over behind the hogback called Honey Ridge, and not enough sense not to use it.

"They make camp for the night," pointed out the Icefalcon. "And see, they're only heaping the sheep carcasses up, near the black tent there." The fact that men had erected the black tent against the side of the largest wagon made his nape lift with horror, and he was mindful that the last of the clones had died the previous day.

Several of the laborers apparently agreed with the Icefalcon's estimation of the proper method of transporting dead sheep. There was conference, heads shaken, argument: "What do they do?"

"The finger game," said the Icefalcon. Behind them among the fallen and dying spruces he heard Cold Death laugh. She was communing with Ingold Inglorion through the medium of a pool of frozen meltwater; over the weeks of journeying she had spoken to the old man nearly every night, and they had become fast friends. "They play it as we would cast a knucklebone, to choose a man for some unpleasant task. Ah," he said, watching one unwilling

man head in the direction of Vair na-Chandros, deep
in conference with Bektis and the trap-mouthed Truth-
Finder. "The matter explains itself. Myself, I should not
only cast a knucklebone but cheat, were it a matter of
speaking to that one."

The chosen unfortunate plainly thought so, too. He
bowed and abased himself profoundly, gestured toward
the dirty-gray piles of dead beasts.

"Are they dogs, that they let themselves be whipped?"
asked Loses His Way, when Vair had made his reply
and the messenger, holding his bleeding face, returned
to inform his colleagues that yes, his lordship really did
want the entire sheep—wool, guts, and all—heaped beside the tent.

"Generally," said the Icefalcon.

The scouts they had sent came back from the glacier.
Vair na-Chandros listened to what they said, then turned
and studied the ice itself. It towered above the camp,
above the hills, an unimaginable opaline fortress whose
translucence shed a queer blanched reflection on the faces
of the men below. Cold-killed spruce, birch, hickory, and
mountain laurel lay in a crushed gray rummage along its
base, mixed with and buried under vast avalanche spills
and chunks of rotting ice.

*A monster,* thought the Icefalcon. A monster that would
in time eat the world.

"He is mad," Loses His Way repeated after a little, "if he
thinks he will get all his possessions to the top."

The Icefalcon shook his head. "Whatever else may be
said of this Vair na-Chandros," he murmured, "he is not
mad."

The boy Tir was escorted from among the wagons. "It is
well the woman is there to look after him," said Loses His
Way. "She is good, that one."

"She is the one who deceived him into leaving the protection of the Keep," retorted the Icefalcon, with whom
the subject of Hethya still rankled.

Loses His Way shook his head. "I have watched her

now many weeks," he said. "People can be pressed into any hunting, good or ill, o my enemy. She cares for the child, and cares more for him each day. She has the way of one who has had a child herself. Has the boy been here, then?" For Tir made signs, pointing along the right side of the talus.

The Icefalcon hesitated, not sure what to say. "It is a knowledge in his family."

"But how can he know what does not exist?"

*How indeed?*

He himself had gone to scout another way up the glacier, on the far side of Daylily Hill, a deep crevice and chimney that could be scaled with the help of axes. The road led to the North, but the end of the road was now covered in the trackless ice. Vair asked another question, and Tir assented, seeming very small and helpless among the men.

*If you strike him again,* thought the Icefalcon, *though he is no kin of mine and has no claim on me, still I will have an accounting from you.*

But Vair did not strike the child. Instead he gestured to Hethya, who even at this distance the Icefalcon could tell was possessed by the spirit—or imitating the mannerisms— of Oale Niu.

"What new hunt is this?" murmured Loses His Way.

Cold Death came over to them, having finished filling Ingold in on everything that had so far passed that day. The old man had finally reached Renweth Vale, she had informed them yesterday, having come down from the north over the St. Prathhes' Glacier, a nearly impassable trek; he had been most interested in Vair's journey.

"Did you see this when you shadow-walked into the camp?" she breathed, and the Icefalcon shook his head.

"It was packed in its boxes in a wagon." His voice was the murmur of ice winds through the naked roots of fallen trees. "I thought the boxes had about them an evil light, like the thing in the tent. Do you know what it is?"

She shook her head.

Under Hethya's instructions, the crates were opened, the pieces lifted out and put together by Bektis and the Truth-Finder, helped by the scout the Icefalcon called Crested Egret, a clever young man who managed to stay at Vair's side without ever incurring his wrath. Tubes of gold of varying thicknesses looped over balls of glass, crystal rods bound in iron and covered over with brittle-looking encrustations of salt.

"Is she indeed possessed of the spirit of an Ancestor of the shamans?" asked Loses His Way, as Hethya moved forward to help connect the many components into one single, sleekly lumpy finger, glittering like an extension of the ice wall itself.

"Either that or some instruction survived, writ on paper or embedded in the heart of a Wise One's crystal, that she studied to lend credence to her lies." The Icefalcon, crouching beside him, rested his crossed hands on his drawn-up knees. "Anyone can make up stories—it is an art among the mud-diggers, and many are adept at it."

"Pah," said Loses His Way. "She has not the look of a woman who tells lies."

*Oh, hasn't she?* he thought. But he only said, "It has something of the look of the things we found in the Keep many years ago. Rudy and Ingold made of them weapons that spat fire at the bidding of the Wise Ones, but they did not work overwell. They needed no Ancestor of shamans to show them how such things were made."

Slowly, with dignity, Hethya walked around the apparatus, touching the tubes and the rods, the balls that fit sometimes into the rods and sometimes into one another. Bektis nodded wisely at her side. Gil, thought the Icefalcon, would be open-mouthed with awe, but to him it was merely what it was, glass and iron, gold and salt, elements of the earth that had existed in their current form only somewhat longer than other formations of the same substances. Hethya emphasized a point with a sweeping gesture that would have shamed a marketplace preacher in the days before the coming of the Dark, and her voice carried dimly across space to the three watchers—possibly to other watchers as well.

Still, it was a wonder when it was finished. It lay glistening in a cradle of geared wheels such as Ingold tinkered with in the crypts of the Keep, haloed, it seemed, by some curious condensation of the thin wicked afternoon light. Tir hung back, as if he would conceal himself between the wagons—he came forward when Vair beckoned, but unwillingly and, when asked a question, would only shake his head.

Hethya and Bektis stood beside the new apparatus. It was Hethya who worked its ivory levers, making the whole of it swing about suddenly, like a live thing, articulate, quivering, balanced to a hair. Bobs and wires whipped like the antennae of an insect, and lights sang from the jewels that hung on their tips.

A strange shiver passed through the Icefalcon, the uneasy sense that Gil-Shalos was right. This was more than elements combined.

There was a silence like the silence before an ice storm, a hushed waiting fear of the unimaginable.

Bektis laid his hands where Hethya showed him—tiny figures, gray and gold, white and red against the flinty gray rocks, the rinsed-out aqua ice.

Then a flash, less like lightning than as if a star had spoken a curse of power, a curse that extended like a tickling feather a delicate, whickering, colorless whisper of unseen flame. The sound that cracked across the valley was, the Icefalcon was sure, only the sound of the rock splintering where the shimmer touched it. A great chunk separated from the wall of the promontory before them, pitching down the scree. Then like the sea-yammer came the wild whinnying of the mules and horses and all the men crying out.

Even old Nargois, whom the Icefalcon had observed to be a man of calm courage, fell back, hands fluttering in the signs against demons.

Only Vair remained where he was, observing with

interest as Hethya moved the levers again. Bektis, who had flinched, stepped forward to lay his hands upon the apparatus again. Another shimmer, as if the air between the crystal horns of the machine and the raw rock wall had flawed, like the break in a pane of glass. The Icefalcon saw a slab of rock jerk outward, break, and tumble free down the slope before he heard the sound of it, a deep, booming crack and the hiss of heat.

"This is bad hunting," whispered Loses His Way, when any of them could speak again.

*Bad hunting indeed,* thought the Icefalcon. Three weeks' journey away that they were, he could not but feel that things would be worse still for the folk of the embattled Keep.

"What did she say?" Gil and Minalde both got to their feet as Ilae emerged from the hidden chamber in the crypt. The young mage stood in the doorway for a moment, a tall gawky girl, and gestured with one long-fingered hand that she was all right.

Encountering Brycothis, the mage spirit who dwelled in the heart of the Keep, was, Rudy had told Gil, frequently a disorienting experience.

Both Rudy and Ingold had tried to describe what it was like; Gil had the impression it was something only fully understood by another mage. Brycothis herself—Gil had seen her image in half a dozen of the ancient record crystals, a rangy woman with smiling eyes and the tattooed scalp of a wizard of those days—had long ago transmuted into something far other than human, a pattern of memories and power whose center lay in the heart of the crypts. Those who entered that center, whose minds touched hers, experienced different things at different times.

"Did she speak to you?" Not that Brycothis actually spoke. Minalde led the girl to the bottom step of the hidden stairway, where she and Gil had waited, and made her sit down.

"Oh, yes." Ilae nodded hesitantly. "I mean, I saw things.

She was there." She nodded quick thanks as Gil handed her the flask of tisane—now lukewarm—she and Alde had been sharing. "But I didn't understand what I saw."

Gil and Alde were silent. Shy and slow-spoken at the best of times, Ilae thought for a while, then said, "I asked her, was there another way into the Keep. And I saw . . ." She spread out her hands helplessly. "I saw the laundry room up on the third level, back behind the sanctuary of the Church."

"The laundry room?" Gil almost laughed.

Minalde asked worriedly, "Are you sure?" Not because she thought Ilae would have been mistaken about anything she saw—wizards as a rule didn't make that kind of error—but simply because it made no sense.

"Sure as I'm sitting, m'Lady."

"But it's in the middle of the Keep," said Alde, baffled. "You couldn't have a secret passage going into it without it passing through my bedroom, or the sanctuary, or Lord Ankres' storerooms . . ."

"Christ, are we going to have to take measurements?" Gil asked, appalled. "That whole area behind the Aisle has been so changed and remodeled, with walls and cells partitioned and knocked together and new corridors put through, we'll never get an accurate reading. There's a dozen secret passages there already, going from one set of rooms to another. I don't even want to think about it."

"And in any case the entry has to be at or near ground level," Minalde protested. "Which means a stairway—maybe in the outer wall? At least we know it's in the rear quarter of the Keep."

"But who would have known of it?" Ilae asked. "And who'd Vair get to turn traitor? And how? It ain't like there's a stranger come, or anybody gone recently."

"If it exists at all," said Gil softly. "I'll tell Janus and we can make a search, and it better be a damn quiet one because the fewer people who know about this one the better. But if there's another doorway, I'm betting it's one only a wizard can see. That means you, Ilae, and Wend outside. You up for it?"

"I have to be," Ilae said simply. "Don't I?"

She corked the flask and got to her feet, preceding them up the snail-shell curl of the stair, the witchlight with which she had illuminated the chamber drifting ahead. Gil and Alde followed more slowly, Alde thriftily blowing out their single candle. The witchlight salted the embroidery of her overgown with sharp white sparks and glinted in the pins that held back her long hair.

When Ilae got farther ahead of them, Alde asked Gil, "Do you think there's a doorway somewhere behind the Aisle? Hidden by spells?"

"I think we'd better look for one," said Gil. "But no. I think it's something different. Something else."

He was the only person who could warn them.

Tir pulled the furs of his little bed nest closer around him and listened to the howling of the wind. It blew strong enough down from the glacier to rock the wagon on its new-made runners, and now and then it shrieked, like the ghost of a tormented man.

He had worked out, pretty much, what he had to do, and he would sooner have walked up and spit in Vair's face than go through with it.

The night was bitterly cold. Maybe too cold to get out of his furs. He might freeze to death. It sounded like a comforting alternative.

He was the only person who knew about the *chen yekas*—that was the term for the machine he'd seen that afternoon, the terrible thing that spit, instead of fire, that cruel strange streak of purplish nonlight. The word was clear in his mind, clear as his sister's name. He was the only person who knew the secret of Vair's *tethyn* warriors, though Vair and Hethya used another word for them that was what Hethya said Oale Niu called them. But *tethyn* was what they had called them back in the deeps of time that his ancestor remembered.

He was the only person who knew the most terrible secret of how it might be possible for him to warn the Keep.

And there was no way out of doing what he knew he was going to have to do.

Before she'd gone out Hethya had untied his wrists. Even though she bandaged them carefully they were always raw and bleeding. Lord Vair checked the spancels on them every day. The thought that Hethya would get in trouble for giving him that fragment of comfort, that scrap of dignity, tormented him. If Lord Vair ever found out about the knife in his boot it would mean a beating— worse than a beating—not only for Tir but for Hethya, too.

But Rudy was dead. His mother was dead, too, Bektis had told him, dead of grief because he, Tir, had been such a fool as to go with Bektis out of the Keep.

It was all his fault. If it was just him, he would deserve everything, including death.

But Wend and Ilae would still be at the Keep. And Ingold was out there, too, somewhere, and those two young wizards would have contacted the old man, first thing, in their magic crystals. At the Keep they still had a chance.

Tir took a deep breath.

Like everyone else in the camp he slept in most of his clothes. Cautiously, moving the way the Guards had taught him, he found his heavy jacket by touch. He'd put it in the same place every night: the Icefalcon had told him about that. No light penetrated the blankets hung over the back and front of the wagon-covers against the cold. He edged among the bags and packets of food, the bundled, dirty-smelling clothes that they'd stripped off the poor *tethyn* when they died. He eased the jacket to him and slithered into it, checked that his mittens were in the pockets, and pulled on both his fleece cap and the jacket's hood. Rudy had told him many times that the world was getting colder and that the lands near the Ice in the North were colder even than Renweth Vale in winter; Tir could not remember being so cold in his life.

In another life, he thought . . . One of those other little

boys had been this cold. Maybe several. He didn't recall
clearly, and sometimes he knew that he didn't want to. He
put on his mittens. He was trembling, and the dull ache in
the pit of his stomach that never seemed to go away was a
churning agony now, but he knew he didn't have much
time. Hethya would be back, at least.

He wadded up his pillow and a blanket to make it look
as if he were still buried under the covers. Then he slipped
to the back of the wagon and listened.

The guard was there. After several minutes he heard
him cough. Somewhere a mule brayed, mournful despite
its blankets in the icy cold. The scrunch of footfalls, and a
man's voice said, "Ugal," in greeting, the guard's name,
the big handsome young man who'd given him the dates.

"Pijek." Pijek was one of the sergeants.

Sometimes after Lord Vair had mistreated Tir, Ugal sent
him bits of dried fruits or sweets but had never actively
taken his part—in fact he sometimes explained why what
Lord Vair was doing was for Tir's own good. Tir didn't
blame him, but he couldn't eat the sweets. Most of the
time he felt so sick with terror that he couldn't eat at all.

Ugal asked, "Has he finished?"

"Still making the rounds." At least that's what Tir
thought Pijek said; the man had an accent of some kind,
and Tir's grasp of the ha'al, though enormously improved,
was far from perfect. "He's asked Yantres and Nicor and
Tuuves, Hastroaal and Ti Men . . ." Tir knew most of the
men of whom they spoke. "Near a score."

"There going to be another fight?"

"Seems like. Nicor said they caught sign of savages.
If"—there was a phrase Tir didn't know—"we're going to
need all the men we can get."

*Savages. White Raiders.*

Tir groped his way back along the long side of the
wagon, carefully shifting the sacks of parched corn and
beans aside. His small body wriggled easily between
them, until his hands encountered the wooden side itself.
It took only seconds to work loose the inner coverings and

worm up under them, over the side of the wagon, under the outer covering, and to let himself drop.

The drop wasn't nearly as far as it had been when the wagon-box was up on wheels. The runners provided better cover, too. After the wagon's dark, the reflected torchlight from the camp seemed bright, the cold cosmic. Tir crouched in the shadows, heart pounding so hard he could barely breathe, orienting himself.

He was on the outside of the circle of wagons. He knew he would be—they always brought them around in a ring the same way. Slunch glowed on the dark slopes of the flooded valley through which they'd worked their way for the past three days. Above them the glacier towered, not a single wall like St. Prathhes' Glacier in Renweth Vale, but a rampart of ice, a universe of cold, slowly devouring the world. He could see where it lay between the Big Guardian and the Little (and some other boy whispered in his mind the names they had borne all those years ago), the land at its feet drowned in milky, shallow pools.

The Ice in the North.

Men stood guard around the perimeter of the camp. Lord Vair's men, his chosen legions, loyal to him, loving him despite what he did to them. Their black helmets were decorated with his bronze peacock crest, through which their hair—white or black, like horsetails—rose in fluttering pennons. The last of the *tethyn* had died yesterday afternoon, though they'd been stumbling for days. Tir thought about the White Raiders, and the fewness of the men left.

Dimly, Tir was aware that a magician, with the right equipment, could make *tethyn* out of men. Someone in another life, someone in the dark of his memory, had seen it done. As he watched Lord Nargois walk from guard to guard, touching this man on the shoulder, speaking gently to that man, he knew that was what the old man was planning to do now.

He'd seen it done. He knew he'd seen it done. Somewhere . . . someone . . .

And he knew he didn't ever want to see it again.

But he had to, so he could tell Ingold what was going on.

That was what Janus, and Gil, and the Guards all said, when they talked about war and scouting in the watchroom after training was done. "If you're alone and can't do anything else," Gil had said once, gesturing with those thin strong hands—broken fingers taped together, wrists strapped up in leather—"don't be a hero. Don't get yourself killed. Just observe everything you can in as much detail as you can, so you can report back."

She'd been talking to a couple of the new kids, the young men and women just being trained in the hard school of warfare; she hadn't even been aware of Tir sitting quietly in the corner by the hearth. "Something that may not look important to you may be a critical piece of information to someone who knows something else."

Ingold would know how to save the Keep.

Tir crawled forward among the shadows, circling until he reached the largest wagon, the one that was connected to the black tent. He'd seen Lord Vair already, coming out of the tent, pausing to talk to Nargois and to Shakas Kar, the southern Truth-Finder with his shaven head and his nasty little hard smile and his crimson belts. Men were dragging a sledge across the camp from the supply lines, the smell of carrion suffocating: it contained the bodies of all the *tethyn* who had died, some of them many days ago.

"Take it in." Lord Vair gestured with the whip that never left him. He never used his right hand, his hook hand, keeping it instead in the folds of sleeve and cloak, as though that whole arm had been consecrated to evil and shame. Ugal and others had told Tir that their lord had lost his hand in cavalry training in his youth, which had for years disbarred him from military command, until the coming of the Dark. "He would have had honor and glory years ago but for that," Ugal had said, apologizing for the commander he loved. "You can see why he is angry."

The tent stirred already with activity, and Tir smelled

from it the dusty stink of the dead sheep and the thick loamy pong of dirt, choking in the fire-touched dark.

"My Lord, I must protest." Bektis appeared from between the wagons, bundled in a velvet coat lined with mammoth wool that came down to his heels. He had a muff of white fur on one hand, the hand where he wore the jeweled Device all the time now, and a dozen sables wrapped around his neck.

"We know how to operate the *dethken iares . . .*" *Only that wasn't the real name of the thing in the tent,* thought Tir. *It was called a* chknaïes. *Who had known that?* ". . . with a single . . . ah"—he glanced at the young guardsman standing nearby—"source." He took Lord Vair's arm, led him a little apart, closer to the wagon beneath which Tir crouched. More softly, he went on, "My Lord, I cannot vouch for what might happen."

"It is your business to know what will happen," snapped Vair. "I thought you claimed expertise in this matter, sorcerer. I thought you said you knew everything of such machines and of the mages who created them." The razor-edged voice sank soft, turning Tir's belly cold and sick. "Is this not then the case?"

"Of course it is the case," Bektis replied quickly. "It's just that it was not considered safe . . ."

"Flesh is flesh," replied Vair. "Did you not say that the dead flesh is multiplied within the vat? That it can only duplicate itself so far with the substance of the victim, but that the machine knows the image of that which is to be created? Is this not then how it works?"

"Of a certainty it is," replied the mage, but his long fingers emerged from the muff to tangle and twist the snowy lovelocks of his beard.

"We need men." Vair's voice was hard now, though no louder than the whisper of the ice wind razoring from the crumbling ramparts above. "The savages gather around us, and it is still some days to our destination. Once we get on the ice we can be taken at a disadvantage. And we must needs still have enough men at our disposal to consummate the taking of Dare's Keep. Now, can it be done as I wish or not?"

"My most illustrious Generalissimo . . ."

"Every machine can be tinkered with, sorcerer, by those who truly understand them. You say this Harilómne did it, this heretic whose studies of the ancients taught you in your turn. Don't treat me like a commoner. Every expert can adjust and change." His voice was like the grip of the hooks in Tir's collar, in Tir's flesh. "This is why one brings experts, instead of leaving them to perish at the hands of those hypocrites who wish to foist blame for their own crimes upon the heads of their tools. Not so, sorcerer?"

Bektis bowed his head. "It is so indeed, Lord."

"Then I trust you will make the necessary adjustments?"

"I will do so, Lord."

"Good," Vair said softly. "Good."

He walked away toward the tent where he slept; Bektis to the camp's central fire, where Hethya stood, warming her gloved hands. Hethya, Bektis, Vair, Shakas Kar, Nargois . . . Tir counted them off on his fingers, then wriggled along the hard-frozen ground to the back of the largest wagon-sledge.

Even the three sides of the wagon-box had been given a petticoat of canvas and goat-hair cloth so that the space beneath, if not precisely warm, was at least protected from the winds. The legs of a table were visible in the long flat rectangle of reddish light burning within, surrounded by a horrible jumble of carrion shapes. On one sledge lay the pitiful sheep, with cut throats and blood drying on their wool; on another, a lumpy mass, covered with a goat-hair blanket, that stank and dripped. A third sledge, behind the others, was heaped with random things, brush and cut wood and even piles of dirt.

Tir crawled to the edge of the wagon-box where the curtains began. There were at least four layers of them, to cut both cold and any possibility of light seeping out. He crawled between them, like a mouse in a bed curtain, until he was behind the sledges with their gruesome burdens, where the smell was awful but the light of lamps and candles did not penetrate. Then he chinked the curtains a little and peeked through.

The iron tub up in the wagon-box, arches looming over it like the ribs of an unknown beast. Two big lumps of gold-woven crystal set at angles to its unarched end and the jointed canopy of glittering mesh suspended above. Steps went up from the tent to the wagon-box, but even after the men who'd hauled in the dirt and corpses departed, Tir dared not emerge to have a closer look. In the main part of the tent there was a folding table, with what looked like a box on it.

He tallied it all in his mind.

And pounding him, tearing him, whispering in the blackness of the back of his brain was the knowledge that he'd seen all this before. That he knew what was in the box on the table.

The curtains covering the entrance heaved and blew. Tir let the hanging fall shut to almost nothing. He had to know. There had to be somebody who knew, who could tell Ingold.

It was Bektis and Nargois. With them was Ugal, big and handsome and friendly, taking off his spiked helmet and looking around him with awed gray eyes. Tir's heart stood still with horror and grief.

*No. Not him.*

But there was nothing that he could say or do.

At Bektis' direction (Bektis never did any work) Ugal and Nargois carried two dead sheep and a great quantity of wood and dirt up the steps, the planks creaking under their weight. They went down for another load, and Tir looked away when they pulled back the cover over the other sledge. The stench, the horrible bloated black bodies with the flesh falling away . . .

He knew he should be brave and look but he couldn't. He kept his face buried in his arms while their feet creaked up the plank steps. He tried not to hear the noise the things made when dropped into the vat. If he threw up they'd find him. That awareness was the only thing that kept him from doing so.

Then he heard Vair's voice.

"Ugal, is it?" There was gentleness in his tone, and affection, like a strong father addressing a son.

"Yes, my Lord." Ugal was delighted with the recognition, delighted that his generalissimo knew his name. He was always telling Tir, *My Lord praised me* or *My Lord spoke to me—I think he knows my name.*

"Do you understand the help I need from you? The magnitude of the task I'm asking you to do?"

"I—I think I do, my Lord. None of us really . . ."

"None of you really knows. No. That is as it should be, but it makes your help—your willingness to help—a gift of trust doubly to be treasured. Please understand how much I value that."

Tir raised his head and looked. The shadows behind the dead sheep were dense as night, and he could open quite a slit between the hangings. He saw Lord Vair touch the young man Ugal's face with his left hand, like a caress.

"Thank you, Lord."

"You understand this will hurt a little."

Behind Lord Vair, Shakas Kar entered the tent, silently.

Vair went on, "It isn't much, but sometimes men have cried out—you remember."

"I won't cry out."

"Sometimes men do," said Vair. "There is a drug, you understand, that weakens the subject; would you be willing to wear a gag? That way there can be no fears, no apprehensions on the part of your friends."

"I am willing to do whatever you wish, Lord, but I promise you, I will not weaken."

"Good man." Vair stepped forward and embraced the young soldier. "Good man."

*No!* Tir screamed, despairing, silent. *Run away, Ugal! Run away!*

Tir watched as the young man stripped, and Shakas Kar

stepped forward with a gag of metal and leather. Bektis offered the young man a cup first, which he drank as if it were sacramental wine. They gagged him then, and Hethya came in, with the haughty mien of Oale Niu, her eyes like stone. She and Shakas Kar brought from the table the black stone box, which contained—as Tir knew it would—a set of needles, some crystal, some silver, some iron, eight or ten inches long and tipped in jewels or beads of glass. These they drove into the young man's flesh, at certain points—*thohar* points, whispered one of those distant memories, bringing with it a shudder of blackness, a desperate desire not to see anything further—while Ugal stood tall and beautiful, naked, head thrown back, wincing a little at the stabs but silent and proud. He had a knotted war-scar on one thigh and another on his left arm, and with his long white hair hanging about his shoulders he seemed like a splendid animal, like a father or an elder brother Tir had always craved.

When the needles were all in his flesh Hethya and Bektis helped him climb up the wooden steps and lie down in the great iron vat with the carrion and the wood and dirt—as a warrior Ugal would have encountered worse. They adjusted something inside. Maybe, thought Tir, so that the needles sticking out of his back wouldn't be pushed crooked when he lay down.

He knew what was going to happen. In the dark of his mind he knew. Some one of his ancestors, under circumstances Tir could not imagine, had seen this done.

Bektis walked over to the head of the tub and stood beneath the hanging swags of iron and crystal net. He closed his eyes. Tir saw Hethya look away.

He was glad it all happened in the tub, where he didn't have to look. He was glad Ugal was gagged, and drugged, too, though the young man did make noises through it, stifled screams and worse sounds, body sounds: squirtings and gushings; horrible, sodden, elastic pops, like leather exploding under pressure, and blood spraying up. Once Ugal's head bounced up over the rim of the tub and Tir had to clap his hands over his mouth, press his eyes shut, swallow back the bile that came dribbling then out his nose.

*I have to do this, I have to do this, I have to do this,* and he clung desperately to consciousness, unable to breathe, his mind screaming. *I have to do this.*

Ingold had to know.

But he couldn't look, while footfalls creaked—Bektis' or Hethya's—and there was a soft noise of squishing, and the plop of something dripping where it had been spattered up onto the canopy. All he could remember was the taste of dates, carried and treasured with a young man's cravings for sweets, all the way up from the devastated South.

Then there was another sound, a muted, deadly whickering, like fire but thinner; an aura of power that raised the hair on Tir's head. He bit down on his own sleeve, sinking his teeth into the dirty-tasting leather to keep from fainting, screaming, crying. In front of him he saw Hethya hand Shakas Kar something—the iron gag. Shakas Kar wiped it down with a rag. From the vat Tir heard the sounds of movement, thrashing, and saw the wagon-bed rock.

*Don't scream,* he told himself. *Whatever you do, don't scream.*

A man's voice cried out random strings of sounds. An identical voice answered, *"Atuthes! Atuthes!"* Tir recognized the ha'al word for *father.* Something bleated, like a sheep with human vocal chords.

Vair climbed the plank steps, swinging his whip a little in his gloved left hand. "Perfect," he whispered, looking down into the vat. "Perfect."

Tir watched—Tir made himself watch—while the *tethyn* all came down from the vat. This part wasn't bad, except that they all had Ugal's face, they all had Ugal's body, though without the scars. Like the Akulae they were hairless, and their skin looked funny, though in the lamplight it was hard to tell what was just tricks of shadow and moisture: patchy, smooth in places and rough in others.

There were eleven of them.

Nargois brought clothing out of the bales along the walls and gave it to them, but they only stood there staring at it stupidly, and he had to show them how to dress. This troubled the second in command. He passed a hand before the face of one Ugal and addressed him. The man answered with a faint, bleating grunt.

"It doesn't matter," said Vair shortly. "They'll fight. That's all that matters. Ugal!" he said, in a voice of command, and they all turned their heads at once, in a single movement.

"It is good," he said to Bektis. "It is good."

The men filed out when they were dressed, lumbering and shuffling in heavy coats, in wrapped rawhide leggings, Nargois nudging them along like a skinny black pale-eyed sheepdog.

*Eleven,* thought Tir. There had never been more than four of any group of *tethyn.* He remembered—out of where he didn't know—that four was all you could get, sometimes only three. Eleven was bad.

When Nargois brought in another young man—when Vair said in that warm, friendly, fatherly voice, "Hastroaal isn't it?" and Hastroaal replied eagerly, "Yes, my Lord"— Tir worked his way, with infinite slowness, back through the curtains, out into the darkness under the wagon, and so through the petticoat around the wagon's bed and out to the outer blackness.

"You understand the help I need from you? The greatness of the task I'm asking you to do?"

"You know I'd follow you to the ends of time, my Lord . . ."

"Good man. Good man . . ."

Tir relieved himself away from the wagons—his bowels were liquid with disgust and fright—and then climbed back into his own wagon, snaking through the provisions to return to his nest of furs. His hands trembled so badly he could barely take off his mittens and coat, and he felt cold through to the marrow. The cold stayed with him, even

under his blankets, growing deeper and deeper so that Tir
wondered if he were dying. He tried to stay awake because
he knew that when he went to sleep he'd remember fully,
remember when he or that other boy had actually seen the
whole thing, actually seen what happened in the iron vat
(which was called a *draik*, he remembered, and wanted to
scream at them, *Stop telling me these things!*).

He woke up screaming, being shaken by a guard, an
older man named Mongret, to whom he clung, sobbing,
feeling as if his body would tear itself apart.

"Is all right, *Keshnithar*," the man soothed him, calling
him by the name some of the guards used when Vair
wasn't there to hear: Keshnithar, Little King, though
sometimes in good-natured jest they called him *Drazha*,
Scarface. "Is all right. Oniox," he called out to another
man who had come by, "get the lady, would you? Our
boy's had a nightmare."

The other guard glanced back at the black tent and
grunted. "Small blame to him. The very air's evil tonight.
She's over there."

"Oh." There was silence, the men looking at each other
through the thrown-back curtain at the back of the wagon.
"Ah. Well." Mongret hugged Tir again, reassuring, but Tir
knew that nobody was going to get Hethya. He wasn't
even sure if he wanted to see her, for her clothing would
smell of carrion and power and lightning, and he didn't
know if he could stand that. "Is just dreams, Little King,"
he added, in broken Wathe. "You all right?"

Tir sniffled, fighting hard not to seem a coward, and
said, "I'll be all right," in the *ha'al*, which made both men
smile.

"That's my little soldier." The men liked him, though
none of them would stand up to Vair for him. He didn't
blame them for this. Neither commented on the fact that
his hands weren't tied. "You want me stay a little, till you
sleep?"

Tir nodded. The man didn't speak the Wathe well
enough to learn anything if he talked in his sleep. Mongret

dried his tears with a rough, mittened hand, and Tir lay down, though he didn't sleep. There was an odd comfort in knowing that whichever of his ancestors it was who had, willing or unwilling, witnessed what he had witnessed—who had seen the skin peel back, the organs burst, the head swell and pop like an overripe grape—had been as sickened, as appalled, as terrified as he; had wished, like him, that he had never seen it. It was as awful for a grown man as it was for a little boy.

It was almost daylight when Heytha returned to the wagon, took off her heavy outer garments, and curled up in her blankets. She smelled of the cheap southern rum from the keg in the back of the food wagon, which they sometimes distributed when the nights were very cold. Tir listened to her breathing. He didn't think she slept. Later on in the morning, when they were breaking camp, Tir saw that the camp was crowded with *tethyn*, over a hundred of them, and all with those strangely patched-looking skins, all with the same few faces: Tuuves, Hastroaal, Ti Men . . . Their eyes were blank, not like the eyes of the Akulae or of the *tethyn* who'd formed the train from Bison Knoll. Those had been slow and stupid but human. Though some of these could speak, others only grunted or made soft noises in their throats. When Tir encountered Ugal, wearing makeshift clothing and rawhide wrapped around his feet instead of boots, he had to run away behind one of the wagons and vomit.

He was still kneeling there, soaked with sweat and shaking, when Hethya found him and told him that she had to take him to Vair. It was time the train moved on, out onto the Ice itself.

# CHAPTER TWELVE

With dawn they brought the Dark Lightning up to the ice face and began to carve.

"Behold their road." The Icefalcon wrapped his arms around himself, shivering. He had already seen how clouds hung over the ice cap, columns of gray and black and dazzling white where the sun struck them. Up on the Ice it would be world-winter indeed.

"It is bad hunting." Loses His Way passed him one of the double-sewn coats of bison-hide and a short-handled war ax. "Never have I seen so bad a hunt. See how the lady holds close to the boy? She fears for him." From a distance he'd become very taken with Hethya.

"She fears for herself. He is in her charge."

Loses His Way shook his head, and for a time they watched Hethya and Bektis, together at the controls of the Dark Lightning. The unholy colorless glim in the air wickered forth, played across the pearl face of the Ice. The notch at its edge deepened, steam gushing to join the cloud cover, and milky water flowed in a sputtering, steaming stream.

"She is wise," he said approvingly, watching her issue instructions to Bektis, who turned the Dark Lightning in its geared cradle, the apparatus moving like a hunting cat seeking prey. They had been busy in the night, for, around them, many new clones affixed leather boots to the feet of the mules and dragged the sledges up the rocks. Vair in his quilted garments of white fur and silk spoke to Hethya, and she returned some haughty reply. "She knows not to show her fear. Does your man in the ice pool know aught of this Dark Lightning, little shaman?"

A few minutes previously Cold Death had blown on and rubbed one of the hard-frozen puddles near their camp, scratching the surface with a pebble and speaking Ingold's name. The Icefalcon had been aware of the sweet high bird chitter of her voice all during the bringing up of the Dark Lightning, as she narrated what she saw to the Archmage of the Wizards of the West.

He saw the old man in his mind, shaggy and scrubby and filthy as Ingold generally was after his journeyings, tucked like an apologetic old dog into some cranny of the rocks close enough to the besiegers to go and help himself to supper at their campfires. If he knew Ingold, the old man was doing it, too, on a nightly basis. The thought brought a pang of envy. The Icefalcon was heartily weary of pemmican.

"Ingold says he has never heard of such a matter." She came to the two men to watch, gloved hands shoved in her pockets like an impish girl. "But he did not seem surprised that the magic of the Ancestors of wizards could be turned to such a use."

"Did he say what he thought," inquired the Icefalcon, "of this woman who claims to be possessed by the Ancestors of wizards? Whether what she says is possible?"

"All things are possible," replied Cold Death cheerfully. "From the remaking of the world to the rescue of this child. Come. If we're to be on the Ice before them, it is well that we start to climb now. We have no Dark Lightning, no magic from the Ancestors of wizards, to help us."

The horses Cold Death turned loose to forage to the south, laying a Word on them to return at her summoning.

Vair appointed ten men, none of them clones, and these took what remained of his horse herd and drove them away south. "A present for Blue Child," said Cold Death, and grinned. "How kind!"

*But not the act,* thought the Icefalcon, watching the beasts grow smaller in the desolate valley's distance, *of a man who had any intention of returning along the road he had come.*

Curious.

The wall of ice that rose beyond Daylily Hill was broken into a succession of chimneys, towers, crevasses and blocks, mushrooms and cauliflowers of ice and fanged overhangs that forbade ascent. Snowshoes weren't the only things the Icefalcon and his companions had worked on in the starlit dark and reflected ember glow. The thinner garments they'd taken from the cache, the empty food bags, and anything they could not use they had sliced up, weaving ropes of the rawhide strips.

Still it was a difficult ascent. The Icefalcon led, hacking his way with an ax and cutting steps for the others, looping the rope that Loses His Way could follow. The food, and the rough sled they had made to drag it, they raised after them in slings, and last of all Yellow-Eyed Dog, puzzled but content to follow Loses His Way.

The world at the top was alien beyond belief, long snowfields alternating with broken hogbacks and chopped zones of ice hills, rough seracs and towers all colorless, cold, and dead in the clouded light. Iron-hued rock ridges carved the distant horizons—the Icefalcon recognized with shock the crests of the Little Snowy Mountains—and dunes of snow rose to the west, hiding the notch carved by the Dark Lightning. Above those dunes, however, billowed columns of steam, marble-white in the grizzle of the sky.

"They'll know they're being followed, do they but look over the crest of those dunes." The Icefalcon contemplated the windblown powder snow, the mush of tracks they had left, and Yellow-Eyed Dog bounding idiotically about snapping at flying flakes. The cold tore at his face despite the thick coating of bison fat and seemed to eat through his gloves. His breath froze hard in his beard, and the air burned not only his lungs but his eyes and his teeth.

"They know it already." Cold Death shrugged. "What are three more barbarian scouts and a dog? Nothing in our tracks says, *Here is a man who has trailed you from Ren-weth Keep.* At least not in a tongue they can read."

The Icefalcon wasn't happy about it—it offended his sense of fitness to leave so much as a mark on the snow—but he knew she was right.

Still, he chose the hardest snowpack and black ice to traverse once they got their snowshoes on and led the way up the wind-carved slopes, single file to obscure their numbers, to a vantage point where they could observe the wagons' ascent.

Fog drowned the space beyond, the ice cut nearly hidden as the columns of steam spread and dispersed. In the dead light it was difficult to judge distances, and the murk made it worse; the sound of water trickling down the artificial couloir came dimly to them, with the sound of axes cutting steps in the snow and voices calling orders. A mule brayed, protesting to the Ancestors of animals at the task it was required to perform.

"Cruel hunting, o my sister," the Icefalcon murmured. "And to what end I do not know. We will now need your wisdom indeed."

They moved thereafter through a world of ice and fog, like wolves pursuing reindeer across the heart of winter. Sometimes they could approach the caravan no closer than several miles, laboring through rough ice and the broken wildernesses. At other times, when snow whirled down or white fog reduced everything to the ghostly still-ness of the gray territory that lies between death and life, they drew nearer, concealed by Cold Death's spells. By night they dug snow-caves in the sides of the long glacial ridges, and sometimes the Icefalcon would hack his way up a serac or block or ice tower, and sit for as long as he could endure the cold, watching the lights of the dis-tant camp.

These were the lands that had been the Night River Country. He knew it, sighting on the familiar peaks in the distance: the Yellow Ancestor, the Peak of Demons, the Peak of Snows, in exactly the distance and relationships he had known, it seemed, since before he knew his name. More than anything that knowledge, that awareness, lodged in the Icefalcon's heart, a buried unacknowledged hurt, like an arrowhead embedded in his flesh; that under the Ice, under his feet, lay the world of his childhood summers, the aspens and the meadows and the place called Pretty Water Creek. The Ice had eaten it. Time had eaten it. Even when, in eons of time, the Ice disgorged it again, it would not be as it had been, but would be scoured and pressed and twisted out of recognition.

He would be gone, too, of course. But those meadows now existed only in his mind, as the faces of the Ancestors of wizards existed only in the gray crystals Gil read in the Keep.

This was not something of which he could speak to Loses His Way or to his sister; maybe not to anyone. Never in his life had he wept for anyone, for to weep was to be weak, and to mourn loss was to give power away to that which was lost, and to Time. But his heart wept for the Night River Country, the home of his childhood that was gone.

In this bitter world, demons glided across the snow. By day they sometimes had the appearance of whirlwinds, and, in the short terrible nights, of flickering lights far off over the Ice. Their voices whined and sang even when the wind was still. Toward evening of the second day on the Ice one of the clones broke from his place in the line of march and stumbled, slipping and shrieking and brandishing his sword, toward the place where the Icefalcon and his companions struggled along on the other side of a flow-ridge.

The man came smashing through the thin crest of the ridge almost on top of the Icefalcon. The Icefalcon had his sword in his hand already and aimed for his neck, but the man ducked at the last moment and the blade caught him on the collarbone. The clone turned and lunged at him again, sword drawn, grinning like a dog, and as the Icefalcon stabbed him through the chest he realized that the man was possessed of a demon.

The demon came out of the man's mouth like a glowing mist that thrashed and clawed at the Icefalcon's eyes and face for a moment and then was gone. The body of the dead clone lay in the snow at his feet.

Shouting on the other side of the snow ridge. The Icefalcon, Cold Death, and Loses His Way fled, sliding and slithering down the ridge, with Yellow-Eyed Dog bounding happily behind. Later, after the sergeant in the red boot-laces had looked at the dead man, cursed about barbarians, stripped off all the clothing and weapons and gone away again, they returned to look at the body.

"He makes his warriors out of air." Cold Death knelt to touch the hairless face, already rimed with frost. "Or wood and dirt and dead flesh, as the case may be. But he can't make a man's soul. It was only a matter of time before the demons found a way into the living flesh."

"Will they seek us out again?" Loses His Way fumbled at his heavy furs, as if to touch the amulet he wore against his skin beneath. "I have an amulet made for me by Walking Eyes."

"Amulets work against demons because the demons are spirit only," said Cold Death, standing up again and grabbing Yellow-Eyed Dog by the ruff to pull him away from the corpse. "The flesh of these things may protect the demons from the amulets' power . . ."

"With Walking Eyes' amulets," the Icefalcon added unkindly, "it wouldn't take much."

There was an outcry from farther off, and the clashing of swords. The three warriors scrambled up the trampled flow-ridge to see what the problem was. Two other clones had attacked their fellows, cutting madly all about them with swords and daggers, the blood like scattered poppies, garish on the snow. Even at the distance of half a mile the Icefalcon could hear them laughing crazily as they were dragged down and killed.

"They eat fear," said Cold Death softly. "Live on it, as
butterflies drink perfumes."

Vair stood over the fallen bodies of the two clone lu-
natics. There was no need to see his face. His whole body
was a threat, a quest for someone to savage. Bektis, beside
him, explained at great and mellifluous length why none
of this was his fault.

In time Vair turned aside, but it was clear from the way
he moved that he was not a happy man.

Later in that same day they reached the far edge of the
snowfield. The ice buckled and faulted in a maze of towers
and crevasses, huge wind-carved ridges interlaced like the
fingers of a hand. This formation narrowed toward the
north, and the Icefalcon guessed it was in fact a continua-
tion of the valley he had known as the Place of the Bent-
Horned Musk Ox, which even in his day had been walled
by hanging glaciers.

The caravan stopped, and Tir and Hethya were summoned. The Icefalcon was able to work his way to within a
hundred feet of them. Tir was saying, "There was a creek
that came out of the hills here. A canyon went back into
the ridges, that way." He gestured with one mitted hand.
The day had cleared with the advance of evening, and the
mountains to the north were clearly visible; about a day
east lay a line of broken-toothed black rocks thrusting
through the gashed jumble of ice. Everything flashed in
the high pearly light, the snow like cloud and the Ice a
thousand shades of blue and green where the wind scoured
it, the mules panting under their fur robes, frost forming
on their muzzles as it formed on the beards of the true
men, the bare flesh of the faces of the clones.

In the wan strange light Tir's face looked like a little
skull amid the gray fur of his hood, nothing left of it but
the great blue eyes and the unhealed tracks of cuts. *Are
they trying to starve the boy to death?* The wounds had the
look of malnutrition to them, and his face was bruised in a
way the Icefalcon did not like.

"Certainly the lie of the ice seems to indicate that the land beneath rises in that direction." Bektis stroked his snowy beard. "But whether we are in fact at the place where we must bend our course eastward to meet the valley of which the child speaks . . ."

Tir took a deep breath; it seemed to the Icefalcon that he was trembling. He closed his eyes.

"There was . . . there were three creeks that came together," he said slowly. "Right here. There was a waterfall, and a pool. We saw a wolf drinking there one night. Daddy—Father—We turned there. The road turned there. We made for that notch in the ridge." He pointed. "We journeyed through the night, and I remember the sound of the water running beside the road."

"And if you traveled in darkness," retorted Bektis spitefully, "where were the Dark Ones? They should have been thick about your train as wasps around honey."

"I don't know!" Tir almost screamed the words. "I don't know! I just say what I remember, and that's what I remember!"

"Don't speak disrespectfully to Lord Bektis." Vair caught the boy under the chin. "He doesn't like it. I don't like it, either, to hear a child of your years lash out like a savage. And stop crying." For Tir had begun to sob uncontrollably. "You're a pitiable thing." Casually, he released his grip and slapped him, in a single move. The slap was hard enough to stagger Tir. Hethya looked away.

"Make your apology."

"I'm sorry, Lord Bektis."

*I will kill him,* thought the Icefalcon, very calmly, seeing the child's face and body, hearing the child's voice.

He understood, and had agreed with, Ingold's decision to remain in Renweth Vale, relayed to him through the usual medium of an ice face and Cold Death. There was no way the old man could have overtaken Vair's caravan in time to be of help. It was clear to them both that there was some threat to the Keep far beyond Vair's eleven hundred henchmen camped outside it, something that in all probability neither Wend nor Ilae would be capable of dealing with. But beneath his warrior's logic, the logic of the Real World, he wished he could at least have the knowledge and comfort that the mage was on the way to help where he could not.

"The three springs are what you remember?"

"Me lord," said Hethya, her Felwoods brogue breaking into Lord Vair's cold, focused scrutiny of Tir, "me mother was a witch of sorts. She could track the course of a stream underground, miles through the woods. Folk were all the time after her to do it for the farms. Could perhaps me Lord Bektis do the same beneath all this ice, and tell us if there are three springs down there?"

Bektis grumbled and began to make passes with his hands above the ice. After a little time he reached into his muff and brought out the crystalline Device, which he affixed to his hand, pulling off his glove to do it and immediately surrounding himself with a heatspell that coalesced in curls of fog. The Icefalcon withdrew silently into the aquamarine chasms of ice, but followed the train as it veered eastward and dug a shelter within a hundred yards of it that night.

The clouds returned with nightfall, segueing into a morning of strange fogs, but by midday there was no further need of Tir's navigation. Through the shadowy grayness and blowing ice the nameless mountain ridge pushed higher, a line of coaly rock like a cresting wave about to break, and at its base lay a great blister in the ice, a huge mound some five miles long, ancient ice, green and black at its heart and unchanging, the slow-moving floes all fractured and broken around its sides.

"What is it?" Loses His Way squinted against the shadowless glare, for in the white world beneath the clouds one was not sure if what one saw was what one seemed to see.

"At a guess," the Icefalcon murmured, "the ice is shaped by something that lies buried beneath."

\* \* \*

"Hethya?" Tir rolled over a little and propped up on one elbow in the wagon's dark. By her breathing Hethya didn't sleep, either, and he wondered if she had the same dreams that he did, about Ugal's head bobbing up over the side of the iron vat, blood-gorged purple flesh bulging out around the iron of the gag, ready to burst, eyes conscious wells of agony. No matter how close he held to her, no matter how many furs and blankets they piled on, he couldn't seem to stop shivering.

Her voice was not the slightest bit sleepy, but muted, so the guard outside wouldn't hear. "What is it, me lamb?" Southland rum whiffed on her breath. It was often so now, at night.

"Did your mama teach you about the machines? About how to work them?"

He felt her breath still. Then she said, "Faith, lamb, me mother was a hedge-witch and a scholar, not one of the great old ones. I've said how it was, when as a little girl this voice would speak words in me head that only I could hear or understand. Oale Niu, now, the great *d'ian sian*, Ladymage and Queen . . . Whyever would you think it was me mother?"

But there was wariness in her voice.

"Well, in the Keep we found these crystals," said Tir. "And Gil and Ingold"—he still couldn't speak Rudy's name—"they found a way to look into them with this black table, and they see a lot of things, things from the Times Before. That's how they learned to bring the potatoes back to life, the earth apples, so everyone could have enough to eat."

His stomach clenched at the mention of eating. He didn't think he'd ever be able to eat again.

"And if your mother was a witch and found some of these crystals, or some other things written about those old machines, I thought maybe she'd have taught you about them. Especially if there were machines like that hidden in Prandhays Keep."

"Well, you're a sly one, and that's a fact," she murmured. "But I'm afraid you're out, me lamb, though it's true the . . . the *dethken iares*"—she carefully mispronounced the words Oale Niu used for the *chknaïes*—"was at our Keep, or part of it was, anyway. Oale Niu, she showed me the way of it, long before Lord Vair turned up with the rest of it all in pieces and jumbled together with bits of other things."

"Where did he get it?" He tried to sound casual and evidently succeeded.

"He's not said—he's a close one, the evil old so-and-so—but me, I think despite what all the southrons say about their land being pure of wizardry from the days of dawn and all that other chat . . . I think there was a Keep there in that city of theirs, that Khirsrit, once upon a time. And when he got driven out of the South by that poor girl he made his wife, bad cess to him, he took what he could."

"And did he take over Prandhays Keep?"

Hethya was silent for a time, running a lock of Tir's hair through her fingers. The iron winds had fallen, and noises could be heard around the camp, the squeak of the guards' boots in the snow, a man cursing one of the *tethyn*—the whole men, the real men, were always cursing the *tethyn*, usually for their stupidity. Hitting them, too, though Tir wanted to protest that it wasn't the *tethyns*' fault they were stupid. It was Vair's, for making them wrong.

Still, there was a tension in the camp, a fear, screwing tighter and tighter. Yesterday a *tethyn*—one of the Hastroaals—had run amok, away from the lines, and had been killed by White Raider scouts not a hundred feet from the line of march; later a Ti Men and a Cia'ak had started attacking everyone in sight with their swords. They were possessed by demons, the men said. Though Vair said this was not so, he and Bektis had distributed the demon-scares that usually hung around the camp on poles and wagon-boxes among the men for the rest of the march.

At least twenty hadn't given them back tonight, when they needed to make a Warding around the camp.

Everybody was scared. And the great silent whaleback of the ice mountain, that giant green-black blister under its covering of snow that overshadowed the camp, made it worse.

And if they knew what was under there, thought Tir despairingly, they'd be more scared than they were.

He shut his eyes, trembling and suddenly sick at the thought, and Hethya, feeling him shiver, hugged him tight.

"Well, and he did take over Prandhays," she said softly, and by her voice she was lost in a bitter dreaming of her own. "This past summer it was, in the days of the harvest, not that there was a great deal of that, and if me mother had lived I misdoubt it would have made a hair's difference. He's been gatherin' his southron troops and the local bandits together there ever since, him and that Delta Islands brute Gargonal, may the flesh rot from their stinking bones."

The hate in her voice made him turn his head, though nothing of her could be seen in the blackness. Her hand felt like a piece of wood, closing on his shoulder.

"Bastards, all of 'em, and Vair the biggest bastard of 'em. I don't know whether he came to Prandhays because he thought he could take it—Mother bein' dead and no wizard to go up against Bektis—or because he'd learned somehow there were bits and pieces of their foul machines left hid there, God knows by who, in the deep of time. But the first thing they did was go lookin' for 'em. And there's more such things, Bektis says, hid away in Dare's Keep, though he doesn't know where—leavin' aside the fact that anyone with a siege-engine or two could take Prandhays, and Dare's Keep, if Vair can take it, is near impregnable. If it hadn't been for me—for Oale Niu, that is—knowing the way of the weapons, I'd be there yet, bein' . . ." She checked the angry spill of words, and her hand jerked a little, then patted his thin shoulder as if just remembering that he was there.

"Bein' treated bad by every man of his pox-rotted regiment, one at a time or all together in a bunch, the pigs.

Don't think hard on me, sweeting. You've got to do what
you can."

Tir nodded, remembering how he had kissed Vair's
boots and told him he loved him before every man of
the camp. "I know," he said. "But the wizards—the old
wizards—didn't put fire-spells around the camp. They
had these round gray rocks in iron holders that threw white
light, and they called the—the thing that spits light, they
called it *chen yekas*, not *karnach* like you do."

"Ah," said Hethya softly. "And what did they call it,
under the Ice, that we're seeking? What was their word for
that?"

Tir said gravely, mischievous for the first time in aching
weeks, "Doesn't Oale Niu know that?"

She tweaked his hair, hard, like an older sister, or his
playmates who were dead. "Don't you be a clever boots
with me, laddy-boy."

Even the thought of it chilled the brief happiness he felt
at teasing again, playing again, remembering what it used
to be like to play. Quietly he said, "*Tiyomis*. That was their
word for the Shadow that Waits at the End of Time."


Bektis and Hethya set up the Dark Lightning on the
western side of the ice hill and began to carve. The notch
grew into a tunnel, steam rushing out in white torrents to
innundate the surrounding world in fog, and the stupidest
clones were sent to bail out the meltwater that collected as
the tunnel grew deep. At the same time the wind eased and
changed direction. The cinder-hued roof of cloud fractured. Lakes of green-stained pale sky shone through.

"There will be a moon tonight," said the Icefalcon.

He and his companions had dug a snow-cave in the
sprawl of crevasse, ice wall, and dune that crazed the glaciers around three sides of the blister of ice. Scouting in
the last of the evening light he'd found signs of the Earthsnake People among the ice and rocks of the rising mountain wall behind; this morning there had been more and,
near them, later prints, prints he knew.

The Talking Stars People. It was difficult to tell much in snowshoes, but he thought he recognized Blue Child's characteristically long stride. Those deeper prints of massive weight would surely be Red Fox, and always close at his side Stays Up All Night, who had been his strongest supporters against her. She would have sent Spider Music and Eyes In Her Pocket and some others after the horse herd, but most of the peoples of the Real World were wary about invaders in their territory, especially invaders whose intentions were not immediately apparent.

It was more than a matter of many wagonloads of forged-steel southern weapons, though that was a consideration even above horses. They had suffered before, from the incursions of the mud-diggers of various sorts. They would not let themselves be surprised or outflanked again.

From the top of the ice tower where they sat, the Icefalcon watched Nargois and Sergeant Red Boots set extra guards and confer worriedly with Vair. Bektis remained within the articulated spiral of the Dark Lightning's cage, like a hermit crab in some fantastic shell. From these, the Icefalcon turned his eyes to the sky, to the guards, to the flawed blue ice. The moon would be in its last quarter tonight, he recalled, but it should rise early and bright.

"Will the weather hold clear tonight, o my sister?"

She considered a moment, then nodded.

"Vair will know that, too," remarked Loses His Way. He scraped a fingerful of sweetened bison fat from the heel of the rawhide bag and passed the bag along to the others. "He's expecting an attack, and I don't think he'll be disappointed."

"Even so," said the Icefalcon. "They will all be on the watch for the Earthsnake People, or for Blue Child, whose coming, I think, will only help us. I think this may be our chance to get Tir out."

# CHAPTER THIRTEEN

Bodiless, the Icefalcon circled the camp.

He found the Earthsnake People, bivouacked at the mountain's feet. The jagged terrain concealed their fires and the snow-caves where they awaited the night. The Dark Ones had taken their shaman seven years ago, as they had taken Walking Eyes of the Empty Lakes People, but his amulets were still strong. Bektis would have trouble putting spells of madness or terror on them.

He saw the Talking Stars People moving in from the higher ground, one by one, Blue Child herself scouting the lead.

Strange, thought the Icefalcon, to see her again, face-to-face.

She did not seem aware of the shadow-walker keeping pace with her over the hard granular snow. She picked the way for her warriors masterfully, out of sight and out of the wind. Her face, like theirs, was greased thickly and wrapped to the eyes in a scarf of knitted mammoth wool stiff with the ice of her breath; all that he could see of her indeed were her eyes. Sky-blue, cold, and suspicious always, demanding of herself the perfection that the Icefalcon had always sought; they hadn't changed. She was a heavy-muscled woman and a tall one, acid scars of battle with the Dark Ones adding to the marks of the old burns. She would be difficult to defeat, thought the Icefalcon, when he issued his challenge—which she must accept if he backed it by the word of Loses His Way. He had been training hard, but she had been living hard, surviving in a world colder and crueler than the world of the Keep.

Leading the people who should have been his to lead.

"I think you don't want me to go because you want to keep me back," Dove in the Sun said to her—he could still hear the girl's voice and see the anger in those sapphire-bright eyes. "You think I'll be a warrior to match you. You're jealous of your standing."

"I'm not jealous." Blue Child's harsh voice was calm. The Dove was the only person in the steadings she'd let talk back to her. "You're too young. You're not strong enough to survive a fight, or an injury. Not quick enough, and not hard enough."

Her eyes had gone past the girl—pretty as a fox kit and as fierce—to the Icefalcon, her rival, watching from the corner by the sod-roofed longhouse of Noon's family, and she'd added, "And don't you let her talk you into taking her, either. She's not ready."

But of course he had. The Dove could talk anyone into anything. Except Blue Child.

Had it been because he loved her? Or because he was angry at Blue Child, who already clearly saw herself as Noon's heir? And for whose sake was the anger—the Dove's or his own?

But in any case, he thought, moving off up the rime-ice on the dune, marveling still that in his shadowy state he left no tracks, it was not his doing that the Dove was killed. She had been speared, she had not the strength to keep her horse from panicking, and both had fallen. And that was all.

But it was he who had had to tell Blue Child that her lover was dead.

Demons floated, whispering, all around the camp.

More of them, now, a dirty brown beating in the air. Sometimes only the glister of disembodied eyes, the

dripping sheen of fangs. Mouths that tore at him, hissed—
lights that jigged insanely over the snow.

That sly fire peered from the eyes of at least eight of the
clones in the camp. Two of them wore demon-scares.
One, seeing the Icefalcon—or the demon within it seeing
him—pointed straight at him and ran toward him, screaming and pointing and giggling. But two of the booted
guards brought up their crossbows and shot the demon
soldier, and the demon rolled forth from the man's mouth
with the coughed blood of his collapsing lungs.

It mauled and tore at the Icefalcon for a moment, but experience had shown him how to put aside at least some of
the pain, how to shut his mind against it. The thing spat at
him and reviled him in Noon's voice and went its way.

The Icefalcon moved on, shaky with shock, with the
fear and cold that were inescapable in the shadow state.
The light was thinning away, fogs and steam drifting between the wagons from the ice mountain where the Dark
Lightning still bored rendered all things strange and flat.
When he passed the place where the clones' bodies were
piled—more had died during the day, though they were
only a few days old—he saw that the bodies, stripped of
their clothing, were piebald, skin like human skin in
places, in others strangely textured, rough and granular, or
covered with a fine fuzz of grayish wool.

He found the wagon where Tir slept, set in the midst of
the camp.

There would be confusion when the Earthsnake People
attacked later in the night. He ghosted from wagon to
wagon, estimating distances, terrain, and what the lighting
would be like in torch-flare and darkness. Judging where
the Earthsnake People would make their attack and where
the Talking Stars People would. Where he could make
his entrance to the camp from the crevasses beyond—
bundled in coats of bison and mammoth fur, one man
looked much like another. Once back in his own body, the
body that now slept in the ice-cave they'd dug last night,
he'd be able to . . .

The hissing of the Dark Lightning ceased. Clones slopped, shivering, into the tunnel with leather buckets—a huge slab of clear ice marked the dumping area of the meltwater they carried out.

Someone said, "Bring the boy."

"And fetch me a tisane, for God's sake!" Bektis called from the metal cage of the Dark Lightning's cradle. He was heavily wrapped in his long coat, his head protected by a series of embroidered caps, scarves, and a hood. On the refugee train from Gae to Renweth after the city's destruction by the Dark Ones, Bektis' collection of warm garments and muffs had been a source of never-ending derision among the Guards. The Icefalcon wondered what these southern warriors had to say about him when Vair na-Chandros wasn't there to hear.

More voices in the tunnel, and churning in the fog that filled it. Bektis had the air of a man at rest and would, the Icefalcon was certain, be occupied with his tisane for some time to come; he wasn't sure whether the dark flicker of the machine's beams would harm him, though it wasn't anything he cared to put to the test.

He stepped into the tunnel's fog.

The walls were slick ice, melted and frozen hard again, and blue as sapphire. The floor slanted downward, straight as if ruled, vanishing into dense fog and darkness. The ceiling dripped with water condensed from the steam, and the clones hurried past, water steaming and sloshing from the buckets they bore. Gil had described such a place in the heart of the Saycotl Xyam, the cursed mountain in the South, and the Icefalcon wondered if Vair na-Chandros sought here the same kinds of demons that had dwelled in those terrible caves.

Vair and Nargois strode past him in the mist, torches haloed in woolly yellow light; Hethya walked behind. "Can you see it?" Vair called out.

Fog hid them, but for fidgeting shapes in the saturated ocher glow.

"There, me Lord. Look where the runes catch the

light. We give it another burst, a short little one—a foot, maybe."

"Don't be absurd, woman, we'll destroy them and then where will we be?"

"For sure your Bektis has never cooked, then. You can tamper with the heat, surely. It's a thing he operates with his mind, after all. Can't he be stopping at a foot?"

A warrior emerged from the choking brume, reflections from his torch frolicking through the mirror-smooth walls as if an army of lamp-bearing demons ran through the ice on either side. Hethya followed him, and Lord Vair, their breaths visible in the cold that flowed down into the tunnel from without. Hethya's round, jovial face had thinned with the journey across the Ice, and there were smudges of weariness below her eyes. Vair looked like a snake mummified in pitch.

The Icefalcon hesitated, looking back into the dripping vapors, then turned and followed them out again.

"You call this a tisane?" Bektis waved the boiled-leather cup at a stone-faced guard. "The dishwater of a poor man's house is stronger! If . . . My Lord," he turned expressively to Vair, with the air of a man more put upon than human flesh can bear. "My Lord, might I please, *please* prevail upon your goodness to instruct your fool of a cook not to drown these tisanes in bergamot! They're undrinkable, absolutely undrinkable!"

Vair took it, tasted, and threw it in the guard's face, adding a terse instruction in the ha'al tongue in which the Icefalcon was fairly sure he caught the word *flog*. To Bektis, Vair said, "Hethya claims that as a sorcerer you should be able to shorten the beam of this apparatus with your mind." He tapped the gold and iron of the intricate frame. It flickered with quicksilver brightness, and the Icefalcon had the renewed sensation that it was a living thing, attentive, waiting to hunt again.

"We can see it through the ice," explained Hethya. "I'd say a foot of ice, not more. Melt it off within an inch or two and we can go after it with hammers."

Bektis looked momentarily nonplussed.

"The beams won't hurt it." Tir stood beside the Dark Lightning's cradle, flanked by two guards, bruised face white and pinched around huge, hollowed eyes. His voice sounded distant, as if he slipped for a moment into some faraway dream. "Nothing will hurt it."

"Pray your recollection is correct, boy," said Vair, and Tir shivered, the movement of his eyes to the big man's face saying everything about what the past month had been like. "Can you do this, sorcerer?"

"Of a certainty, my illustrious Lord." Bektis drew himself up with an air of injury not noticeable prior to Tir's reassurance that whatever lay within the Ice would not be damaged by Bektis' miscalculation. "A foot, you said?" He stroked his beard, the huge crystals on his hand shining among the niveous river of silk. "Perhaps it would be best to touch it with the beams to a distance of ten inches or so and have the men remove the final few inches with hammers." He nodded grave approval of his own wisdom. "I believe that would be best."

Hethya rolled her eyes.

Bektis drew a few deep breaths, as if collecting his strength for some mighty effort, then with dramatic suddenness spread his hands. The crystals flashed in the last pastel whispers of daylight. With disembodied eyes, the Icefalcon saw the cold blue energies that came flickering out of the ice from unknown depths, saw the crystals in the iron nets stream with sparks as they drew in the forces of the air—heard, too, a kind of dry, crinkling glitter, like galaxies of suspended needles brushed by wind.

Bektis shut his eyes—*If he thought he could get away with crying "Abracadabra" like a street-conjurer, he'd do it,* reflected the Icefalcon—and laid his hands on the bubble-thin ball of iridescent glass that seemed to be the apparatus' heart . . .

The Icefalcon saw the energies flash and change. With a vibration that tore at his nerves, he felt the beam of darkness lance out, a touch, a breath; a hissing deep within the tunnel, white light glaring in the clouds of mist, and steam rolled out, a dragon's sneeze. Then Hethya took a torch from a guard and strode down into the mists, and, at Vair's signal, the two warriors followed, axes in their hands.

Her voice floated back, "We've got it!"

Vair took Tir by the hand; the boy's face went rigid as carved bone at the touch. Even Bektis disentangled himself from the latticed gold and iron and followed them into the luminous blue tunnel, leaving the guard who had come up at that moment with a second tisane to stand waiting, cup steaming in hand.

Like a cat's ghost the Icefalcon trod softly in their wake.

The tunnel itself was close to a hundred feet long, and mist reduced visibility to inches. Voices echoed wetly; there was a dripping of water, the crunch of axes, and the thin *splish* of a boot in a puddle. Clones bore dripping buckets past, and though there was no perceptible sensation of heat, the air felt damper. Shapes clarified in the vapors, and the Icefalcon arrived at last at the tunnel's end and saw what it was that Vair sought.

Even as men chipped at the edges of the ice, white rime was forming again on what the Icefalcon could see was a pair of enormous, coal-black doors. It seemed to him that he could see, too, through the heat-cleared ice, the black wall in which they were set. It stretched away on either side, vanishing into the glacier's green eternal midnight.

Black wall, black door, untouched and unscathable, and underfoot, beneath a heap of ice shards and mush, the suggestion of steps leading down.

The goal of the journey was a Keep, long ago covered over by the Ice in the North.

"Open it, child." Vair's voice clanged on the diamond silence, a hammer affixing shackles, an ax striking a door.

The Icefalcon, a wary distance from Bektis, could see Tir trembling, his breath a plume in the light of torches and magic. "They open out," he said, his voice tiny in the still-

ness of watching, of awe. "If they weren't locked from inside, it still took a wizard to open them."

"Lord Wizard?"

Bektis self-consciously adjusted the crystals on his
hand—the Icefalcon wondered whether the wizard had
had that look of haggard thinness, of wasted flesh and
waxen skin, the last time he had seen him close. He made a
great flourish of his arms and a dozen graceful gyres with
wrists and fingers, lights sparkling and leaping from the
gems he bore. The right-hand leaf of the dark portal grated
against the ice where it hadn't been completely cleared. A
shower of scrapings rained to the muck and water and re-
freezing slush.

Everyone stepped back.

The slit of darkness was like looking into the deepest
heart of the earth, where the Dream Things wait forever.
Bektis made another gesture, outer sleeves emphasizing
his thin arms. The slit widened.

The smell rolled forth. "Mother of Mercy!" Hethya
coughed and gagged.

Foul and green and thick as soup in the air, it seemed
to clog the lungs like sewer water, a summer-smell of
garbage long forgotten, borne on a rolling wave of heat
that made the fog swirl and then thicken still more. At the
same moment a tendril of vine dropped through the crack
of darkness: gray, desiccated, bearing on it still the deformed pads of what might have been skeleton leaves, the
bumpy and twisted nodules of what could, three thousand
years ago, have been fruit.

After a second of shocked stillness, Bektis sent witchlight drifting through the doors. It showed those closest
the tunnel that would lead to the inner doors.

Vair said, "Good God!"

But what lay beyond, thought the Icefalcon, was not
something that had ever been created by any god—at
least by none that could by any stretch of imagination be
called good.

Like a second door behind the first, the passage was

barricaded with vines. They had a shiny look in the white
witchlight, like the scarred flesh of a mummy's fingers:
dried, withered, even in death tough as wires when the
guards came hesitantly forward and hewed at them with
their swords. They sheeted the floor and walls above an in-
describable mulch underfoot of vines, leaves, and fruit
from which white ferns sprouted that had never seen light,
mingled with pallid fungal growths that seemed to shift
and bulge with the bending of the torchlight. The inner
Doors at the end of the passage stood open. Vines flowed
out of the utter dark beyond like a filthy flood frozen in
mid-spate, knee-deep or higher, silent, blanched, dead.

"It's impossible," whispered Vair. "What plants grow
without light of the sun?"

"The Keep was reared by wizards, Lord," said Hethya,
her voice the voice of Oale Niu. Vair shot her a sidelong
look, suspicious and shaken, his hand straying to the topaz
demon-scare he wore. "Else why are we here?"

Beside him, the Icefalcon heard old Nargois whisper,
"Why indeed?"

"Get some men in here." Vair recovered his composure,
glanced back at the older man. "Clear this, and have them
start bringing the gear in." He walked ahead, straight
white form glimmering, boots crunching and slushing in
the rotted vines. The others followed, Tir and Hethya
holding hands tightly and the guards looking as if they
wished they could do the same.

Cold air seeped after them into the passageway, fog
condensing like a convocation of ghosts. The ghosts
drifted on their heels through the inner Doors, over the
guardian tangle of vines, and into the Aisle.

Bektis flung up his hand—jewels flashed, and witchlight
drenched the darkness and hurled it to flight. "Mother of
Sorrows!" Hethya cried, and made a protective sign.

Fully the rear third of the Aisle was choked with what
appeared at first, in the hard glow of the magefire, to be a
single monstrous organism: bristling, feathery, colorless
against the ebon walls; five levels tall to the vaulted night

of the ceiling a hundred feet overhead and stirring with
movement and furtive sound. But the Icefalcon saw—they
all saw, with the strengthening of Bektis' magelight—that
what at first appeared to be a homogeneous wall was in
fact an impenetrable tangle of ash-hued vines that varied
in thickness from the width of a child's finger to cables
greater than a man's waist, of strange-shaped balls of fuzz
and bristle that might have been leaves or spores, of pen-
dant clots of moss that had taken on the bizarre shapes of
giant fruits or carcasses hung to cure. Molds and lichens
pillowed everything in a pale upholstery that glittered
with moisture; weird bromeliads sprouted from them in
spiderlike profusion only to play host themselves to
thread-fine mazes of pale-glowing fungus.

Arms and limbs and tributaries of this bleached jungle
looped through the doorways of the cells that faced onto
the Aisle and cascaded from the windows of the second
and third levels; the whole of the floor was covered in
stringy, wormlike tendrils. Where streams of water flowed
across the floor of Dare's Keep, here lay only crisscrossed
seams of plant life, burgeoning out of the old channels like
hedges and reaching all ways across black stone. When
the heat spilled through those empty eyeless windows,
those gaping black doorways, drawn by the bitter cold
of the Doors opened after all these millennia, the vines and
the molds and the bromeliads stirred and muttered with its
passage, and the great soured noxium of decay surged
over the men and the woman who stood, shocked speech-
less, in the heart of that vast internal night.

But the Keep was whole. Thousands of tons of ice lay
above its roof, pressed on its walls—had so pressed for
three thousand years, as if the building lay at the bottom of
a frozen sea. But the Keep was whole.

"It is good." Vair's yellow eyes shone as they traveled
over the cyclopean walls, the stairways that circled up
through towers of openwork, the bridges spanning the
Aisle, rank with hueless fern and fungus and curtained
with gray stringers that reached to the floor. "Impervious,

like Dare's Keep, in which one can raise and provision
an army and laugh to scorn any who come against one. It
is good."

As if in response to his words a chime spoke, echoes re-
sounding, musical and yet queerly atonal, with a flat dead-
ness that gritted on the nerves. At one side of the Aisle a
vast series of wheels and gears had been built into the
black stone of the wall, powered by water trickling from
basin to basin, the basins cracked so that the water
streamed down the stone.

To the nearest guard, Vair snapped out an order, flap-
ping a hand at Hethya: "Cia'ak will go with you while you
select a suitable room for yourself and the child. Qinu . . ."
He signaled up another man, rapped out words in the
ha'al, the Icefalcon hearing (he thought) *clothing* and *bed*.
This was something on which he had not counted, and
after a moment's hesitation, he followed the guard into the
passage once again. More men entered, hacking at the
vines with axes and dragging great mats of them not out,
but in toward the Aisle.

At the outer end of the ice tunnel the messenger spoke
to Nargois, who waited with a great crowd of clones
bearing axes, torches, bundles of weapons and gear. The
elderly second nodded and began to issue orders. The
Truth-Finder detailed men to the largest of the wagons and
instructed the clones in unshipping the vat and its accom-
panying equipment. The expedition's priest, with his servant and three clones, bore down the tunnel the portable
altar and velvet-draped equipment deemed necessary for
the approval of the Straight God.

It was at this point—though the dim slice of moon still
lingered well below the hills—that the camp was attacked.

The first person to be aware of the attack was Nargois,
one moment giving instructions to the perimeter guards—
he, too, seemed confident that the attack would come with
moonrise—the next moment looking down with widening
eyes at the brown-feathered arrow sticking out of his
diaphragm, as if he could not believe what he saw. A

second arrow went through his throat under his left ear, probably before he was aware of any pain from the first, and then the Earthsnake People and the Talking Stars People were in the wagon circle.

Sergeant Red Boots shouted an alarm, dove behind the cage of the Dark Lightning issuing commands, and battle was locked. A stray arrow went through the Icefalcon's chest, a weird cold wickering that caused no pain. Demons flickered and danced in the fog-wraiths that haloed the torches and billowed pale underfoot. Mules shrieked and dragged their leads, Alketch warriors and wolf-silent Raiders dragging them in two directions. Clones grabbed up provisions and dashed for the tunnel while another sergeant tried to organize a defended retreat; arrows felled them, and fur-clothed shadows caught up the bundled swords, axes, and armor they bore and wrenched the weapons from their dying hands. The priest came out of the ice tunnel and cried something, and a demon-ridden clone raced up to him, shrieking, and sank an ax into his chest.

Blue Child axed Red Boots through the shoulder against the Dark Lightning's cage, took a sword-thrust in the double hide of her jacket, and slashed the man's face open with her knife. Her followers and his were running to join battle—she kicked the man out of the way in a spray of blood and swung herself into the Dark Lightning's cradle, laying her hands on the glass ball at its center in the way that showed she'd been watching Bektis all the time.

The Icefalcon knew Blue Child was incapable of activating the apparatus, but he was the only one that wise in the ways of magic. Every southern warrior of the dozen closing in hesitated—and every one was taken in that hesitation by one of Blue Child's band, with the neatness of dancers in a cabaret.

The Earthsnake People had made their appearance by this time, slithering under the wagons out of the snowy dark. Some killed, others only seized whatever weapons they could. Though they were still outnumbered by the

clones, the combined forces of the two Peoples proved
sufficient to force the southerners from the wagon circle.
Torches toppled in the snow, the dimming light adding to
the confusion. Men hauled whatever weapons and provisions they could down the tunnel, the circle of defenders
shrinking around it, hampered by the possessed clones in
their own ranks.

The Icefalcon raced down the ice tunnel through a
melee of fog and torchlight, flying arrows and struggling
men, feeling as if he were in a dream, except that his
dreams seldom featured anything so weird as that glimmering corridor of mists. He could not communicate with
Tir, but should the boy be enterprising enough to chance
an escape in the confusion, he wanted at least to be by
his side.

Near the Keep's Doors he met Vair na-Chandros, dark
face twisted with rage as he shouted orders and lashed
with his whip at the men struggling past him under their
burdens. Bektis scurried in the generalissimo's wake,
wrapped so thick in spells of protection against anyone's
notice he was to all intents and purposes invisible. But to
the Icefalcon's bodiless consciousness the ward-spells,
guard-spells, arrows-miss, and calamities-hit-someone-
else appeared as a fluttering mass of plasmoid light, and
the old man, clutching frantically at the crystal Device
strapped to his hand, had the appearance of a demon-fish
of the southern seas, which attaches seaweed ribbons to itself in order to increase its bulk and pass for a being too
formidable to eat.

He would, the Icefalcon guessed, barely have the concentration to throw illusion, confusion, fear, or much of
anything else at the attackers, so desperate was he to
remain unseen. As well, he thought. He would not like to
lose someone like Red Fox to a jackal like the Court Mage.

The Aisle was a madhouse, men throwing down their
burdens, snatching up weapons, running back up the
tunnel. No sign of Tir or Hethya, but among the men,
demons buzzed, shrieking and dodging when someone ran

past with a demon-scare. Booted men and other clones were killing the possessed clones systematically, like men butchering rabid animals; five or six lay bleeding about the floor, the demons that had been in them romping madly in the jungles that dangled down the walls, shaking the vines and screaming with laughter.

The Icefalcon thrust aside the cold embrace of a demon that, unnervingly, took the shape of Dove in the Sun and fell upon him, weeping and biting; he felt the pain of the bites but knew it wasn't real. The pain of seeing her face again wasn't real, either, or so he told himself. Tracks in the creepers showed him where people had gone, through a door at the front end of the Aisle, into the caliginous passageways that in the Renweth Keep would have been first level north.

A corridor curtained with a tapestry of pallid vines and fungus like cobwebs; a slit of torchlight limning a door. Ancient wood, but still stout. Cold Death had told him it was dangerous to tamper with the shape his consciousness told him it wore, but he had passed through tent curtains and wagon-tops without trouble, and the wood proved no more difficult.

Hethya and Tir were inside.

The ax-wielding warrior was still with them, one of the booted men, long black hair hanging loose around a brown face and profound uneasiness in his eyes. Tir and Hethya sat on their blankets, looking around. Cold Death had told him that it was possible for a shadow-walker to enter dreams, and in fact his original intent had been to scout the camp and wait until Tir fell asleep, then brief him on the lay of the ground, and how they should meet, in a dream.

But the boy clung close in Hethya's arms, wide eyes staring past the dim glow of the little hemp-oil lamp, listening to the distant clamor in the Aisle. Hethya murmured, "There's no need to fear, sweeting," and pushed back his hood from his forehead and stroked his hair. The Icefalcon saw that she was in truth a handsome woman.

Though there was the hardness in her eyes of someone who has been had by a hundred bandits, there was neither cruelty nor spite.

"I'm not afraid." Tir shook as if with bitter cold.

"You know these Keeps were built all alike, with but the one set of Doors. And even were they not, it's all buried under the ice, you know. All this"—she gestured about her, to the lichens that padded the wall and the ceiling, the lianas coiled at the base of the walls like the shed skins of serpents—"all this looks creepy enough, to be sure, but it's just plants, and mostly dead ones at that. They must have grown up from the tanks in the crypts, as you were telling me of, back at your own home Keep. There's naught in it to fear."

His lips formed the word *no* without sound.

"He's a snake and a beast, our Vair, but he'll not be lettin' aught befall us so long as he needs us—and need us he does still. There's a secret yet here in this Keep that he's after finding, a secret he says'll get him back into power in the South, and him that furious at his wife that she drove him out."

Her voice sank to a whisper, though it was clear the guard knew no Wathe. "You just go on doin' as I've done, me honey. Lead him along, that there's always one more secret to find. As for this . . ." Her voice grew stronger again, and she shrugged.

"That old fraud Bektis is fond enough of his own skin, and he listened deep, to every sound and whisper, before puttin' foot through those Doors. You can trust he'd have heard anything bigger than a mouse. When all's said it's naught but an empty building."

Tir closed his eyes, and a shudder passed through him; for a long time he said nothing. Then, "No."

"No what, lambkin?"

He shook his head, his mouth set, trying not to show fear. His voice was barely to be heard. "Not empty."

# CHAPTER FOURTEEN

From the Keep of Shadow, the Icefalcon passed into the Keep of Dreams.

Prandhays Keep, he thought, and looked about him at the walls of wood and wattle, stained bright yellows and oranges under centuries of torch smoke and grime. They had glowstones there, more than at Dare's Keep, and the decayed chambers whose arches and doorways and internal windows looked into one another like a warren of coral were brightly lit. The chamber in Hethya's dream was nearly as brilliant as daylight.

Hethya's mother was there. How the Icefalcon knew this woman was Hethya's mother he wasn't sure. Perhaps the knowledge was part of walking in someone else's dream. Her eyes had the look of Hethya's, green-gold and tip-tilted, and her hair had once been the same cinnamon hue. Even faded as it was, it retained the curly strength and weight, piled in random rolls on her head and bristling with sticks of wood and metal to keep it out of her way. She was beautiful like Hethya, but thin.

"They're fools," she said. "Idiots!" Like Hethya she used her hands when she spoke. "They should be learning about these things, not trying to figure out how to extract the magic from them to heat their rooms or make their little vegetable patches grow! That wasn't what these things were made for!"

"Well, Mother," pointed out Hethya, "we don't know what they *were* made for."

She was younger then and trimmer, and there was a

lightheartedness in her eyes that had disappeared over the intervening years. The yellow silk gown she wore was new enough that the Icefalcon guessed she dreamed of a time six or seven years ago, the Time of the Dark or just after it. She had a child on her knee, a year or two old, dark-haired and green-eyed, reaching with round pink hands to snatch at the braid she dangled in play as she spoke.

"We know why some were made." Hethya's mother flicked with the backs of her fingers at the pile of scrolls on the desk before her: heaps of them, tablets and codexes and books. Gil-Shalos, thought the Icefalcon, would perish with envy at the sight. "Most of this is rot, rubbish, but some of it, my girl . . . Some of it has told me some most interesting things."

"Such as?" Hethya hoisted the child on her hip and crossed the cell to stand by her mother's chair. For a time the two women studied the scrolls with heads together, the child grasping and reaching for the older woman's hair-sticks, the resemblance clear between the three dissimilar faces. In the corners of the cell, and through the archways and half cells and vestibules opening from it, the Icefalcon glimpsed dim half-familiar shapes: the sections of canopy that had been over the iron vat in the wagon, the half-assembled midpart of the Dark Lightning's cradle. There was a black stone table in one of the vestibules that the Icefalcon recognized, such a table as Ingold and Gil-Shalos used to read the smoky polyhedrons that held the records of the Times Before.

If bandits had taken Prandhays Keep, the Icefalcon could guess what had become of that child, what had become of Hethya as well.

When the armies of humankind were being raised for an assault on the Dark, Ingold and Alde had both sent to Degedna Marina, landchief of the Felwoods, begging for all and any machinery or relics of the Times Before, for any mageborn they could find. Degedna Marina had dispatched a small force of her warriors—and those of her lesser lords—but denied finding such mechanisms in any of the three Felwoods Keeps. No wizards, she said, dwelled among those who survived.

Hethya straightened up, began a sort of dance with her child on her hip to make the toddler laugh. She stopped at the sound of a sharp scratching by the cell's curtained door, called out gaily, "I'm coming, Ruvis."

"Ruvis, is it?" Her mother looked up, exasperated, amused. "Mal Buckthorn just brought you back here an hour ago!"

"Shh! Ruvis'll hear you!"

But her mother had kept her voice down, evidently knowing her daughter well. Hethya put the child in a cradle wrought of forest twigs and ancient goldwork, tucked it up with a sheepskin and a bright-patched quilt, and said, "You be me good, little dumplin', till I return, me peach, me blueberry." She checked a mirror, readjusting the jeweled comb in her hair. "Dub Waterman's coming by for me around midnight, Mother. If so be he gets here before I get back, tell him I've gone out for a few minutes to fetch you some lampblack from Oggo Peggit in the Back Warrens and I'll be right back . . ."

Her mother rolled her eyes, "You are incorrigible." But she laughed as she said it and kissed her and tousled her hair. And because this was a dream the Icefalcon felt Hethya's sorrow and the pain of her loss and knew the grown Hethya, the woman Hethya, wept in her sleep.

He stepped away from her, back into the Keep of the End of Time.

They lay together in their cell, Hethya and Tir, the child snuggled in the woman's arms. The earlier guard had been replaced by a clone, who sat just outside the shut and bolted oak panels, staring indifferently at the dirty torchlight on the opposite wall. Only the thinnest fuzz of hair covered his scalp, but what was unmistakably a patch of wool grew from his cheek.

Within the cell, an oil lamp burned, a grimy fleck of

fire in the close-crowding shadows. Tir, too, dreamed of a Keep.

Not Dare's Keep, not the Keep the mage Brycothis had surrendered her human life to enter as Heart-Mage and core. The Icefalcon recognized the Keep of the Shadow, though the vast Aisle was cleared to its rear wall and the light of glowstones outlined from within a patchwork of balconies, open archways, winding staircase, and a rose window like the lost sun of summer. The streams on the black stone floor spoke with gentle music; the voices of the men who walked there echoed very softly, like single pebbles dropped into still ponds.

Tir was there. Sometimes he looked like Tir—Tir worn to his bones, sunken eyes desperate in a scarred face—and sometimes he looked like someone else, a sturdy boy just coming into adolescence, with the dark-gray eyes of the House of Dare and black hair growing unevenly out of what had been a close crop. He walked in the wake of two men and looked about him as he walked.

One was a burly middle-aged warrior whose initial pug-faced ugliness had been recently augmented by scars and burns. The Icefalcon recognized the wounds. He carried such marks on his chest, right arm, and hand from the acid and fire of the Dark Ones. Most adults in the Keep did. The other man was small and fine-boned, his shaved skull illuminated with the intricate tattooing that Gil-Shalos said was the mark of a mage in the Times Before.

"I know you weren't ready for this," said the scar-faced warrior. "But with Fyanach's death I don't think we have a choice."

"No," the mage said in a voice that could have been contained in the smallest of pottery jars. "No. And I understood there was the possibility when I assented to come." But there was stricken pain in his eyes. He was fair-skinned and, like his friend's, his face and scalp and tattoo-written hands were crossed with burn scars and the pink, brittle flesh of acid scalds, the track of battle against the Dark Ones. "Will they ever know?" he asked.

"Some will." They weren't speaking in the Wathe, or the ha'al, or any tongue the Icefalcon had ever heard. He knew his understanding of it came only through Tir, who remembered in his dream. "It's not a knowledge many share, even at Raendwedth."

The name meant *Eye of the Heart*—the capacity to read a person or situation clearly—coupled with the locative for mountains; the Icefalcon hadn't known that was the derivation of Renweth Vale's name. "There have been too many corrupt wizards, too much evil magic. Too many hate magic on principle now, and small blame to them. So it's not a knowledge that can be shared. But some will always know, down through the years. Your name—and what you do—will not be forgotten. That I promise you, Zay, my friend."

"I do not . . . want to be forgotten." Zay rubbed his chest, half unconsciously, as if to massage away some cold or grief. "And Lé-Ciabbeth?"

"I'll tell her."

The great clock spoke, hard leaden chimes that flattened on the air.

"She'll want to come here," said the scar-faced man after a time. "I'll detail warriors to escort her, as soon as they can be spared."

"No." Zay stopped and caught his companion's arm, desperation in his face. "Too long."

He led the ugly man across a succession of footbridges, down the vast plain of the floor, through a silence that diminished their footfalls to a thrush peck against rock, then up the double stairway that curved to a pillared door at the Aisle's inner end. In the Keep of Renweth the territory at the end of the Aisle on the first level belonged to the Church and that above to the Lady of the Keep.

The two men stopped again at the top of the stair, on the threshold of a triple archway. "You'd best go back, son," said the warrior, speaking to Tir. "In time you'll know this secret, but now is not the time."

"But something might happen to you, Father." Tir

spoke in the cracking voice of adolescence, and indeed as he spoke he wore the form of that other boy, in his black kilt all stamped with stylized eagles of gold. "Isn't that why you brought me? So I'd know, in case the Dark . . . ?"

"It is the Dark we fear here, son. The Dark, and what they might conceivably learn." The father stepped away from his friend to put a hand on the son's shoulder. "After I've spoken with the other mages at Raendwedth, we'll see."

But the Icefalcon felt Tir's memory—the memory of stories he'd heard about his own father, his real father, Eldor Andarion, seized and borne away by the Dark Ones to their hellish nests—and after the two men vanished through the right-hand archway, the boy crept stealthily in their wake.

The northern end of the Keep beyond the Aisle was the headquarters of the Keep's ruling landchief, containing the chambers where his warriors slept and the rooms where his weavers, potters, smiths, and bakers dwelled with their families and plied their trades. Here—as in Renweth—there were audience chambers great and small, conference halls, even chambers spelled with Runes of Silence against the working of wizardry, which could hold the mageborn prisoners within their walls. There had always, the Icefalcon deduced, been renegade shamans.

But unlike Renweth, this Keep was new. In Renweth over the countless years, families and clans had broken walls, enlarged cells, put in new stairways to suit their convenience—diverted the water pipes and run conduits off public fountains and latrines, installed false ceilings to create storage lofts, knocked out new doors or blocked old ones up: in general behaved like people making themselves thoroughly at home.

In the Keep of Dreams, corridors still ran straight and wide. Doorways were uniform and uniformly equipped with wooden louvers—(*I'll have to tell Gil-Shalos all this*)—and no pipes ran along the high black ceilings or the walls along the floor.

No bindweed tangle of ramose chaos; no torches.

Only glowstones in mesh baskets casting pale clear shadows as mage and warrior entered a cell *(fourth on the right after the pillared audience chamber),* mounted the spiral stair there, and, in the small conference chamber above, worked a catch behind a sconce on the wall to open a hidden panel.

They ascended a farther stair, and the boy who was also Tir watched them from below. He was tall enough— barely—to reach and work the lever behind the sconce. The stair was narrow, concealed within a wall, the Icefalcon guessed. He wondered if there were a corresponding route in Renweth and what its goal might be.

Here the goal was disappointing: a round vestibule entered, and exited again, by two doors that were only the width of a man's shoulders and barely six feet tall. What seemed to be a long conference hall lay beyond, though there was no table there, no chairs. Its eastern wall contained an archway flanked with frost-white pilasters in whose core seemed to be a half-seen spiral of broken fragments of iron and rock. The archway led through a smaller chamber, likewise bare and likewise giving by a similarly pilastered arch into a third still smaller, and so into a fourth. Fearful of being seen, the boy remained hidden in the gloom of the vestibule, watching his father and the wizard Zay slowly pace the length of the first hall, then pass between the pillars to the second. Their voices were too low to be heard, but he saw Zay gesture, desperate, demanding, his shadow swooping huge over the wall, though what he demanded the boy did not know.

Around them the Keep slept, secure against the Dark Ones that haunted the lands outside. Tir turned away, afraid to follow further, and descended the secret stair.

The Icefalcon waited for him at the bottom.

*"Icefalcon!"* The boy flung himself at him, sobbing with relief, grabbed him hard around the waist, and pressed his wounded face to his belt knot, clinging as if he'd never let go. "Icefalcon, get me out of here! Get me

out of here! They killed Rudy, and Mama's dead, and they're going to break into the Keep and kill everyone because Vair thinks there's more weapons in the Keep, and he needs a place to raise an army that has food and can't be broken into like Prandhays . . ."

"Easy." The Icefalcon awkwardly stroked at the boy's dark hair. "Easy." He had always abhorred weeping children and was uneasily aware that such overwhelming emotion could decant the boy into wakefulness again. It might be hours then before he slept, and the Icefalcon had information to impart, and the cold pain, the ache of concentration, was beginning to saw at his consciousness.

"Your mother's not dead. Nor is Rudy, though he was badly hurt."

Tir lifted a face wild with hunger and the fear of belief. The Icefalcon felt a cold lance of fury at the man who would put that look into a child's eyes. "Lord Vair said . . ."

"Lord Vair's a liar."

Tir pressed his face to the Icefalcon's side and again burst into tears.

"Tir, listen. Listen." *We don't have time for this.* The Icefalcon patted the brittle little shoulder blades and wished Hethya were there.

*And why didn't she wake Tir if he was sobbing in his sleep? Stupid wench, probably deep in some dream of tupping Ruvis or Mal or Dub or Dare of Renweth or Sergeant Red Boots or the Alketch Cavalry Corps . . .*

"Tir, listen to me." The storm seemed to be subsiding. "I'm here to get you out, but you must help me. Can you do that?"

Tir looked up at him again, wiped his eyes, and nodded.

"Good boy. I'm separated from my body now—my people call it shadow-walking—but I think I can get you out of this cell. I'm going to leave you now and scout a place outside the Keep where you can hide, a place for me to meet you and a route to get there. Then I'll return, tell you where to go, and get the guard to let you out."

"No," whispered Tir. "No, Icefalcon, please. Vair . . ."

He stammered a little, as if his throat closed in protest against even forming the name. He swallowed, mopped his cheeks, and made himself go on. "Vair will make me tell. About the stairway. About the rooms. That's what he's here for. That's what he wants."

"What lies there?" The Icefalcon's pale brows knit. He thought he'd had a clear view to the back of the succession of chambers and had seen nothing.

Tir shook his head violently. "He'll make me tell," he whispered. "Bektis will make me tell. There's a spell they can do . . . Icefalcon, *please*."

The boy began to tremble and hiccup, and the Icefalcon patted his shoulders again. "Sh-sh. Very well." He was thinking fast—and in truth, until he knew what Vair intended he did not know how much time he'd have. "How well do you know this Keep? Is there a place on the first level where you can hide? Close enough to the doors that you can get there quickly?"

Tir nodded. "There's places Bektis can't find me. Places magic doesn't work. Up there"—he pointed up the concealed stairway—"is one of them, but it's all grown up with plants in real life."

"Can you find another such? Good. When I leave you, you must wake and slip away as soon as the guard opens the door. Go quietly, so not to rouse Hethya."

"Can Hethya come with me? Icefalcon, please!" he added, feeling the warrior stiffen, and grabbed a handful of wolfskin vest as if he feared the Icefalcon would thrust him away. "She's sorry, and she hates Vair as much as I do, and she only helped him because she was afraid not to. He'll hurt her real bad if I run away and she doesn't. Please."

"And if she decides it's in her best interests that neither of you flee?" He still remembered her in the high Vale, soaked with the clone's blood and clutching her hair in false terror. Remembered her gazing down at the Keep and declaiming in the voice of Oale Niu.

"She won't. Please." His eyes filled, and he blinked

hard to keep them from running over: not a child's bid for pity, but fear for the sake of one who had been his only comfort. "She helped me, Icefalcon. I can't leave her."

He sighed. This was getting more and more complicated. "Let me speak to the wench."

She was dreaming about Ruvis. Or Mal or Dub or goodness knew who else—someone with long blond hair and muscular buttocks. The Icefalcon poked Hethya in the shoulder with his toe. She wriggled out from under and sat up, startled and protesting, hay in her rumpled hair: they were in a barn loft, sometime before the rising of the Dark. Wide windows opened to night and summer hay, and in the moment before Hethya's face and body assumed their present-day appearance she seemed no more than a girl of seventeen.

*And beautiful,* thought the Icefalcon. *Gay and wild as a pony in springtime.*

"You?" she said, clearly discomposed. She frowned. "You're the one . . ."

"Who rescued you in the Vale at the last quarter moon, the more fool I."

She scratched hay and flowers out of her hair and pulled up her bodice to cover a sailor's paradise of breast. Her handsome lover folded away into a trick of the moonlight.

"I can get you out of the cell," the Icefalcon said shortly. "Will you go? Tir can lead you to a hiding place while I find a route to get you to hiding outside the Keep the next time they open the Doors. Tir seems to trust you."

The lush mouth tightened down hard, and she looked aside. "Poor infant. Poor little child."

"Poor child indeed if he's got only you to guard him," retorted the Icefalcon, and she looked back at him in a flash of anger. "Or would you rather continue Vair's doxy?"

She struck at him, mouth square with anger and teeth bared, and he caught her wrist and twisted her out of his way. She pulled free, rubbing her wrist—in the dream they both had physical form or a very strong illusion of it—

banked rage like the dying fires of a burned house in her eyes. "And what choice have I, me lanky boy? To be killed by his troops the way they killed half the other women at Prandhays, after they'd raped the lot of us six ways from the backside of next week? To be made a slave to them or sold to some bandit troop for enough mules and sheep to mount the siege at Renweth and bring His Foulness this far?"

The Icefalcon asked quietly, "Is that what happened to your mother?"

"You leave me mother out of this, boy-o." She looked away, breathing hard, her face half veiled in the tangle of her hair.

"Me mother died the summer before last," she said finally. "Or that time of the year that should have been a summer, with the wheat rotten in the stem and us killin' the very cats for meat. There was fey wicked things in the woods then that killed some in the Keep—two of the little children and one of the herdboys that was Mother's pupil in spite of all his parents had to say about witches and souls. They killed Mother, too, I think—the things in the woods."

She brought up her hand, chewing her thumbnail, red mouth pulled down, ugly and hard.

"When old Vair and his stinking lot came marching up the road, there wasn't a great deal to be done nor any to say 'em nay. Her La'ship had made the Keep strong against the Dark Ones, but it'd been broken far back in the days, repaired strong, and broken again—Mother'd found the signs of it all around the walls, she said. It was nothing to Bektis and his putrid crystal Hand."

She sighed, looking down while she jerked the laces of her bodice tight. The Icefalcon propped a foot against a winnowing fork and rested his right hand on his sword-hilt. Even as a disembodied spirit within a dream he did not discount the possibility of attack.

"Mother always said the more we knew of the Keep—the more anybody knew of anything—the better everyone's chances would be. She'd always studied everything she could lay hand to. When she found all them papers and scrolls and tablets of gold and glass buried in the vaults of the Keep, she wouldn't rest till she'd read every one. She was like that. I don't know if you'd understand."

"I understand." The Icefalcon saw again Gil-Shalos' formidable collection and ink-stained, bandaged fingers.

"Well, there was a deal of apparatus in the Keep," Hethya went on. "Things Degendna Marina didn't tell the Lady Minalde about, and we kept finding more. Men would hunt for it in the vaults and in these sort of tombs in the hills north of Prandhays. Somebody found if you buried bits of it under your fields the insects wouldn't eat the corn—at least that's what they claimed. Or that it would draw deer into traps, or put under a mattress would let a man be seven times a hero in bed, though *that* was wishful thinking so far as I could ever tell. Still, those who found the stuff, for all me mother's pleading and her La'ship's orders, they'd break it up and sell the bits to any who'd aught to trade for it: a bit of land that bordered the spring or a cell closer to the fountains or the latrines, or maybe just a fine iron pot. I bought back pieces of it for her, whenever I could. I told her I traded sewing for it."

Her eyes met his, steadily, jeeringly, daring him to speak.

He only said, "Ah."

"Well." She let out her breath. "And for nothing, in the end of it all. Mother had parchments, drawings of these things, and how some of them worked, all written out as far as she could figure 'em, though they could only be worked by wizards. She said a lot of the instructions weren't clear even at that, or had gone missing over the years." She waded through the hay to the loft windows, jade moonlight and oceanic dark.

"Like it?"

The Icefalcon followed politely. Stubble meadows and neat orchards lay half guessed behind hurdles of withe, fruit gleaming faintly among inky leaves. Sheep grazed the stubble. Somewhere someone played a mandolin; a drum tapped dance rhythms.

He thought, *The heart of mud-digger laziness.* But there was pride in her voice.

"Father loved this farm, put his heart and his sweat and his soul in it. He kept asking me when I'd decide which beau to wed so he could train him up in its management, the way he tried to train me. Poor Dad."

She shook her head. "I was too much Mother's daughter to be a yeoman farmer, but I hadn't her power. Even all her reading, I just followed what I chose of it, for the fun of the thing. I never knew all those lists of True Names she was after memorizing, nor could tell a sassafras from a dogwood. But when Vair and his boys showed up and started lookin' about for anyone they could sell, I rolled up my eyes and went into a fit and gave it all to 'em about Oale Niu. She was originally a princess I'd made up stories about, I and me girlfriend Lotis, when we were little—later on I told 'em to me daughter. Lotis was dead by the time Vair came."

She looked back over her round white shoulder at him, watching his reaction from under thick lashes. Below them her father's land lay still and sweet, like the Night River Country before the coming of the Ice.

Should someone enter his dreams, he wondered, would they walk through the flowering reed beds along the Night River or see otters there playing in the birch-fringed pools?

"Is that what you were after learning, me bonny iceberg? Who this slut is that lets Vair tell her what to do?"

"No," the Icefalcon said, more quietly than he had spoken at first. "What I want to know is, will you hide with Tir in the Keep until I can get you both out? Look after the boy? Not hand him over to Vair to save your own skin?"

Hethya sighed and pressed her forehead to the wood of the window frame. " 'Tis madness." She sounded weary unto death. "He'll find us in time. He needs the child. Whatever it is the boy knows he won't be letting him go."

"The Keep is large," said the Icefalcon. "Tir knows it. You don't happen to know what it is that Vair is so eager to learn?"

Her head moved again, *No*. "I'm not so sure the child himself knows, poor little lamb, for all that Bektis was after telling our stinkissimo about the memories of the House of Dare. If their memories were so bloody exact, why didn't old Eldor remember how they'd put the Dark Ones to rout, instead of lettin' a thousand men die that could have stayed in Prandhays and kept the bandits away? Liars," she whispered, shutting her eyes in despair. "All of 'em, liars."

Sadness crept into the darkness, the hopeless grief that colored her dream. Far off, as if on the other side of the trees, he saw the reflected glow of flames in the sky and heard the shouting of warriors looting, the screams of women.

"Will you go with Tir?" he pressed her. "Help him to hide? Not give him over to Vair? You know once Vair's forced what he wants of Tir, you'll just be handed over to the troops again."

He felt the flash of her hatred for him, for speaking of it, but he only spoke truth and she knew it. At length she let her breath out in a sigh and said, "Aye. Aye, friend ghost, you open that door for us and I'll do it. How much worse can matters get?"

The Icefalcon forbore to enlighten her on that head and said only, "Good. Wake now, and wake the boy. By the next time you sleep I'll have scouted a way through the warriors outside."

The Icefalcon's one fear, as he stepped through the desiccated wood of the door, was that the clone had succumbed to possession of demons or that he had been joined by another man. There were demons in the corridor, tiny floating lights that sometimes had the appearance of eyes, and a cold

and sluggish elemental of some kind, hissing and whispering in a circle around the warrior and reaching out to
pinch his toes. He was one—the Icefalcon remembered—
of a clone group of thirteen, and by the dull glaze of the
man's eyes the Icefalcon guessed he wasn't far from a state
of permanent dream. In any case it shouldn't be difficult to
step into the dreaming halls of that vacant awareness.

Nor was it. At the last instant before going in the Icefalcon smelled what was in there, but it was too late to
stop: he should have realized, he thought, that having no
mind to speak of, the clone would recall its only memory.

Pain. Over, and over, and over.

As when the demons ripped his flesh, it did little good
for the Icefalcon to tell himself that this was illusion, and
somebody else's illusion at that. The pain drowned him, a
vat of fire and worse than fire: blinding, specific, agonizing. The pain of the skin bursting at every needle's
entry point and peeling slowly back. The pain of every
sinus and cavity of the skull bloating up with blood until
the membranes burst. The pain of every nerve-fiber out-
lining itself in scalding heat, searing into a pain-ghost
strong enough to reduplicate its image down to the
smallest screaming shred of oozing flesh . . .

*Not real. Not real. Not real.*

Disorientation, horror, cold, and the laughter of demons
who'd seen it coming.

Mind, consciousness, concentration crumpling under
the blinding assault, the Icefalcon could only speak to the
hazy fragments of consciousness that remained in the
clone:

"Unbolt the door behind you, then walk to that first corridor and go down it until you reach a wall." He could
barely get the words out and then dropped out of the man's
dreaming, to lie sobbing on the black stone floor while all
around him the demons shrieked and bit each other with
laughter and the sodden elemental rolled over onto him to
see if there was anything of him it could absorb.

*Oh, get off me, you stupid wad of slime.* The Icefalcon

slid wearily aside. *And the pack of you have my permission to sodomize one another repeatedly with splintery sticks.*

Howling with mirth, the demons manifested the ghostly echoes of splintery sticks. The Icefalcon looked away, repelled.

He couldn't imagine any being sufficiently stupid as to obey his bald and desperate instruction, but then, Gil frequently told him he had no imagination. Very much to his surprise, the clone got to his feet, slid back the door bolt, and ambled through the daisy chain of demons and down the corridor, to vanish around the first available corner. The Icefalcon started to repeat Rudy Solis' favorite expression of astonishment—*Well, I'll be buggered*—looked at the demons, and said instead, "My goodness me."

As he got to his feet the door opened.

Hethya looked scared, but, curiously enough, considering all he'd been through, Tir only wore an expression of quiet alertness, with a trace of the inward look he got when he went fishing through the ancient darkness of other people's memories. He whispered, "This way." Hethya paused long enough to check the lamp—which she had almost covered with its pierced lid—and latch the door again before she followed.

Demons frisking around him, the Icefalcon made his way down the hall to where the clone stood, facing the blank black inner wall of the Keep.

*It will hurt. I will let the pain pass through me and give it to the Watchers behind the Stars, who eat pain.*

He stepped into the man's dreaming again, fast, and said, "Turn around, go back up this corridor and to the latched door again. Sit down outside it as you were."

He still lay on the floor, groggy with shock, trying hard to keep his spirit from dissipating until the pain's echoes lessened, when the clone and its attendant pack of demons rounded the corner.

*So much,* he thought, *for that.*

It took him a little time, pacing the Keep's straight black corridors, to find Tir and Hethya. Even as a shadow-walking dream, he moved as he had in his waking body, though he could stride faster than they because of his height.

The Keep might be intact, but it was a crazy-house nevertheless, clogged with foliage, corridors and stairs blocked entirely by lichen and molds, by mushrooms colorless as dead men's flesh and the size of newborn lambs. In some rooms light shone, curious and sickly and from no apparent source, and these rooms were choked thick with growths that then spread through corridors. In others—and not necessarily those near the outer wall of the Keep—there was no heat at all and frost coated the walls three and four inches thick, the ceilings turned to wildernesses of icicles and the floors to knee-deep mountains of cauliflower ice.

Tir and Hethya had to turn back repeatedly, either because the corridors were clogged or because they could afford to leave no track, either in frost or leaves.

"The Icefalcon said—in my dream he said—Rudy and Mama were still alive." Tir's voice was tiny, a despairing whisper of hope as they stole through the square-cornered warrens. "He said Vair was just lying. Do you think that was true? Don't step there," he added, pulling Hethya back from a stretch where ice sparkled in a sugary shroud. "We have to go around again."

"Me blueberry, I don't know." Hethya squeezed his too thin shoulder. Her breath was smoke in the firefly glow of their lamp. "Vair's a born liar sure enough, but a born liar can still tell the truth, and Bektis hit your friend with enough levin-fire to stop a megathere in its tracks, and that's a fact. Sometimes it's best just to put it from your mind, sweetheart, and not tell yourself yes or no. Your ma may still be alive, and him just sayin' she's dead so you won't try to get away back to her, but it's a bad world, and bad things happen. Can you put it aside, tuck it up in a little box in your heart, till it's time to find out?"

Tir swallowed. "I can try."

The Icefalcon followed them until Tir, after long trial and error marked by two more dim chimes of the endless clock, found the cell he sought, a double in the far front

corner of the second level, marked with Runes of Silence
and reached by an inconspicuous stair whose entry was
hidden by one of those tricks of shadow and perspective so
dear to the mages of the Times Before. There he left them
and started back the short way for the Doors, having no
fear of leaving his footprints in the frost. Being only
shadow himself he saw clearly in darkness, but it seemed
to him, descending the hidden stair and striding quickly
along the straight silent passageways, that the darkness
lay somehow thicker than it had, thicker than it should.

He paused, tingling in all his nerves. Far off, at the end
of the corridor, something moved: three violet lights, not
the marshfire flicker of demons, but something else. Then
darkness again, and a moment later, soft and thready, a
breath of a whistled tune.

The cold that had tortured him since the shedding of his
flesh redoubled, curling around the shadows of his bones
and clutching tight. Not fear, he told himself, but reasonable caution made him back away and seek another route
downward to the Aisle and the Doors.

Not fear at all.

But as he hastened along the corridor the Icefalcon
heard the ghosts of demon laughter and the slow, horrible
knocking that seemed to come from nowhere, a giant fist
hammering the stone. Somewhere a man cried out in fear,
and when he passed a wall white with frost the Icefalcon
saw clumsy words scrawled in the white crystals, higher
than a man could reach. There were no footprints on the
frost below.

Tir was hiding in this haunted place. The Icefalcon
quickened his stride for the Aisle.

There was torchlight there, and hemp-oil lamps. Voices
echoed far less than they did in Renweth, for the sharpness
of the sound was absorbed by the muck underfoot and the
leathery monstrosity growing into darkness. Even the voices
of enemies were a comfort after the darkness, the sight of
men engaged in mundane tasks like sorting weapons and
boots and blankets under the eye of their sergeants.

As the Icefalcon watched, another clone dropped his load of cornmeal, flung up his arms, and fled away into the chamber's vast darkness, leaping and dancing and shrieking with demon laughter. The sergeant in charge turned uncertainly toward a doorway behind whose brittle, decaying louvers the white glow of magefire burned. But in the end he hadn't the courage to enter. From that doorway the Icefalcon heard Vair's harsh snap of orders and the scrape and chink of metal.

They were setting up the vat, thought the Icefalcon, and wondered what substance the generalissimo would use this time to flesh out the numbers of his creations. The Talking Stars People had gotten most of the mules.

Not that the Icefalcon had any intention of lingering to find out. The naked cold of being bodiless had grown to a torment, and the ever-present sense of suffocation, the formless anxiety and grief, were making it harder and harder to concentrate. He felt weary and scraped, exhausted and craving sleep—Cold Death had warned him against sleep.

It would be night outside. His mind was already charting the passageway between the two sets of Doors— cleared now of weeds—gauging the hundred feet of slick blue ice tunnel to be negotiated . . .

He stepped between two clones and laid his hands on the locked inner Doors.

And could not pass through.

The shock was an abrupt one, almost physical. After a little practice he had moved through wood or stone or metal like a ghost—matters of the physical world as irrelevant to him as the pains of demons.

But the Doors were magic. The wall in which they were set was magic, wrought long ago to forbid the passage of the Dark Ones. Probably—although he certainly meant to check it inch by inch—the whole of the outer wall of the Keep was so imbued with spells.

As long as the Doors were shut, he was trapped.

# CHAPTER FIFTEEN

"I will eat them all!" The deep toneless shouting hammered flatly on the black walls, echoing from some remote place. "I will eat them up!"

"What's he saying?" Tir asked almost without sound, not sure if he understood the ha'al speech correctly. There was a goatish sound to the words, not human at all.

Hethya turned the horn cover of the lamp just the tiniest bit, uncovering only a hole or two, enough to outline the white leathery leaves, the unspeakable shapes of the fungal horrors that crusted the snout of the fountain where it emerged from the wall.

"He's talking of eating everything or everybody." The words were a bare whisper. They'd already learned that sound carried farther in the straight halls of the Keep of Shadow. "He's gone mad, I think. It'll be one of the clones."

While Tir stayed back with the lamp, Hethya edged between the obscene jungles to what had been the fountain's basin and dipped both their water bottles full. Some of the leaves were white, others black and shiny as jewels or furred like bison, shapes barely recognizable as what had been the leaves of potatoes, or peas, or squash. "Faith, you'd think they'd die in the dark, after all these years."

"They grow on magic." Tir drank gratefully from the dripping bottle she handed him. "They should have dirt and stuff to eat, too, like we do at the Keep—Lord Brig showed me, he's in charge of the crypts—but there's magic here, too." He shivered, and it seemed to him that the bleached leaves moved. "The magic is still alive."

"Faith." She hooked the water bottles to her belt, listening. Far off came a dull pounding, like a moron child beating on a wall, but huge and viciously strong. As she moved off Tir caught something, some anomalous shape, from the corner of his eye and turned back to look.

For a moment there was a trick of shadow, of the movement of the lamp no doubt, where the tangled vines swung and clustered around the fountain, so that Tir's heart stood still with terror.

But there really wasn't anyone there.

Not a gleam of bald-shaved head or deep-sunk watching eyes.

The noise he'd thought for one instant to be a soft-whistled tune was only the wind moving through the corridors.

The thought came into his mind, *You'd be happier away from the light. Happier in the dark alone.*

Tir knew he would be. Since leaving the dark warm protection of the Keep of Dare he had encountered nothing but pain and terror and grief, and he never wanted to go outdoors again.

Still, he turned away and hurried after Hethya, and tried not to listen to what was almost a voice, whispering among the leaves in the dark.

They had to open the Doors sometime.

The Icefalcon stood, his whole existence a hideous wrack of anxiety, in the lambent golden shadows of the triple cell Vair had taken as his theater of operations, watching the generalissimo and his tame mage argue.

"Savages!" Bektis' gray velvet sleeve bellied like a wing with the theatrical indignation of his gesture. "Savages! Too stupid to consider using the apparatus for their own advantage, though of course they never could. But they don't know that. And they're too stupid even to try!"

Vair regarded him narrowly across the table set up at the

head of the vat. "And this is what you see, is it, sorcerer, in that scrying glass of yours? That the *karnach* no longer exists?"

"My Lord, the White Raiders began dismantling it before our Doors were even sealed! They've smashed the luminar—broken the core rods—" His honey-flower tenor went squeaky with fury, the only time the Icefalcon had truly believed him to be a mage as Ingold was a mage, with a mage's instincts. "What they couldn't break they tipped into crevasses in the ice! It is gone, my Lord! Gone!"

"And so you don't have to put yourself in peril by attempting to retrieve it?" Vair cocked his head, primrose eyes cold. "Is that what you're telling me?"

Bektis drew himself tall, his beard rippling with the jut of his chin. The Icefalcon noted briefly that Bektis' beard, though waist-length and white as winter ermine, was perfectly combed and bore none of the matted and sweaty appearance of the hair and beards of Vair's warriors. He must work at it for hours a day. Even Vair's long gray hair, though dressed back in a ridge, looked as if he'd been through a battle. Perhaps a spell kept the wizard's beard clean?

"What I'm saying is truth, my Lord!"

Vair lowered his eyes again, counting out the crystalline needles from their box. He worked deftly, moving them onto the tabletop with his single hand. The Icefalcon, his mind still charred by the memories of the clones his shadow had spoken to, could barely look at them, could barely endure remaining in this room. The doorway and the ceiling's four corners were strung with demon-scares, which was a relief, for it was growing more and more difficult to push aside the demons and elementals that oozed through the clogged darkness and snuffed among the bleeding lichens.

"Truth includes the fact that you turned tail quickly enough when the Raiders charged. I thought you had spells of illusion, spells of fear."

"Spells of illusion and fear only guarantee a battle if the enemy isn't ready for them, Lord. The Raiders have followed us since we came onto the ice . . ."

*Longer than that, old man.*

"And they quite clearly have a shaman of their own." He fussed at the gold-mesh straps that held the crystalline Device to his hand, and the Icefalcon, close to him for the first time, saw that the edges of the thing had worn the flesh into oozing blisters on wrist and fingers and also, he now saw, beneath the jeweled collar that was evidently part of the ensemble.

*He must be sleeping in it.*

Yet there was no sign of padding, no sign that he had put a bandage or wrap of any sort between his skin and the enchanted metal and stone.

"Without the power of civilized magic, you understand, they were no match for me . . ."

"But they were strong enough to frighten you?"

"There was no point in continuing."

"Hear me, Bektis, Servant of Illusion." Vair raised his head from his counting, and his voice was level, chill as iron left outside to freeze. "And hear me well. I saved you from the wrath of the Bishop Govannin for one purpose and one purpose only, that you assist me in retaking my rights to the lands of the South. You proved useless against that bitch Yori-Ezrikos in open battle, even with that precious bauble of yours."

Bektis clutched his jeweled hand to his breast, irrational fury blanching his face. "I would scarcely say that saving you, and twelve hundred of your men, from being slain by your wife was 'useless,' my Lord. Nor the knowledge I've given you about the weapons and Devices that may still exist, hidden in Dare's Keep. And this bauble, as you call it, is the Hand of Harilómne, greatest of the . . ."

"I don't care if it's the second-best festival hat of God's Mother. Your Harilómne, for all his talk of studying the Devices of the Times Before, may have been as great a faker as yourself. I'm a patient man, Bektis. You will help me in this matter now, or you will find that my forbearance runs thin. Do you understand?"

"*You* do not understand . . ." Bektis was still clutching at the Hand of Harilómne, trembling with rage. Then he seemed to recollect himself and lowered his eyes. "I understand, my Lord."

"Good." Vair returned to sorting the needles, white-gloved fingers arranging them by crystal, iron, gold. "Now you inform me a new band of Raiders is moving up from the south. So we have little time. As soon as it grows light you will cast your illusions, make the Raiders outside the tunnel believe there is something—a stray mammoth, perhaps, or something else edible—that they must seek a good distance away. Near a crevasse, if possible, where we can gather up their bodies from the bottom. I need men, Bektis." He pushed the last of the needles in its place, with obsessive neatness, and raised his eyes again. "Four more of the Hastroaals have died and two of the Ugals gone mad."

"My Lord, I warned you about mixing the flesh of the source with other things."

"And despite your warnings I have eighty men where I would only have had a score. To accomplish the taking of Dare's Keep I will need as many again, and again. Have the Raiders gathered up the bodies of the slain?"

Bektis inclined his head. "They lie in a crevasse in the ice, not far from the tunnel mouth. Not deep." He still toyed with the Hand, stroking the smooth facets of the jewels, as if for reassurance.

"Good. And they'll certainly be fresh. You're to go with Prinyippos and his party when they fetch them and retrieve any fragments of the *karnach* that you can find."

"My Lord . . ."

"At dawn, Bektis." Vair started for the door. "That's— what? Two chimes of the clock from now?"

Bektis inclined his head again, not looking happy. "Two chimes it is, my Lord. But . . ."

Vair turned like a panther, a sudden swirling movement

that startled even the Icefalcon, his left hand jerking free the curved sword at his waist. His draw was slow, the Icefalcon noted—it was hard to bring the hooks to bear to steady the scabbard—but there was trained and deadly speed as he dropped to fighting stance: "What was that?"

Bektis had fluttered back, startled, out of the way, and only shook his head. "What was what, Lord?" His voice squeaked with panic.

Slowly Vair straightened and walked back to the table where he had been arranging the needles.

In their midst lay a woman's comb, black horn set with three garnets. There was nothing in the least odd about it—Vair sheathed his sword awkwardly to pick it up—except that it had not been there before.

Demons fed on the magic buried deep in the walls of the Keep. Knockings and murmurings filled the darkness. Climbing the stairs that Tir had climbed in his dreams, traversing passageways knee-deep in dead black brittle vines that made not a sound under his shadowy feet, the Icefalcon heard them. Lights flickered among the choking plugs of lichen and fungus, glistened on the beards of icicles that depended from cracked ceilings and broken fountains. In the Aisle, or in those chambers where the clones stacked weapons and food, small objects would sometimes rise up and fling themselves against the walls. One man ran shrieking into the corridor, striking at something no one else could see as the marks of teeth appeared in his cheeks and hands.

The Icefalcon moved on. The chambers that had been clear in Tir's dream, behind the triple archway and the rose windows on the Aisle's northeastern wall, were an impassable bolus of mutant groundnut and squashes through which he slipped like water.

*Vair will make me lead him there,* Tir had said.

*But why?*

The hall of the crystal pillars was dead to magic and clear of the encroachment of vegetation. So was the round

vestibule with its tiny doors—from whom did they expect
an attack this deep in the center of the Keep? The Dark
Ones could change size at will. Another chamber close by,
spherical and small, a round lens of heavy crystal in one
wall that showed the hall of the pillars—the Icefalcon
looked but could see no Rune of Silence worked into its
doors or walls. Something that by its leaves had once been
a bean plant had filled most of one wall with clinging runners and the floor with a mulch of stinking decay.

A guardroom?

The clock chimed dimly in the distance. Warily, the Icefalcon passed through the vestibule's door, and despite the
pain that grew steadily in him, the ache and coldness that
more and more threatened to swamp his concentration, he
felt also the tenseness of danger, the sense of something
waiting for him in the dark.

Waiting, he thought, for a long time.

But even the eyes of shadow that could see demons saw
nothing amiss. Bare black walls, bare black floor. From
the door he had a clear view through all the archways to
the end of the succession of ever-shrinking rooms, and all
were bare to the walls. To the best of his recollection it had
been so in Tir's dream.

Or had he, the Icefalcon, shadow-walker and interloper,
seen only part of the child's dreaming memory?

Had there been something in that final chamber, hidden
behind the two men whose shadows lurched across the
walls?

Or did he dream, too, now?

He walked the length of the great chamber, passed between the crystal pilasters, crossed the smaller room behind. A sound made him turn, but there was nothing. Only
the blank ebon walls.

More slowly he walked on, and from somewhere he
heard the thread of someone whistling—a phrase of music,
then silence.

A smaller room, crystal pillars, a chamber smaller yet.
Beyond another arch another chamber, dark and tiny and

anonymous; another arch. The cold in the core of his mind was almost overwhelming, icy panic and growing darkness, and a sense that he trod where he should not tread.

*Go back.*

*Go back or die.*

Was it his ancestors who spoke to him? Black Hummingbird, who had first slept on the slopes of Haunted Mountain, to hold the shell and the iron flower that let him hear the voices of the Stars? One of the Dream Things—the Flowered Caterpillar or the Mouse's Child—that sometimes lied and sometimes told the truth? Or something in the blackness, something that was trying to keep him from this final secret, the secret Tir had begged not to be forced to reveal?

It seemed to him that more crystal pilasters glittered before him, a double line of them. Surely there had been only four rooms, three archways? He counted three or four more before him, and a guessing of others beyond.

A trap?

A man sat in the darkness before him, a little to one side of the next arch.

There was something very wrong with the darkness, something amiss about the shape and perception of that chamber and the next. Voices seemed to be murmuring all around him, a mutter of anger, desperation, and a loneliness that had long ago plunged over the black edge of abyssal madness.

*Go back. Go back right now.*

The man before him stood. "Nyagchilios?" He spoke his true name, the name of the pilgrim-falcon in the tongue of the Talking Stars. "Icefalcon?"

The Icefalcon retreated, terror of a trap flaring in him, a trap whose nature he could not even guess. But he knew, as surely as he knew the name the man had said, that if he lingered even another few moments he would be caught in some unguessable doom. Carefully, never turning his back, he edged away, through chamber after chamber, toward the door.

The man—or illusion, he wasn't sure which—took a step or two after him, then stopped. But the Icefalcon could see him between the pilasters as he retreated, see him clearly in the dark: the broad shoulders beneath a ragged mantle of brown wool, the close-cropped white beard and the face gouged with scars and creases and laugh lines. Blue eyes that hid terrible knowledge under wise brightness, like sunlight on the well at the cosmos' heart.

If any illusion could have called him into the gullet of a snare, thought the Icefalcon, it would have been that one. Because of all people he could have summoned to his aid, the first on his list would certainly have been Ingold Inglorion.

The second chime sounded as the Icefalcon emerged from the narrow door of the vestibule. He hastened down the hidden stair, passed like a fleeting ghost through the jungle of vines. It was in his mind to make a detour and fetch Tir and Hethya, but aside from the fact that they would undoubtedly still be awake, it would do them little good to walk straight into the arms of Bektis. Who he needed now, he thought, was Cold Death. There had to be a way to send warning to Blue Child and her band that the illusion of the hunt they pursued would lead them to disaster. Possibly Cold Death knew it already.

The Doors stood open. Lamps gleamed in the dense white mists of the passage, in the ice tunnel that stretched beyond. The cold there cut his brain like a knife, but he welcomed it: he was out of the Keep, out of the trap of its walls, running now for the sleeping flesh of his body like a jack hare running for his burrow, with the glowing hounds of hell coming behind.

The bright glare of morning smote him.

He was free.

Another war band coming up, he thought. Some scouting or hunting party that had cut the trail of the Earthsnake People and followed to see what hunting they sought in the Ice in the North.

What hunting indeed?

He would not, he thought, pausing, be able to see them once he returned to his flesh.

It was dangerous, the tearing and weight of exhaustion and pain tightening on him like the tightening of the torture boot or the rack.

Still, he was going to be coming back this way in his human flesh to lead Tir and Hethya to freedom. After a moment's thought, the Icefalcon flung himself skyward, flying the way Gil-Shalos—and long ago Dove in the Sun—had told him that they flew in dreams.

The ice dropped away below him. Seracs reared like fortresses, arêtes and nunataks traced in black the shape of buried mountains behind the green-white blister of the ice. Higher the Icefalcon rose, through a gray mistiness that almost hid the land. It would be easy, he thought, to become lost here, to become lost entirely from his body. To rise and rise, above all cloud, until his soul united with sun and air.

He understood suddenly that the pain and cold and loneliness he felt were the result of trying to hold the shape of the body that lay somewhere in the Ice. The terror and suffocation would last only as long as he clung to the memory of that shape, clung to the illusion of lungs and heart, the intention of returning to that abandoned flesh. Indeed, they were nearly unbearable now. If he embraced the sunlight and the air, he would be free.

Or was that another illusion of the demons of the air?

He looked about him, as his namesake would look about for the white hares of the ice.

He saw the crevasse where Blue Child had tipped the broken Dark Lightning: no child of the Real World would hold a weapon that could so easily be taken back by its original owners and turned again. Antlike men slipped and fell near the crevasse with the clumsiness of those who had never navigated on snow, hauling what pieces they could find or dragging the bodies of the slain.

To the west he saw Blue Child's band—nowhere near any crevasse—and among the rock ridges southeast of the Keep's bubble the dark ragged assemblage of the Earth-snake People. Far off, coming up from the south on the trails left by the others, was the new band, well over two hundred strong. The Icefalcon flew toward them, effort-less as a silver rag of cloud. From the air he recognized Breaks Noses, younger brother to Loses His Way, war leader of the Empty Lakes People. Bundled thick in double-sewn fur and mammoth wool, others followed him: Buttonwillow, Spindle, and Doesn't Bathe. The friends and kin of Loses His Way. And with them Beautiful Girl, the mother of Twin Daughter—the wife of Loses His Way.

Cold raked him, tearing his attention, shredding his mind. Terror swamped him, and he was falling again, plunging toward the white and blue and black of the broken ice. Gray things and darkness clotted his sight and the laughter of the winds his hearing.

Elementals.

It was hard now to pull his attention away, hard to fight clear of the terror, to remember that he had no bones to break. He couldn't breathe, and weariness rent him be-yond bearing. He saw the shadow-form of his hands and arms that had once been clothed in wolf-hide tunic, in the appearance he knew, torn tatters of ripped clothing, flesh gone and bones bare from biceps to wrist. Something like a vast spider of cloud and ice-fog clawed out his entrails, and he could not think his body whole again. Elementals vast as mammoths walked over the snow below him like pond-skimmers, waiting for him to land.

*Go away. Go away. Go away.*

He leveled out a few feet above the snow, hearing them like swarming bees above his head. A flying tangle of shreds and bones, he skimmed the broken whiteness, dodged be-tween hummocks and ridges, seeking the crevasse where his body lay. The thoughts of the air and the brilliant, hurting sunlight frightened him now, and he found himself crying for the comforting armor of muscle and bone.

Voices below, cold and hard as the shattering of glass. A bellowed war cry and the clash of steel. Light exploding among the gashes in the ice, and columns of steam, hard and nearly tactile, marble and diamonds and then gray, all-choking fog.

Dread such as he had never known slammed his heart.

He dropped to the ice at the head of the crevasse, leaped down the jagged blocks as though possessed again of human legs and human muscles. Tracks of booted feet marred the snow before him, booted feet and those bound in rawhide. Another levin-bolt and the crack of thunder, another billow of steam. The Icefalcon raced between the narrow sapphire walls, hearing a man curse in the choking mists. "Little bitch got away."

*No,* thought the Icefalcon. *No.*

"Don't kill that one." He heard Crested Egret's voice as he came around the projecting shoulder of ice and saw four or five clones holding the struggling, thrashing Loses His Way, dragging him down with their sheer weight. Two clones lay dead in the crumble of snow, and a third sat bowed over, his back to the frozen wall, numbly clutching his belly.

Bektis emerged from the fog, stuffing his chilblained hand, the Hand of Harilómne still flashing on his fingers, into an ermine muff. The smoke of a heat-spell surrounded him, mingling white with the general vapors as he scrambled down from where the deeper gash of the chasm narrowed and ascended. He was panting and looked put out. Even his beard was mussed. "You should have those guards of yours flogged," he snapped at the little officer. "The fools let her slip by!"

Crested Egret's expression did not change. "I'll see it done, Lord sorcerer." He had a prim voice—he was one of the Alketch who, like Vair, had kept up shaving even in the wilds and battles of the North. "Which of them failed you?"

Bektis hesitated a moment, looking from man to man of those standing near, then said, "That one, that one, and that one," pointing—at random, the Icefalcon thought. Two of the men looked startled and angry; the other, a clone, seemed barely aware that he'd been singled out. Before anything further could be said someone called out, "Here's another!"

*No. No. No.*

Steam still poured in a misty river from the ice-cave where they'd spent . . . last night? The night before? Two clones emerged dragging something. Loses His Way flung himself against his captors like a chained bull and bellowed.

They were carrying the Icefalcon's body.

"Dead, sir," said one of the clones. The Icefalcon knew those words from his time in the South.

"Your little pretty-boy, is it?" another added in a kind of mixed dialect as Loses His Way wrenched at the hands that held him. "Not bad," said someone else, or something along those lines; there was crude laughter and jostling.

Crested Egret silenced them with a couple of flat, yapped orders, and they bound Loses His Way, not without difficulty, and slung the Icefalcon's body on the sledge with the two dead clones and the wounded man. All the men worked together to drag the sledge back out of the crevasse, slipping and skidding and falling on the ice.

*No.* The Icefalcon was trembling, or would have been, he thought, had he flesh to tremble in. He ran back along the mist-drowned crevasse, seeking Cold Death—meltpools and scars, blue as glass, showed where Bektis had struck at her with the lightning of his crystal Hand, which had evidently been designed for single combat and spells rather than armies or groups. But of Cold Death herself he could find nothing.

The fog was thick here, and demons slipped like lampreys from the ice walls, reaching out to him with thin white hands of pain.

*Cold Death!* He tried to call his sister's name. *Cold Death!*

But there was nothing. Frantic, he turned and ran after Bektis and the retreating guards through the bloodstained snow to the blue tunnel, keeping as far behind them as he dared. Hurting, shaken, and more frightened than he had ever been, he saw before him the black Doors of the Keep framing torchlight within. The dead chime of the clock reached out to meet him, and as the warriors dragged their booty through—living and dead and one body that was not quite either—the Icefalcon slipped in after them and heard the Doors shut again behind.

# CHAPTER SIXTEEN

"Huh," said Hethya. "So it's yourself again."

She'd been dreaming about her daughter and the forest Keep. Dreaming about the rooms that had been carved off the crypts in those long years between the time when the Dark Ones had returned to their underground realms and the time when the forest Keeps had ceased to be fortresses with the return of order and the rule of the High Kings of Gae.

She'd been playing hide-and-seek with her child while her scholar mother investigated the caches of long-buried junk at the bottom of those twisty wooden stairs: hibernant glowstones gone dark with time, old chests of brown brittle scrolls, broken furniture and hidden doorways concealing still-deeper fastnesses, still-more-curious treasures. Her daughter could only toddle but staggered with a child's blithe tumbledown delight among the shadowy warrens, barely illuminated by the lamps that Hethya and her mother bore; her laughter was gay in the dark.

But with the Icefalcon's appearance in the crypts of Prandhays Keep Hethya transfigured once more to a woman of thirty, a little blowsy, a little haggard, with bitter eyes and the dirty hair of one who has traveled far and hard. She put her hands on her hips, and leaned her back against a plastered archway, and asked, "And what is it you'll be wanting now?"

It was hard to speak the words. "Your help," he said. "Please."

The Icefalcon took her hand—his own no more than

shreds of flesh clinging to white bone—and led her across into the Shadow Keep, dark tunnels cancerous with fungus and strange white ivies. He was very cold now, disoriented and weary beyond speaking, every wound and gash given him by the demons of the misty air open, bleeding, weakening him; drawing away his concentration from the task of keeping bone and flesh clear in his memory. The sun kept coming back into his mind, and the free flight in the air, the desire to dissolve and to sleep.

He was beginning to realize that he might not make it back to his body. If it were destroyed he knew he would not last long but did not know what would become of him in that event.

"Did you find a way out?" asked Hethya. A reasonable request, but in his weariness he felt a flash of dull rage at her, a desire, unprecedented in his experience, to strike her across the face.

"No." It was unworthy of a person of the Talking Stars—and also a pointless expenditure of energy—to show anger. Also, he would not give her that. So he kept his voice neutral. "I was unable to leave the Keep until the Doors opened, and then I found Bektis had encountered Cold Death: she fled from him, I know not where. Here."

There was a guard outside the door of the triple cell where the vat and its horrors had been set up, one of the very few that still possessed a solid door. The corpses of the slain had been dragged there and heaped in a corner; bundled bales of dead foliage and whatever else could be gathered: fungus, the last of the wood, a dead mule. A new, stout bar had been slotted into the makeshift sockets on the door, though the Icefalcon knew that Loses His Way was bound. Had he not been, the wood, long dehydrated in the cold, might not have held him.

Because it was a dream the Icefalcon passed easily through the thick wood, and Hethya stepped gamely behind.

"Faith!" she whispered, shocked.

Not, the Icefalcon was certain, because of the bodies.

Anyone who had passed through the Time of the Dark had seen bodies, in all stages of decomposition and ruin. Certainly this woman had seen worse if she'd watched the making of the clones. Even the fact that the clones had begun to decay in the warmth of the Keep was something she already knew. She went over to where the Icefalcon's own body lay on the pile, forehead and eyelids smudged with the remains of Cold Death's ward-spells, and touched his face, something the Icefalcon found extremely disturbing.

"Faith, are you a ghost, then?"

"No." He said it a good deal more vehemently than he had intended. "I am alive, only separated from my flesh for the time being." It crossed his mind to wonder whether that was in fact the case. Whether removal from the ice-cave, and from Cold Death's spells, had in fact killed the life-spark of the emptied flesh so that he would return only to die as the body died.

*Could* he return at all without Cold Death's help?

"But I can be of no help to you if I return to my flesh in a locked room with guards outside. You will have to get me out."

On the floor beside the piled corpses, Loses His Way lay chained, spanceled the way the Alketch spanceled deserters or criminals, wrists locked to ankles, with a cord around his neck tied to the short chain that joined the ankle manacles, only long enough to permit him to breathe as long as he did not struggle. While the Icefalcon watched, Loses His Way tried to twist free his wrists nevertheless, veins bulging out at his temples with the tightening of the noose, until he dropped back limp again, chest heaving with the thread of incoming air.

"Leave it, me bonny," said Hethya softly, going to kneel beside him. "Leave it, you great fool. You'll only murder yourself." Her hand reached again, touched the blood-smeared red-gold hair.

The Icefalcon heard footfalls in the corridor and stepped back, shadow hand touching shadow sword. Hethya, her

eyes on Loses His Way's face, swung around in shock
as the door opened and Vair na-Chandros strode in at
the head of a small squad of warriors, and her hand went to
her mouth. "They can't see you," pointed out the Icefalcon, catching her arm to steady her. It interested him
that for once she did not scream. "This is only a dream,
you know."

Vair gestured to the dead. The clones, without a word
spoken, began to strip them, pulling off footgear, weapons,
furs. He glanced down at Loses His Way and said to Bektis
in the Wathe, "What do you think? The lords of the bor-
derlands tell me that White Raiders are without loyalty to
their own people and can easily be turned to fight against
other Raiders."

"This has been my experience as well, illustrious
Lord." As usual Bektis bowed a little as he spoke. Though
immaculate as always—and still smoking very faintly
with a personal heat-spell—the Icefalcon thought there
was a suggestion of tension to the corners of his eyes, that
the lines of strain were cut very deep indeed in the high
dome of the forehead, and when he stroked the Hand of
Harilómne his long fingers trembled. "Indeed, for several
years there was a barbarian in the High King's Guard, and
he showed no compunction in turning his sword against
his own brethren. They are utterly without loyalty."

"And you are utterly without brains," the Icefalcon said,
"if you don't know the difference between my kindred the
Talking Stars People and such cowardly vermin as the Salt
People, the Empty Lakes People, and the Black Rock
People who attacked the lands of the Wathe. And twice so
if you think that I would raise my hand against the children of my own Ancestors, you witless dotard."

"Faith, is that a fact?" asked Hethya, surprised.

Did she really believe that such obvious trash as the
Black Rock People could be related to the People of the
Talking Stars? The Icefalcon opened his mouth to flay her
ignorance, but Vair went on: "To be sure we could use

another whole man in our forces, if we could be sure of his loyalty."

"Loyalty?" roared Loses His Way, heaving furiously in his bonds. His voice came out hoarse from strangulation. *More's the pity,* reflected the Icefalcon, *that he didn't strangle himself into silence.* Noon had always taught him that the longer an enemy thought you could not understand his speech, the better off you would be. "Loyalty to you, you night-walking jackal? You murderer of my kin? Before I'd take one step back at your orders I'd walk over a cliff!"

The Icefalcon closed his eyes in momentary pained annoyance.

"So you know our tongue." Vair stepped close to the bound man, his white cloak falling over the bulging, straining arms. "Your kin were fools to attack. As they shall learn."

From his belt he unhooked his whip and slashed Loses His Way hard across the face. The warrior stared up at him with blazing azure eyes and, unable to spit in the face of the man standing above him, spit instead at his groin.

Vair's mouth worked once, sharply. Without another word he began to beat the bound man before him, lashing at his face and shoulders with the whip until blood ran down into the tawny beard, then, when the whip would not cut through the tough hide and fur of Loses His Way's clothing, kicking him hard and systematically in the belly and back. Neither man made a sound.

When Vair was finished and stepped back, trying not to pant, Loses His Way raised his gory head and through the broken stumps of his front teeth, spat at him again. It was blood this time.

Vair's voice was shaking with anger. "My Truth-Finder Shakas Kar," he said, "will give you far more time than you will wish to regret that."

As he turned to go Loses His Way spat once more, the red gobbet striking the hem of the snowy cloak. Bektis and

the clones departed in their lord's wake, the clones with
their arms full of clothing and weaponry.

"He is a fool." The Icefalcon looked down at the big
man lying, panting, his cheek in the puddle of his blood.
"But at least this matter diverted Bektis from looking at
me, whom, beard or no beard, he would probably have
known." He looked down again at his own body, naked
now like the others. Would he die, he wondered, in the
cold? "And he might have seen the Runes of Ward on my
face. It certainly kept any man present in such fear of
speaking that no one remarked that I had no wound.
Come."

He took her by the hand again and led the way into the
corridor and down to the cell where the clones were
dumping coats, shirts, long strips of rawhide binding, and
the rag stuffing they wore beneath for warmth. The cell's
door had long since crumbled, so they stationed another
guard before it, another clone. But while the men were still
unburdening themselves the slender scout Crested Egret
strode down the corridor, all his creamy braids fluttering
like pennons, and called out "My Lord! My Lord, the boy
has escaped!"

Vair swung around, and his gold eyes seemed to pale in
the glow of Bektis' witchlight, to pale and grow smaller,
like an animal's that is about to attack. "And how is this?"
he asked.

"My Lord, the man on guard doesn't know. He's one of
the Ti Mens; he says he's been sitting there the whole
time."

Vair's teeth showed white where his lips pulled back
from them: "Does he now? Maybe Shakas Kar can jog his
memory a little."

The Icefalcon personally couldn't imagine torturing a
man so obviously incapable of remembering information,
a man moreover who hadn't the smallest benefit to gain
from helping the prisoner escape. Bektis, Crested Egret,
and at least two of the nonclone warriors present all
thought so, too, for there was a general intake of breath . . .

And a general exhalation the next moment, words unsaid.

Ti Men the guard, the Icefalcon gathered, was in for a very bad few hours.

"Bektis . . ."

"I shall begin scrying immediately, my Lord." Bektis almost dropped to his belly in his haste to anticipate Vair's demand. "At once. But I beg you to remember, there are chambers in this fortress that were wrought to be proof against magic, proof against scrying as well."

Men were already hastening away to the search, Crested Egret summoning the guard from the weapons cell, explaining—in careful detail and words of one syllable— to the remaining clone on guard that he now had to watch both doors.

"And can you find these chambers?"

"Of course, my Lord. Of course." Bektis would have made the same prompt and affirmative reply, thought the Icefalcon, had the question involved eating the moon with a cheese-fork.

He hastened away with as much dignity as a man can retain when on the verge of breaking into a panic run; the Icefalcon did not blame him. Nearly everyone else had fled. Vair turned to follow; one last clone warrior emerged from the storage cell, handsome young face creased in puzzlement, clearly oblivious to all that had passed in the corridor. He held out to Vair something that caught the torchlight in a spangle of black and green: a child's velvet slipper, sewn with emeralds. Too small to be Tir's or anything like Tir's. The very workmanship was strange, a remnant of some forgotten world.

"It was in there," said the clone, pointing back into the cell. "In the middle of the floor."

Vair turned it over in his gloved fingers, staring at it for some time with his strange golden eyes. Then he threw it aside and strode down the corridor. The clone picked it up and followed, still holding the pretty thing in his hand.

Only the single clone guard remained, outside the door

of the vat-room. A flame of demon-light whisked around the corner, out of sight. Far off the Icefalcon heard, or thought he head, a muffled voice whispering words that he could not quite make out.

"We'd best work fast," said Hethya. "We're aye and far off up on the second level, and the boy's been a good little scout about not leaving tracks, but we can't push our luck too far. What's your plan?"

"I think I can get this man to go to the latrine around that corner there and take off his weapons and his clothing."

"As you did with the poor sod that was on guard over me and Tir?" She shrugged. "Sure and I've known men who did stupider, under the impression it would please God or their fathers."

She followed him around the corner to the dark latrines, one of the few on this level not entirely choked with boscage. "Should be easy enough to hide here. You might look up where they're keeping the food and get *those* guards to wander off as well. Or have 'em carry it up and leave it somewhere on the second level, on silver trays and with a bit of wine and perhaps a couple of dancin' boys into the bargain."

She winked at him; the Icefalcon merely looked coldly down his nose at her and led her back toward the dark stairs, the foliose tunnels of frost and darkness. "It's hard on the child," she said after a time of climbing stairs in silence. "He's brave as a little soldier, but now and then I see in his eyes somethin' that makes me fear he'll never trust again."

"And whose fault is that?"

"And what good would it have done me to say *No, I'll not do it?*" Her autumn eyes turned suddenly hard as glass. "Or to have Bektis open up with that sparkler of his once we were in the Keep and scorch poor Lady Minalde and everybody to a whickerin' crisp, and me with 'em, if I'd said a word wrong during that meeting? Me mother always said to me, 'Wait and watch. No matter what they do to you, if you're living you can still do somethin' farther on down the road.' Which you'll have to admit you can't do if you're dead, me bonnie barbarian. And neither the boy nor his mother were kith nor kin of mine."

The Icefalcon opened his mouth to reply but closed it again. By the lights of the Talking Stars People, Hethya spoke the truth. Noon would have advised him so as well. At length he said, more quietly than he had intended to respond, "What you say is true. But I think that, far up the road, that may be what Bektis believed as well. One must know when one has gone down a road far enough."

Tir sat awake in the double cell on the second level front, at the top of its hidden stair. They'd dispensed with the lamp to save oil, kindling instead a small fire of broken-off vines and dry moss and the shards of the decayed wooden doors. Hethya lay asleep, muffled in quilted coats—in her dream-shape she wore the bodice and petticoat and a sort of rough jacket that she'd had on in her dreams of Prandhays Keep. The Icefalcon watched as her form faded from sight at his side and her eyelids stirred on her body of flesh. There was a change in the texture of the air as her dreams melted into the reality of the Keep.

"Will you be well here by yourself?" she asked Tir, after she'd explained to him what the Icefalcon had said and what she had to do. "Old Vair's got men out searching, but half of them are clones, and once he splits up a man into all those parts it's like he's divided the poor soul's brain among 'em as well as his spirit. I doubt they'll find you here. You're not afraid, are you?"

Tir shook his head, though his eyes seemed huge, haunted in the tiny face.

Seeing in them the lie, Hethya knelt beside him and took him in her arms. "It'll be all right, sweeting."

"I know," he whispered. "It's safe here."

" 'Course it is," she said. " 'Course it is. Vair couldn't find this place in a year of market days."

Tir relaxed a little and nodded. Hethya touched the wick of the lamp with a spill from the fire and made sure that there was enough wood to last for a time and that the light of the little blaze could not be seen from the corridors. But by the way the boy looked around him as Hethya and the Icefalcon, visible and invisible, left the chamber, the Icefalcon had the sudden, irrational impression that it was not Vair whose coming Tir most dreaded.

*I did this before. The pain did not kill me.*

The Icefalcon stood for a long time in front of the clone in the corridor, gazing into the man's dulled eyes.

Memory of agony. The only dream he had, played over and over: skin flaying off, blood bursting the flesh . . .

*I did this before.*

He felt shredded, ice-cold and ill. The thought of dropping again into the mind of a clone turned him sick.

*And what would be so bad about dying anyway?*

At least the man wasn't possessed by a demon.

He waited until the man's eyes glazed with inattention, then stepped close, across the wall of dreams.

He could barely get the words out, drowning in pain doubled and redoubled to the screaming abysses at the core of the world: "Vair wants you to go to the latrine, take off all your clothing and your weapons, and walk away down the corridor beyond as far as you can, then stop."

He ripped himself free, lay shuddering on the floor, cold to his bones and gasping . . .

And the clone waked, blinked, and looked around him, frowning. Then he shook his head and settled back against the wall.

*He* would *be one of the brighter ones.* Or maybe he'd paid attention to what they did to Ti Men.

Had he had a sword of steel instead of shadow, the Icefalcon would have lopped his head off from sheer pique. Had he had a sword of steel instead of shadow, he reminded himself, he would not be having this problem.

Hethya would be in place beside the latrines, waiting. How often did they change the guards? How often did an officer come and check on them? Especially now, with Tir missing?

It was like waiting for the bison to go back to grazing, like waiting for the wind to shift so you could inch closer to a drinking deer. The Icefalcon had hunted injured, had lain for hours hungry and cold, motionless to surprise prey. This twisting, screaming ache within him wasn't much worse than that, he told himself.

Only waiting, as a hunter waits.

The clone's attention drifted.

The Icefalcon wondered if he could alter what he looked like in the man's half dream.

To look, for instance, like Crested Egret.

One hunted raccoons by making a noise like a raccoon.

"Vair wants you to walk to the latrine, take off your clothes and your weapons, and walk away into the corridor beyond."

For a terrifying moment, confused by agony and shock, having made himself look like Crested Egret, the Icefalcon could not remember what he looked like himself. His mind groped, fumbling for a memory, any memory . . .

Demons shrieked somewhere near, cold fire pouncing.

He writhed out of the way, calling to mind Cold Death's voice and his own recollection of the person who heard her, who was her brother. There were demons all around him, grabbing at his thoughts, tearing and slicing at him with pain and confusion. He thrust them away, but the pain remained, wounds opening and closing in his phantom body: spent, bleeding, trying desperately to breathe. Terrified with a sense of how close he had come to death.

And the clone was walking away toward the latrine.

The Icefalcon followed shakily, first on his hands and knees, though he got to his feet in a few yards—not that Hethya could see him, of course. He watched from the darkness as the man obediently disarmed and undressed and wandered naked into the blackness and jungles of the farther corridors. Hethya was out of the side passage and pulling on the man's sheepskin coat almost before the clone had turned the next corner, fumbling in her haste to wrap the rawhide on over her own boots, wadding her disheveled auburn braids up under the fleece cap. "Whatever else can be said of you, me lanky boy," she addressed the air around her, "you're a damn good dream-speaker." She strode back along the corridor, clumsy in her borrowed gear, to the barred door, shoved the latch aside. "I hope to meet you face-to-face when you're not a corpse or a ghost . . . There."

She snatched up the guard's abandoned torch, blew out her lamp again, stepped through into the triple cell, and made a face a little at the growing odor of rot. The torch's light ran redly over the curves of glass and gold, slick and cold on the quicksilver lining of the vat. The needles on their table grinned, demon teeth. Loses His Way, panting like a trussed bull, half rolled up onto one shoulder, squinted at the light, defiance still in his swollen eyes. Near him the Icefalcon's body lay pale among the darkening corpses, long braids like age-bleached serpents with their rawhide thongs and tangled bones.

"He's all yours, me hearty." Hethya stood aside from the door.

The Icefalcon stepped forward, reached down to touch his own face, his own hands . . .

And felt nothing.

It was a stranger's body.

The face was his; his the blood moving slow as a winter stream in the veins. Bones, muscle, sinew . . . But it was as if he could no longer remember the language he had spoken as a child. Could not recall the route to a valley he had visited at the farthest edge of his memory.

The terror was like a blow over the heart.

"Come on." Hethya glanced over her shoulder at the open door, stuck the torch in a wall sconce, and crouched to slap the still face. "Wake up, boy-o, there's a good lad. Open your eyes, curse your lizard-eating heart . . ."

"He is dead," Loses His Way mumbled through puffed

purple lips. "A shaman cursed him to his death, cursed his flesh and everything it touches . . ."

"That's not the story his ghost told me in me dreams, handsome."

Loses His Way's blue eyes flared, caught between astonishment, hope, and suspicion; Hethya was already cutting the cord that stretched down his back, fumbling in the guard's coat pockets for the key to the spancels.

"He says he'll be able to get back into his body, not that I think he can do it without a good dollop of witchery for a shoehorn. Me mother was always on about idiots thinkin' there wasn't a thing to magic but sayin' the words of a spell." She pulled the chains away and thrust her shoulder under that of Loses His Way as the warrior tried to rise and stumbled, limbs cramped and feeble from the binding and the beating he had undergone. "Can you help me get him out of here?"

"Where?"

*Remind me never to put you in charge of my horses,* thought the Icefalcon in disgust. *You'd trust a demon who pointed out a waterhole.*

Loses His Way tried to pick up the Icefalcon's limp body and staggered, dropping it to the floor—

*Thank you very much. When I get back into my bones, I'll find half of them broken.*

"I'll take him—no, I know how to carry a man. Next room along, gather as much of the clothes and gear as you can, boy-o—you know how to get in touch with this sister of his? This shaman that served him his eviction to begin with?"

Loses His Way shook his head. "She fought this Wise One Bektis and his gem of lightning but was driven back, burned by his fires; hurt, I think."

Hethya cursed and manhandled the Icefalcon's body up across her shoulders. "Well, we'll just have to do what we can. There's no chance he's off waitin' elsewhere for us, is there?"

"Were it me, I would not."

They stepped into the corridor, Hethya watching nervously in both directions while Loses His Way gathered up clothing from the other room, then made their way swiftly down the first crossing passage that would take them out of the general area, shadows lurching in the torchlight in their wake. The Icefalcon was filled with a kind of fascinated dread at the sight of his own face cold and slack against Hethya's shoulder, his own braids dangling down, the scarred arms and calves loose and lifeless. Twice he came near, reaching into the flesh, and twice stepped back, defeated, alien, and desperately frightened.

Like a ghost he could only follow, in the shadows behind the torch's light.

The old man was there.

Huddled beside the bead of lamplight, Tir felt him, out there in the corridor, waiting.

The room was safe. It had been spelled against the scrying of wizards, and the spells held true against other things as well.

But he was there.

Closing his eyes, Tir looked down into memories, as if looking into a well, though whether they were his own or the old man's he didn't really know.

The long-haired warrior, the man that other boy had called "Father," stood before the chair where the old man sat. They were back in the chambers with the crystal pillars: the third chamber, which came right before the fourth one that was so shallow it was barely a niche.

The old man he had seen in his visions of the caravan train, the old man who had been one of those to set out the flares against the Dark Ones. The magelight feather above the aged wizard's head gleamed on the blue patterns of his scalp, the heavy overhang of his tall brow, the questing jut of nose. He looked up, and Tir could not see other than shadow in the sockets of his eyes.

Gently, Tir's father said, "It's time, Zay."

Zay made no reply.

Tir's father licked his lips. "We can't wait any longer."
His long hair was dressed up in a comb, black with garnets
that glinted like droplets of blood.

"No." The old man's mouth formed the words, but there
was no sound to them. His sigh, though not great, was
louder, like the tearing loose of the soul from its moorings
in flesh. "Just . . . till morning comes. Please."

"We'll take the road in the morning," said Tir's father,
and Zay looked up at him more sharply, hearing something in his words beyond what he said. "There is no other
way," the long-haired warrior went on. "As long as
we know so little of the magic of the Dark Ones, we
cannot risk—we dare not risk—using the shorter path. Lé-
Ciabbeth . . ." He hesitated over the name. "Ciabbeth did
not come?"

Zay shook his head again, and his voice was only a fragment, a splinter of bleached glass. "No."

There was long silence. Then the long-haired man said,
"I'm sorry. Truly, truly, I am sorry, Zay. But there can be
no more delay. Too many lives depend on it, not only
the lives of those here now, but their children, and their
grandchildren—all the generations of humankind who
will shelter within these walls. They will thank you, and
bless your name."

The old man nodded. "And that," he murmured, "will
make it better, I suppose?"

Tir's father said, "If I could do it, Zay, I would."

Zay looked up into his face, bitter, weary beyond
words—Tir didn't think he'd ever seen such wormwood
wryness in human eyes. "Yes," said Zay softly. "I believe
you would, Dare." He got to his feet, straightened his dark
robes around him, his hands fumbling. "Ciabbeth . . ."

"When she comes," said Dare softly, "she will thank
you, too."

Tir shivered as the men walked away between the
crystal pillars. The cold seemed to grow on him, the cold
of memory in that place, and it seemed to him that he

heard someone's voice whispering, *She never came. She never came. She never came.*

The whispers seemed to echo from the dark beyond the room where he now sat, the impacted blackness that not even the fire's tiny light could dissipate. It seemed to him that cold flowed in from that blackness, a cold worse than the bitter chill of the frost-stricken chambers, a living cold, malicious and vile.

Footfalls that weren't really footfalls. Bitter hatred, wormwood resentment.

*She never came.*

A badness deep and rotted, a badness that collected in pockets in the turnings of corridors, the neat cells that no one had lived in long enough to make their homes, in the black well at the heart of the crypts that Tir knew plunged down eternally into darkness.

*Fickle, wretched, cowardly whiners . . .* The resentment was a stench imbued deep within the stone. *Ingrates. Cowards and ingrates.*

From the corridor came, with the cold, a thread of whistling, a half-identifiable tune.

He'd heard that tune. He knew it.

Was it a tune? Sometimes it sounded like an old man's voice, whispering in the nightmare blackness.

Names, Tir thought. Sometimes, in those bad places that he hurried Hethya through, he could hear that hoarse, muttering voice telling over names in the dark. He didn't think Hethya could hear. It terrified him because he knew those names. He could see their faces in his mind and knew what had happened to them. Could see the things they wore—a child's black shoes sewn with green gems, a woman's fan—things they'd left behind.

And above everything else, the anger that soaked every stone, every wisp of lichen, every vine and mushroom as poison soaks a sponge, imbuing its every fragment. Anger and resentment and hate.

And magic that lived on.

# CHAPTER SEVENTEEN

*Wait. They will open the Doors again. They have to.*
She was out there somewhere. She could restore him.
Couldn't she?

The Icefalcon waited. Aching with the demon wounds
and cold to the core of his heart, he trod the spatchcock
light and shadow of the haunted Aisle and listened to the
men searching the Keep's darkness around him. Now and
then lights flickered in the skull-eye windows, high up on
the Aisle walls, or in the doorways that weren't blocked
thick with vines. Sometimes a man would emerge from
one and cross the lumpy, tangled mess of the floor, holding
aloft a torch or a lamp. *And may our Ancestors help us all
if some fool of a clone drops a brand into this dry bramble!*
Water dripped and trickled down the wall below the water
clock, and occasionally the great flat leaden chime would
speak, marking time as it had marked it, meaninglessly,
for years beyond years.

Night lay thick in the corners, more dense than any
darkness outside. Sometimes demon-lights drifted into
sight or slipped like glowing insects among the colorless
monstrosity of growths that choked the eastern end of
the vast space. Sometimes the Icefalcon heard what he
thought was a tune whistled, or a voice whispering, far off
or just behind his shoulder.

He would not, he thought, like to be searching alone in
those empty, icy halls.

White light flared in a window on the second level, a

brief burst that died away, then a moment later revived. Magelight?

After a moment's hesitation—he found himself fearing to leave the Doors, like a haunt trapped eternally in one corner of one room—the Icefalcon left his post and mounted a winding staircase hung with brittle lianas, counting doors along the corridor at the top until he found the place.

Bektis stood alone in the empty chamber, summoning light.

Or trying to summon light.

The old man had suspended a curtain before the door of the cell, not thinking, apparently, of who could see through the window of the Aisle. He had taken off the Hand of Harilómne, and the Icefalcon saw how horribly the flesh underneath it had blistered from chilblain and the constant rubbing and tearing of the gold mesh straps, the heavy jewels. The Hand, and the Collar that went with it, lay in the corner of the room farthest from the door, resting on an ermine muff. Every few seconds the Court Mage's eyes would stray in that direction as if, contrary to the evidence of his own senses, he needed continuous reassurance that they were there.

At the moment the Icefalcon entered the room, Bektis was performing the motion—without his usual theatrical flourishes—associated with the summoning of light. It was a gesture that Ingold Inglorion had reduced to a small opening of the fingers. A sort of sickly blue twilight flickered in the room, spotted here and there with hazy zones of brightness that ranged in size from that of a man's palm to only a few hanging sparks. They faded almost at once. The floor was written over with the chalked Circles of Power, rubbed out and scrawled again, earth and silver and blood. Bektis repeated the gesture, not flourishing but large—a beginner's gesture, the Icefalcon guessed, like a child imitating his elder's spear-cast before his muscles are trained.

A little marshfire dribbled down the walls.

Bektis pressed his hand to his mouth, and his whole body shivered, like a tapestry shaken by wind.

His gaze went back to the Hand and the Collar, and in his eyes the Icefalcon saw the sick expression of a drunkard who has been vomiting for days offered a brimming cup of raw gin. And he understood.

And like the drunkard, Bektis walked over to the alien jewels, lifted the Collar, and put it around his neck again. When he raised his beard out of the way, the Icefalcon saw where the metal and gems had chafed the crêpey wattles of that pallid throat; his mouth flinched and tightened with agony as he buckled the straps of golden mesh around his fingers and wrist. His whole body trembling with defeat, Bektis made the summoning gesture again, and magelight filled the room, refulgent, warm, more gorgeous than the sun.

Bektis pressed his hand to his eyes, then to his mouth again, trembling so hard the Icefalcon thought that he would fall and breathing in single, desperate gulps. Steps sounded in the corridor—Vair's, the Icefalcon thought. Bektis didn't hear until they had nearly reached the curtained door, then he spun, his face resuming its usual hauteur as the blanket slashed aside and the generalissimo stood framed against the pitchy gloom beyond.

"Where have you been?"

"The clamor of the men in the Aisle disturbed my concentration, illustrious Lord." Bektis stroked his beard and looked as if he had not, moments ago, been on the verge of weeping with despair. "I thought that might have been a reason that I was unable to locate the boy."

"You should have spoken to Prinyippos about it," said Vair. "He'd have silenced them." He nodded back to the hall behind him, and the scout Crested Egret stepped out of the shadows and into the glow of the cell. "And have you had better results here?"

"Not yet, Lord. All the Keeps were wrought with chambers of Silence, chambers where Runes were laid to prevent wizards from . . ."

"Don't tell me how the Keeps were made, you old dribbler. Ezrikos' palace in Khirsrit is built on the crypts of a vanished Keep. I've been through them a hundred times. They have to come out for water sometime."

"And when they do, I will find them, Lord. But there's a magic in this Keep, a power beyond my experience . . ."

"I'm beginning to think common demon-scares are beyond your experience. This band of Raiders that's coming up from the south . . ."

He laid a hand on Crested Egret's shoulder, and the slender young man almost preened himself at the attention from his lord. "You say the White Raiders have magics of their own. How can you be sure that when you lay the illusions on Prinyippos here to lead them into the trap, the member of the band whose form he's taken won't *be* there to give him the lie? That would make mice-feet of the business when I can least afford to lose that much flesh."

"Do not trouble yourself, Lord." Bektis raised a soothing hand. "The illusion with which I shall cloak Prinyippos is a strong and singular one, not a battle illusion. Battle illusions are by nature more diffuse. This new-arriving band shall be met by Prinyippos before they have time to join with their kindred . . ."

*The Empty Lakes People are* not *our kindred!* the Icefalcon wanted to shout at him.

"And Prinyippos shall wear the form of one of those I killed when they attacked me on the knoll where I camped, west of the mountains. If he will but stay for a few moments, I'll demonstrate. The chasm into which he shall lead them is close enough to the Keep to lend verisimilitude to his story of its being a secondary entrance, and it will require no great exertion, either on my part or that of your men, to collapse the ice above them and bury them."

"And you can dispose of the ice afterward?" Vair stroked the ends of his graying mustache; he had shaved again and dressed his hair, but still looked somewhat worse for the journey. "It will do me little good to slaughter two hundred men if I cannot have their flesh for the *dethken iares* afterward."

Bektis straightened his shoulders indignantly. "My Lord, even without the weaponry of the ancient ones, I am not without resources. My power is more than sufficient to clear the ice from the chasm after it has done its job."

"That," said Vair softly, "is well, sorcerer. Because I need flesh to multiply my men into an army capable of conquering Dare's Keep. And every delay increases the chances of something going awry, of that coward Gargonal abandoning his part outside the walls of the Keep or of those bitches in the South, Empress and Bishop, getting wind of my plans. The last thing they want me to have is a fortress that cannot be breached and a steady supply of food. I need not explain to you, I think, what will happen to you if they overcome us?"

The Court Mage looked away and cradled the bloodied crystals of the Hand to his breast. "No, my Lord."

"Then find the boy and find him soon. The spells you spoke of will break the information out of him quickly enough."

"Yes, my Lord."

"How soon until these new Raiders come close enough that Prinyippos can reach them?"

"From observing them in my scrying glass, my Lord, I should say that the chimes here will sound five times. On the fifth chiming, we should send out Prinyippos. It will be about the ninth hour of the day then and thus close to twilight when he leads them into the ice chasm."

"Good. Prinyippos, have a company ready to go out at that time." At least that was what the Icefalcon thought Vair said—he understood the words for *company* and *go out* and did not hear any numbers in the locative of time.

He didn't need to know that Prinyippos' words were "Yes, Lord." The young scout all but rubbed Vair's legs and purred.

Flesh to make more warriors. Warriors to invade the Keep.

But he had the apparatus of the vat—the *dethken iares*—by the time he conquered Prandhays Keep. For what reason had he come north to this place? And even with hundreds of extra men, he must know the Keep's walls were impenetrable?

Tir knew something. Something that would enable Vair to break the Keep.

Bektis would find the boy, that he did not doubt. Whatever the Hand of Harilómne was doing to Bektis' powers, when he wore the thing it multiplied his own abilities a dozenfold, at least in certain situations. Neither Hethya nor Loses His Way would be able to protect the child, and the Icefalcon had begun to understand that without the ability to return to his own body, his hours were numbered and leaking away fast.

Vair was going to trap and kill the Empty Lakes People.

Ironic, thought the Icefalcon, treading the stone corridors of the Keep of Night—easier to follow than those of Dare's Keep, at least in his bodiless form. The only reason the trap would work was because the warrior whose face Bektis knew and was at this moment reproducing for Vair's edification was, by chance, a member of that same people. The Talking Stars People or the Earthsnake People would kill the imitation warrior out of hand.

He passed through curtains of hissing, colorless squash tendril, traversed fused clumps of creeper and rock-tripe, cells packed thick with toadstools or white plate-fungus, as if in a dream, knowing no human body could go that way. It worried him that this was growing easier, as if the bonds to his own flesh were dissolving. Demons crept through the moss like ants and tormented him with their bites and their poisons; it was harder and harder to tell himself that the pain was illusory.

He could end the pain. Sometimes he thought about it so desperately that all that kept him from dissolving was the knowledge that if he did so here in the darkness, he might not even be united with the warmth of the sun.

Only the chill of the ice-ridden night beneath the glaciers, forever.

The pain was real.

Dove in the Sun stepped forth from the wall, the Dove with her chest opened and organs glistening through the smashed ribs, the Dove with blood on the wild roses twined in her sun-bright hair. "Why didn't you come back for me, o my kinsman? Why didn't you even look?"

That pain was real, too. It was hard to force himself to remember that he didn't have to stop and explain to her. As a child of the Talking Stars, she would have known, lying alone on the ledge beneath her dying horse, that her wounds were hopeless. He passed her by, and her voice followed him down the corridor.

"Why didn't you even come to hold my hand as I died?"

He had no reply to that.

Then he came to a shattered black hell of frost curtains, hanging spears of ice lengthened to bars across corridors and throughout cells, hollow columns of water frozen harder than iron.

Words whispered there.

And an old man waited among cold-killed vines the thickness of a horse's neck, among translucent sheets of dribbled ice and obscene dead mushrooms.

An old man with his tattooed hands folded, as if sourceless light fell on them and left the rest of him lapped in darkness. The Icefalcon could see with the eyes of a ghost, and those eyes were blinded to the old man's face. For some reason he knew he was ruinously old, white hair grown out shabbily around the base of the skull to a spiderweb cloak over the bent shoulders. Nails uncut for years beyond speaking twisted back on themselves, vile as the curves of the perished vines.

His teeth were not human teeth. His eyes no longer human eyes.

"You came back." The voice was the glowing slime that drips from rotted meat. "You came back after all."

The Icefalcon felt the hair lift on his scalp. "I have never been in this place before, old man." Everything in him, ghost though that everything was, screamed at him: *Flee. Flee. Get out of here at once.*

"And they didn't tell you of me?" When the old man moved, his robes made a noise like thin paper, eroded by eons of time.

"They told me nothing, old man. Forgive me if I speak disrespect."

"Forgive you?" The old man put his head to one side, and there was something horribly wrong about the glisten of the unseen eyeball. "Forgive? I was told . . . I was told my name would be remembered. That I would be thanked. That I would be thanked forever."

He moved toward the Icefalcon, extending one thin arm, the crooked nails bobbing and trembling like twigs.

*"I was not thanked,"* he whispered. "And she never came, though the way was open. The way was always open. She never came, and they all departed, all left me, after what I had done for them. And now . . ." He smiled. "Now that you're all back, I'm going to make sure that no one ever leaves again."

He giggled, reaching out, and into the Icefalcon's mind flashed the image of himself, his phantom consciousness, being absorbed into these black walls. Not to die, but to remain, forever, listening to the old man telling over names to himself in the frozen darkness.

Logic dictated immediate and precipitate flight, and the Icefalcon fled. Behind him he could hear the old man creaking with shrill laughter. "You think you can escape?" Glancing over his shoulder he saw the fragile form lift like a blown sheet, whirl through the air toward him, white hair swirling, skeletal arms outstretched. "You think you can escape me?"

They blew through corridors blocked with foul vegetation, past fountains knotted with ice. In one huge cell that was little more than a seething hairball of lichen and vine, three clones were struggling, fighting their way inward, not outward, at the whispered lurings of demons. The men were weeping with fright and pain, trying to escape the leathery tendrils around them. The old man turned aside at the sight of them, laughing when the demons tried to flee.

"Not so fast, my little tender ones." He fell on them like a fast-moving hawk. The demons tried to slip through the walls, and the black stone refused to let them pass. The last the Icefalcon saw of the old man, he was holding the littlest of the demons between his two hands, eating its head while the clones wept and groaned among the bonds that clinched tighter and ever tighter around them, strangling out their lives.

In the hidden chamber on the second level, the Icefalcon's body lay wrapped in spare coats and clothing, his weapons in a pile at his side. At least they had that much sense, thought the Icefalcon, trembling with cold and exhaustion. The sight of a Wathe-forged sword, its hilt stamped with the emblems of the Guards of Gae, would have given Vair more information than he should have.

Tir sat still, racked with a slight, constant shiver. Hethya was arguing with Loses His Way. "And I suppose all those double and triple and umpty-upple warriors of Vair's are just going to turn their wee faces to the wall and fall asleep?"

"Pah! Insects. The boy must be fed. Us, too. Else we will be unable to flee, unable to help ourselves or anyone else." Loses His Way's face was frightful, a swollen mass of purpling flesh that gaped in six or eight places where the whip had opened the skin. Blood caked his beard and his braids, and the few teeth he had left in his mouth were ragged chips.

"Should we leave this room we'll be walking into places where Bektis can see us, does he care to look into that crystal of his. That he's been busy about this and that is all that's saved us, but every time's another risk."

"So ask this Ancestor that dwells in your head, this Ancestor that guided you into alliance with the Father of All

Traitors, to tell you where safe places can be found! *She* knew this place."

Hethya straightened her back, her face altering to the cold, haughty countenance of Oale Niu, and she opened her mouth to reply. Then she thought again, and her shoulders slumped; her red lips closed. "Would I could," she said softly. "There is no Ancestor. Your lanky pal figured it. He'll tell you the whole of it when he finally comes back, if he comes back."

She sighed, all fight gone, and turned her face. She still wore the clone's overcoat and wrappings and would easily have passed for one of Vair's warriors in the dark. Her mouth tightened hard, not to give anything of herself away, but Loses His Way saw, and the anger went out of his face.

"There," he said gently, and stepped to her, putting a comforting arm like a bear's great forepaw around her shoulders. "There, Little Ancestor, there's no need to weep."

She shook her head violently. "It's tired I am, that's all," she said, tears creeping down her cheeks.

"I know."

"I just . . . I did try."

The broken, toothless mouth moved into what had once been a smile. "I know. And you did well. As well as any warrior."

"I'm sorry, sweeting." She looked down at Tir, defeated. "You've met His Nastiness. It was join with him or . . . well, have happen to me what I'd rather not have happen."

"It's all right." Tir's voice was tiny in the gloom. "I knew you made it up." He stepped close to her on her other side, put his arm around her waist as he did with his mother, and leaned his head against her hip. "Way back at Bison Knoll I knew."

Hethya laughed a little, wept a little, returned the pressure of his embrace, and with her other hand patted the big, knotted hand of Loses His Way.

"I did what I could."

Loses His Way smiled, and even through the blood there was a warmth to it, like the sun's *ki* in whom the Icefalcon's people did not believe. "We all do what we can, Little Ancestor. You kept the boy alive. No small thing in dealing with that carrion eater from the South. You did well."

Tir went on, "And I don't know if . . . if Bektis will be able to see us, even if we leave this room, or if they'll be able to find us even if he does see us. The old man might not let him."

"What old man, sweeting?"

The Icefalcon had come close and had tried already, vainly, to enter the body lying cold and still in its nest of furs. Pain throbbed and cramped him, worse and growing worse still, agonizing, nauseating, flesh shredded, teeth marks showing on the exposed bones.

Was this why he couldn't return to his own flesh?

Had he destroyed his ability to do so when he'd taken on the form—for seconds only—of Prinyippos in order to command the clone?

Or had he simply been away from his body too long?

*You think you can escape?* the old man had screamed after him with peals of mocking laughter.

And the voice of the clone shouting dumb echoes of voices in his head: *I will eat you all.*

Despair closed over him, the knowledge that he would die here in the darkness. The knowledge that it was over.

"The old man in the Keep," whispered Tir, and his words brought the Icefalcon back to awareness of his surroundings, of these three people beside him, with whom his life was entwined. "The old man with the tattoos all over his hands and the big long fingernails . . ." His little pink fingers described the obscene curves of the overgrown claws, and the Icefalcon thought, *He's seen him, too.*

"He lives in the Keep."

"You mean a ghost?" asked Loses His Way doubtfully.

Besides being a White Raider, his swollen, bloodied face was something from a nightmare, but Tir seemed to have taken his horrible appearance in stride. Loses His Way and Tir drew Hethya back to the little fire, and the chieftain selected a couple more fragments of wood to feed the blaze.

The boy shook his head. "He's alive," he said. "That's what the whole thing was about. He's been alive . . ." He broke off, groping for words, struggling to make them understand, to understand himself.

Loses His Way and Hethya traded a look of incomprehension, then looked back at the child. "You mean he was living here before we burrowed through the ice?" Hethya asked gently. "How did he get here, sweeting? What did he eat? Not those filthy plants, to be sure."

"I can't." Tir buried his face in his arms. "I can't say."

She stroked his black hair. "There, there, it's all right," she murmured. "You don't have to say."

She looked up at Loses His Way again. "Your lanky pal's a sort of ghost, though he says he's alive, too. He comes to us in dreams."

"Shadow-walking," agreed Loses His Way, nodding.

"Here," Hethya said, and looked around her suddenly. "What am I thinking?" She pulled a rag from her pocket; wet it from her water bottle. "Let me at least clean you up and make a civilized man of you."

The chieftain grinned a little as she daubed water on the rag and very gently began to wash the cuts on his face, and he said, "Ah, never will you make a civilized man of me, Little Ancestor."

"Civilized man—now there's a contradiction in terms."

And both laughed a little, the sparkle of their eyes meeting on the outer edge of pain and death and dark.

"Now, I may not be some reborn mage of the Times Before," she said when she had finished, "but me mother taught me a bit of meditation. It always pays, she said, to know how to calm your mind. Lord knows I'm not going to sleep in any hurry, but meditation may serve for him to speak to us at least."

Loses His Way nodded. "Our shamans do the same if a shadow-walker becomes lost. It is not something my people do often, you understand—shadow-walk, that is—for it is very dangerous." He nodded down at the Icefalcon's body. "As we see."

"He'll be all right," whispered Tir anxiously, "won't he?"

Hethya's glance crossed the warchief's; it was Loses His Way who replied. "That we do not know, Little King. It may be that he will not. But if anyone can return after this long, it is the Icefalcon."

He grinned with his broken teeth and puffed lips, blackened blue eyes dancing in the flittering light. "He would not have it said of him that he permitted even death to get the better of him, so of course he must return."

Tir giggled. *And what is wrong,* demanded the Icefalcon, *with striving to be perfect in survival? For there are times when only the perfect survive.*

But he was glad that Tir had lost some of his look of fear.

"It would help if we had smoke," said Loses His Way, "or some of those herbs that the Wise Ones burn to dissociate the mind from the flesh."

"You're telling me, laddy-o." Hethya sighed, and closed her eyes. "You're telling me."

"The Wise Ones taught me this . . ." Loses His Way gravely touched her face and temples, her hands and arms, at the points of relaxation, the nexus of the body's energies. The tension in Hethya's shoulders eased, and some of the grimness left her face.

"What is it?" whispered Loses His Way, seeing Tir flinch.

"That's where they put the needles in," the boy replied in a strained undervoice. "When they make the *tethyn.*"

"They are the map of the body, the sources of its energies. Anything can be used for evil as well as good, Little King."

In the corridors far off the chime spoke, and once the Icefalcon heard the rustle of hide-shod feet, two or three turnings away, and a mutter of scared voices. But they faded—evidently the ventilation in this chamber was good enough that the smell of the smoke did not carry— and the dense silence returned, thicker, it seemed, than before. Hethya never dropped into sleep. The Icefalcon sensed her mind always working, dragged away to one course or another despite the discipline—which, he guessed, she had never practiced as the Wise Ones practiced it.

In the corridor the vines rustled, a sighing of movement, though there was no wind.

*You think you can escape?*

"What was that?" Hethya's eyes popped open.

Tir whispered, "The old man."

Loses His Way made a move toward the fire. "Don't be an ass," breathed Hethya, her hand on his wrist. "He'll see in the dark."

The warchief was on his feet already, drew his sword, stepped to the doorway, a bearlike bulk in the gloom.

"Out the back," said Hethya. "We can . . ."

"We can't leave the Icefalcon." Tir was on his feet, too, trembling like a leaf in a winter storm.

"For pity's sake, laddie . . ."

"He's a Guard," said Tir. "I'm his lord. I can't."

Hethya made a move back toward him. "Too late," murmured Loses His Way, firelight tracing the blade's edge as it lifted to strike. "Can you see him? White hair, like a ghost in midnight."

Silence flowed out of the dark of the corridor, a long thinking silence, palpable as the ever-thickening cold. Far off a demon bobbed, backlighting the spiderweb of white hair, the dark shape cloaked in magic. Somewhere a voice whispered, thin and envenomed with rotting hate.

There was another rustle, sharp as the hiss of a snake.

Then two soft swift steps, a dark bulk emerging from darkness . . . A muffled curse, and Ingold Inglorion threw himself through the door, white hair disheveled and drawn sword flickering with pale light. He rolled under Loses

His Way's strike and turned, panting, to stand for a moment in the doorway, facing out into the haunted abyss.

For a moment it seemed that the shadows reached out to him, surrounded him, smothering and evil . . .

Then it seemed that something altered, shifted, and there was only darkness again.

"Dratted plants." Ingold turned; his voice was like flawed bronze, brown velvet, and rust, unmistakable. "To think I once liked salad. Miss Hethya—or should I say Lady Oale Niu—I do hope you have something with which to make tea."

# CHAPTER EIGHTEEN

"It was you that I saw." The Icefalcon pulled the thick mammoth-wool coat closer and experimentally flexed his hands. Though this part of the Keep wasn't noticeably cold, he could not stop shivering. It seemed to him that he would never be warm again. "In the chamber with the crystal pillars—last night? The night before?"

In the dark of this place it was difficult enough to keep track of time, even without the nightmare of suffocation, cold, demons, and terror. An echo of pain remained, a phantom imprint burned in his mind. Every few minutes he would feel his own arms again, not trusting himself to believe that there was flesh over the bone.

"That was me." Ingold dug into one of the packets of food he'd brought in his knapsack, which he and Loses His Way had retrieved from the corridor while the Icefalcon, numb, dizzy, and feeling like a piece of very old driftwood on a beach, lay staring at the ocher firelight patterns on the ceiling, blinking now and then and rejoicing obscurely in the friction of a real eyelid over a real eye. "Have a cake."

The old man extended a potato cake to him. The Icefalcon devoured it ravenously and immediately felt queasy at the revival of digestive organs. He wasn't about to say so, however. He was the Icefalcon—and food was food.

"You might have informed me," said the Icefalcon, "that you'd followed us after all. Your presence would have been useful in any number of instances."

"I'm very sure it would have been," Ingold replied soothingly.

"I take it your interesting little accounts of the Siege of Renweth were fabricated from reports sent to you by Ilae and Wend?"

"By no means." The wizard took a bite of dried apricot—apricots grew well in the Keep's crypts, along with grapes, cherries, and several varieties of nuts. Other than the usual cuts and scratches gained from cross-country travel and sleeping rough, and a bandage around one hand that the Icefalcon remembered from his vision in the pillared chamber, Ingold did not seem much the worse for wear: shabby and unprepossessing as an old boot and several times tougher.

"Four days ago—which was the last time your sister spoke to me—I was in the Vale of Renweth, readying the latest of my half-dozen attempts to draw off General Gargonal's troops long enough to let me slip through the Doors. That one succeeded, I'm pleased to say—it's quite surprising what men will believe if you take them off guard in the middle of the afternoon. When you saw me, I was in one of the laundry rooms in the Royal Sector, specifically, the chamber Brycothis designated, or seemed to designate, as the Renweth end of what Gil refers to as a transporter.

"Surely you knew it had to be something of the kind," he added, seeing the Icefalcon's expression of startled enlightenment. Gil had told a number of tales that involved transporters. "Vair na-Chandros is many things, but he isn't a fool. Of course the only reason he would take such a troublesome journey would be if he thought there was a way from here straight into Dare's Keep. Even with the Hand of Harilómne, Bektis couldn't have overpowered Ilae, Rudy, and Wend together, and the wards on the Arrow River Road were strong enough to have warned us of the army's approach in spite of all Bektis might do."

Ingold extended his hands gratefully to the fire. "I guessed as soon as Wend told me Tir had been kidnapped that it had to be something of the sort, and Cold Death's information only confirmed my suspicions. Vair sought such a thing at Prandhays first, didn't he, Hethya?"

"I don't know what he was seeking after at Prandhays." Hethya, still sitting in the circle of Loses His Way's arm, raised her chin from her fists. She had been staring dully at and past the cell's obsidian wall, as if defeated or expecting punishment; there was a questioning look as she met the wizard's bright-blue gaze.

Whatever she saw in Ingold's eyes must have encouraged her, for she sat up a little straighter and said, "That Bektis, he went through every stick and stitch of Mother's scrolls—dragged 'em all down and spent all the winter at 'em, the ones she'd never known the tongues of—while Vair and Bektis hauled me out of me cell every couple of days and asked me this and that, and me never knowin' what it was they wanted to hear or what they'd do to me if they didn't get it."

Her nostrils flared, and she fell silent again, the twist in her lips a line of ugly memories.

"Now you speak of it, they did ask me about travel between Keeps—they asked Oale Niu, that is—and I kept sayin' there wasn't much, there wasn't much. Stands to reason, you see."

She shrugged and took another bite from the dried fruit that Ingold had passed all around. "You'd never want to get farther than you could find shelter at sunset. I would have said, 'None at all,' but Mother did find some pretty old scrolls of what she said looked like copies of copies of things from far, far back, talkin' of travel, so there must have been some. You'd never have got me out."

Her eyebrows, coppery in the glinting amber light, pulled together. "Two accounts, they was, and both of 'em full of fightin' off the Dark with torches and wizards puttin' up flares all round the camps, and such, though we had no way of knowin' how far after the coming of the Dark those were written, nor who'd been at 'em and changed 'em around since. People do, you know," she added. "Mum found two or three times, where she'd have a tale written one way, and then another one fifty or so years later, where somebody'd changed it."

"That," the Icefalcon said haughtily, "is because civilized people make up so many stories to amuse themselves that they do not understand truth when they encounter it. Among my people it would not have happened."

"Among your people all you talk of is animal tracks and the weather, I've heard."

"Of a certainty." Loses His Way looked wounded by the distaste in her voice. "How else can you know where to hunt, or what the pasturage for your horses will be, or where the game will graze did you not know where the rains have been in the spring? How can you tell which herds travel where unless you know the tracks of their leaders and where they went last spring and the spring before? And besides," he added, "they are friends, those leaders. The herd of Broken Horn, the great rhinoceros of the Ten Muddy Streams Country, I have followed his tracks for fifteen years now. I know where he is likely to lead his people in seasons when the rain comes before the Moon of Blossoms and when it doesn't fall in the Twisted Hills Country until after the New Moon of Fawns."

"Be that as it may," said Ingold, turning encouragingly to Hethya. He had experience with the peoples of the Real World once they got on the subject of weather and animal tracks.

"Be that as it may," she said. "I cribbed pretty heavy off those travel stories, and Vair, he never could get around me."

"And I take it," said Ingold, his deep, scratchy voice a little dreamy, "that one of those two travel tales concerned this place."

"Aye," Hethya said softly. "Aye, it did that."

Far off a man's voice could be heard shouting nonsense words, or perhaps crying out in another tongue. Ingold lifted his head, blue eyes wary under eyelids marked with tiny, hooked, vicious scars; listening. Sorting sound from sound, as mages did, sorting the darkness with his mind. The Icefalcon thought of those endless hallways stretching away into shadow, the chambers glimpsed in confusing dreams, rustling with lubberly vegetation that crept with demons, into which men bored stubbornly, stupidly, working their way inward, not out.

*I will eat them all.*

His memory had curious gaps in it, but some images were branded into his consciousness: an old man gripping a struggling demon between his hands, grinning as he tore chunks of its glowing, plasmic pseudoflesh with his misshapen teeth and drank of its life.

The Keep was coming to life.

There was something he was forgetting. Something he'd heard. Bektis cradling blood and jewels to his breast. Prinyippos preening himself. Vair . . .

*You think you can escape?*

"I couldn't say I'd been one of them as had left this place, see," Hethya went on after a moment, "because I didn't know how long after the coming of the Dark that was. And I didn't know what Bektis knew. But Bektis already knew that this place *had* been left, for whatever reason: left standin' empty, he said, and the people all just walked out and shut the doors behind 'em. God knows why."

"I can guess," said Ingold. "We came very close to it ourselves a few years ago—leaving Renweth, I mean. An ice storm killed all the stock and most of the food plants. This far north, with the Ice advancing, it was bound to happen. Or maybe there was sickness."

The Icefalcon sat up a little, his back propped against the wall, his sword near his hand—he was never completely comfortable unless his sword was near his hand and he had a dagger where he could get to it fast—and accepted another potato cake. In the back of his mind a name tugged at him, a half-forgotten vision of a warrior and a child. "Who was the old man?"

"Zay." Tir looked up, a little surprised that none of them knew, none of them remembered. "His name is Zay."

Once Hethya spoke of it, Tir recalled very clearly the caravans from the Keep of the Shadow straggling into Renweth Vale over Sarda Pass.

He didn't remember whose memory it was. The glaciers were low on the mountains, though not as low as they were nowadays. The mountains themselves looked different, waterfalls down bare rockfaces where trees grew now. The air was very cold. He remembered how his breath—that other boy's breath—smoked and his fingertips hurt within his gray fur gloves. He remembered how few they were, only handfuls of women and a couple of children. The men had all perished, victims of the Dark.

He did know that whoever it was who had originally seen this emigration had known that these were the people from the Keep of Tiyomis who didn't know about Zay. He—whoever he was—could not remember all those other little boys, all those other young men, whose glimpsed recollections lurked in Tir's mind. He, whoever he was, had been untroubled by the nightmares of acid-blood stink on the wind, the dreams of driving an ax home into another man's helmeted skull on the field of shouting battle, the sudden terrors of attempted murders long past: a happy and thoughtless young man.

He hadn't known about Brycothis, either.

Tir said, "Zay was like Brycothis. He was one of the wizards who raised the Keeps."

He spoke from the shelter of Ingold's arm, tucked beneath the old man's mantle like a chick under its mother's wing. Clinging to the old man, delirious with relief at the familiar smells of wood smoke and soap, of chemicals and herbs; the smells of the Keep. After the first hysterical hugging, he'd stepped back, knowing a wizard needed space to work in. But he'd clung to the old man's robe when Ingold went out into the corridor again, down to another cell to work the spells to summon the Icefalcon back to his body, spells that couldn't be worked in the Silent room. He'd had to bite his lip and then his hand to keep from speaking.

At last, when Ingold rose from the Icefalcon's side, wiping his face, Tir had whispered, "Is Rudy okay?"

"Rudy is well." Ingold had ruffled Tir's black hair as he said it; there was no lie in the blue eyes. "I worked a healing magic on him as soon as I entered the Keep, before coming here. He's weak—he was badly hurt—but he will recover. The first thing he did when he woke was ask after you. Your mother is taking care of him and praying every night for your safety."

So his mother was all right, too.

He wanted to kick Vair for lying.

*No,* he thought. *He wanted to . . .* There were other things, adult things, evil things, that he wanted to do to Vair. Things that frightened him, turned him sick even to consider.

He pressed his face to Ingold's side and tried to push the thoughts away, to look aside from those dark places where others before him had looked.

Ingold was here. Everything was going to be all right.

"Brycothis told the other mages about—about entering into the Keeps," he said after a time. "About becoming part of the heart of the Keep. Giving up their bodies, and their lives, so their magic would link the Keeps with the magic of the earth and the stars forever. Some other wizard was going to do it . . . Fyanin? Fy-something. But he died on the way, when the Dark attacked them at that hill where we were.

"There were a lot of Keeps," he went on, looking from face to face of these people who surrounded him, these people he loved—even Loses His Way, who had scared him at first. "But there weren't a lot of mages. The bad king killed them. And some of them were bad themselves. And a lot of them they couldn't spare because they needed them to fight the Dark. But Zay rode north with . . . I think with Dare of Renweth . . . and Fyanach because Zay was from the North, from the Valley of Shilgae, which was real rich then. They were his people. He was their guardian."

"And they left him," murmured Ingold. "They left him alone."

The Icefalcon frowned. "He must have known why."

"Must he?" Ingold widened his eyes at the young man. "Why do you say that? When someone hurts you—hurts you very badly—do you ever really derive any consolation from the knowledge that they were only acting as they felt driven to act?"

The Icefalcon saw again Blue Child's eyes meeting his across the longhouse fire. Sometimes the Wise were too damned perceptive.

"And he has been here," he said. "All this time."

His mind returned to the eclipsed shadow, the wobbling fingernails, the vile glimmer of unseen eyes. He thought about the evil slow-growing plants that choked the corridors and chambers, about the spots of deadly cold. It was as if, he thought, they were locked in the body of a beast long dead, wandering in a vast, stilled, ebon heart.

"Was this Far-Walker, this *transporter*, ever used?"

Ingold shook his head. "I don't know," he said. "If it was, it fell out of general use long ago. Certainly no record of it survived, not even in the archives of the City of Wizards."

He wrapped up the rest of the potato cakes and stowed them in his knapsack, which he shoved into a corner. He had always, thought the Icefalcon, looked more like a beggar than a wizard, except for the sword he belted at his hip. And indeed, within this chamber where the Runes of Silence were written he was not a wizard, only a very tough old man.

He settled now by the fire and extended his palms to the warmth. "I've never seen mention of it in any of the record crystals, either, and most of those were made well before the coming of the Dark Ones. Perhaps it was originated by the mages of that time but in the end considered too dangerous. The Keeps depended for their safety on absolute impregnability. One set of Doors, and those locked and guarded with the most stringent of magical wards. And nothing else, as I knew to my sorrow, from those nights sleeping cold on the mountainside and stealing food from Vair's troops to stay alive. Fairly good food, too, if you knew which mess to visit—though one produced meals that tasted excellent but made me truly ill afterward."

"Ah, that'll be me cousin Athkum." Hethya nodded. "They took him on as a cook—as a slave, of course. Cousin Athkum was another of me mother's pupils, though not to magic born. He was a dab hand at herbology and healing brews, though. I'd be surprised," she added casually, "if any of them live much past the end of summer."

"Good heavens," Ingold murmured, alarmed.

"You probably didn't take enough to hurt you." Hethya shrugged. "By the time enough accumulates in their systems—he says brown-cap mushrooms are the best— he'll be far away. It isn't as if they didn't ask for it."

"I suppose not." Ingold shuddered a little. "I shall take steps to invoke spells of healing on myself the moment I'm out of this room. As for the transporter, it may only have been an experiment and never used at all. In any case, all knowledge of it was lost at the Renweth end. This may have been deliberate, for the archways of crystal that seem to have demarcated its resonating chambers were bricked up and plastered over. Brycothis directed Ilae to it, of course, but she could make no sense of the images she placed in her mind. It was only when you, Icefalcon, came through the wall as I sat meditating there that I realized how the function and shape of the room had to have been changed."

"Can we go back?"

"We can," Ingold said slowly. "It would be best if we can do it without showing Vair where the transporter lies. I'm fairly good at covering my tracks, but magic won't work in the chamber itself nor in several of the corridors round about it, and I'm not sure that four adults could pass those corridors again without leaving traces that could be deciphered in the frost and the vines. That's what he wanted you for, wasn't it, Tir?"

The boy nodded. "I had to get away," he said. "I couldn't let him—I never will let him. He's evil. He's going to make more soldiers and take them to the Keep . . ."

"Out of what, pray?" demanded Hethya scornfully. "Mushrooms?"

"The Empty Lakes People," said the Icefalcon.

The others looked at him, silent with shock.

"They're on their way here, two hundred of them," he said. "I'm sorry. I . . . ." He shook his head, angry at himself for not speaking of it before. Like a single black comb on the table of crystal needles, like a dream about Bektis summoning light, the conversation had slipped away in clouds of demon-laughter and pain.

"Breaks Noses leads them. After four more chimes of the clock Bektis will lay a glamour upon Crested Egret— Prinyippos—so that he can lead them into a crevasse in the ice, where they will be killed by an avalanche. Vair will use their flesh as he used the flesh of the sheep, he says, to manufacture ten or twelve or twenty warriors, where before he could only call forth four from his iron vat.

"And with that many warriors to assist in the search," he added reasonably, "stupid as they are, it can only be a matter of time before they locate the transporter without the help of our lad Scarface here."

Hethya said, "T'cha!" in offense, and slapped at his foot, which was the nearest part of his body to her. But the Icefalcon saw Tir's fleet shy grin and the duck of his head, as the deformity and shame transformed to something men envied, the mark of battle survived.

"And where," Ingold asked gently, "does Vair keep this vat of his?"

Three corridors away from the dark triple cell beside the Aisle, Ingold paused and closed his eyes, dreaming or meditating or doing whatever it was that Wise Ones did.

When they turned the final corridor, it was to discover the door guards of the cell gone. By the muddy boot prints there had been two of them this time, Vair evidently having learned a lesson about single guards in that corridor. The Icefalcon felt a twinge of irritated envy toward people who didn't have to step through a slashing fire-fall of pain in order to send the clones on some sort of wild-goose chase to the farthest latrine in the Keep, but he put it aside as illogical.

Ingold paid for his powers in other ways.

Neither the Icefalcon nor Loses His Way breathed a sound as they traversed the short stretch of corridor and Ingold slipped back the door bolt. The wizard paused on the threshold, like a cat balking at the entry to a haunted room. Then he stepped in, moving with a wariness that made the Icefalcon uneasy. Anything that scared Ingold Inglorion was indeed to be avoided at all costs.

Whatever it was, he noticed that Loses His Way didn't seem to sense anything amiss. Saving, of course, the smell of old blood about the *dethken iares*, which was almost drowned in the overwhelming stink of the clones' corpses. Creepers had already grown through the doorway, probing into the brown mess. The chieftain muttered, "Pfaugh! This is ugly hunting. He will make warriors of those?"

"Of their flesh, yes." Ingold was clearly fascinated. "I've read very old accounts of this procedure, though its use was lost with the technology of this apparatus. These"—he lifted the crystal needles from their table, turning them to the dim feather of magelight that floated above his head, angled the glass beads on their heads to catch some gleam within them—"went into the nerve points of the body, the crystal into the head and shoulders, the iron into the limbs, the gold into the abdomen and organs."

He moved from object to object, running his heavy-muscled hands along the twisted glass and iron of the arches surmounting the tub and the visceral-looking glass tubes. "The power was aligned through the canopy,

though they've got it sourced wrong. Those two crystals at
the foot belong on either side of this sphere here, in an
equilateral triangle. Once that was done the power was
self-aligning, and a circle chalked round the whole would
close the circuit and start the process working. I wonder
where Bektis learned of it?"

"Wherever he found that gem he wears on his hand, be-
like," said the Icefalcon. "He calls it the Hand of Harilómne. It grants him greater power than ever I saw him
use."

Ingold, leaning over the vat to touch the brownish film
that seemed to emerge from the quicksilver lining itself,
looked up swiftly, and his white brows pulled together.
"Yes," he said, and there was old knowledge, old anger in
his voice. "Yes, I know what the Hand does. And it
probably isn't what Bektis thinks."

The Icefalcon leaned his back against the doorpost. He
found that even the walk down to the chamber had winded
him. His calves ached and felt on the verge of cramping;
annoying, he thought, and something he should be beyond. "I thought you said the Devices of the Times Before
were beyond your ken."

"Many of them are. But Harilómne was hardly a mage
of the Times Before, and he left accounts of his Hand—
and of this Device, as it happens, which he tried hard to
duplicate before he was driven out of the West of the
World by the Council of Wizards. I should imagine your
girl Hethya's mother encountered an incomplete copy of
his work on what he called the Cauldron of Warriors,
hidden away at Prandhays Keep."

"She is not *my* girl," said the Icefalcon indignantly, but
Ingold had already turned back to the vat and was studying
the pattern of tiny lights that gleamed starlike in its lining.
The Icefalcon followed him and saw that the bottom was
an inch or so deep in the brownish ooze that filmed the
sides. He shrank from the thought of touching it, even
should the salvation of his soul depend upon so doing.

There was evil here against which rivalries for love or

power, revenge, or the falsification of a sacrificial omen were the spites of a pettish child. A true evil, a monstrous and vile greed that disregarded all but itself.

"What does the old one do?" Loses His Way nodded toward Ingold, his voice low so that the mage would not hear. "What does he need to know, other than that this thing must be destroyed before Vair can make use of it again?"

Ingold moved on, fingering tubes and cylinders, and glanced calculatingly back at the chamber's door. Knowing him, the Icefalcon realized that the old man was wondering if there were a way of stealing all or part of the apparatus, a way of carrying it intact back to the Keep of Dare, to be studied and preserved.

He came swiftly around the end of the vat and closed his hand on the heavy wrist. "Destroy it," he said.

Later he realized that the fault lay in them both. Ingold for not simply destroying the thing at once—provided that such a thing were possible—and himself for distracting the mage and for a fatal second tying up Ingold's sword-hand and his own.

"Fool, Inglorion!" thundered a voice from the direction of the door. "Ten times a . . ."

Had Ingold not needed to shake free of the Icefalcon's grip he might have leveled his staff, fired off a spell of lightning and ruin, a moment faster. As it was, Bektis had time to duck, slipping back out of the doorway and slamming it shut. The blast of power Ingold hurled crashed the door open again, demolishing the heavy wood in the process; the Icefalcon stepped back from the wizard at the same moment Loses His Way stepped forward; Bektis' return blast of lightning caught them both.

Loses His Way went flying over the pile of corpses and against the wall, gasping with shock. Ingold staggered, catching himself on his staff for balance, and Bektis, in the doorway once more, cried out words in a voice of power, words the Icefalcon had heard before. The Court Mage lifted his hand, and the Icefalcon could see it encased in the gold-woven crystal Weapon of Harilómne, chilly light lancing, flashing through the matrices of power and showing up the bones within the flesh.

Ingold flinched, ducked, holding up his hand. Fire shattered around him, ripped long scars in the black stone of the floor. He hurled something—cloud, darkness, a smell of dust and blood—and dimly through blindness the Icefalcon saw Bektis' free hand move, trailing light from its fingertips like an acrobat making patterns with ribbon.

The patterns traced and scattered, spreading out across the black walls of the room itself, engulfing Ingold like a reaching hand. Ingold rolled to his feet and tried to rush the older mage, sword held high, and the Icefalcon realized an instant before it happened what Bektis was doing and cried out, "NO!"

Bektis turned in a swirling extravaganza of cloak and beard and slapped his right hand, the Hand of Harilómne, outspread into the center of the rushing pattern of color drawn from the walls. Ingold had almost reached him when thin blue lightning fingered out from the ceiling, the walls, from every corner of the chamber, stitching into the old mage's body like needles. Ingold stumbled, fell, got to his feet, and came on again, but shreds and shards of something that wasn't light and wasn't darkness seemed to peel from the very fabric of the Keep, ringing him in a nimbus of burning. He fell again, and Bektis removed Hand and Weapon from the wall and stretched forth his other hand, signing the flaring, chittering darkness to depart.

It did not.

Lightning flashed and wickered from the ceiling again, driving Ingold back along the floor. The old man rolled, tried to get to his feet, face set in shock and pain. Loses His Way charged Bektis with a roar of rage and was stabbed through with a finger of crimson fire from the crystal cap on the wizard's finger, dropping him in his tracks—the Icefalcon edged along the wall, sword drawn, waiting for his chance to strike.

Ingold tried to stand again; it was as if he were being devoured by a half-seen holocaust of stars.

Bektis took a step toward Ingold and said, "Stop it."

The lightning continued. Shadowy forms dipped and wavered around Ingold—he must have been using some kind of counterspell, for the Icefalcon could see his hands and lips move, even as he tried to get to his feet, gather his strength. Harsh half-seen flakes of light pushed him steadily back, toward the far wall, Bektis advancing . . .

But Bektis' hands fluttered uncertainly. In the reflected glare the Icefalcon could see that the Hand of Harilómne had crazed, like glass heated and suddenly cooled, the crystal clouded and dead.

Bektis' dark eyes were wide with terror and doubt. "Stop it," he called out again, speaking to the walls, the ceiling, the whole malevolent Keep itself that seemed to be bending and bowing toward him, funneling into the room like the heart of a killer storm. *"Stop it! I command you!"*

A darkness seemed to lift out of the rear wall of the cell, dry and ancient, covering it from the Court Mage's witch-light and from the illumination of the lightning that played and struck and slashed around Ingold's retreating form. The Icefalcon saw Ingold's face, sweat standing on his forehead and eyes wide with desperation; saw his lips move in the words of counterspells, holding off the lightning as best he could. Sheets and threads and arrows of purplish quasi light whirled around him like blown leaves, leaving black burns where they touched; cold filled the room, rolling in waves from the dark at the far end.

And there was a voice, the Icefalcon thought. A voice that laughed a slow, dry laughter, building in an almost silent crescendo of glee.

"Stop it!" Bektis' voice was almost a scream. He gestured wildly, and the grayed chunks of burned crystal fell from his hand in bloodstained pieces that shattered on the floor.

Loses His Way, staggering painfully to his feet, started

to rush forward to Ingold's side, and the Icefalcon grabbed his arm and dragged him back, behind Bektis, toward the door. A final flare of lightning sliced down, catching Ingold full in the chest. He staggered back and seemed to fall into where the wall should have been and wasn't.

Falling back into the engulfing darkness that a moment later was gone.

Ingold was gone, too.

Purple threads of lightning flowed around the ceiling of the chamber, down the walls, across the iron sides of the vat. Harmless, heatless, an echo of desiccated laughter.

The Icefalcon closed his grip hard on Loses His Way's arm and fled.

# CHAPTER NINETEEN

The Keep was alive.

Blue worms of phosphor fleeted along the join of the ceiling, slipped away out of sight into the wall. Somewhere far off, knocking could be heard, tapping and pounding on the black walls in blackness; once one of the walls of the Silent cell on the second level bled a little, liquid black in the dim pulse of the little fire, but red when Hethya went and touched it and brought the smear of it back to the fire on her fingers. She said, "T'cha!" and quickly wiped it away, but not before Tir saw.

The whole Keep was whispering. Names, Tir thought—the names of those who had departed. The names of those who had gone away. Sometimes it whistled, a sad little tune, an air Tir almost knew.

And sometimes it was only silent, and that silence was worse than anything. One could almost see in it the lifted ironic brow, the wet silver eye beneath.

Hethya raised her head sharply. Picking up one of the swords the men had left, she crossed to the cell's door. For a time she listened, face profiled in the ocher glow that twined her curls with brass and laid a thread of fire along the blade's edge. "Now what would they be after?"

Far off, almost unheard and thrown from wall to wall in a distant ripple of echoes, Tir could hear the barest strain of sound: a trumpet being blown.

"It only needed that," panted Loses His Way, "to make the hunt complete."

291

The Icefalcon, concentrating on igniting the oil-soaked end of a stick from his firepouch without putting out the hot little banked coal, muttered, "The hunt is far from complete." To his huge annoyance his hands were shaking and would not stop. Even the short run through the darkness had winded him, and the presence of enemies who might appear at any moment made him edgy as a panther. "Myself, I would not advise you wager any substantial sum on old Ingold being dead."

"Dead or living, he's of no use to us." Loses His Way pushed back the aureate mane of his hair, loosened from its braids during the beating and streaked with gore and filth, but still brilliant as summer light. "Can this shaman Bektis turn the very walls against us?"

The Icefalcon shook his head. "The Hand of Harilómne—the crystals he wore that shattered—were a spell of summoning, of focus, by which he made himself stronger. Being a fool, he summoned and focused the Ancestor of Shamans, Zay, he who sacrificed himself to become the *ki* of this place. Now that he has brought him to life he cannot send him away."

Lights flitted through the corridor, pale violet flames that lost themselves among the pallid spill of dead vines and mushroom forest growing from the cross corridor before them. It might only have been the quiver of the tiny flame on the end of his match, but the Icefalcon would have sworn the vines were moving.

Loses His Way used a colloquial term, common in the Real World, which meant "stands downwind from mammoths."

The Icefalcon looked around and knelt to hack chunks from the stringers of dried vines growing along the base of the wall. "The boy might know where that gulf of darkness would take him."

"And what then?" demanded the chieftain. "They will be sending forth this decoy soon. Without your shaman to aid us . . ."

A trumpet sounded in the Aisle. A peremptory note, the

call the Icefalcon recognized from the presence of the armies of the South at the Keep of Dare seven years ago. "It is a summons."

"That?" Loses His Way bridled. "Only fools would summon their warriors so, where anyone can hear."

"They are fools," said the Icefalcon dismissively. "And what enemies have they that they would fear in this place?"

The blue eyes narrowed, suddenly the eyes of a beast. "Us," he whispered. "O my enemy, they have us."

Cautiously picking their route so as to leave no track, the Icefalcon and Loses His Way took some time to find a stair to the second level upon which they would not meet Vair's warriors, most of whom were assembled in the Aisle when the two enemies slipped into a cell that had a window.

Extinguishing the torch and leaving only the single match burning, propped against the wall by the door, the men crept to the square outlined in dull red light and, looking down, saw the crowd gathered almost directly beneath them, where the vines had been trampled flat into a stinking mush. The bald pates of the clones caught a glister of the torchlight. They seemed, the Icefalcon saw, to herd instinctively together, like with like, brothers seeking the comfort of their brothers without knowing why, twelve or sixteen or in one case eighteen together, staring stupidly before them. The Icefalcon counted the heads of the whole men, the tufts of white or black or red hair still pulled up in topknots or lying loose on their shoulders: the men who moved briskly and spoke among themselves, glancing all the while at the dark Doors, the solemn lunacy of the water clock, the vast seethe of plant life at the Aisle's end.

Such a man was talking to Vair, his voice loud enough to carry to the unseen watchers above.

"Demons led them," he was saying, and gestured to two clones standing nearby, staring about them foolishly. Brother-clones, the Icefalcon saw, White Alketch with

their fair skin scratched and torn from vine shards and
thorns. "It's a long way around, going in through the back
because of that, my Lord." He nodded toward the hueless
tangle of the jungle—though the Icefalcon didn't understand many of his words, his gestures made clear enough
what he said. "But there are no vines around the place itself." *Hï ekkorgn*—selfsame place—the Icefalcon recognized too the word for *vines*. "It's just as my Lord Bektis
described it, my Lord: four chambers leading one out of
the other, with pillars of crystal flanking the arches." The
gestures of his hands—one, two, three, four—made his
meaning unmistakable.

"They've found it," whispered the Icefalcon, and he felt
a cold grimness settle around his heart. "The transporter
Vair has been seeking. The road that leads directly from
this place into the heart of the Keep."

"How do you know?"

The Icefalcon shook his head. Vair was speaking to
Bektis now, more quietly. "How far are these barbarians
from the crevasse's head?"

"As I see them in my scrying stone, my Lord, they come
on quickly." Bektis didn't look a hair the worse for his
battle with Ingold: long hair combed smooth over his
shoulders, beard like a curtain of snow. The Icefalcon noticed, however, that Bektis kept his right hand tucked out
of sight in his ermine muff.

"Can Prinyippos reach them from here?" Vair, too, was
uneasy, watching the black Doorways, the colorless vines,
like a man expecting attack. "If Inglorion knows of our
presence here, whether he came through the Far-Walker or
followed you over the mountains, you can believe he will
relay that information to the Lady of the Keep."

"My Lord, I tell you there is little to fear from the man
now. I wounded him, unto the death, I think."

"So you have told me." Vair's eyes returned to the
wizard's, with a coldness in them the Icefalcon could
sense even from his high coign. "But you told me also that

you were not pursued. You told me that Inglorion himself
was in Gae."

"He *was*, my Lord. On that I will swear."

"Then he came after you, Bektis, with truly enviable
speed. Perhaps he was even here before us. In either case
we have no time to waste."

"As you say, my Lord." Bektis managed to make a gesture of submission without taking his hand from his muff.

"It is best," Vair said, "that the matter be pressed to conclusion without delay. Is Prinyippos ready?"

Bektis smiled, a hint of smug triumph in his eyes.
"I trust," he purred, "that my Lord will find my work
satisfactory."

He held out his hand, and a slim form stepped from the
door of the nearest cell. That door was almost under the
window where the Icefalcon and Loses His Way watched,
so they didn't see the scout until he reached Bektis' side.
Beside him, the Icefalcon felt rather than heard the thick
hard jerk of breath.

It was Twin Daughter.

Twin Daughter as she had ridden to battle on Bison Hill,
when all she thought was that here was an easy raid. Twin
Daughter with her three flame-bright braids wrist-thick
over a coat of mammoth hide, her scarred oval face thin
with hardship and brown with the sun-glare on the ice.
The Icefalcon felt the movement of his enemy's arm
against him and glanced sidelong to see Loses His Way
reach inside his coat to touch the spirit-pouches that hung
around his neck.

"I thought you said this Bektis had lost the greater part
of his power?"

"He made this glamour before, to show it to Vair,
wanting his praise," the Icefalcon whispered. "It did
not take much to renew now, like a banked coal being
breathed once again to life."

"Not bad, my Lord, you must admit."

Twin Daughter said something to his lord in a teasing
voice, flirting with him, and Vair's dark face split with a

lewd grin. The Icefalcon did not understand the idiomatic speech, but the tone was that of a woman of the streets, bantering a customer, and he felt Loses His Way shiver.

"She looks good enough to bed," purred Vair, and put a hand on Twin Daughter's—Prinyippos'—cheek. The counterfeit woman simpered and made a play of eyelashes, and the men around them hooted and laughed. "Of course," Vair added with a grin, "she did before."

"Hyena." The voice of Loses His Way was soft, like the first cracking of the ice underfoot, when a traveler is too far to reach shore before it gives. "Scum."

"She is dead." The Icefalcon turned his eyes away, not wanting to see what he saw in his enemy's face. "She lies beyond his dishonor."

"Even so," he breathed. "Even so."

"You will go with Prinyippos," Vair continued, turning to Bektis. "At a safe distance you will follow to maintain this illusion that you keep on him. Mongret, Gom, Tuuves . . ." There was a stirring—the first man stepped forward, but Gom and Tuuves were clones, and nearly a dozen of each tried to amble to the front. Vair seized one of each name, gestured the rest back as if they had been beggars importuning him in the street.

"My Lord," said Bektis, "you know the strength of my illusions. The caving-in of the crevasse can be accomplished as easily from within these walls as without. May I remind my Lord that the wizard Inglorion is still somewhere here."

"I thought you had killed him, Bektis." The gold eyes cut to him, a flint knife gashing flesh. "And yes, I know well the strength of your illusions. When the avalanche is accomplished and all the barbarians are dead, you will return and inform me. I will send you out again with the larger party to recover the bodies. I trust you will find some way to keep the barbarians engaged outside until the matter is accomplished."

"My Lord," said Bektis stiffly, "they have not yet returned."

"Excellent." Vair folded his arms, his hooked hand as always out of sight within the folds of his cloak. "I trust I have no need to remind you of the probable fate of a mage who through spells forbidden by both other wizards and the Church influenced not only the choice, but the date, of the succession of the Prince-Bishop of the Alketch should that mage find himself abroad in the world without a protector?"

Bektis' mouth tightened under the flowing beard, his dark eyes filled with loathing and fear. "You have no need to remind me, my lord. Nor do I need reminding that rightness and legality consist not in what one has done, but whether one holds a position of power."

Vair smiled. "Good. But I shall remind you nevertheless should you show signs of absentmindedness. Be prepared to depart at the next chiming of the clock."

The Icefalcon and Loses His Way watched while further dispositions were made, four men set to guard the great Doors while others were sent out searching again. The Icefalcon caught the word for what his people called *innyiasope*, yellow jessamine, a potent poison frequently used to deprive mages of their powers, and guessed that Ingold was their quarry. The old man had been hurt already by the pent rage and magic of the Keep of Shadow. Gil-Shalos would kill him, thought the Icefalcon, if he let Ingold come to further harm.

Beside him, Loses His Way asked in a low voice, "How much ill can this Bektis do?"

"Because he has not the Hand of Magic does not mean he is without power," replied the Icefalcon. "My sister tells me that there are herbs a Wise One may chew to temporarily increase power in times of need or restore it when after too great an exertion it fails, though the cost is terrible afterward." He watched the graceful white-haired Wise One make his way to the nearest stair. "I have known Bektis many years, and he is a man who is never without such an expedient. He may have used such to renew the illusion existing on Prinyippos the Crested Egret. In any case, men can start an avalanche in this country as easily as magic."

The chieftain chewed on the ends of his mustache, staring out into the torchlight, which faded as men dispersed into the mazes once more. One of the searchers halted in crossing a toadstool-choked watercourse, reached down to lift something from the bridge—a cup, the Icefalcon saw, one of those weird apports that were, like the knocking, signs of the growing strength of the mad *ki* within the dark.

At last Loses His Way sighed, his broad shoulders slumping, and he said again, "Even so. My enemy, see the boy bestowed somewhere safe and fetch Hethya to this place at the sounding of the next chime. Tell her to come armed."

The Icefalcon raised his brows. "If you think the three of us capable of defeating four warriors with a full view of the Aisle and a wall at their backs . . ."

"Just fetch her."

There was a note in his voice that made the Icefalcon turn and a look in the chieftain's eyes—resigned, defeated, sad—that made him pause. But there was nothing he could say to his enemy—who was not his kinsman—nothing he could ask that Loses His Way would answer. So he only asked, "Will you need light?" and, at Loses His Way's assent, slipped into the corridor again, down two turnings to where the gray cold-dried plants lay thick and came back to kindle another torch.

Then, slipping quietly along the endless crisscrossed junctures of the halls, detouring twice, thrice, and many times again to avoid the plants or the ice that would leave mark of his passing, he made his way to the hidden stair that led to the chamber of Silence.

An hour, he thought, for Prinyippos to reach the Empty Lakes People. An hour or perhaps two to convince them of the truth of his assertions, to explain how he, Twin Daughter, had come to this place. The Stars alone knew how he was going to do that. Breaks Noses was a seasoned warrior and a skeptical man: the Icefalcon had fought him in a dozen minor raids and wars. He would sniff cautiously at a trap before stepping inside.

But the shaman of the Empty Lakes People was long dead. The wolfskin leggings and tunic that Twin Daughter appeared to wear were the very garments in which she had ridden to her death: a Wise One, whatever else one might say of Bektis, was always keenly observant. Her hair had the same bright hue, like the grass on the southern slope of the Twisted Hills in the Moon of Farewell, and braided into it were the hand bones of a man who had long ago stolen her horses in the forty-mile dry stretch between Angry Creek and the Place Where We Catch Salmon.

Prinyippos would come out of seracs that marked the buried mountains and speak to the Empty Lakes People with Twin Daughter's voice. Even the mother of Twin Daughter would believe.

Perhaps especially the mother of Twin Daughter.

The Icefalcon quickened his stride. Everywhere, now, he had the sensation of being watched. Where he turned to avoid a tunnel filled for thirty feet and no farther with bars and sheets and spears of ice, he saw by his feeble matchlight that the icicles bled.

What would Prinyippos say to them? he wondered. The Keep was buried under half a mile of ice. They had been tracking the great party of men and mules, drawn by rumors of southern weapons of tempered steel. Would he say to them, "There is a great house, a great city, of the mud-diggers, where they have these weapons under slender guard"?

There would be no difficulty in finding a crevasse suitable for a trap. They were everywhere, waiting innocently for an unwary foot above. It did surprise him a little that Blue Child had let her warriors be drawn off by a promise of mammoth, mirages being what they were in this land. Still, he had been hungry enough to go hunting a putative lemming, from time to time.

Two turnings to the left in pitchy gloom, the pattern of

lichen and fungus familiar on the wall beside him. Frost here—turn aside. A trick of shadow concealing the doorway, then up steps, endless and spiraling, the smell of dust and death and rotting plants rising around him like the slow heat of a stove.

Blue fox fire outlined doorways and turnings, then vanished. Nearly on top of him something screamed in the ragged voice of a puma, what felt like claws raking his face. The Icefalcon's sword was in his hand and he was cutting, a checked stroke to avoid damaging the blade on the wall . . .

And of course it met nothing. There was the puma scream again, claws ripping his sleeve. He felt them catch and pull, felt the seep of hot blood underneath, but there was no cold—the sleeve hadn't been torn. If it wasn't exactly an illusion, he thought, forcing himself to walk on, it was meant for the same purpose, to get him to run and lose himself in the labyrinth. The demons, too, took strength from the magic of the Keep.

The thing screamed in his ear for another dozen yards, then let him alone. He heard it scream again, muffled by distance and by turnings; heard a man's shriek of terror and the thunder of running feet.

*Fool.*

"What happened?" gasped Hethya when he came into the chamber of Silence. He put up his hand to his face, and his fingers came away bloodied.

"Demons. I need Hethya to help me, Scarface. The warriors of Vair are hunting for Ingold everywhere on this level." Time enough later to tell the boy Vair had found the transporter. "Is there some safer place where you can hide?"

Tir nodded. "There's a room above this one, on the fourth level. You can't see the door. You have to count steps. Fifteen from the last corner before the wall. You can't see the door from inside, either."

"Will you be well there?" Hethya asked worriedly, as if,

thought the Icefalcon, Tir hadn't thought the matter out before speaking.

Tir nodded. "I'll be fine."

"You won't be afraid?"

"No."

"And what did you think the boy would say?" whispered the Icefalcon as they ascended a stone thread of stair to the level above. "*Yes, I'll be terrified?* Of course he will be afraid." He watched while Tir counted careful steps and then pushed at the black stone of the wall. The wall yielded nothing. The Icefalcon paced off fourteen of his own long strides and tested the wall. As with Ingold's body, his hand seemed enveloped in shadow—it was indeed difficult to see anything in the dim lamplight—and he stepped through into a close-smelling blackness.

He reached back immediately and drew the others in, Hethya holding up the lamp. A ribbon of water ran down the wall into a basin, and where the water came out, lichen and fungus and the ubiquitous vines choked the ancient spigot. The whole room was foul with leathery leaves. The Icefalcon thrust his sword into every vine and clump of toadstools, paced off the confines of the room, then cut the dead vines away, clearing a space for a fire and at the same time making something to burn. He was very tired now and though food had made him sick before, he felt the need of it desperately, muscles aching and all his flesh deathly cold. His hair had come unbraided from the snatchings of demons, hanging down his back in a cloak the hue of moonlight and getting in his way every time he turned his head.

He kindled a little fire and laid down two sticks of vine to show where the door was on the inside. "We'll be back," he said.

Tir looked hopelessly tiny and hopelessly young. "I'm not afraid."

The Icefalcon kindled the vine-stem torch. "You may be the only one in the Keep to be saying that. Sleep if you can."

Though the dreams in this place, he thought, were not something that he would wish upon a friend, or on a friend's son.

"They've found the transporter," he said to Hethya as they descended again. "Loses His Way has a plan, he says, to keep Vair from getting more men, but the Keep will need to be warned, if we can devise it."

In the corridors of the second level a clone crawled along on his hands and knees, bawling out names at the top of his lungs. Elsewhere footsteps raced by them, ghostly and bodiless but fleet with the speed of panic, and the Icefalcon thought he heard the tearing intake of breath.

The Keep was alive.

"I never thought that it would be like this," whispered Hethya, hurrying at his side. "Never."

"And what did you think it would be like?"

"Like home, mostly." Hethya shook her head. "Only musty, empty. They can't have stayed here all that long, it's so . . . so tidy. I don't know if you've been to Prand-hays Keep, me lanky friend, but it's a fair warren, worse than Renweth, at least what I saw of Renweth. Fat chance I'll ever have of them invitin' me back when this is over, and small blame to 'em. Mother . . ."

She hesitated, her breath indrawn, then let it go. The Icefalcon touched her arm, holding her back. Something moved in the corridor ahead, near the rectangle of wavering light that marked where the Aisle would lie. His sword was already in his hand. He scanned the walls quickly, looking for another door, a way to get behind whatever lay ahead of them.

A voice whispered, "Icefalcon."

Loses His Way. He felt Hethya's breath come in for reply—they'd doused the torch some way back—and he squeezed her arm, hard. There was more than one in the corridor.

From another shadow, the same voice breathed, "It's all right." There was no mistaking the voice of Loses His Way.

"By the Corn-Woman's hair-sticks, man, we have no time!"

The voice—the same voice as the first two—spoke from yet another shadow, and they all stepped forward at once, outlined against the flickering reflections of the torchlight in the Aisle. Cold passed through the Icefalcon like the onset of mortal sickness.

He made himself step forward, say, "I'm here."

Beside him, Hethya whispered, "Dear God in heaven," and he heard the rustle of the mammoth-wool coat she wore as she made a sign to avert evil.

But evil had already come—and gone.

There were four of him. Them.

*No. My enemy, no.*

The process of shredding, of peeling the flesh from the screaming bones, remade as well as made. All four of Loses Their Way had their teeth once more, and none bore the bruises of Vair's beating. He looked different, with neither hair nor beard, the broad face far younger, the strong chin and generous mouth odd and prominent. The Icefalcon wondered if the scar he'd given Loses His Way at the Place of the Sugar Maples was gone.

The words of Tir came back to him: *That's where they put the needles in* . . . And Ingold: *The power is self-aligning* . . .

Who knew what he had learned from watching Bektis in the chamber before Hethya rescued him or what Tir had told him of what he had seen?

His people being lured into danger, his daughter dishonored by Bektis' illusion . . .

*O my enemy, no.*

They had divided his clothing among them, like the sons of a man who has died. One wore his boots, another his shirt of wolf-hide, another his leggings, under a makeshift assortment of garments stripped from the corpses in the vat-room, the commissariat where clothing and weapons were stored. One of them carried all four spirit-bags, still bound at his belt.

They were all armed, too.

Hethya's eyes were wide, suddenly filled with tears. "O my friend," she said softly.

Loses His Way—one Loses His Way—shook his head: "Woman, we have no friends among the people of the Real World but our kin." He spoke slowly, laboriously putting together the words with wits divided and dulled, and his voice was sad. "This my enemy"—he put a heavy arm around the Icefalcon's shoulders, hugged him hard— "he is dear to me as a son, but he is my enemy. My kin would kill him the moment they saw him."

He drew their swords. "It is done," he said. "Vair and his warriors will be in the Aisle soon. And . . ." He frowned, groping for a thought that escaped him, and another of him said, "The Talking Stars People. The Talking Stars People will be back."

"Ah." He nodded. "Yes. They are chasing a mammoth that doesn't exist." He smiled, and a flicker of his old self glinted in the blue eyes. "And well served. My enemy, let us go."

The Icefalcon and Hethya pulled up the hoods of their coats, so when the six of them crossed the Aisle—four hairless clones and another who wore the rawhide footgear of the clones—none of the four clones on the Doors would notice. Not that they would anyway.

The fight before the Doors was short and sharp. Other Alketch warriors were scattered about the Aisle and came running, but the cavern was long, and in the juddering gloom it took a few moments before any of them realized anything was amiss. By that time the Icefalcon and Loses Their Way had pulled open the Doors.

Men fell on them from behind, and the Icefalcon turned, cutting and striking, his body falling into the practiced routines driven into him by Gnift, Swordmaster of the Guards, and before him by Noon and the other warriors of the Talking Stars People: feint, dodge, bob, slash, ducking to use his long legs to sweep the opponent's feet from beneath him, cutting with the dagger in his left hand.

Loses His Way grunted in agony as a sword plowed up under his breastbone; the Icefalcon felt a sharp regret to see the light vanish from those blue eyes. But at the same instant Loses His Way half turned in the long black tunnel of the gates, and cold air swirled through as the outer doors were pulled open. Loses His Way slashed the throat of an Alketch warrior, turned almost in the same movement and jerked free Twin Daughter's spirit-pouch from his belt, threw it whirling down the dark gate tunnel.

Loses His Way in the outer Doors caught it, shoved it through his belt in the same instant that Loses His Way who had thrown it—the man born in magic and pain, but man nonetheless—took an Alketch hatchet between his shoulder blades, having taken his eyes from his enemies to make his throw. The Icefalcon gutted the man who killed him a second later, but it was too late and he knew it. Loses His Way collapsed on the inner threshold of the Doors, body spasming. There was understanding in his eyes the second before the awareness went out of them, understanding when the Icefalcon, Hethya, and Loses His Way, taking advantage of the fact that the next Alketch warriors were still some thirty feet away, turned and fled back into the hidden and secret halls.

Loses His Way, warchief of the Empty Lakes People, flopped a few times on the steps of the Keep as his lungs tried vainly to expand in his rib cage, then died alone.

"The spirit-pouch will—will break the illusion." Stumbling at the heels of the Icefalcon and Hethya as they wound their tortuous way through crossing corridors, Loses His Way brought out the words with effort, something memorized carefully and only half comprehended. "The spells of Bektis, the spells that make Breaks Noses and the others believe that this Prinyippos is Twin Daughter, will not endure in the presence of a part of her, the soul of her, the spirit that remains in the spirit-pouch. If he can reach them . . ."

He turned and looked back over his shoulder, though all sight of the Aisle had been obliterated behind the ebon walls, the endless night around them. They were in a place of thick growth, dead vines crunching beneath their feet, and the creepers rustled with the movement of demons, droplets of what looked like blood on their leaves.

"He'll reach them," said the Icefalcon. "If he is as strong as you, my enemy, and too stupid to know when to quit, he'll reach them."

"Did it hurt you," Hethya asked softly, "when the other two died? Your—your other selves?"

A foolish question, thought the Icefalcon—they were separate people after all—but Loses His Way said, "I felt it. I . . . it is a loneliness. Worse I think than when Twin Daughter died, or her sister, who perished when they were only babies."

He looked down at her, a big generous kingly man, and oddly, no less so now, bald and shorn and stripped of the spear-point of his wit. His heart remained a king's heart. "I feel—empty. Hollow. As if all chance of ever being whole again were gone. But of course it was gone when I . . . when I climbed into the vat."

"Do you remember it?"

The lampflame wavered on glittering ice; the Icefalcon turned aside, guiding them, counting doorways and turnings. A great confusion filled him, horror and regret that he knew he should not feel—Loses His Way was his enemy after all. But he could not rid his mind of the clones' dreams of agony, the only memories they possessed.

In the darkness men's voices called out distantly, footsteps thudded far off; someone cried out in horror, cut short. Like a breath of wind a low laugh seemed to hover on the edge of hearing.

"Not really. Just . . . like a beating in childhood. I don't . . ." Loses His Way turned, sword in his hand, listening, but only silence breathed from the choked passageway to their left, the wilderness of stalactites and wrinkled frost-mounds to their right. "I don't remember. Is all well with you, my friend?"

The Icefalcon opened his mouth indignantly to disclaim friendship with any member of the Empty Lakes People but said instead, "All is well." He had a slash through his coat, but the tough mammoth-hide had taken the force of the cut, which had not penetrated to the skin. His face smarted from the claws of the demons, and he felt cold to the marrow of his bones.

"What now?" asked Hethya as they climbed the last long stair.

"The transporter must be guarded," said the Icefalcon. "No magic will work in that chamber, so even if Bektis returns you will have little to fear. They so wrought it that one man outside could defend the vestibule from an army arriving by transporter—and of course any similar defense in the Keep of Dare has long since been taken out by those silly laundresses who have the rooms now. But such defenses work the other way as well. Vair may have men there already, but with luck they won't realize Loses His Way is anything but some White Alketch clone until it's too late."

Loses His Way grinned. "Now this," he said, "this sounds like good hunting. I and my other selves, we will need to split our tally of enemies killed when we come before the *ki* of battle," he explained to Hethya. "Naturally I need to kill a good many more, and an army coming at me through a single door . . . Ah!"

"I couldn't help but be noticing," said Hethya, "about this '*you* will have little to fear.' And just where does this *you* come out of, me lanky boy?"

"It comes out of one of us having to find Ingold and find him quickly," retorted the Icefalcon. "He must have told someone at the Keep of Vair's intention, so if worse came to the worst they will not be taken completely unawares, but without Ingold we cannot warn them, by transporter or by other means. The boy Tir may recall something of where he might be, something of this Keep."

They reached the last turning of the corridor. Darkness stretched all around them, waiting. Somewhere the

Icefalcon could hear Zay whistling, that maddening, haunting tune. On the floor before him glinted a handful of jewels, a woman's headdress and rings, pale-green jewels whose heart glinted black as mile-deep ice. Whose?

Stepping around them, he counted out fourteen of his long strides, picking by touch the pattern of lichen and molds on the wall, familiar now.

"We are here, Scarface; we've sent an envoy to the Empty Lakes People. Now we need . . ."

He stepped into the little room and stopped.

Tir was gone.

# CHAPTER TWENTY

Tir waited a long time.

Far off he could hear the voices of men calling and the ghostly chiming of the clock. These didn't frighten him the way the whispering did, endlessly telling over in darkness the names of people whose faces Tir remembered but whom he'd never met. The voice was tiny, but it was right there in the room with him, like a worm-stuffed rat crouching in the corner.

Sometimes the voice said other things to him, too. Things about what Vair would do to him when he caught him. Things about his mother beating him for being stupid when he got back to the Keep. Things about Hethya and the Icefalcon being dead.

It was illusion and Tir tried to ignore it, but time stretched out, and it might have been true. Vair was out there, and the image of the Icefalcon's body—cold asleep, as he had been when Hethya and Loses His Way brought him in—would not leave his mind. He loved Hethya, and since everything and everybody else he loved had been taken away from him, why not her, too?

Curiously, he knew exactly where Ingold was. He didn't know whether this was something he remembered or something the Keep told him, but he knew where he was and how to get there. After Renweth, the Keep of the Shadow was ridiculously easy to navigate, or would be except for the vines.

It was just that he had an idea of what the place was and didn't want to go there.

The Icefalcon had said, *Wait.*

Tir drank a little water from the bottle at his belt and waited, trying to shut the voice from his ears.

But there was something wrong with the room. It seemed smaller than it had a few minutes—but how many minutes?—ago. The crinkly mats of fungus on one wall, the blobby lichens on the ceiling, appeared thicker in the tiny flare of the lamp, and it seemed to him that they'd begun, ever so slightly, to pulse. And there was something he couldn't see moving in the corners.

There was another place that was safer.

Safe forever, within enclosing walls, where he'd never have to go outside again. Wind and sunlight and open air tangled with the images of Vair's hand and Vair's voice, and the terror that other boy had felt in the open—waiting in the circle of the wagons for the Dark Ones to come— merged with the gnashing onslaught of pain and grief and guilt and dread.

Darkness safe and still. Darkness where nobody could get to him again, nobody could hurt him, ever. Darkness warm within these walls.

The Icefalcon and Hethya and Loses His Way were dead—he had a horrible dream-vision of the chieftain dying on the threshold of the Doors, gasping for breath that would not come, a hatchet stuck bloody in his back. They were never coming back for him.

And that was all his fault, too.

Only Vair would come. Any minute. Any minute.

Unless he got out fast.


"Huh. I thought White Raiders were supposed to be able to track fish through water." Hethya folded her arms and contemplated the black stretch of corridor, barely to be seen in the guttering flicker of the makeshift torchlight.

"A dog of ten thousand Ancestors cannot track a ripe fish if that dog's nose is covered." The Icefalcon spoke without even raising himself up on his elbows, stretched full-length among the scuffed creepers, the broken mosses, a burning vinestalk held in one hand a little over his head. "Someone passed here since you and I departed to meet Loses His Way near the Aisle. But whether that someone was child or grown, woman or man, coming first and then going away or emerging from the room and fleeing, I cannot tell from these few marks in this light."

"Could someone have found the room?" she asked, moving after the Icefalcon as he proceeded up the hallway, snakelike on his belly, checking and studying each inch of the broken tracks through the vines. "Entered it and taken him away?"

"Indeed someone could," the Icefalcon replied. He spit a stray strand of his hair out of his mouth. "Whether they did or not is another matter."

"There was no sign of struggle." Loses His Way appeared from the nearest crossing corridor, another vinetorch in his hand. The instincts and training of a tracker were deep in his core; it would take more than the horror of cloning, of having his soul and self divided, to rob him of that. "The moss and fungus on the walls is thick. It would take a print easily."

"Were Tir a man grown I would say it pointed to his leaving of his own accord," agreed the Icefalcon. "But a child is easily overcome. Easily fooled as well, though less so, I think, with that particular child. There." He stopped in the crossing of another passageway, rising to his knees and holding the torch aloft. "At last. See how the stems and broken leaves lie, outward into this corridor where the floor is clear? There is no sign of someone coming inward. More, the fanned-out stems and broken leaves aren't much. Small size and slight weight. He departed alone, of his own will, I think."

"Why?"

"Thought leaves no track." The Icefalcon crawled a few more feet, examining the floor, which in this portion of the corridor was hard black stone, unyielding of any mark. A little farther on, lichens blotched it and the walls. Tir had gone carefully, but not carefully enough.

"There. That's his foot." The Icefalcon looked up. "The ceilings are high, but had a man borne that little lamp I think the smoke would have marked the fungus." The thick, whitish growth clumped the ceiling overhead, like the wrinkled bellies of pigs. "Demons may have found him there and frightened him into leaving, but he didn't flee in panic. See how the heel of his foot is marked as deep as the toe? He seeks something. Look how he's tried one passageway, then turned back."

"And you said thought leaves no track?" Hethya scuffed along after him, amused.

The Icefalcon raised his brows. "There is nothing here of the boy's thought. Only what I can guess from his actions. If I saw an antelope's track going toward Cranberry Pond, then turning so suddenly that sand was kicked up toward the pond, I would surmise that the beast smelled a dire wolf in the serviceberry thicket between the two maple trees there." He rubbed his eyes, which burned from lack of sleep. His body ached, and the very small amount of pemmican he'd consumed from the last of Loses His Way's stash had ceased to deliver energy a long time ago.

"And how d'ye know it was a dire wolf and not a saber-tooth or a wee bit of a bobcat, me lanky boy?"

"Because a family of dire wolves have hunted for twenty years among the serviceberry thickets on that side of Cranberry Pond. And what of Oale Niu?" he continued, resuming his careful quest along the passageway. "What has she to say of where the child might seek safer refuge, here in the Keep of Night?"

Glancing back at Hethya's silence, he saw the woman duck her head, her rich mouth tightening ruefully in the flickering torchlight. "Oale Niu would say," she said, "that Tir's headed inward to the heart of the Keep. That would be my guess, anyway. Everything me mother learned of the Keeps seems to indicate that places where power centered seemed to lie in a sort of pattern throughout but cen-

tered on the midline in the middle third. And the center of
the Keep's pattern was the heart of the Keep."

The Icefalcon nodded. "The laundry rooms in Renweth—
which is where the transporter lies—are on the midline,"
he said. "And the chambers where Tir hid lay at the corners. It makes sense."

He got to his feet, wiping some of the muck from his
hands on his wolfskin tunic, and moved carefully on.
Tracking by the dim flutter of the torchlight was giving
him a headache—even moonlight would have been pref-
erable, being more stable. But Noon always said that the
times when one's life depended most on tracking, the light
was usually bad.

"I'm glad I don't have to deal with Oale Niu anymore,"
sighed Hethya. "She was such a stick."

"She served her purpose." The Icefalcon never thought
he'd achieve tolerance for what this woman had done, but
he found he could not dislike her. "And you did her well."

"She was me Aunt Flory." Hethya laughed a little, drew
herself up to the posture associated with the mage of ancient times, and intoned, "Unless that girl is made to wear
a corset, Uranwë, she will have no better posture than a
peasant. 'A tree may be bent by a child, if the child but
bend a twig.' Uranwë was me mother," she added, a little
sad. "I always pictured Oale Niu in me mind with Flory's
face, and the way Flory did up her hair, in a lot of loops
round her ears."

She paused, seeing the Icefalcon's raised brows, and explained, "It helps to picture someone you're tellin' a tale
of. It makes for a better tale."

"I have never understood," said the Icefalcon, exasperated, "why civilized people wish to make a 'better' tale of
something which is not true. It is useful to tell lies to one's
enemies, but civilized people make a virtue of falsehood."

"Ah, it's not a falsehood, me lad," she sighed. " 'Tis an
art, like singin' or dancin', for the joy of the thing, and the
beauty alone. And there's times when it's more. Sometimes when a person's in grief or in pain, that beauty'll

carry 'em through until the pain gets less and they can go on. And sometimes when their mind is goin' in a circle of rage or hurt, they can find rest in some image, some way the words gyre, until they can think clearer and find a way through."

Gil returned to his mind, the intensity of her blue eyes in the glowing magelight as she wove her tales of men who could fly through the air and princesses who led armies through starry darkness to victory with the help of farmboys and smugglers and men wrought of metal and wire. Rudy, he recalled, had told a tale once, of a king stranded for twenty years on a desert island inhabited by two magical spirits and of the man who came to find him and fell in love with his daughter. "Cool, punk," Gil had said. "I didn't know you'd ever read *The Tempest.*" "What tempest?" Rudy had replied, startled. "I'm talking about *Forbidden Planet.*"

A drift of voices sounded in the darkness, soft at first but growing nearer. There was a cell several yards up the corridor whose door still partially survived; the Icefalcon indicated bare patches in the floor, and in three tiptoeing leaps made it to the place. Hethya followed so clumsily he wanted to strangle her—any competent enemy could have read her tracks—with Loses His Way helping her over the longest jump.

Fortunately, the voices belonged to clones, hacking free and gathering into blankets all the vines, all the lichens, all the monstrous, deformed toadstools that they could from the corridor. The Icefalcon cursed as they casually obliterated all trace of the child's tracks. He would be hours picking up the trail again.

Beside him Hethya whispered, "What are they doing? They can't be going to eat that stuff."

He clapped his hand over her mouth—the woman would talk through the ruin of the world—and waited until the clones finished their harvest and staggered trying to balance their torches with the unwieldy loads.

"No," breathed the Icefalcon. "Bektis has returned and

informed Vair that there will be no fodder for his black vat."

"Then I succeeded." Loses His Way's blue eyes shone in the tiny seed of the surviving matchlight. He shut them then for a moment, breathing deep, remembering past the nightmare wall of pain. "It was not in vain."

"But he's gatherin' up that garbage naytheless."

"This is Vair we speak of," the Icefalcon pointed out. "He will have his men, and he will have them soon. He knows his time is short. I think, my enemies, that we must give over our hunt for Tir, at least until we hold the transporter chamber. Then I will return to this place and take up the hunt again."

"The trail will be cold," Loses His Way warned.

The Icefalcon gestured at the mess of scraps and shards the three clones had left. "It cannot possibly be colder than it is now, and it may be that the delay will cost us the Keep of Dare. Come. The scout who found the place said it was roundabout to avoid the vines that grow in that whole part of the Keep. It will take us some little time to find."

In the event, it did not take him as long to locate as he feared it might, though over the next two hours Hethya had a good deal to say concerning the parentage and eventual destinies of Vair na-Chandros, the Icefalcon himself, and the builders of the Keep of the Shadow. The explanatory gestures of the scout when talking to Vair had indicated, as such gestures subconsciously do, not only the manner but the direction of his search, and the scout himself had taken not the slightest precaution to cover his own tracks, those of the two demon-led clones who'd first discovered the place, or those of the three guards Vair had subsequently dispatched to keep watch in the room. It was easy not only to find the place once they cut the man's trail but to determine how many guards were there.

The fact that Vair needed all his nonclone warriors for other things helped, too. None of those on guard so much as questioned when Loses His Way—bald and beardless and clothed pretty much like everyone else in Vair's party—entered, greeted them with grunts, and killed two of them before any realized what was going on. By that time the Icefalcon and Hethya were through the narrow door and it was all over.

"Trust Vair, the bastard, not to provide the poor souls with a bite to eat on duty," sighed Hethya after searching the bodies. "Not that I didn't appreciate the pemmican back a while ago, me dear . . ." She flashed a quick grin at Loses His Way. "Just that it's worn off, if you take my meaning. Me mother would tell me to be glad I'd had that, and stop complaining."

"That," said the Icefalcon, hauling the clones over into a corner, where they could not be seen from the vestibule, "was said by the Ancestor of All Mothers to the first child born in the world. Personally, I derive little consolation from the knowledge that I have been hungrier in my life."

He moved along the walls of each chamber in succession, torch in hand, examining the place as a wolf would examine a trap. It was as he had seen it in his shadow state, a succession of four chambers, each smaller than the last, dwindling in length in accordance with what he vaguely recognized as some mathematical ratio and connected by open archways flanked with pillars of what appeared to be frosted glass. The last chamber of the four was noticeably colder than the other three, and there was a smell there, curious and disturbing, that he could not identify but that made his flesh creep on his bones. He walked quickly out of it, back to the small watch fire where Hethya and Loses His Way awaited him, and looked back over his shoulder two or three times, troubled by the impression that when he did so he would see nothing but darkness at his back.

But there was always only the rear wall.

The vestibule was, like the suite itself, clear of growths of any sort, a circular chamber some twenty feet in diameter—he could recall no corresponding room in the Keep of Dare—whose inner doorway would barely admit a man. Stepping into the corridor outside, he followed it to where a thick plug of vine had been chopped clear, admitting to the second, spherical vestibule.

*The Wise One stands here,* thought the Icefalcon, raising his torch to look around. *From here he works the spells that enable the transporter to function.* Light glimmered, as through a window, and, turning, he saw that there was a window indeed, a convex crystal set into one wall that showed the length of the transporter suite, down to its farthest end. Though he had seen no corresponding circle of crystal in the first of the transporter chambers, it was clear that this was where the window opened: he saw plainly the small fire, the dead clones, Loses His Way standing beside the door that was narrower than his own shoulders.

Hethya went to him and put her hand on that massive back, speaking to him, the Icefalcon thought, though he heard no sound. Loses His Way turned, his blue eyes gentle in the firelight, and sad.

She asked him something, raising her hand to brush cheekbone and jaw with the backs of her fingers, and the firelight touched her curls with carnelian and put specks of sunset in her eyes. There was a wistfulness there, and a hope that tries not to hope. Loses His Way smiled, took the hand still raised in his rough fingers, and shook his head. Then he brought her hand to his lips and leaned down a little—for he was a very tall man, even against her height—and kissed her forehead.

But what she asked him, and what he replied, the Icefalcon never knew.

Tir hid for a long time in the darkness. It was peaceful there, and safe. The moss on which he curled was soft beneath his body, the air warm. He slept deeply, dreamed sweetly of long uninterrupted peace. When he woke, he was dimly aware that Vair was furiously angry with Bektis, berating and coldly cursing him for . . . for what? Tir didn't know, but Bektis' clothing and beard were dotted with blood, and he was flecked all over with ice and snow. In any case, it didn't trouble him.

Vair would never, could never, find him here.

No one could.

He became aware of the stirring, the angry susurration of the vines. They didn't stay still. Even the dead ones didn't stay still. They shifted and moved, growing tighter and tighter in certain corridors. Lights crept and stole through them like glowing worms, and Tir became dimly aware that the activity was concentrated, concentrated in a corridor a level down from him and some distance away . . .

Cold. There was cold growing in that corridor, even as the vines choked and knotted tight. Wind poured through them, wind that came out of nowhere, enough to tear the flesh from the bones. Water gushed down among the vines, first in drowning torrents, then slowly lessening to a steady trickle as the cold grew.

The Keep, Tir realized, was trying to kill someone there. Strangle them, blind them, kill them with cold.

He was overwhelmed with the urge to go back to sleep.

"Tir?" The word was gasped, nearly soundless, close to the hidden door of the cell. "Tir, are you there?" He knew the voice, soft and husky and perpetually half breathless, now breaking with exhaustion and strain. The Icefalcon.

The door of the cell itself had long ago perished, but the open doorway was concealed within a curiously obscuring gloom, like many of the doors in the Keep. Tir wasn't sure how he himself had found it. Maybe the Keep wanted him to. He couldn't see it now from his bed of mosses, even with the glow of the little fire he'd made: it looked as if there were just wall there. Obviously the Icefalcon couldn't see the fire either.

Silence pressed, a waiting silence, watching. If he answered, thought Tir, he'd then have to do something, leave this place, go outside, be hurt again. The Icefalcon had tracked him as far as this corridor, but the floor of the corridor—far back along the wall on the fifth level—was slick and smooth and would take no tracks. He could stay here in silence. In time the Icefalcon would go away.

But the Icefalcon was a Guard. And as Lord of the Keep, the Guards were Tir's servants. The Icefalcon would probably go on hunting for him until the Keep killed him.

Very slowly, Tir got to his feet and walked to where he had marked the door.

"I'm here," he said, and in speaking felt as if he were giving up silence and peace and warmth forever.

He reached through the door to show him, his arm and hand vanishing into dense darkness. A moment later ice-cold fingers took his and the Icefalcon stepped out of the black curtain of gloom. He was soaked and shivering, a rime of ice on his long pale hair and beard, his face a mass of scratches and his throat bruised black, abraded as if thorns had gripped him like strangling vines. Tir expected him to be angry, to demand why Tir hadn't spoken up before—he'd been calling out softly in that corridor for quite some time.

But he said nothing, only looking around fungus and shadow, gray eyes listening, as if he, too, could hear the whisper of the Keep. Then he looked down at Tir and, reaching out—fingers trembling with cold and exhaustion, something Tir had never seen in this toughest and most aloof of warriors before—touched the half-healed gashes on Tir's face and the black tangle of hair that fell down over his eyes.

"Is it well with you, Altir?" he asked, and Tir nodded.

"I'm sorry I didn't say anything before," whispered Tir. "I . . ." His throat closed up. He couldn't explain why he hadn't, why he didn't want to go back. Why he was afraid.

The Icefalcon gestured the explanation away. "You did speak," he said. "It is all that matters. Did you hide here from demons? They can't really harm you, you know." There were claw marks and what looked like bites on his face, and Tir had seen some of Vair's warriors in the corridors—when they could not see him—and knew that what the Icefalcon said wasn't entirely true anymore. At least not here.

He shook his head. "Vair," he said, not sure if that was what he meant. "I didn't want Vair to find me." He could have left it at that, but it wasn't the entire truth. "I didn't want anybody to find me."

The Icefalcon knelt by the tiny blaze, held out his hands to it. The white fingers, impossibly long and strong, were chapped and red with the cold, bleeding around the nails, and Tir felt overcome with shame again that everyone had had to try to rescue him when he'd been stupid enough to be kidnapped in the first place.

"Because you went with Bektis?" asked the Icefalcon, studying his face in silence for a time.

Tir looked away.

"He fooled me, too. We all make mistakes, son of Endorion."

"But we can't afford to," said Tir. "You said that yourself."

"Some of us are wrong sometimes, too," the Icefalcon said a little ruefully. "I think your mother will be more angry with me for bringing an enemy into the Keep than she will be with you for being deceived by that enemy. As a grown man and a warrior, I should have known better, especially as I knew Bektis for years before the coming of the Dark Ones. The world is as a rule unforgiving, but sometimes we are fortunate enough to redeem our mistakes. We are more fortunate still to be forgiven even without that restitution. Even, I think, Hethya will find it so."

Tir looked up quickly, trying to read the enigmatic eyes. "Do I . . . Do I have to go back?"

He didn't know what it was that he feared out in the open spaces of grass and sky. Not the Dark Ones. Not even Vair and his hooks, not really.

"Don't you want to go back?"

Tir was silent. He'd always felt a little afraid of the Ice-falcon, awed by the tall young captain's aura of quiet danger; had feared that haughty intolerant perfection. But Rudy always said, *Tell what you see . . .*

"I just want to be safe," he said, so softly he hoped the Icefalcon wouldn't really hear. "It's like I don't even want to see Mama or Rudy or anybody. Like I don't want friends anymore or anything. I just want nothing more awful to happen to me."

What he thought that might be he didn't know and prayed the Icefalcon wouldn't ask him.

But the Icefalcon only said, very softly, "Ah." Just that, and then sat silent for a long while, memories of his own altering for a time the gray chill of his eyes.

"Everyone has to go back, son of Endorion," he said after a long time. His words came hesitantly, as if he'd suddenly forgotten the language. When he thought about it, Tir realized he'd never heard the Icefalcon talk for very long at a time, and not about anything but tracking and weaponry and food, the everyday concerns of the Guards.

"Sometimes when we have been . . . hurt—betrayed . . . Sometimes when we think we have brought our ill down upon our own heads . . . It is difficult then. Sometimes it takes a long while to turn around and face what we fled. We don't even need to defeat it. But we must be willing to look at it once again."

Tir whispered, "Oh," and stood for a time while the Icefalcon returned to warming his frozen hands and the steam rose off his wet icy clothing. The thought that the Icefalcon might have been hurt once, or be frightened of anything, was new to him, and unsettling.

"Can we get out of here?" he asked softly, and the Icefalcon glanced up from the heart of the blaze. "Out of the Keep, I mean? Go . . . Go back?"

"Not until we find Ingold," he said. "That is the one thing remaining, son of Endorion: to find Ingold. For without him we have no hope of turning aside Vair before he crosses over into the Keep of Dare."

# CHAPTER TWENTY-ONE

There were five levels of the crypts below the ground, even as there were five levels above, and Tir and the Icefalcon followed the vines inward to the Keep's heart. In places vines lay like combed hair, wrist-thick, calf-thick, thigh-thick along the base of the walls, under ceilings where molds moved and murmured to themselves and dripped blood on warrior and child as they passed below. It was as if the plants that had once been cultivated in the hydroponics crypts had gone mad when the Keep went mad, growing and growing in the blackness and bringing forth nightmare fruit of shapes unseen in the sane or waking world.

In the vines, in the fungus, in the frost-locked chambers where no footfall marred the white glittering surfaces of the floors, apports appeared and disappeared: a man's boot. A hair ribbon wound around a stem of wild roses, the blossoms still fresh. A scroll of strange gold letters. A cooking pot wrought of metal the Icefalcon had never seen. Somewhere water gurgled, and in its voice the Icefalcon heard the mutter of names.

Demons kept putting out their torches and picked and tore at the Icefalcon's hands and face and hair while he patiently rekindled sparks in tufts pulled from the desiccated moss. After having his spirit-body gutted, torn, dismembered by demons for endless hours, these efforts at distraction did not impress him.

There was a sixth level, below the crypts and the sub-crypts, at the bottom of the lowermost stair. Nitre gleamed blue on the rock walls, and the air was frozen with a crushed eternity beneath the ice. Tir led the way silently, tracing memories of some ancient and unimaginable errand, and the Icefalcon trod silently after him, his hand near his sword-hilt but knowing in his heart that there was nothing there a sword could stay. At the bottom of an endless stair lay only a cavern lit by the phosphor-glow of nitre and lichens, and in that cavern a pit that fell away to nothing. Wind roared there, and water, too, the Icefalcon thought, and the vines that had lain along the wall the whole of the final stairway spread out and hung over the pit's edge, gray and dry and dead.

A bronze ball floated suspended in the pit, almost below the reach of the wind-snatched torchlight. The bronze had been cracked, perhaps with age; stained and green and falling to pieces, but the magic that had been in it endured. It was just large enough to contain a man.

"Altir, my dear boy." Ingold had managed to hook one elbow over the edge of a great crack in the bronze ball's top and haul himself up from within it. His face was scratched, and there was blood in his hair—demon-lights floated around the ball, and the Icefalcon could half see their plasmic shapes crawling over the curving surface—but his voice was cheerful.

"And the Icefalcon, too. You have no idea how pleased I am to see you both."

"I can guess." The Icefalcon hunkered down at the pit's edge—warily, because demons would probably consider it the ultimate in hilarity to grab his ankles. "Have you made tea?"

Ingold got his other elbow up and rested his chin on his crossed wrists. His hands were in bloody shreds. He must, the Icefalcon thought, be using all his magic to keep the ball from falling into the pit. "You know, I intended to," said the wizard apologetically, "but the stove in here won't light and the only tea I have with me is a second-rate Round Sea red, which I know you don't drink."

Eyes wide, Tir whispered to the Icefalcon, "There isn't

really a stove in that ball, is there?" and the Icefalcon shook his head. "I didn't think so. There used to be chains here. They sometimes hung prisoners over the pit with them."

"Nice people," commented the Icefalcon, standing and handing Tir the torch. The boy was trembling with weariness—as was the Icefalcon himself—but there was no need to tell him to be careful. They'd all been walking around knee-deep in tinder for days, and even at the Keep of Dare, where the black stone of the walls would not burn, children were taught from earliest childhood to be extremely careful with open flame.

As he moved cautiously along the wall, probing with the sword-tip under the debris of muck and dead vines, he called out, "Any particular material or link size of chain you wish?"

"Well, you know," replied the wizard judiciously, "when I'm in danger of being dashed to pieces I generally *prefer* to be rescued with a fifty-fifty alloy of bronze and silver, oval links rather than square, and no longer than two inches, but since I've been here for some hours I'll settle for anything you find."

He turned sharply and gestured with one hand as lightning sparked from the wall of the pit. The white glare showed up the lines of exhaustion gouged in his face and the grim fear in his eyes. The forked spear veered aside inches from him, but as it did the bronze ball dropped several yards, then caught itself, almost dislodging Ingold in the process, and slowly rose once more, like a blown-up bladder.

"It is not a good thing," said the Icefalcon, digging cautiously under the leaves with his left hand, "to let down your standards." Dead tendrils of vines clung to the chain like black wires as he pulled it free, the metal clinking softly. His muscles ached to his back teeth with the effort of dragging it to the edge of the pit.

"I won't tell anyone if you won't."

"Is there a post or a ring in the floor that we can fix this

to?" asked the Icefalcon, looking down at Tir. The boy
looked terrified as well as beaten with fatigue, but the silly
banter of the adults—which Ingold and the Icefalcon had
been trading since their first meeting on the training floor
at Gae—seemed to calm him. He thought a moment and
went to show the Icefalcon the place; when they came
back the chain was gone.

"It's heavy," consoled Ingold, in response to the Icefalcon's remarks. "It probably wasn't apported very far."

The Icefalcon hated Zay with a great, weary hatred.

They found another chain—not the same one—buried
under moss, and the Icefalcon kept hold of it this time,
wrapping and knotting it through one of the rings in the
floor. He wasn't sure whether the chain would reach, but
he wasn't about to trust knotting it to the vines. More
lightning burst and flared from the sides of the pit, drawn
to the ball by the magic Ingold was putting out to hold it
aloft; the effort of turning it aside made the ball itself pitch
and dip nearly twenty feet.

"Rudy says levitation's just about one of the hardest
magics to do," whispered Tir worriedly. Wind had begun
to rise, swirling up out of the pit. The creepers underfoot
twitched with a dreadful serpentine life.

"So I have heard, too." The Icefalcon dragged the chain
to the lip of the pit, gathered loops of it in his hand, gauged
the distance to the ball. "Can you bring that thing up a
little?"

"I'll try." Ingold inched himself up gingerly onto the
top curve of the broken ball. Wind caught in his long white
hair, his tattered robes. "I thought you pitched thirteen in-
nings against Lord Ankres' guards last summer for the
championship."

"I was pitching a baseball, not a chain." Rudy had been
responsible for the Keep baseball league—it was Ingold
who'd slugged in the winning run. The Icefalcon had
held out for weeks against participation in what he haughtily referred to as a "silly child's game," until Gnift the
Swordmaster had informed all Guards that they *would*

participate—he needed a winning team against Lord Ankres. The Icefalcon had been the star pitcher ever since.

The chain fell short five times, lightning searing and slicing its way up the length of it as it dropped down against the side of the pit. The sixth time Ingold caught it, levin-fire sizzling as the old man's bleeding hands wrapped around the links; the spells to turn it aside released the bronze ball from its suspension and it dropped from beneath him. Ingold swung in a long pendulum swoop and fell, hard, against the side of the pit, clinging there with demons dragging at his ankles and the freezing wind raking him. Tir screamed, "Ingold!" in terror.

"I'm all right," came Ingold's voice, half drowned in the spectral howling. "I'm all right."

Beside the Icefalcon, Tir was white as a ghost; the Icefalcon pretended not to see and called down, "I know you're all right, old man, but don't hurt the chain. It's expensive."

It was very seldom that the Icefalcon—or anyone—could make Ingold laugh out loud, but that one succeeded. His laughter came ringing up out of the lightning-slashed maelstrom of the pit, followed by a soldier's epithet. The metal clanged softly against the stone as the wizard started to climb.

Wind redoubled around them in fury, ripping at the torch flames and nearly rocking the torch from Tir's hand. The Icefalcon staggered, caught the vines at the pit's edge for balance, and then pulled his bloodied hand back with a curse. Driven leaves slashed their faces, blinding them, colder and colder . . .

Then the wind abruptly ceased. In the stillness that followed, mist began to rise from the vines underfoot, from the fungus clumped along the walls, from the pit itself.

The Icefalcon spun, rising to his feet, sword in hand, heart hammering. "Get back from the edge of the pit, Tir," he said softly. "But don't go far from me. Old man, get up here."

In response there was only the zapping hiss of lightning below.

"Get up here!"

A shadow in the mist, forming slowly. Stringers of white hair and glabrous flesh peeking through holes in black rags; the glint of crystals . . . The Hand of Harilómne? The smell of him, thick as the reek of a privy years uncleaned. The shadow opened its mouth, but all that came out was a hiss.

The Icefalcon didn't dare take his eyes off him to see where Ingold might be. He heard the chain clank again, and the chill flare of lightning illuminated from below the mists that now filled the pit. Gil had told him once that the best bet when confronted by an angry wizard was to get him talking; the Icefalcon, no conversationalist, groped madly in his mind for something to say, something to hold this spirit of insane power distracted until Ingold could arrive.

"As you see," he said, "we have not escaped you after all."

Zay's head turned. The eyes that regarded him were white pits of mindless rage.

"I wonder that you will let those others depart, the black generalissimo and the men he makes from mushrooms and filth. He does not regard you, does not even know your name."

The old face, wrinkled beyond humanity, did not alter its expression, but the mouth opened a little, showing the brown broken stumps of teeth, and he hissed again. Then the chain clanked, and Zay's hand flashed up with reflexes a young warrior would have envied, and fire roared across the dry carpet of the floor like a drench of water hurled from a basin.

The Icefalcon grabbed Tir and dove for the half of the floor uncovered by vines, striking the rock hard and rolling. There was a clashing of chain and then Ingold's voice crying out words of ward and protection and the roll of oily heat. Looking back, in the flaring crimson light the Icefalcon saw Ingold, standing on the lip of the pit, wreathed in fire and smoke, and before him himself: senile, filthy, reeking, drool dribbling from a toothless mouth, blue eyes blind and wandering, but the face his own. Flame swirled in columns from the floor again, and Tir screamed in pain: spots and threads of fire burst to life all along Tir's arm, across the Icefalcon's shoulders and thighs, then quenched suddenly with the lifting of Ingold's hand.

The flames shrank to fingerlets in the vines, died to a bed of throbbing coals, though blazes continued to gutter and flicker all around the room's walls, and smoke filled the air.

A woman now stood before Ingold. Gil-Shalos, sluttish and loose-mouthed and obscene.

"Zay," Ingold said patiently, though he was panting with exertion and sweat streaked his soot-grimed, blistered face. "It is you that I wish to see." He stood perilously near the edge of the pit, driven back by the flames, holding up his hand to shield his eyes.

*He's holding Zay's attention,* thought the Icefalcon. *Holding him so I can get Tir out of here.*

Looked at logically, what good that would do if Ingold were killed he couldn't imagine.

Still he calculated the route, not a good one—past Zay, along the wall where the fires still smoked and sputtered, up the stairs . . .

Wind roared up out of the pit again, slashing at Ingold's beggarly rags, almost rocking him from his feet. Sleet mixed with it, chips of rock, dead leaves, sparks, and stinging insects. The Icefalcon pressed Tir's face to his chest and bent down his head, blind, frozen, waiting to get the strength, to find the moment, to flee. Trapped by the vines in the corridor outside Tir's hiding place, he had felt the power of the Keep: the cold, the icy wind, and the water that had poured down over him from the broken pipes had sapped most of his strength.

Zay's strength was endless, the strength of madness, night, cold, rage.

And in the end, flight would do no good.

*Keep him talking,* Gil had said.

The wind increased, blackness at the world's end. The hate of three thousand years in solitary hell. Cyclone fury that would shred flesh from bone. The Icefalcon closed his fingers hard around the vines of the floor to keep from being blown into the pit and pressed Tir to him until he thought their bones would lock.

Stillness fell. An angry whisper among the vines. The Icefalcon was aware his hands were bleeding. In the cold black darkness images flooded into the Icefalcon's mind: the Dark Ones surrounding a camp in open country, the Keep of the Shadow looming tall and cold above a valley where three springs glinted diamond-bright in gray rock. A wolf surprised where it fished in one of those springs. The white hard moon ringed in ice and ringed again with the huge frost-flashes of moon dogs halfway across the sky.

Men and women packing, loading food and clothing into hampers and bins. A girl in her teens pressed back against a corridor wall in the Keep, a basket of laundry in her arms and her hand clamped tight to her mouth as pale-blue lights ran along the wall into darkness. Knockings in the night.

A child crying as her bedclothes caught fire.

They had left because he had begun, slowly, to go mad.

The Icefalcon suddenly understood why.

Smoke and mist funneled down on Ingold again, a black whirlwind like a dust devil through whose ragged fringes lightning flared blue and deadly. Wind and lightning drove him to the edge of the pit, wind and lightning and concentrated malice, blinding and tearing and cold. Now was the time—Zay's mind centered on destroying the rival mage—Noon or any other of the people of the Real World would have told him to flee. But instead the Icefalcon stood up and shouted, "Zay!" at the top of his soft voice.

The howl of fire and darkness, smoke and nightmare, drowned his words.

"Zay," he cried again, pitching his throat to the cutting edge of flint, "Zay, she tried to come! Lé-Ciabbeth tried to come to you!"

He hoped to his Ancestors—not that they were ever very helpful—that he had the name right.

The smoke and lightning died. The whirlwind grew still. A leaf skittered, came to rest among the dead snake-skins of the vines. Ingold, driven to his knees on the pit's edge, looked up in considerable surprise but had the good sense to say nothing.

Stillness filled the room, stillness and darkness broken only by the flickerings of the fires in the corners, the malign whisper of lightning deep in the pit.

Anger.

He felt as he felt in the summer hunting on the plains, when the sky turned green and hail slashed sideways over the grass and the long yellow-brown funnels of the cyclones began to finger silently from the clouds.

Anger black and aching and filled with loneliness.

*Not one of them remembered. Not one of them remained. She did not come.*

The Icefalcon tried to assemble in his mind what Gil-Shalos would have made of the story, how she would have threaded together the half-guessed clues of Tir's dreams, of the apports, of Vair's and Bektis' words and things Hethya had told him or Loses His Way.

"Lé-Ciabbeth tried to come to you, Zay," he said slowly, as before him the shape grew into being again, solidifying with a horrible gradualness from shadow and darkness and the choking smolder of the fires in the room.

"When the transporter, the Far-Walker, would not work, she tried to come overland. She died in the badlands, far to the south of here."

The weight of the anger focused, mad but calm. Conscious as he had never been in his life of his naked helplessness, the Icefalcon reflected that the problem about keeping a wizard talking to you was that you called your-self to his attention, and there was very little use in being a perfect warrior if one was going to be so stupid as to do what he was doing now.

The whispering was within his mind, but he knew it came from the sick-gleaming silver speck of a moist eye, peering at him out of shadow. *How did she die, bar-barian? How do you know this?*

Gil would ask, *Was she a mage or not a mage?* It was important to the telling of the tale.

Also, the Icefalcon reflected, to his continued survival. After this he would stick to the truth. It was easier.

He thought about tracks and trails long left cold. "I do not know this, Ancestor of wizards," he said. "My people found her bones in a stream cut on the hill that lies three days' walk west of the great pass of Renweth; her bones, and her jewels, green as spring leaves with hearts black as summer night, jewels such as none of us had ever seen. These we buried with her bones . . ."

Did the Ancestors of the Times Before bury their dead? Why hadn't he ever asked Gil that?

He didn't know why, but something made him add, "At the far end of a box canyon, near a stream, where the wild roses first show themselves in spring." And he saw the place again in his heart.

Long stillness, slowly deepening—*they can find rest in some image,* Hethya had said, *until they can think clearer and find a way through.* There was a sort of whisper in the darkness, a little sound, *Ah . . .*

The stillness spread like the ripples of a pond, to all the corners of the Keep.

The Icefalcon said—for himself, for the Dove, and for that vanished lady—"Forgive her that she failed."

*She never came. She never came.*

But now there was only deep sadness in the thought, and that deepening calm, as if the whole Keep might slide over into sleep and dreaming. The Icefalcon saw again those years in the Keep of the Shadow, the knockings in the darkness growing louder and more angry, the unexplained little fires, the things falling down, disappearing, moving. The madness that was Zay's only refuge from regret.

"You waited a long time for her, Zay," came Ingold's voice, gentle out of the darkness, like the voices heard in one's mind in dreams. "No one could blame you for your anger. But now it is she who waits for you."

Black rage swelled again, suffocating; the air lambent with fire. The chain where it hung down the side of the pit jerked and rattled, and for an instant the smoke collecting ever thicker above their heads bellied and dipped, whirlwinds reaching down.

Then that silence again, and stillness, as Zay let his anger go.

*I don't know the way out.*

"I do." The mage's deep, flawed voice was genuinely sad. "And I will show you."

The Icefalcon wasn't sure then what he saw—but then one wasn't, dealing with the Wise. He thought Ingold made a gesture with one hand, sketching lines of light that stretched out from his fingers, past where the wall had to be, into zones of the air that glittered as if jeweled. He thought he saw stars, but they were deep in the earth and that was impossible.

The lines were already fading when a voice said, far away, *Thank you.* Darkness streamed back, darkness heavy and breathless, darkness without relief—darkness dead, at rest after three thousand years of madness and pain. From the last flicker of light the voice whispered, *Repay?*

Ingold started to shake his head and to lift his hand in benediction, when the Icefalcon spoke up again.

"As a matter of fact," he said, "there is one last thing you can do for us."

"I have never in my life," whispered Ingold, as he and the Icefalcon, with Tir scurrying between them, strode up the dark stairs to the Keep of the Shadow above, "heard such a farrago . . ."

"Don't give me that, old man. I've heard worse from you in drinking games with the Guards." He wiped a trickle of blood off his forehead.

"And you're making a lot of assumptions about what everyone is able to do in that scheme of yours." Ingold was digging around in his various satchels and pockets for something to bandage his hands. "Particularly me."

The Icefalcon raised his eyebrows. "Are you not the greatest wizard and swordsman in the West of the world?"

"What, out of twenty-five survivors? There's an honor for you. And given the fact that . . ."

Ingold stopped short on the stairs, looking upward, and the Icefalcon, following his gaze, felt a sinking dread.

Red light smote their faces as they rounded the curve of the stair, a crimson glare that illuminated from below the billows of smoke that drifted in the dead black air. Heat condensed in the narrow space—heat and the soft far-off roaring, like the beat of the sea.

The Icefalcon whispered, "Damn."

Ingold nodded. "Damn indeed." There was no need for further words between them: they both knew what had happened.

The fires started by Zay in his battle with Ingold had spread.

The Keep of the Shadow was burning.

# CHAPTER TWENTY-TWO

"You have to hold them." Ingold stopped, leaning on his staff, which had appeared as an apport at the bottom of the first flight of steps. He was gasping for breath in the heat, and even here, at the far back of the third level, the orange glare of the Icefalcon's torch illuminated ropes of smoke twisting overhead. "The blaze will reach the Aisle soon. Vair must know already that he has to leave by the transporter or die."

"How much time will you need?" Though he would have died rather than admit it, the Icefalcon was grateful for the halt. He was shaking with fatigue, the sweat that poured down his face stinging in the cuts. They had been forced repeatedly to turn aside, to seek ways past corridors or stairways that were already infernos. Twice Ingold had put forth the power of his spells to get them through red holocausts of flame, but after hours in the pit his own strength was half spent and there was more to accomplish.

The wizard shook his head. "If Zay's instructions were accurate, not long." He coughed, pressing a hand to his side, sweat-mixed blood and soot a glistening mask on his face. "But Bektis will almost certainly be in the control chamber. Do what you can." He slapped the Icefalcon's arm, as if the request concerned the polishing of boots before suppertime. "Altir? I think it's best if you come with me."

Tir nodded. He had been silent through the battle in the subcrypt, the race up flight after flight of steps, clinging to Ingold's hand. His blue eyes, nearly black in the torch-

light, streamed tears from the smoke, and the breath sawed
audibly in his lungs, but his face was expressionless, filled
with a stoic resignation.

"You'll keep Vair from getting to the Keep?"

"I will, my Lord." The Icefalcon laid a hand on the
boy's shoulder. "That I promise you."

Watching them hurry down the corridor, wizard and
child together in the faint glow of blue witchlight that Ingold summoned before their feet, the Icefalcon reflected
that the past month of Tir's life would have been considered rough even for a child of the Talking Stars People,
and the boy had acquitted himself well.

He couldn't track as well as a child of the Real World, of
course.

The Icefalcon turned and headed for the transporter
at a run.

At the next crossing of the corridors he stopped again,
flattened into the shadows. Men filled the passageway before him, coughing in the smoke. Torch-glare caught bald
heads, naked faces, eyes staring glazedly at the bent
sweaty necks of the men in front of them. Someone yelled
an oath in the ha'al tongue and the men stopped, jostling,
and began to mill—fire ahead?

The Icefalcon doubled back, sought yet another way
around.

Fire was spreading. Grown by the stubborn, angry
magic of the Keep of the Shadow, the gourds and bean
plants, the groundnuts and potatoes, had penetrated every
crypt, every level, even ventilation shafts and water pipes.
Some still lived, knotted in spongy symbiosis with fungus,
lichen, moss, and toadstools, and slowed the fire's spread
while emitting suffocating billows of smoke; in other
places wizened vines made fuses along which the flames
raced faster than a man could run. Twice and thrice the
Icefalcon was stopped by walls of flame, hearing behind
him all the while the panicked shouting, the bellowed orders of Vair's army as it, too, sought a way to the transport
chambers that now were their only hope of egress and life.

The Icefalcon wondered if Ingold would make it through the blaze to the round chamber where the spells of the transporter could be worked—wondered if Zay had spoken the truth to the old man in the end or had decided to play one last devil's trick on them all.

Which, he reflected, would be just like the old bastard.

A corridor lay open before him, walled both sides in fire as the vines along each wall burst into flame—roofed with fire as the fungal mat overhead ignited. Flakes of flame snowed on the Icefalcon as he wrapped his scarf over his mouth and nose and ran, praying the passageway wouldn't end in another incendiary wall.

Behind him he heard someone yell. *Of course*, he thought. *They think I know the way.*

*Let's hope they're right.*

"Man, we'd given you over for dead!" Hethya sprang to her feet. "We were giving you another few minutes . . ."

The Icefalcon pitched gasping through the vestibule door and whipped sword from sheath—"They're behind me!"—and turned even as he cried the words to slice the first man through the door behind him. More yelling, more milling in the vestibule—weapons thrusting through the narrow opening; seize, slash, block. Blood gouting out in streams and a severed hand flying against the wall like a swatted bug.

"Mother of Tears!" cried Hethya, and Loses His Way demanded, "Where's the boy?"

"With Ingold" was all the Icefalcon had time to rasp as a halberd opened his leather sleeve.

"He's safe?"

"God, no," panted the Icefalcon. "Don't be a fool."

"Oh," she said, evidently realizing the absurdity of the word in the circumstances. "Sorry. If you've got any brilliant strategies at this point, boy-o," she added a moment later, "how about trottin' 'em out?"

Smoke poured from the vestibule, thicker and rank with the smell of new burning. The air was like an oven, the floor underfoot hot through his boot-soles.

"A curtain wall would help," panted the Icefalcon. "Machiolations. Boiling oil." It was impossible to breathe.

"We'd have that if we hadn't eaten all the pemmican."

The Icefalcon sliced hard at the next head to appear through the doorway, had his blade intercepted on a two-pronged halberd. The inexperience of the clone that wielded it was the only thing that saved the Icefalcon from having the weapon wrenched out of his hand; he was able to slip in under the shaft and slash the man's arm with his dagger, then pull free. Instinct made him keep low—Hethya's sword-swipe at the next enemy would have taken his ear off.

"Waste of good food," he said.

The ventilation shafts gushed nothing but smoke now; the Icefalcon felt his skin blister in the scorching air.

"Can we ourselves use the Far-Walker?" asked Loses His Way. Blood streamed from his chest and arm where a lance had pierced. "Get out of this place and warn the people of the Keep?"

"We can't activate it." The Icefalcon hacked again with his sword, his arms like lead. "It takes a Wise One to do that." Blood spouted over him from the man whose throat he opened; someone in the rear rank pulled the dying clone aside.

"And that's what Ingold's gone to do?"

"Don't be a fool, woman," snapped the Icefalcon. "The last thing we need is to open the way into the Keep with Vair right outside."

"Well, I've no intention of roasting to death to save your lot!"

"You think Vair will spare you?"

There was an outcry from deeper within the vestibule, beyond the heads of the crowding clones. The clones themselves—hundreds of them—were barefoot, scantily clothed, their skin patchy and odd-looking, greenish even in the livid light, or the slick, vile orange of the monster toadstools. Now and then during the confused struggle in the doorway the Icefalcon had the impression that one or more would suddenly go berserk in the vestibule, turning on his companions, slaying and being slain or rushing out into the bellowing furnace of the corridor.

Then a voice cried beyond the press, "Put down your weapons!"

The clones in the doorway ceased to fight, fell back untidily to show the defenders Vair na-Chandros, his white tabard soot-blackened, a tulwar in his hand. Bektis stood beside him, smutted, filthy, gasping—holding Tir against him with one hand, a silver knife at his throat.

Vair's teeth glinted under pulled-back lips. "Get back," he said. "Let us pass or the boy dies."

"I thought you said," began Hethya furiously, and the Icefalcon said, "Shut up!"

His eyes met Tir's. The boy's were stretched with panic under a mask of smoke and blood. Anything could go wrong in any hunt, thought the Icefalcon. All it would take, in that maelstrom of smoke and heat and darkness, would be for Ingold to lose his grip on Tir's hand; for the old man to have been overcome by fumes, or fire summoned by Bektis, or some trap in the Keep itself. Bektis was weakened and in no good case to fight, but then Ingold wasn't, either. The Court Mage would have found it easy to lure the child to him in the confusion.

The Icefalcon stepped back. Tir screamed, "Don't let them! Let me die, I order you! Please! Don't let . . ."

Bektis shook him, hard. "Be still, boy."

The Icefalcon retreated, sword pointing out, Hethya and Loses His Way closing in on both sides. Vair stepped through the vestibule door, clones surrounding him, their stupid gazes wandering. Some were beginning to rot already, stinking appallingly above the calcifying heat.

"Good." Vair's eye traveled calculatingly around the big chamber, seeking other defenders, finding none. "Very good. Prandhays Keep has been broken, time and again through the years; its walls would never stand against the Devices that harridan wife of mine, Yori-Ezrikos, now commands. But Renweth . . ." He smiled under his dark mustache, though he was panting for breath in the heat. "Renweth is another story. Whatever weapons we find there, Bektis, in Renweth we will have a base to raise and provision the force I will need to march south and retake what is rightfully mine. And who knows what Devices are hidden there."

His lips parted in an ugly grin as he thought of the twelve-year-old girl he had raped on their wedding night, the girl who had hated him so much that she'd murdered the son she bore him. And the relish in that grin, the vile amusement, made the Icefalcon realize that by comparison Blue Child's ferocity was as innocent as summer rain.

"I look forward, Bektis, to seeing Yori-Ezrikos again. Is the way open, Bektis?"

The mage edged at his heels, long white fingers closed around Tir's jaw in a strangling grip. "The way is open, my Lord. Behold."

He lifted the hand that held the silver knife and made a pass in the air, speaking words that sounded nothing like Hethya's made-up tongue of the Times Before. Behind him the columns of crystal, ranked room to room in a line, flickered with cores of greenish light, and threads of starshine seemed to race along the floor between them. A hot, quick flicker of light flashed, far back in the dark, and the smoke that bellied thick beneath the high ceiling stirred, then streamed inward, pouring between the pillars through the second chamber and the third.

As he had in his shadow vision, the Icefalcon half discerned more pillars than there should have been, a fourth and a fifth and a sixth pair, and on past into darkness.

Vair gestured to the clones. "Go," he said. "Kill all that you meet."

"I trust," said Bektis smugly, "that your Lordship is well satisfied?"

His attention was on Vair, in anticipation of an accolade that, the Icefalcon reflected, he should have had more sense than to expect—and in that moment of distraction, Tir acted. With the neat speed of a man's, the boy's hand dropped to his boot-top and the next second there was a dagger in it, a dagger with which he slashed across the back of Bektis' hand. Bektis screamed, jerked back, and the boy was free, running.

The Icefalcon was moving, too. In a single long leap he reached the child's side, seconds before Vair's left-handed fumble for his sword. The Icefalcon's sword tangled with the dark commander's blade, flung the weapon aside, and struck back the blade of the nearest clone's attack as his momentum carried him, and Tir, out of immediate danger.

Vair screamed, "Stop him! Kill him!" as the Icefalcon slapped into the wall between Hethya and Loses His Way, sword pointing outward once more.

Bektis, clutching his bleeding hand to his breast, snarled, "The room's under a Rune of Silence, fool!"

Behind the Icefalcon, Tir was sobbing, "Stop them! Please, stop them!" and struggling to push through, as if he would attack the clones himself, but none of the three warriors made a move.

"There's nothing we can do," said the Icefalcon softly. He had already caught, above the stench of smoke and rot and burning, a smell from the inner chambers of the trans-porter, a smell green and anomalous, that told him that all was not as Vair supposed it to be.

But he couldn't say so, could only hold Tir fast, while behind the shoving ranks of clones Vair struck Bektis a blow that knocked the old man to the floor. Swords, hal-berds, spears in hand, the clones shuffled through the pillars, disappearing along the lines of green light and starshine into darkness.

Tir struggled, weeping, in the Icefalcon's grip.

"There's nothing we can do."

Something beyond the vestibule outside caught with a deafening roar. Heat, exhaustion, and the strangling smoke made the Icefalcon light-headed, and he saw Hethya stagger and Loses His Way catch her on his unin-jured arm to keep her on her feet. For a moment, when there was a gap in the line of clones, the Icefalcon thought

Vair would order his men to take the three of them and Tir—wasteful, in his opinion, but then Vair was wasteful.

But Vair seemed to realize what that was likely to cost in terms of men and in terms of time.

"Come, Bektis," he said softly to the trembling, furious old man who lay sprawled at his feet. "They'll follow us through. They must, or die. As you must. What about it, wench?" he called to Hethya. "Will you take servicing my men above death by fire? And you, Little King—if you hurry, you'll be in time to watch me rape your mother."

Dagger in hand, Tir flung himself in soundless rage at Vair. The Icefalcon dragged him back, holding the struggling child against him as the tall man turned, laughing, toward the crystal columns, the retreating lines of light. His white-cloaked form blended into the shambling lines of the clones, visible among them for quite some time, fading back and back into the shadows.

After a long moment Bektis pulled himself to his feet, leaning against the wall and holding his ribs, a look of loathing and defeat in his eyes. He staggered into the marching line of the clones, catching their sweaty shoulders to hold himself upright, and was gone.

"Hyena," gasped Loses His Way, his breath like a bellows in the airless heat. "Coward and pig." His eyes never left the shambling ranks, shuffling, coughing, pouring sweat and staggering now as they passed through from the vestibule and down the length of the chamber to the first pair of pillars, the second . . .

Tir wept silently in the Icefalcon's grip.

"But he is right, my friend," the warchief murmured. "What will you? It is follow or die."

"Well, there might be a certain amount of satisfaction in following, of course." Ingold stepped from the rear ranks of the clones—who didn't appear to notice him—and strode quickly to Tir, dropping to his knees before the boy and putting his hands on his shoulders. "My dear Tir, thank God you're all right!" Blood covered one side of his face and a fresh wound put streaks of gore in his hair, where the whole of him wasn't nearly black with smoke and ash. "Forgive me! I never imagined the corridor to the control chamber was booby-trapped like that."

Tir flung his arms around the wizard, clutched him desperately with his face buried in the threadbare robes.

"It's all right," said Ingold. "It really is all right. I'd never have brought you with me if . . ."

"I'd have thrashed the life out of any man who'd send a child into what we just came through!" protested Hethya.

"No one in the Keep will be hurt," Ingold murmured, face bent over the weeping child's head. "I promise you." He held out his hand to the Icefalcon and used his grip on the young warrior's arm to get to his feet. "We really have got to get out of here. The Aisle's in flames. I think I can damp us a way through to the Doors, but I'm afraid we're all going to get singed."

"Vair . . ." sobbed Tir. "Ingold, Vair said . . ."

"It's all right," said the wizard again. "Vair's not anywhere near the Keep of Dare. In fact he's farther from it than ever. As a final favor to us, Zay of Tiyomis told me how to change the destination of the transporter before he . . . he died. And he is dead," he added, as Hethya's lips parted in surprise. "He left behind enough of his power to operate the transporter one final time, but, as I said, it opens no longer into the Keep of Dare. That was the Icefalcon's idea," he added, and Hethya regarded the Icefalcon in surprise.

"So you've turned tricky in your old age, have you, boy-o?"

With dignity, the Icefalcon replied, "Something I overheard Vair say while I was shadow-walking made me think there was a more suitable destination for him."

"What, you've found a way for the transporter to send him straight to Hell?"

"Nearly," said the Icefalcon after a moment's reflection.

Loses His Way wiped the sweat from his stubbly brow. "Where have they gone?"

"To the crypts of what used to be the great Southern

Keep of Hathyobar," said Ingold, and coughed on the smoke. "It stood on the shores of the Lake of Nychee, on the site now occupied by the Imperial Palace of Khirsrit."

"Where this lady Yori-Ezrikos dwells?" asked Hethya. "That hasn't much use for our boy Vair, never mind that he's her lawful wedded husband?"

"The very one." Ingold smiled. "I was pleased to hear that Vair is looking forward to an encounter with her because he is going to have one a great deal sooner than he looked to."

# CHAPTER TWENTY-THREE

There were spells of inconspicuousness a truly Wise One could place upon a man so that he might spend a day and a half in the camp of his enemies without them noticing that the person to whom they were bringing food, wrapping in blankets, sitting beside a fire—with whom they shared accounts of the game to be found on the Ice in the North: ice camels, lemmings, caribou, and once a pure white megatherium—would in any other circumstances be painted all over with messages to their Ancestors and have his bowels pulled out through his nostrils.

The Icefalcon was grateful for this circumstance. He was very, very tired of fighting.

He had no idea who the Empty Lakes People thought he was and didn't care. Nor had he any idea by what spells of illusion Ingold had guaranteed the absence of the Talking Stars People when the little party waded through fog, smoke, and steam up the dripping, hip-deep meltwaters of the collapsing gate-tunnel to the outer world again.

Mostly, once he woke in their emergency camp of snow-houses southeast of the ice-blister, the Empty Lakes People didn't address the Icefalcon by name at all. But the forms of speech they used toward him all indicated that they thought he was one of their kin.

The idea offended him deeply, but not deeply enough to buy his own death by mentioning it. He noticed they addressed Ingold, Tir, and Hethya as their kin as well. Cold Death they did not appear to see at all.

Cold Death was sitting by him when he woke up again,

most of her hair on one side singed off from her fight with
Bektis but otherwise looking much the same. "How is it
with you, o my brother?" she asked, and offered him a flat-
baked cake of honey and fried insects, a specialty among
the Empty Lakes People.

He was so exhausted and so hungry he even took it. "As
well as can be expected after my own sister runs away and
leaves me to die."

"Has it taught you a lesson about shadow-walking?"

"Yes," retorted the Icefalcon. "Never to put you in
charge of it again."

And she laughed.

Later that day she helped him stand, and they emerged
from the snow-house where he had lain and walked together along the shore of the steaming lake that now
stretched for miles along the feet of the black rock mountains. The great ice-blister still rose in its center, and steam
and smoke poured from a thousand rifts and crevices in its
sides. The waters of the lake churned now and then as
crevasses or pockets in the underlying ice collapsed, and
columns of steam would jet upward, marble-white in the
hard arctic sky.

"Ingold tells me that with the magic of the mad Ancestor gone out of it, the Keep itself will collapse." Cold
Death folded her arms, a look of sadness in her button-
black eyes. The day was warm, for the Ice, and the warmth
rising from the lake made it more so. Her breath barely
showed when she spoke, and she'd put back her hood, the
burned patches and blisters on her scalp showing through
a thin stubble of new-grown hair.

If she'd escaped serious injury at Bektis' hands at all,
thought the Icefalcon, she must be a far, far stronger
shaman than he had ever suspected.

"The heat will burst the stones," he said. "Gil-Shalos
tells me that the Keeps that were ruined—Prandhays
and Black Rock and Hathyobar—were those where no
Wise One surrendered life to keep the magic alive. They
crumbled, as all things do with time."

"Me mother said Prandhays probably burned at one time." Hethya came over to join them, Yellow-Eyed Dog trotting at her heels. Prinyippos' illusion had begun to come to pieces—Loses His Way had said—the moment Twin Daughter's spirit-pouch was brought into his presence; it was Yellow-Eyed Dog who'd brought down the scout when he'd tried to flee. The Icefalcon wondered if the illusion might have stood up more strongly had Bektis still had use of all his powers. Breaks Noses and his band, Loses His Way added, had never before had a warrior of the Alketch to torture; they'd prolonged the process as far as possible in a spirit of inquiry.

The Icefalcon wished he had been there to see it, though during Loses His Way's account—technical and detailed as all such accounts were among the folk of the Real World—Hethya quietly got up and left.

She seemed recovered now, though, bundled in the coat of megatherium wool and looking a little rested. "Me mother says she found signs of burning where the stonework was repaired."

A particularly violent upheaval tossed great cakes and shards of ice to the surface of the milky waters, bubbles heaving and bursting with fog that melted imperceptibly into the miles-wide shawl of vapors covering the land.

"That has to be the Keep itself." Hethya tucked her gloved hands into her armpits for further warmth. "I imagine it'll all freeze hard again once the fires are quenched. And give all the tribes something else to talk of besides caribou tracks and megatherium dung."

"You underestimate my people, Ancestress," replied the Icefalcon gravely. "Should a chunk of rock the size of many houses fall out of the sky and make a hole in the earth, it would not hold for them such interest as a change in the seed content of musk-ox dung. Nor should it," he added. "One must, after all, know what plants grow in one's own range."

She glanced at him under her eyelashes to see if he were jesting, and he turned his face haughtily away.

The Empty Lakes People gave them provisions and sleds for their homeward journey and agreed to accompany them to the edge of the Ice. This was, the Icefalcon guessed, due to the persuasions of Loses Their Way. He saw the two clones many times, walking on either side of Breaks Noses, or sitting, talking quietly, with Beautiful Girl by the fire or at the shore of the steaming lake, Yellow-Eyed Dog lying happily at their feet.

Hethya also spent time with Beautiful Girl and seemed to get along well with her, but it was clear to the Icefalcon that Loses Their Way had no eyes for any but their wife.

"She understands that we must die soon," said Loses Their Way on the second day. "In a way I think I will be glad."

And his brother-clone nodded. They, and the Icefalcon, Hethya, and Cold Death, had gathered near the fogbound shore of the lake. It was already freezing fast, sealing in the Keep of the Shadow with all its secrets and the burned shell of an old man who had given more than he was capable of bearing.

"When we—when I—when those others—died," said Loses Their Way, "we felt it. It was—a dying. A wound that cannot be healed. We are not whole men."

"We are glad," added Loses Their Way, "at least that we helped our kin. That our names will be included in the Long Songs. And that we could see our brother Breaks Noses and our beloved Beautiful Girl, that we can die in our lands by what remains of the Night River Country with the aspens green with summer."

The Icefalcon opened his mouth to point out that the Night River Country was and always had been the range of the Talking Stars People, but he had affection for his enemy, so he did not. Instead he said, "I am glad for you, too, o my enemy. It was a good hunt."

Loses Their Way smiled like a sun god through a gold bristle of stubble. "I will tell you a secret. There is no such thing as a bad hunt, o my friend."

"Your sister tells us that the Talking Stars People have returned at last to this place," said Loses Their Way.

The Icefalcon looked sharply at Cold Death.

"They are camped on the other side of the lake, among the broken ice, near where the tunnel was," she said. "At least the mammoth I summoned for them to chase were real, and not illusion like old Pretty-Beard's."

"If you wish," said Loses Their Way, "I will linger when my people move on and go with you to their camp to tell them what I heard of Antlered Spider concerning the dream-powder given to Noon in the Summer of the White Foxes. With this evidence, even the evidence of an enemy, they must at least give you a hearing and a trial. Do you feel strong enough, my friend, to take on Blue Child in a single match?"

The Icefalcon rubbed his hands, bandaged and bruised within the marten-fur gloves, flexed the ache and the lingering weakness of fatigue in his shoulders and arms. "I have waited a long time," he said quietly, "to meet Blue Child again."

Beneath the cold brilliance of the arctic stars he thought about Blue Child.

About Noon and Dove in the Sun.

About the Place of the Three Brown Dogs and the Valley of the Night River, the Haunted Mountain and the place called Pretty Water Creek where the Talking Stars People had their horse pens and falconries, where the white dogs of the Talking Stars People lay dozing in the ember-colored grass between the longhouses. About the sweet taste of milk curds and mead and maple sugar, and the soul-encompassing sting of cold water after a sweat-bath, and the smell of blood and wood smoke under starlit skies.

Across the steam of the lake, thinned now to a scrim of luminous white, his eyes sought for sight of Blue Child's camp—not that even a child of the Talking Stars could see their camp. The marmoreal landscape was still, and in the sky the stars spoke the sweet fragile language that humankind could no longer comprehend.

They remembered him and knew him. There were brothers and sisters who would welcome him back. He would at last be their chieftain, as Noon had been. From the Ice he would lead them south, to their new hunting lands, for what remained of his days and theirs.

If he survived the fight with Blue Child.

He flexed his hands. The training with the Guards of Gae was rigorous, though not, he thought, so fierce as the life lived by every child of the Talking Stars. He had trained as a Guard in part so that he would not lose that edge of strength. In his heart, he had always known that he would come back.

In spite of the food and the rest, weariness dragged at him, the inner fatigue that is not cured by a few days' rest. Rising from his blankets that morning had been like pushing a very large stone up a steep hill.

But she had been living in hardship and cold as well. Wounded, for all he knew, during the fight at the gate.

It was good odds that they were even.

He flexed the ache from his shoulders and rubbed his burned face, tender around the scraggly mess of beard. It would be strange, he thought, to be home again. Though he would never admit it to anyone, he would miss Gil-Shalos' stories—useless as they were—and the sound of Rudy's harp, and Janus' jokes, and, in spite of himself, going down to the crypts to observe Ingold's newest inventions.

To ride with his brothers and sisters again. To lie in silence among his silent hounds. To track caribou across bad country and to know that he had them.

To be one with his people again, with their narrow dreams hard and focused as diamonds, with the bitter beauty of the dying land.

If he survived.

He looked up, aware that he wasn't alone.

"Will you go, o my brother?" Her face was a dark pearl

in the midst of an explosion of black fur, gleaming a little with starlight and mammoth grease.

The Icefalcon raised his brows in surprise. "I did not think there was question, o my sister. I am the Icefalcon. I would have been chief among our people. Blue Child robbed me of what would have been mine. Do you question that?"

She shook her head. "I believe that you would have been chieftain of our people," she said. She sat down next to him on the broken projection of black rock that thrust up through the snow—the tallest peak of a mountain ridge buried beneath the all-devouring ice.

"And even after eleven years, I think you could have that again. Maybe more surely because you are a man now, with a man's strength and the core of a man's experience. They will listen to your voice in counsel and follow you in war. But you are wrong when you think Blue Child robbed you out of greediness, to have what you deserved."

"For the sake of Dove in the Sun, then?" She had been much in his mind since the confrontation with Zay in the subcrypts, as if the love he had once borne for her were growing back, mutated by understanding into a different form.

Cold Death sighed. She was a long time silent, her arms folded, a stubby little figure in her heavy coat. "You are my brother," she said at last, "and I love you. But you are not a leader."

The Icefalcon drew in breath to protest, then let it out. In all his life he had never known Cold Death to be wrong. He sat silent now, looking across into her face.

She scratched her nose and pulled her hood more closely over her shagged hair and the naked patches in her scalp. "There are those who lead," she said, "and those who follow, and those who walk alone. You walk alone, o my brother. Blue Child is a leader. She destroyed you, not out of malice, nor for jealousy's sake, but seeking the good of our people. Your adherents liked you and would have followed you in council and fought for you against her and against their kin and brothers as well. Noon liked you. You have charm, chilly bastard that you are. The Blue Child has none. But she knew she would be a better leader *for the people*. Do you understand?"

The Icefalcon was silent.

"Were you a leader," Cold Death went on quietly, "you would now be leading the Guards. Were you a leader, you would have gone back for Dove in the Sun when she was wounded."

"She could not have been brought back," argued the Icefalcon. "She was dying. I could not endanger the hunt for her."

"You could have sent the hunt back to safety and made sure that she did not die alone. Blue Child would have, even when there was no hope of saving her, even in the face of possible death herself."

The Icefalcon thought about that, silenced once more.

"The child Tir would have."

For a long time he simply looked down at his hands and the dagger he held in them. At the dim starshadow on the snow. But he saw Eldor Endorion, and Loses His Way, and even Zay of the Keep of the Shadow at the End of Time, who took on the burden that his shoulders were not strong enough to bear. At length he said, "She could have told me that."

"Would you have listened?"

Dove in the Sun laughing as she rode out with his hunting party. Blue Child's face, ugly and craggy, across the longhouse fire, calculation in those wolfish ice-blue eyes.

Noon weeping as he stepped from the darkness into the red light of the fire and held out to the Icefalcon the white shell.

Stays Up All Night, and Fifty Lovers, and Red Fox, all ready to fight Blue Child's friends for him. Ready to divide the tribe, or to split off from it, at a time when the harshness of the winters and the thinning away of the herds as they migrated farther and farther to the south were threat enough.

And for what? he thought. For what?

He walked by himself. He had always walked by himself. He knew this of himself; Cold Death was the same way. He had dealt well with his kin and his friends, but in a way he had always felt separated from them. Unlike Zay in the dark beneath the Keep, this isolation was a thing that he knew and loved.

But it was hard to think that he would not walk by himself in the Night River Country again.

Cold Death was gone in the morning. The day was clear; only the thinnest mist of steam rose from the center of the lake, and already the ice was blue and hard on its verges. Even with the clearing of the steam he could see no sign of the camp of the Talking Stars People, but he knew he had but to circle the lake and they would find him.

The Empty Lakes People were breaking their camp to go. Unsurprisingly, none of them mentioned Cold Death's absence. Such were her spells that the Icefalcon doubted they'd even been aware of her presence.

It mattered little since he knew he'd see her again.

"I think she departed so that she would not see the fight between Blue Child and myself," he said to Hethya, binding up their provisions of frozen caribou meat. "She considers Blue Child a better leader for the Talking Stars People than I."

"Well, that's damn cold, I must say!" Hethya bridled. Even under a coat of grease, thin with fatigue and criss-crossed with bruises and demon-bites, her face had a flirta-tious prettiness. She would do well, the Icefalcon thought, at the Keep. "There's a sister for you!"

"I have learned," said the Icefalcon gravely, "never to gainsay my sister."

The others, he had noticed, steered clear of the subject of Blue Child. Ingold had not said one word that indicated that he expected the Icefalcon either to go or stay—Ingold was good at that—but had merely gone about selecting

such provisions as the Empty Lakes People could spare
and seeing them packed.

Now the old man came over to him, leaning on his staff,
Tir walking in his shadow. The boy had had very little to
say at first and showed a disinclination, even during the
daylight hours, to leave the snow-house. Hethya, and
Loses His Way, and Beautiful Girl had spent a good deal
of time there with him, and he looked a little better now, as
if he were eating again, though the Icefalcon suspected he
still had nightmares and would for many years to come.

At least he remembered, thought the Icefalcon, what it
was to have friends and to value them above the solitude
of complete safety in a fortress, and that was something.

In the cool gray sunlight the half-healed gash on his
face was a great jagged red double line, scabbing and
horrible to look at. The children back at the Keep would
love it.

With them walked Loses His Way, and it was he who
spoke. "My friend," he said, "shall we cross over to the
camp? Your kindred should be astir by now." It was an
hour or so after dawn—a sly dig, since the people of the
Real World would take shame to themselves to be still
sleeping after the first whisper of light.

Among the other sleds, Loses His Way called out, with
Yellow-Eyed Dog gamboling and biting at snowflakes
like an idiot, and Loses His Way turned to grin at him, and
waved.

He had, the Icefalcon calculated, only a few days to
live. Yet he would lose one or perhaps two of them—
perhaps all, if the Talking Stars People took exception
to his entry into their camp—to help him, should he ask
for help.

So that he could return to the people he had left, to the
life of the Real World, that he himself so treasured.

To give him the gift of choice.

"Go with your kindred, o my enemy," the Icefalcon
said. "I have nothing to say to Blue Child, nor to any of the
People of the Talking Stars."

The hairless brows shot up. "You will not go?"

"The Night River Country is gone." He hadn't thought to say that, which was closest to his heart, especially not to this man, and, looking up, the Icefalcon saw the understanding and the shared grief in his enemy's blue eyes. Loses His Way made as if to extend his hand to him, and, embarrassed, the Icefalcon stepped back and drew himself with dignity to his full height.

"I may be a barbarian," he added coldly, "but I am not insane. We hunt that we may survive, and it is clear to me that survival is a thing more assured in the Keep of Dare than in the Real World now. Everything that once we knew lies under the Ice. In two years the Ice will spread farther, and stranger things than the Dark Ones and the slunch and cloned warriors will yet walk this beleaguered world. A man would be a fool to dwell in a place so deadly when he could have safety and comfort elsewhere."

The warchief grinned a slow grin into the red-gold stubble that would never grow out into a beard. "Even so," he said, and held out his hand. "I see that living near the Wise Ones you, too, have become wise. Then good hunting, o my friend, on your new hunt. Do not forget us who are fools."

The Icefalcon turned around and considered Ingold, and Tir, and Hethya, looking at him also in surprise. "Come," he said coolly. "There is a long road yet back to Sarda Pass. It is time we were gone."

Scrunching stolidly along on his snowshoes, Tir released the hem of Ingold's robe and dug into the hard-packed surface with his staff. The sunlight frightened him at first—the open air frightened him, filling him with panic he did not understand—but over the past two days he had begun to remember how it had been before Vair, before the Dark.

Last night Ingold had looked into his scrying crystal and spoken to Rudy, who had reported all things well at the Keep. The besiegers outside, he had said, had begun to fall

sick; Wend had reported half a dozen of them deserting
over the lower pass to the River Valleys in the night. There
were mass graves now in what had been the orchard before the Summerless Year. Ingold was making plans about
what to do with the rest of the besiegers when he, the Icefalcon, and Hethya returned to the Vale, but Tir was wondering if there would be anyone left for them to deal with.

Except, of course, Hethya's cousin, cooking poison
mushrooms in his pots.

Ahead of him he watched the silvery braids plaited with
bones, the lanky gray back bent to the harness of the
sled—with his left arm only engaged, the right always free
for his sword—and beside him the golden-brown, stocky
form that was Hethya. Once, to his surprise, he heard the
Icefalcon laugh.

"Ingold?"

"Yes, my child?"

Tir kept his voice politely down so the Icefalcon wouldn't
hear. "Is that all he really thinks about the Keep?" he
asked worriedly. "Just that it's safer than staying with the
Talking Stars People? Does he really care that little about
his family? And about us?"

Ingold smiled down at him. "He cares too much about
them, and about us," he said gently. "There is a saying that
one can't go home again. That isn't entirely true, but the
person who goes home is often not the person who set out
on the quest and the home he returns to not the place he
left. You'll never get our Icefalcon to admit that he's
changed since he's been among us; you'll never get him to
admit that he suspects that he might not be happy again in
the Real World. I'm a little surprised, frankly, that he ad-
mits it to himself and has chosen his happiness above his
pride."

Tir was silent, thinking about that, trying to emulate the
way the Icefalcon moved on his snowshoes, the way the
old man moved next to him. It sounded lonely. "Why not
admit it?" he asked worriedly. He would be a king, he
thought. He would need to know these things.

Ingold smiled, his blue eyes bright. "Because it isn't the way of the Talking Stars People to acknowledge that their way is less than perfect," he said. "And because the ways and the world of our childhoods always seem more perfect than our lives as adults. But mostly . . ." In his eyes Tir could see the affection that he bore the strange cold warrior who had always stood aloof from them all, "because he's the Icefalcon, and, for him, that has always been enough."

# ABOUT THE AUTHOR

At various times in her life, BARBARA HAMBLY has been a high-school teacher, a model, a waitress, a technical editor, a professional graduate student, a clerk at an all-night liquor store, and a karate instructor (she holds a Black Belt and has competed in several national-level tournaments).

Born in San Diego, she grew up in Southern California, attended U. C. Riverside, specializing in medieval history and spending a year at the University of Bordeaux in the south of France; eventually, she earned a masters degree in the subject. She now lives in Los Angeles, California.

# DEL REY® ONLINE!

## The Del Rey Internet Newsletter...

A monthly electronic publication e-mailed to subscribers and posted on the rec.arts.sf.written Usenet newsgroup and on our Del Rey Books Web site (www.randomhouse.com/delrey/). It features hype-free descriptions of books that are new in the stores, a list of our upcoming books, special promotional programs and offers, announcements and news, a signing/reading/convention-attendance calendar for Del Rey authors and editors, "In Depth" essays in which professionals in the field (authors, artists, cover designers, salespeople, etc.) talk about their jobs in science fiction, a question-and-answer section, and more!

Subscribe to the DRIN: send a message reading "subscribe" in the subject or body to drin-dist@cruises.randomhouse.com

## The Del Rey Books Web Site!

We make a lot of information available on our Web site at
www.randomhouse.com/delrey/

- all back issues and the current issue of the Del Rey Internet Newsletter
- sample chapters of almost every new book
- detailed interactive features of some of our books
- special features on various authors and SF/F worlds
- ordering information (and online ordering)
- reader reviews of upcoming books
- news and announcements
- our Works in Progress report, detailing the doings of our most popular authors
- bargain offers in our Del Rey Online Store
- manuscript transmission requirements
- and more!

## If You're Not on the Web...

You can subscribe to the DRIN via e-mail (send a message reading "subscribe" in the subject or body to drin-dist@cruises.randomhouse.com), read it on the rec.arts.sf.written Usenet newsgroup the first few days of every month, or visit our gopher site (gopher.panix.com) for back issues of the DRIN and about a hundred sample chapters. We also have editors and other representatives who participate in America Online and CompuServe SF/F forums and rec.arts.sf.written, making contact and sharing information with SF/F readers.

## Questions? E-mail us...

at delrey@randomhouse.com (though it sometimes takes us a little while to answer).